HIS LADY TO PROTECT

JUSTINE COVINGTON

Pat —
Thank you for every
word of encouragement on this
journey. It has been the
foundation on which this book
was written!

With love —
JCovington

JC BOOKS

ISBN: 978-1-7333322-1-7 (paperback)

Edited by Alida Winternheimer at Word Essential
www.wordessential.com

Copy edited by Julie Glover

Cover design by Mariah Sinclair at The Cover Vault
www.thecovervault.com

To David, my very own HEA.

CHAPTER 1

"To Napoleon." Nate Kinlan, Earl of Rainsford and intermittent agent for His Majesty's Home Office, lifted his snifter of brandy and uttered what he hoped was a convincing lie. A lie designed to entrap Captain Alastair Cressingham in a web of treason. Yet despite their best efforts, the Home Office had been unable to pin Cressingham with solid evidence. The man was more cunning than a fox.

"To Napoleon," Cressingham said in a deep, gravelly voice. He raised his glass and tossed the contents back, then thumped it down on his large mahogany desk. Cocking a bushy eyebrow, which only exacerbated the lines on his weathered, wrinkly face, he gestured to the marriage settlements covering the surface. "I want to make sure you clearly understand the terms before we draw the ink."

"Of course." Nate took a small sip of the amber liquid, then set it down, needing his wits about him. He'd been at this game with Cressingham on and off—mostly off—for three years, only recently having been re-recruited by the

Home Office. There was no question he would help, although doing so made him feel like a fish on land. A career spy he was not.

The captain rose, standing for a moment between the two branches of candles on either side of his desk, which barely illuminated the dark, walnut-paneled room. The floor-to-ceiling bookcases that flanked each wall, stripped bare of every volume the Cressingham family had ever owned after he'd taken up residence, reminded Nate of the charred, blackened skeletons he'd seen on the field in Spain, and he shivered involuntarily. This room had once been a place of happiness and light. Now, no number of candles could chase away the penetrating darkness.

The captain's barrel-chested frame was encased in a well-tailored blue coat, a stiff, white neckcloth tied neatly and without affectation at his slightly jowled throat. He limped around the desk clutching a marble-tipped cane, his gait the result of an old-and-oft-discussed war wound, and stood over Nate, his dark, cunning eyes glistening with intelligence.

Nate had to force himself not to shrink into the worn leather armchair. Damn, the man could be intimidating.

"In allegiance with his magnificence, the Emperor Napoleon, you agree to marry my niece, Susannah, and turn over to me her entire dowry of ten thousand pounds. I will then move her funds to an account on the Continent, where L'Empereur will make use of them to aid his escape from Elba and initiate a return to power." A sly grin emanated from Cressingham's lips. "Naturally, that latter bit of information isn't in the settlements...only that you forfeit her dowry."

Nate, uncomfortable with Cressingham towering over him, rose from the cracked leather chair, took another sip of his brandy, and set the glass down. "Naturally." Boot-to-boot, he had only a few inches on Cressingham, but it was enough to dispel his sense of inferiority. "Out of curiosity, when do you expect him to make a go of it?"

Cressingham scoffed. "Oh, not until early summer, at the earliest."

Nate nodded. He hoped so, for it would give him plenty of time to prepare. He gestured to the settlements. "Once this is signed, we'll have the banns read. The ceremony will take place at my estate in Sussex, after which I will post up to London to facilitate the transfer of her funds."

"Very good." Cressingham's tone was all business. "Now then," he said, clapping Nate on the back, "sign this. Make it official." He held out a quill.

Nate faux-smiled and accepted it. Dipping the quill in the ink pot, he leaned over the desk and scrawled his name at the appropriate spots on both copies of the settlements. Standing, he handed Cressingham the quill and watched as he did the same.

When he was done, Cressingham dropped the quill on the desk, then extended his hand, his large chest proudly puffed out, a smug-yet-sinister gleam in his eyes. "It seems we have an agreement."

Nate shook Cressingham's beefy hand as needles of apprehension pricked under his skin. *This close.* He'd brought the Home Office closer than they'd ever been to catching Cressingham. And Nate was now one marriage vow away from what he considered a much more important goal: keeping his promise to Ben, his best friend and Cressingham's nephew, to protect Susannah. It didn't bother Nate that he was marrying her without having seen her for years. He'd known her most of her life. She would make a competent wife.

"Now," Cressingham said, gesturing to the door, "shall

we dine? I have a little something special prepared this evening."

"Oh? Excellent." Nate exaggerated his enthusiasm even as he sighed inwardly. What he really wanted was to escape to the comfort of his library at Rainsford House and pour himself a glass of Martell 1795. He did not fancy enduring another poorly cooked meal in a home that harbored uncomfortable memories while sharing the company of a human parasite that not only grated on his nerves but made him long to reach out and strangle him.

You promised Ben.

So Nate allowed himself to be led by Cressingham to the small but well-appointed dining room, resigned to a dull evening of listening to the captain puff up his own consequence and make insipid small talk.

But when Nate crossed the threshold after Cressingham, he was startled to see a person sitting at the dining table, facing away from him…a lady. It took only a moment for him to realize who it was, and his stomach twisted with anxiety. There at the dining room table, her dark, upswept hair shining in the candlelight, sat Susannah Cressingham.

His adversary's niece.

His best friend's sister.

His future wife.

Nate could scarce draw a breath, his feet seemingly frozen to the floor. When had she come to town? She was supposed to be in Northumberland, at his great aunt's home acting as her companion until they wed. He'd made sure of that.

Cressingham didn't slow down. Leaning heavily on his cane, he entered the dining room and hobbled to the head of the table, barking orders to Bertram, his short, black-haired butler-cum-footman, to hurry up, bring the first course, serve the wine.

"And you, you silly chit." Cressingham sneered at his niece, pulling a white linen napkin off the table and snapping it at her. "Stand up and welcome Rainsford. Surely no introduction is necessary."

Turning in the intricately carved chair, she looked up at Nate, and with treacle-like slowness, she stood, her gaze riveted to his.

Nate's heart nearly stopped dead in his chest.

By God, she was beautiful. More than beautiful. *Exquisite.* Susannah Cressingham had transformed, shedding her former awkwardness like a butterfly sheds a cocoon. She was a lovely creature. Tall. Pert nose. Creamy skin. Thick, brown hair. Eyes like dark pots of honey. Curves that would make a eunuch hard.

A wave of white-hot desire shot through him. *Bloody hell.* He was supposed to marry the girl, not desire her. Forcing his mind and body to function again, he stepped into the brightly lit room—such a contrast to the study— until he was within arm's reach of her. He bowed, the bright candlelight making it impossible for him to ignore the well-cut bodice of her lilac-colored gown or her long, delicate, and very bare arms. "Miss Cressingham. Well…" He noticed the way her brown eyes sparkled with…anger? Suddenly nervous as a schoolboy, Nate was unsure of what to say. *How are you? You're back in London? Have you heard from your sister?* "Three years is a long time. Did you miss me?"

Imbecile. Nate gave himself a mental slap. Could he have said anything more stupid?

But Susannah, her face changing from an ever-deepening shade of pink then rose then flush, did for Nate what he'd only thought about. Like lightning, her hand flew, cracking him on the cheek.

The sting radiated down his neck. Nate flexed his jaw and covered his cheek with his hand. He deserved that. He'd never said anything so inane in his life. And the last time he'd seen her hadn't been under the best circumstances.

Captain Cressingham grabbed Susannah's arm, dragging her away from Nate. "What the devil do you mean by—"

"Thank you, Captain, but that's not necessary. You may release her."

Cressingham scowled but did as Nate asked. "I thought sending for her from that old goat she's been playing companion to would be a nice surprise." He harrumphed. "Had I known she'd behave in such a boorish way, I wouldn't have bothered."

"I appreciate the gesture." Nate nodded at Cressingham, then gave Susannah a peace offering smile, but she continued to glare at him, her eyes sparkling with a degree of rage that left him feeling slightly off-balance. Her bitterness certainly made sense, although Nate felt stupid for not expecting it. After what had happened the last time they were all in this house? He chided himself for his lack of foresight. "I suggest we all take our seats." Nate moved behind Susannah's chair and held it out. "Miss Cressingham?"

Susannah hesitated, then, with a characteristic lift of her chin he had always found endearing, she resumed her seat. Nate clenched the back of her chair, trying not to get lost ogling her soft, white shoulder or the ample swell of her breast. A rush of heat and pressure flowed to his groin.

How *bloody* inconvenient. He had to treat this as the business arrangement it was. Nate took his seat, laying his napkin in his lap and silently praying he didn't make a tent out of it.

Cressingham pointed his fat finger at his niece. "You owe his lordship an apology."

"Nonsense." Nate affected nonchalance with a shrug. "She was merely expressing her overwhelming emotion at seeing me." He smiled politely at Susannah, but she refused to meet his gaze. Smart girl. It was best he ignore her, too, lest he get lost in her beautiful brown eyes.

Bertram entered the dining room from a side door, his arms laden with a silver tray carrying three bowls of steaming liquid. He set the tray down on the sideboard with a clatter.

Nate smelled beef and his stomach roiled. Cressingham's cook left something to be desired, like taste. Or flavor.

Cressingham prodded Bertram. "Be quick about it, man."

"Yes, Captain." Bertram set the bowl of soup down in front of Nate. He bowed, then did the same for Cressingham and Susannah. Turning back to Nate, he asked, "Would you like wine, my lord?"

Nate nodded and Bertram filled both his glass and Cressingham's, then filled Susannah's glass with what looked like lemonade.

"Will there be anything else, Captain?" Bertram asked.

"No. You may go."

With a swift bow, Bertram left the room.

"At last." Cressingham reached for his glass of wine. Forgoing a customary toast, he took a large gulp and set the glass down with such force that wine sloshed out, smattering the white tablecloth with dots of red. "Now we can talk business."

Susannah, who'd kept her eyes down and her hand moving mechanically from her bowl to her mouth, suddenly set down her spoon, wiped her lips with her napkin, and rose from the table.

Cressingham frowned. "Where the devil do you think you're going?"

She looked at her uncle and shrugged. "You wish to discuss business. Females are rarely privy to that. Besides, I've lost my appetite this evening." She spared a glare at Nate, making his heart skip a beat or twelve, despite her damning look.

Her uncle harrumphed, the sound something akin to a dog with a hairball, his eyes sharp and greedy and amused. "Well, *dear niece*." Sarcasm dripped from his voice like tallow from cheap candles. "Seeing as the business concerns you, you will stay."

She stood still for a moment, as if weighing what to do, but then resumed her seat, delicately laying her napkin in her lap. "Very well." Her behavior was genteel, but her voice cut like a diamond. "What is this business?" -

Nate's hand, halfway to his mouth with a spoonful of the tasteless soup, froze in place. *Hell.* Hadn't Cressingham told her they were marrying? He lowered his spoon and looked around the epergne at the center of the table to his host.

Cressingham, his fat hand clasped around his wine glass, ate up the scene before him with hungry eyes, which darted from Nate to Susannah, then back to Nate. He looked like a child ready to burst with a secret.

Bloody hell. If Susannah didn't know Cressingham had promised her to Nate, he certainly didn't want the captain spilling the news. Turning to her, Nate said, "Miss Cressingham, I am glad to be able to tell you—"

"You're getting married, chit," Cressingham shouted, cutting him off.

Bastard.

Susannah sucked in a breath. Quick, sharp, punctuated. Then all at once, the color left her face, leaving her looking as if she'd succumbed to typhoid or the grippe or an overzealous blood-letter.

Nate had seen that look on her face once before. Instantly, he was transported back in time to that day three years ago when he left this very house, taking her brother Ben away to protect him from Cressingham's imminent threats, yet forced to leave Susannah and her sister, Isabela, under the captain's dubious guardianship. He remembered her...a frightened sixteen-year-old, eyes round and wide and uncertain, her face pale as linen. She'd kept a death grip on his hand as she ran through a litany of questions about where he was taking Ben, why she and Isabela couldn't leave with him, and when they would see their brother again.

Nate also remembered that he'd made a promise to keep her brother safe, and a pang of guilt shuddered through his body. The expression on her face that day had been ironed in his mind like newsprint, never fading, never rubbing off. Now he was seeing it again, and it ripped his heart to shreds.

But then...her color returned. And so did the look she'd given him when he first entered the room. Eviscerating him with her eyes. Her spine was so stiff, her body so hard, she could have shouldered the pyramids.

Tension vibrated off her in waves, and Nate's instincts went on alert. She was going to run, and if she did, he would follow her. He didn't want her to leave before he explained the arrangement as best as he could without telling her the truth.

Her eyes took on a tenacious gleam, her countenance a mix of incredulity and something Nate didn't like.

Disgust.

She directed her glare at Nate. "I'm to marry you?"

"Yes." Marriage to Susannah was not only part of the scheme to catch Cressingham, but also a sacrifice he was willing to make to fulfill his promise to Ben. Although, to be honest, after seeing her again in all her unexpected beauty, Nate didn't think he was sacrificing anything. "Your uncle and I have already signed the settlements. After all, a long-standing friendship exists between us. We thought it an excellent match."

"And an excellent deal." Cressingham's whispered remark made it to Nate's ears.

Susannah's head whipped around. "I beg your pardon?"

Cressingham reached for his wine, taking a dignified sip. "Nothing that concerns you."

She frowned, her hands gripping the edge of the table. "Of course this concerns me. You said so yourself. I am entitled—"

"You are not *entitled* to anything." Cressingham's tone was low but forbidding, as if he were daring her to challenge him.

Susannah inhaled through her nose. "Very well. I *wish* to know what *his lordship*"—her voice was laden with derision—"is gaining from this 'arrangement,' for I'm getting nothing."

"As I said, niece, that is not your concern."

"Then I see no reason to sit here and be a part of this." She threw her napkin down and rose to leave.

Nate jumped out of his chair, nearly knocking it over, and raced to the doorway, propping his arm against the wooden doorframe to block her in.

She gasped at his quick move, stopping just shy of touching his arm. She did not raise her eyes to his, but kept them focused on the floor.

He leaned down to whisper in her ear and caught her scent. Roses and lavender and everything feminine and sweet, and for a moment, a sense of lightheadedness overcame him. It was unexpected, unavoidable, and almost more than he could bear. In a low voice only she could hear, he said, "This will work out, Susannah. I promise you. But you have to trust me."

Susannah shook her head even as her eyes glistened, her lips trembled, and her throat worked repeatedly. He watched her swallow, swallow, swallow, as if their betrothal was somehow stuck in her windpipe.

Dammit. He could handle her anger better than her tears. He needed her alone. Taking her by the arm to escort her out of the room, he immediately wished he hadn't. Heat coursed up his arm, sending a shock-like kick to his heart, which began pounding in double-time.

He could not lose control over his emotions now. Leaning behind Susannah, he spoke to Cressingham. "If you would please excuse us, I think your niece and I need a few minutes to get reacquainted. May we go into the sitting room?"

"Yes, of course. Take all the time you need. And do whatever you must in order to 'acquaint' her to you." Cressingham laughed, clearly amused at Susannah's discomfort.

Nate fought the overwhelming urge to plant him a facer.

He steered her across the hall and slid open the pocket doors to the sitting room. One branch of lit candles stood on a table in the middle of the powder-blue room, and another on a side table, casting grey shadows in the corners. He gestured for Susannah to enter, but when her feet didn't move, he put his hand on the small of her back

and propelled her forward, then closed the doors behind
them.

"Susannah, I…" God, what should he say?

But Susannah turned to face him and narrowed her
eyes. Any trace of tears was now gone. She crossed her
arms under her bodice, which should have made her seem
formidable, but merely drew Nate's attention to her
breasts.

"My lord," she said, her voice hard. "My uncle may
have arranged this"—she flung a hand out wildly—"betrothal. But he has not asked me my opinion on the
subject, and I assure you, I have one. There is nothing you
can offer that would induce me to accept your hand. You
possess no qualities that I would find suitable in a husband.
You lack honor and integrity. You have betrayed my family.
But perhaps, most significantly, I cannot marry a man I do
not trust."

Nate's gut tensed, but he pushed the anxiety aside.
What mattered right now was that she willingly accepted
him as her betrothed. His ability to catch Cressingham
depended on her not being a hostile fiancée, for sparks
between them would attract too much attention from the
ton, attention Cressingham wished to avoid.

"You don't have a choice," he said matter-of-factly.
"You are not of age. Your uncle, as your guardian, is the
sole arbiter of your fate."

Her eyes flashed in the dim candlelight. "Hear me, my
lord. My answer will be no. *Always.* I will never trust you
again. I don't care what my uncle does, but I will never
marry *you*." She turned away.

Nate felt a pang in his chest, her words stabbing him
like a knife in the heart. But the feeling was quickly swept
away by another, more resolute one—he would have

Susannah whether she wanted him or not. For if she didn't accept him, Cressingham would give her to someone else, just as he had her sister.

And that was not a fate Nate could live with.

CHAPTER 2

SUSANNAH STARED at the wall of what used to be her mama's sitting room, arms crossed, trying to control her breathing. Her racing heart. Her electric reaction to the Earl of Rainsford. Rain. *No, Nate.*

Good. Lord.

She hadn't seen him in three years. *Three.* And of course, thanks to the ample candlelight in the dining room, she could tell he was as devilishly handsome now as he was that day he left her. Tall like the mast of a ship, eyes dark like the night, hair wavy like the hills, and a physique that stretched the limits of his tailor's work, making him seem larger and more alive than ever before.

But she *hated* him to the depths of her soul.

Didn't she?

She ran her hands over her bare arms, trying to still the thrilling *frisson* that raced under the surface of her skin. Pinching the fabric of her silk gown between her fingers, she rubbed it repeatedly, trying to shift her focus away from Nate. To turn off her body's reaction to him.

She forced herself to look about the room, which bore

the stamp of her mama's gracious personality and impeccable style, and Susannah's heart clenched with loss. The room was small, suitable for no more than eight guests, but its quaint size and large, south-facing windows had always given it a cozy, comfortable feel. Susannah couldn't count the number of times she'd curled up in the large window seat with a book from her father's study, basking in the warm sun, absently listening to her parents engage in idle chatter. She would give anything to hear their voices again.

The walls, hung with light blue silk damask, had never felt cold or threatening—until now. The gold-leaf Italianate furniture, set in two conversational groupings, could have doubled as holding cells in a prison, cornering her into a disastrous future. And the austere, white plaster coffered ceiling, which reflected the candlelight, mirrored the barren marble tabletops and empty mantel. Susannah swallowed the large lump in her throat as she recalled how, shortly after her parents died, her uncle had ceremoniously stripped the room of the heirlooms and *accoutrements* her mother's family had carefully transported from France during the Revolution. She might be back in the house she grew up in, but it was certainly not her *home*. Her uncle had taken care of that, removing everything—books, portraits, knickknacks—that held meaning for herself or her sister, Isabela. Susannah inhaled deeply, in part to calm her nerves, but also to try to capture what she was certain was the lingering scent of her mother's perfume, Lily of the Valley.

"You're beautiful, poppet."

His comment caught her off guard, as did his long-ago endearment for her, and she felt a pang in her chest as if it had been punctured by a jouster's lance. Those treacherous words, and the nickname he'd given her so many Christmases ago. The mere sound of it on his lips was almost more than she could bear.

She couldn't fall victim to his charms again. *Hate. Hate. Hate.* Perhaps if she kept saying that to herself, she would believe it. She had to believe it, or she would be smothered by her own love for him.

For she *had* loved Nate. Fully and completely. Which had made his betrayal even more painful.

She had to steel herself against him. Susannah turned slowly, her back straight, her countenance hard like marble. "I'm not 'poppet.' Don't address me as such."

"You never minded before." His voice was husky.

"I'm not the same girl I was then. You may address me as 'Miss Cressingham.'"

He shook his head and came towards her. "I can't call you that. It's for strangers. Mere acquaintances."

Susannah's pulse jumped and she immediately stepped backwards in retreat, wanting to be as far away from him as possible. For each step he took forward, she took one back, until she butted up against something. She gasped, flicking her gaze over her shoulder at the sky-blue silk *chaise longue* behind her. Drat!

Nate kept coming, his eyes never wavering from hers. "I suppose I could continue calling you Susannah. You are, after all, an old family friend." He slowed his pace and his words, his eyes flashing hot with something Susannah couldn't identify. "But I much prefer 'poppet' because"— he held out his hands expectantly—"well, we both know the answer to that."

Susannah's face flamed at the reference to their Christmas kiss under the mistletoe long ago. Just before Nate reached her side, she darted around the chaise, putting it as a barrier between them. She knew it was nonsense, for Nate could easily scale the chaise in one jump if he wished. But she needed something physical to separate them into enemy camps.

Hate. Hate. Hate.

"You're nothing like the man I remembered." *Liar.*

Nate stood on the opposite side of the chaise, the shadows in the room making his cheeks and chin stronger, more handsome. "No, I'm not, poppet." He crossed his arms over his wide chest. "I have changed. I admit that. But so, I think, have you."

Susannah forced herself to look at the Persian rug covering the floor. The coffered ceiling. Anything but him. "Nonsense. I'm the same girl I was before."

"Oh, no you're not. You're a lady now." His voice softened. "You're also angry. Confused. Worried. And I don't blame you a bit."

Nate's empathy was unexpected, triggering a flood of sorrow that came over her like a titanic wave crashing over a breakwater. She couldn't succumb to it. She must not. Susannah clenched her hands together so tightly that her fingers throbbed. In a voice laced with anger, she said, "Your kindness is a bit late, my lord. You needn't bother with apologies."

Nate relaxed his arms and started walking around the chaise. "I am not apologizing for the past, poppet. There were reasons things happened the way they did. Even your brother did not object."

Susannah scurried away, taking refuge behind another chair. "He didn't know he was going to die. I doubt very seriously he would have gone with you if he had."

Nate halted, and Susannah felt momentary relief that his pursuit of her was over, until she noticed his eyes flicking down to the lower shelf of a side table. There, he did it again.

She looked down to see what could have caught his

attention and froze. Lying flat on the shelf was a small portrait of her brother, Ben. A large lump formed in her throat as her insides churned and turned. It must have been overlooked when her uncle had ordered the room cleared. Susannah hadn't ever noticed it before. How could she have possibly overlooked that?

The painting had been done before their parents died, right after Ben's first year at Oxford. It was a lovely, vibrant watercolor, small and framed in gold. It captured very well Ben's hard blue eyes and serious countenance.

She reached down, hands shaking, breaths coming in short, raspy pants like there wasn't enough air in the room, and picked it up.

Her eyes welled up and over, leaving wet trails down her cheeks. *Oh, Ben.* Slowly, without taking her eyes from the small painting, she came around the table towards Nate.

"Susannah…"

She looked at Nate with a hot intensity, her hatred flaring up to an explosion that would make Guy Fawkes envious. *This* was the fuel she needed to keep her anger alive. She flipped the portrait around, her fingers digging so hard into the edge of the frame they hurt. But she relished the pain, for it made her anger hot. Susannah shoved the portrait towards Nate, wanting him to see the life he snatched away from her. "My brother is dead because of you."

"Susannah—"

"Don't 'Susannah' me." Trying not to cry, she pushed it at him again, her eyes still tearing. "You lied to me that day you took Ben away. You promised me you'd bring him back safe. You *promised.* And you let him die."

Nate shook his head. "It's not like that. I got your brother out of the house before your uncle killed him."

"Uncle wouldn't have killed him. But you did, taking him off and buying him a commission."

Nate put his hand up, pushing the portrait of Ben down. "I didn't take him off. It was Ben's idea."

"Liar." Susannah pulled it out of his reach and thrust it at him yet again. "I won't let you hide from what you did."

Nate shook his head, dismissing her accusations. Turning his back on her, he walked to the tall window and stared out at the street, arms crossed defensively, saying nothing.

Susannah positively shook with rage, tears coursing down her cheeks. Why didn't he defend himself? Was silence his only ally? Did he not care what he had done to her family? How his actions had reverberated through both her life and her sister's?

He faced her. "I did nothing"—he spoke almost as if he'd heard her questions—"except protect your brother." His voice was quiet, solemn, reverent.

In whispered tones, she asked, "Then why is he dead?" Susannah propped the portrait against her hip with one hand, and with the other, she gently ran her fingers over the painting. Inside her, cold, cavernous emptiness pressed hard upon her heart. "You could have told us Ben died," she said softly. "You could have grieved with us, comforted us. You could have told us all would be well." Her eyes shot up, burning and teary. "Instead"—her voice took on rapier-like sharpness—"you abandoned us. You went to fancy soirees and hobnobbed with affluent friends, including my uncle. You had neither the decency nor the honor to tell Isabela and me to our faces that he died. And your family." She choked back another sob. "They did…nothing."

"Nothing? My sisters were at school with you."

"They never once offered condolences. Never once asked me to visit. And your mama—"

"We all did what we could." Nate turned his back on her again. "We, my family and I, had your best interests at heart. I can say that only so many times."

"The best for whom? You?" She laughed, bitter and derisive. "It certainly wasn't for Isabela and me. With you and Ben gone, Uncle didn't waste any time marrying her off to the highest bidder."

Nate turned, opening his mouth like he was going to speak, but clamped it shut, giving her his back again.

She was glad. It didn't matter what Nate said. Nothing would change her black opinion of him.

She set down the portrait of Ben, then wiped her wet cheeks with the palms of her hands. Looking around the familiar sitting room, now a grey, shadowy shell of the sanctuary it used to be, she brushed away a fresh trickle of tears. Susannah's mother had entertained her lady friends in this very room, most especially Nate's mother. How many afternoons had they spent here drinking tea, doing needlepoint, singing, painting, laughing like schoolgirls? A pang of longing came over Susannah. She'd been back in London for a week after being gone nearly two years, and she'd instantly gravitated to this space. To her mother.

But her mother. Her father. Ben. All gone. Even Isabela, who had been forced to marry a Jamaican landowner. Turning to Nate, she asked, "Do you know I haven't heard from Isabela in three years? My uncle and her husband take our letters." Her voice thinned. "I don't know if she's well. If she has children. How she's been treated." She swallowed. "If she's alive."

Silence greeted her. Cold, uncaring silence.

Anger spiking, she strode towards Nate, grabbed him by the arm, and pulled on his sleeve to get him to face her.

"Did you hear me?" Her voice quivered. "I don't know if she's—"

"I heard you," Nate said hotly, his eyes sparkling. He shrugged her off. "All evening, I've heard you. Now I need you to hear me. I am more sorry than I can say for what has happened, but I can only tell you so many times that there was a reason for it."

"Then tell me," she pleaded. "Why are you hiding it from me?"

Again, Nate returned no reply.

"I don't understand why you can't tell me anything." She clenched her hands by her sides, frustration quaking under her skin. She would not strike him, even though she wanted him to physically feel all the hurt she'd been living with for the past three years. Taking a steadying breath, she said, "Please. Tell me the truth. Tell me—"

"Stop," he admonished. Taking her by the arms, he pulled her to him, his eyes pleading as they stared into hers. "This cannot go on."

Afraid he would try to kiss her, Susannah fought against him, squirming and pulling and kicking, not wanting him to have this power over her. "Let me go."

Nate turned her so her back collided with his chest, then took both her wrists in his hands and wrapped his arms about her, straitjacket-like. He squeezed her, forcing her to still. "Susannah, please listen to me. Hear me." He bent his head, his hot, whispered breath in her ear. "I did what had to be done. Someday you'll know why. But right now, this is about you and me." He squeezed her harder, almost shaking her. "We are getting married. We have to. I've signed the marriage settlements this evening." He gave her one more squeeze, gentler this time. "I promise you will not regret it."

Susannah bit her lip, resentment building like floodwater behind a dam; however, she would *not* cry. Instead, she tried to pull loose again, but his grip was strong. In the fiercest voice she could manage, she spat out, "I will not marry you." *I cannot marry you.*

"As I said, you don't have a choice. It's either me or another man your uncle picks. Do you fancy a husband like your sister's? Drunk? Dissolute? Who will keep you separated from her?"

At this, Susannah stilled. Good God, she had no alternatives. No choices. No control. No future. Except to be forever bound to the man she used to love. The man she hated. She had to hate him. Of course she hated him.

Her body began to shake with huge, wracking sobs. Didn't he understand? She just wanted her family back. Tears coursed from her eyes and dropped off the tip of her nose. She wailed out her pain, so real and so visceral she physically ached. For long moments she continued like that, her body limp in Nate arms, shaking with the sorrow she'd kept pent up for so long. Why wouldn't he let her go? Let her crumble to the ground so she could be swallowed up by her misery?

Eventually, Susannah noticed a cooing in her ear. A soft *ssshhhh*. A warm hand rubbing her arm even as the other one encircled her waist.

"*Ssshhh*, poppet. Please don't cry." Gently, he scooped her up in his arms and moved to a nearby chair, settling himself down with her on his lap.

Susannah struggled, wanting nothing to do with him, to say nothing of the impropriety of his actions, but Nate held her secure. "Please don't fight me. I am not your enemy."

Was he mad? Of course he was. Not only that, but he was in league with her uncle and whatever nefarious schemes he was planning.

"Poppet, I want to help you. Truly I do. I have an idea."

She moved again, but Nate wouldn't let her go. While still holding her with one arm, he pulled out his handkerchief. "Here. Use this."

Reluctantly, Susannah took it from him and wiped her wet face and blew her nose, then folded it into her still-shaking hand. "Let me up, please."

"I will. But first, I want you to listen to my idea."

She tried to stand up. "I don't care about any ideas you have. You are devoid of honor, as far as—"

"I will tell you about your sister." Nate pulled her back onto his lap.

Susannah ceased her struggles and twisted around, trying to make eye contact with Nate. "What did you say?"

Nate took a deep breath, then relaxed his hold on her a bit. "I know you're not keen on this marriage. I'm sorry to take you by surprise. That was not what I'd intended. I thought your uncle told you about this when he and I first agreed to it a few weeks ago."

"No one told me—"

Nate put his finger on her lip, and the touch nearly scorched her. She pulled back, but his hand followed, tracing the outline of her mouth, his eyes tracking his finger. A warm, fluttering sensation spread through Susannah's body and she cursed herself for it.

As if realizing what he was doing, Nate withdrew his hand and cleared his throat.

Susannah felt the loss immediately. She remembered the last time he had traced her lip like that. Right before he left with Ben. She knew now that he'd done it to distract her, to draw her attention away from the chaos around them at the time. It had worked then just as it worked now.

Only now, she despised herself for loving the feel of his finger there.

He cleared his throat, his eyes on hers. "It seems your uncle has not been informing you of much, whether about your future or your sister's fate. I can remedy that, to a certain extent, but only if you're willing to offer something in return. A quid pro quo, if you will."

Indignant, Susannah tried to stand. "I am not interested in being your—"

"Oh, for heaven's sake." Nate clamped his arms around her, pulling her down onto his lap again. "Do stop being so righteous. It's nothing like you're thinking." He sighed. "Would you please hear me out?" He drew another deep breath, then exhaled.

For the first time, Susannah heard fatigue in Nate's tone, and her heart felt a bruise. Very well. She could listen. Then tell Nate to jump in the river. "I will hear what you have to say. But this is not proper, me sitting here."

Nate opened his arms, and Susannah quickly rose, taking a seat on the *chaise longue* that sat kitty-corner to Nate's chair. She folded her hands around the handkerchief Nate had given her and inclined her head. "Before you talk about this quid pro quo, I want to know more about my sister. How is she? Is she well?"

Nate patted her knee reassuringly. "Your sister is as well as can be expected, given her circumstances and the tropical climate. But you'll be happy to know that she's in the family way for the first time."

A jubilant thrill of excitement exploded within Susannah, and an instant smile formed. A niece or nephew? Oh, thank heavens. Isabela had always wanted to become a mother. She said a silent prayer for her sister's safety—and that of the forthcoming child.

Nate's eyes darkened. "I should caution you, though… there may be complications."

Susannah's excitement cooled quickly. "What do you mean, complications?" Her voice vibrated with panic.

He sighed. "Unfortunately, the Jamaican climate has forced upon your sister a sickly constitution, which has only worsened over time. She should be well into her confinement by now, but last I learned, she was not enduring the pregnancy well."

More tears fell down Susannah's wet cheeks, and she felt suffocated of air. "When was that?"

"About three months ago."

Susannah clenched her hands together into a tight knot. "Why are you telling me this?"

Nate paused as if his next statement carried with it the fate of the world. "Because I'm willing to take you to your sister after we marry."

"To Jamaica? But—yes!"

"Wait, poppet." Nate cupped her small hands in his large, warm ones. "Remember, there is a condition attached to my offer."

Her eyes narrowed. "Ah yes. Your quid pro quo." She paused, and when he said nothing, she raised her shoulders expectantly. "Well?"

Nate held his breath for a moment, then let it out in a *whoosh*. "I want no discord or animosity during our betrothal. Because our families used to be close, it's not wholly out of character for the two of us to have kindled a mutual affection based on past acquaintance. Therefore, in exchange for seeing your sister, I would like you to pretend this is a love match…both in public *and* in private."

Susannah's world shifted on its axis. *Love match?* Her worry over her sister's fate was quickly thwarted by a thrilling, white-hot passion that swept through her body. *Love Nate?*

Then logic took over…and with it, anger.

Was he mad?

"Pretend this is a love match? Are you quite insane? I don't love you." *Never mind that pretending to love you would kill me all over again.*

He gave a half-laugh. "I don't love you, either."

Stung by Nate's frankness, a galling prickle came over her.

"But we can masquerade at love, surely. We can smile at each other. Hold hands—in the privacy of a carriage, of course. Or a sitting room." With an unwavering gaze, Nate pressed her hands.

Susannah couldn't move, couldn't breathe, couldn't think. She could focus only on Nate's hand touching hers.

As if testing the waters, he said, "We will keep it simple. Gentle affection. Perhaps I can kiss you…here?" Nate slowly—ever so slowly—raised her hand to his mouth, pressing his scorching lips into her skin, and her insides warmed again.

"Or kiss you here?" He leaned closer to her, taking his time, giving her space and a chance to pull away, but she did not. She could not. He moved closer, closer, closer as her eyes fluttered closed. His lips pressed gently into her temple. Then her cheek. Then her mout—

"I beg your pardon," said a voice from the doorway.

Susannah inhaled quickly then jumped up out of the *chaise longue*, nearly falling over in the process. She turned towards the door to see Bertram enter carrying a tray with tea.

"Your uncle requested I bring this to the sitting room, although I have kept your plates warm if you prefer to finish dinner."

"Of course. No." Susannah, her voice uncertain, shook her head, confused by Bertram's interruption. "I'm not hungry." With a wave, she gestured to the table near the other furniture grouping. "Set it there if you please, then leave."

Bertram placed the tray where directed, then left the room, sliding the doors closed behind him.

She didn't dare look at Nate, for her cheeks flamed hot with embarrassment. How could she have let him almost kiss her? That surely would have been her downfall. The man was far too dangerous for her own good.

And yet, he offered her something she never thought possible…an opportunity to see her sister. *Her sister with child.* Susannah would have to pretend to love a man she once loved. No, hated. Drat, she had to keep reminding herself of that, because she could love him again if she wasn't careful.

It seemed no matter what choice Susannah made, whether seeing her sister or protecting her own heart, she would be hurt, for if she chose one, she would surely lose the other.

"Poppet, let me help you. Show me affection, let me do the same, and I will take you to Isabela."

Nate's concerned gaze only confused Susannah more. Why did he care? Could she trust him to keep his word? Why was he willing to help her when he was so clearly in her uncle's pockets?

Uncertainty whirled through her like a quickly moving hurricane, but she tried to focus. *Isabela will be a mother. My sister and her baby are what's most important right now.* When put in that context, her emotional storm cleared, and Susannah knew what she had to do. Play a role. Pretend to love. And trust Nate…just for a short time.

Because she would die if she never saw her sister again.

CHAPTER 3

THE NEXT AFTERNOON, Nate sat back against the cushion in the family's stately landau, put his head down, pinched his nose, and closed his eyes, willing his younger triplet sisters to simply *be quiet*.

"Move over, you're taking too much room."

"But there are three of us crammed in this seat. Where do you expect me to go?"

"Stop crushing my gown. Were you raised in a byre?"

Nate soaked up the sun's warm rays through the open top, a welcome change to the recent cold. His concentration flitted from his sister's chatter to the loud calls of street hawkers to the creaks and clops of carts and horses. Anything to distract him from memories of Susannah.

When Cressingham had casually revealed his plan to marry Susannah to someone in exchange for her fortune to benefit Napoleon, Nate quickly volunteered himself as a willing groom, then promptly informed the Home Office. Lord Sidmouth, the Home Secretary, had hesitated, fearing Nate was condemning himself to a life of marital doom, but Nate had insisted his future was none of Sidmouth's business. And when Nate had brokered the settlements, it hadn't mattered one whit what Susannah looked like. That he was finally able to fulfill his promise to Ben was all that mattered.

Then he saw her. So grown up. So spirited. So surprisingly beautiful.

Not two minutes after their reacquaintance did he decided to spend as much time with her as possible. He would bring her to every play, musicale, Venetian breakfast, ball, card party, luncheon, soiree, rout, masquerade, opera, and dinner party he could snag an invitation to. And even those he couldn't.

Their first public outing was to be an afternoon ride through the park in Nate's phaeton, giving him the freedom to be affectionate towards Susannah that he would not have had if they were in Cressingham's company. He also wanted to break down her formidable walls, and he still had to discuss with her the terms of their agreement, for they hadn't finished that conversation last evening. At some point, he'd have to formulate an excuse to Cressingham for their lover-like behavior. He couldn't have the captain thinking he was sympathetic to Susannah.

But right now, he just wanted to enjoy her.

"Aaaaack," screamed Juliana, the eldest triplet, jumping up from her seat and throwing herself on Nate.

Stiffening in surprise, Nate tried to catch his sister, who scrambled around on his lap like a rabid animal. He swiveled his head left to right, looking outside the carriage, wondering what it was that had scared her. "What the devil—"

"A mouse," she shrieked. "There's a mouse in the carriage!" Juliana burst into tears, hiding her face in Nate's neck and grabbing the lapels of his coat as she dragged her feet onto his seat, pinning him down.

Minerva, the second oldest, stood up quickly, pulling her skirts above her knees. "Where? Where is it?" she asked anxiously.

Anna, the youngest of the three, burst into a fit of laughter, rocking back and forth on the seat, her hand covering her mouth. "Oh, you two," she said between giggles, reaching over for a little brown ball of fur. "It's not a mouse. He's my pet. Samson."

Leaning over to inspect it, Minerva, whom they all called Minnie, said, "It's a mouse."

Nate, holding a still-shaking Juliana, had to hide his face behind his sister's head so they couldn't see him smile. When he'd regained his composure, he asked, "Anna, where did you get that thing?"

Scooping up her pet, Anna held him in her hand, her finger gently stroking his head as his nose twitched curiously. "In the trap. His little leg is broken, so he can't get around well."

Juliana shuddered. "Get it out of this carriage at once. I hate vermin."

Anna shoved the tiny brown mouse towards her sister's face, frowning. "He's just a little thing. He won't hurt you."

"Ohhh," Juliana moaned, hiding her face in Nate's coat once more. "Disgusting creatures."

"Anna, put it away or give it to Thomas," Nate said with a sigh. It was pointless to ask her to get rid of Samson. Anna had a special place in her heart for all creatures, particularly broken ones.

"But—"

"You heard him," Minnie said. "I don't overly care for them, either."

"Oh, very well." Anna slipped the mouse into the large pocket in her skirt. "I've got food in here, so he'll stay put."

"He better." Minnie gingerly sat back down on the carriage seat next to Anna. "Come now, Jules." She patted the empty space beside her. "You won't see him again."

Slowly, Juliana extricated herself from Nate and took her seat, wedging herself as far into the corner as possible while wiping her damp face. "That little rodent better not show his whiskers."

Anna harrumphed. "Only if you're bothersome."

Nate, trying to straighten his disheveled neckcloth and waistcoat, frowned. "Enough, girls. Jules, Anna has promised to keep him out of sight." He gave Anna a stern look, but it was just for effect. "Now then, if you three can't sit quietly, I will let you down here and you can walk home with Thomas." He looked over the open back of the landau at the footman, who was suppressing a grin.

How the devil he'd gotten roped into bringing his sisters along with him on today's outing through Hyde Park he could not fathom. One minute he was walking out the door, telling his family he was taking Susannah for a ride in the park, and the next minute, he was waiting for the grooms to unharness his matched pair from his phaeton and hitch up others to the landau.

Anna sniffed. "You have no compassion for small, injured creatures, Jules."

"No, I don't," she retorted. "Why don't you sit over there with Nate, anyway?" Juliana gestured to his bench. "Then that wretched rat can scare *him*."

"It's a mouse, Jules, not a rat." Minnie turned to Anna. "Do move over, if you please." She wrenched her gown from underneath Anna's bottom. "Goodness, you're as wide as a horse."

"Then you are, too, for we are all the same height and build, even if we don't look exactly alike," countered Anna.

Nate glared at the three of them. "Girls, this is my last warning. I came out today to enjoy time with Miss Cressingham, and if you keep going on as you are, you're going to ruin my afternoon, and hers. And I will *not* like that."

The carriage drew up outside the Cressingham home on Little Windmill Street, and Nate gave them a stern look. "No complaining. You wanted to come along on this outing. Keep your hands and words—and mice—to yourself. Bite your cheek if you must in order to not rip into each other. Am I clear?"

Three auburn heads nodded.

The footman got down from his perch, opened the carriage door, and put down the step. Nate exited to the pavement and walked to the front door, with its cracked paint and rusty knocker. Cressingham certainly hadn't maintained the family home as Susannah's parents had. His heart pounded in his chest, and a cold sweat came over him. Good lord, what was wrong with him? It couldn't be nervousness about seeing Susannah again. Behind him, he heard the girls giggling, and he turned to glare at them, their heads together like they were scheming against him. Then he straightened his coat and rapped on the knocker.

Bertram answered the door and, without a word, showed Nate into the front hall, then disappeared into the back of the house.

Susannah stood near the staircase, tying the ribbon of her straw bonnet under her chin. A pang pierced Nate's chest like he'd been shot, and his breath hitched. Lord, she was beautiful, dressed in a lovely peach gown with a matching pelisse, the color warming her complexion. He felt as nervous as a schoolboy, but he pulled himself together and greeted her. "Hello, poppet."

"My lord." She did not look at him.

Nate frowned. Her formality struck him as wrong. "Won't you call me 'Rain,' as you once did?"

She finished tying off her bonnet, then pulled on her kid gloves, still averting her gaze. "No. 'My lord' is the best I can do for someone who has lied to me."

Damn. She was still angry. Of course she was. But her anger wouldn't serve their purpose. "I'm not sure how it will sound if we're supposed to be advertising a love match, yet you call me 'my lord.'"

Nate immediately wished he hadn't said anything, for her face went dark. This was not the tone he wanted to set for the day. "I apologize." Before she could speak, he proffered his arm. "Come, I have a surprise for you in the carriage. One I was not expecting—or really wanting—but it's a surprise nonetheless."

She took his arm, her eyebrows raised in curiosity. "I'm not sure I'm going to like this surprise."

Bertram had come back into the hall, and he held the door for them as they exited the house. Nate and Susannah descended the steps as his sisters stood on the pavement before the carriage, two of them waving to Susannah.

"Miss Cressingham," called Anna in an exuberant voice. "Susannah! Hello. It's been so long."

Susannah gave the slightest pause in her descent before continuing. Under her breath, she asked, "Your sisters?"

Nate directed her a sideways glance, a bit taken aback at her hesitant reaction. After all, she and his sisters had played together as children and had attended finishing school at the same time. "Yes," he said quietly. "Not my idea. I'd much rather have you to myself. However, when they learned I was coming to see you, they insisted on accompanying me." He squeezed her hand. "You used to be good friends. It will be all right." When she slowed her descent, he added in an undervoice, "We have an agreement that you'll pretend to love me, and that especially applies when before my family."

He felt Susannah tense, but then she relaxed and painted a saccharine smile on her face. "As soon as we're married," she whispered, "we're leaving for Jamaica."

Nate kissed her hand but said nothing. He guided her to the carriage, holding fast her hand, which rested on his arm.

Susannah looked up at him. "We *are* leaving as soon as we're married, aren't we?"

"We can talk about that later."

She tried to pull her hand away, but Nate kept it clamped to his arm. Susannah was clearly dissatisfied with his answer and would likely want to argue the point right here on the pavement. Fortunately, he was rescued by one of his sisters.

Anna came forward with her hands extended, a broad smile lighting up her face. "Oh, Susannah. I can call you that, can't I? I must tell you how excited we all were to learn that you're marrying Natey. And how sly of you. Why, he never mentioned anything about you before."

Susannah took Anna's hands and smiled forcibly through cheek-to-cheek kisses. "Hello, Lady Anna. Believe me, I was surprised as any of you."

"Pish-posh, please call me Anna, just as you did when we were young." She patted Susannah's hands, then released them when Minnie elbowed her.

"My turn." Minnie also clasped Susannah's hand in welcome and kissed her cheek. Her smile was genuine but more reserved. "It's so lovely to see you again. Why, it must be two years at least since we were all at Miss Glover's School."

"I believe you're right." She turned to Juliana, who came forward as well.

"It's high time Natey got married, and I'm glad he's marrying you." Juliana kissed her cheeks in welcome.

"Thank you, Lady Juliana."

She waggled her finger at Susannah. "No. Don't you dare. Juliana suits me fine." She looked around at everyone, her hands on her hips. "Well, are we going? We'll miss the crowds." She turned and marched towards the carriage, and Thomas helped her into it.

Susannah flicked a glance at Nate.

He shrugged. "She's gotten more high-handed since leaving school."

His fiancée tried to suppress a smile, and Nate's heart soared. He'd made her laugh, even if she hadn't done it out loud. Perhaps this day wouldn't be so bad after all.

Anna reproached her sister. "Jules, how rude. For heaven's sake, you can't simply walk off like that and leave us standing here." She shook her head at Juliana, who now sat in the open-air carriage, then beamed and gestured to Susannah. "Shall we depart? I do want to see who's out today."

"Likely no one," Minnie said in a pragmatic voice. "It's too early in the Season."

"Enough, girls." Nate sounded weary, even to himself.

The girls climbed into the carriage and settled themselves on the rear-facing seat. Nate helped Susannah in, then sat as close to her as he could without actually being in her lap. His leg rested against hers, and he held her hand tightly in his. Something about this seemed right...as if it were the culmination of an event he'd been waiting for for years. Yet he felt the tension in her body, like a leather strap ready to snap. Nate raised her hand to his lips and kissed it. Surprisingly, she met his eyes, and Nate tried not to laugh at the anger that flashed in them. He gave a slight cough as a reminder of what she agreed to. She must have gotten the hint, because her body relaxed a bit, her eyes softened, and she even smiled, causing Nate's heart to pound.

He tore his gaze away from Susannah to find all his sisters looking at them, grinning from ear to ear.

The carriage weaved its way through the heavy street traffic towards Hyde Park. His sisters chattered like seagulls the entire way about everything they saw, sharing all the latest *on dits*. Susannah, on the other hand, sat in stolid silence next to him, only nodding when necessary. Nate regretted capitulating to his sisters' demands to join them. He should have made this first outing with her a private one.

Thankfully, in short time, they were parading through Hyde Park. Dozens of other carriages made their way in a circuitous route around the park, from stately landaus sporting family crests, to barouches, hired carriages, and even individuals on horseback and on foot. Above the clatter of hooves and the whinnies and nickers of horses could be heard the shouts of acquaintances calling out greetings, high-pitched feminine laughter, and men offering salutations in deep, jovial tones.

It did not pass Nate's notice that several acquaintances —some familiar and some not—paid particular attention to his betrothed as they passed by in their carriages. A few gentlemen pulled out their quizzing glasses to give Susannah a harder look. Nate was both annoyed and proud that his fiancée was garnering so much attention. Then again, he had announced their engagement in *The Times* that morning.

"When are you getting married?" Anna asked, interrupting Nate's thoughts. Her hands were clasped in front of her, her eyes sparkling.

His mood lightened. There was no mistaking Anna's views on the match. "They will call the banns on Sunday. Three weeks." Nate looked down at Susannah. "I hope that is acceptable?"

Susannah nodded. "Yes."

"And I assume you'll marry at Langley Park?" Anna's voice carried hope.

"That is what I intend." A pang of trepidation reverberated through him. He hadn't thought to ask Susannah what her preferences might be. Nate glanced down at her again. "If you're amenable to that."

Susannah looked up at Nate, and the fire was back in her eyes. "I don't have a preference where we get married, *my love*. Only that we do. As quickly as possible."

He stifled a grin at her pointed remark. "Whatever my lady wishes."

Anna released a huge, happy sigh. "Oh, I love a good romance. How fortunate that the two of you found each other again. And to fall in love so quickly."

"From a purely scientific standpoint," Minnie said, "love at first sight is very rare."

"Do not start prosing about science." Juliana raised her hand in warning. "You will put us all to sleep."

Minnie huffed and crossed her arms, which she quickly had to uncross after Anna complained about being cramped.

"Well, I think love at first…reunion, because you do know each other, of course, is entirely possible." Anna clasped her hands together under her chin in a love-is-so-wonderful way. "So, how *did* you two find each other again?"

Nate looked down at Susannah, a flitter of panic stirring his blood. She looked up at him, her brow cocked questioningly. They hadn't prepared for this inquiry. Hadn't talked about the necessary details to make the farce seem real. He scoured his brain for an acceptable answer, but Susannah merely smiled at him, then turned to the girls. "He's been frequenting our home for dinner, being an acquaintance and friend of my uncle."

Well done. Nate opened his mouth to add to the story, but Susannah clenched his hand, demanding silence.

"I have been gone since leaving school, working as a companion for an elderly lady in Northumberland, and only just returned to town."

At the mention of Northumberland, Nate tensed. He had arranged the position for Susannah with his great aunt years ago when Cressingham had asked what he should do with his niece. Because Nate's aunt was practically forgotten in society, he'd been confident Cressingham would never make the connection that Nate had sent Susannah where he could keep tabs on her.

His sisters were another story, however.

Sure enough, Anna pounced, sitting upright in the carriage. "Oh, how interesting. Where were you? What was the lady's name? We have an—ow!" Anna frowned, leaning over to rub her shin.

Nate leaned over, too, and glared at her, willing her to keep her mouth shut. Anna always said too much, too often, just like Mama. In a somewhat insincere voice, Nate said, "Oh, I'm sorry, sister. Did I kick you? My apologies."

"Yes, you did kick me. Why on earth would you—"

"Isn't that Lord Castlereagh?" Minnie asked, nudging Anna. "I didn't know he had returned from Vienna." She looked pointedly at Nate, and he smiled gratefully.

The other occupants of the carriage turned to the right. Sure enough, Lord and Lady Castlereagh soon drove by in a stately barouche, his lordship ordering their carriage to stop when they drew near. Nate did the same.

Castlereagh raised his hat. "Rainsford. Pleasure to find you out today. I see you have your delightful sisters with you." He nodded at the girls. "Ladies, a pleasure, I'm sure."

The triplets all nodded in return and murmured their greetings.

"Welcome back to England, Castlereagh. Excellent work you've been doing, negotiating the peace. I've been following it closely." Nate nodded at Lady Castlereagh. "My lady, lovely to see you again. Glad to be back in England?"

"Always. Travel is so tedious these days." She gestured to Susannah and smiled. "Might we beg the pleasure of an introduction?"

Nate took Susannah's hand into his own, puffing out his chest with pride, and gazed at her. "My dear, may I present Lord and Lady Castlereagh?" He turned to the Castlereaghs. "I would like to introduce to you my fiancée, Miss Susannah Cressingham."

Lady Castlereagh smiled, but it seemed shallow. "It's a pleasure to meet you, Miss Cressingham."

"Likewise, my lady." Susannah's voice was low and quiet, but at least she sounded happy.

Lord Castlereagh raised his hat in salute. "Miss Cressingham, a pleasure." He looked at Nate, his expression guarded. "Cressingham, eh?" He paused. "Is she by chance related to a Captain Cressingham?"

Nate felt Susannah's hand stiffen. He tightened his hold on it while keeping up his friendly smile. "Yes, she is his niece and ward."

"I see." Castlereagh put his hat back on his head, his eyes flicking to the very curious stares Nate's sisters were giving him, then he relaxed his demeanor. "Of course. I know of him. A capital fellow."

Nate blinked rapidly. That was a lie if ever he'd heard one. Castlereagh must know Cressingham was a threat. But was Castlereagh aware of the work *he* was doing for the Home Office? Or did he think Nate was sympathetic to Napoleon as well? There were certainly individuals in high society who proclaimed an affinity for Boney, but an affinity was one thing. Treasonous activities were altogether different.

"When did you become engaged?" Lady Castlereagh asked Susannah.

"Last evening, my lady." Susannah's smile now looked forced. "I was quite surprised by it."

"Happily so, I hope?"

Susannah looked up at Nate, her lips curled in a lovely smile that did not reach her eyes. Clenching his hand, she turned to her ladyship. "Of course, my lady."

"Our families have been friends for years," Anna piped up. "It was a love match a long time in the making." She beamed at the Castlereaghs.

"Is that so?" Her ladyship smiled. "How lovely that you are joining two families of such long-standing acquaintance."

Juliana leaned forward. "My sisters and I attended finishing school with Miss Cressingham, as well. And our mothers were the dearest friends, as were Nate and Miss Cressingham's deceased brother, God rest his soul. So, as you see, it was destiny."

Nate looked appreciatively at his sisters, pleased by their show of solidarity towards Susannah. The girls all wore genuine smiles, but he could see in their eyes a fierceness, a protectiveness, and his heart filled with pride.

He turned his attention back to Castlereagh. "Are you in England for good?"

His lordship shook his head. "Unlikely. I'm to give my report to Parliament, but depending on whether Frederick Augustus accepts our terms, I may have to return."

"I wish you good luck in your endeavors, Castlereagh." Nate nodded towards her ladyship. "Ma'am. I hope we will see you soon."

Lady Castlereagh gave a dignified nod of her head. "Of course."

"Ladies, a delight." Castlereagh bowed to Nate's sisters. "Rainsford, congratulations again. Miss Cressingham, a pleasure. I wish you both very happy."

"Thank you." Susannah's cheeks pinked.

Nate admired her slight blush. He had to fight the urge to lean over and kiss the hell out of her. But he nodded to Castlereagh. "Thank you. I'm very delighted she accepted."

The Castlereaghs quickly moved off, and Nate's carriage proceeded through the park.

"Well," said Minnie once they were moving again, "I don't think Castlereagh approves of your marriage, Natey."

"No, nor do I." Juliana crossed her arms, but only until Minnie complained.

Nate didn't think so, either, but he said nothing.

Anna leaned over and patted Susannah on the hand reassuringly. "Don't worry, Susannah. We love you, and we're so happy you're going to be a part of the family."

Before Susannah could answer, Juliana interrupted them. "Natey, I see our friends over there, about three carriages over." She pointed to a group of girls and their ladies' maids. "Can we visit with them for a moment?"

They could visit with them for the rest of the afternoon

as far as Nate was concerned. He wanted nothing more than some time with his new fiancée. "Of course." He eyed Thomas, who nodded and jumped down, ready to accompany the girls. Within minutes, they were on their way.

Nate was finally alone with Susannah. Turning to her, he took her hands in his, but her question stopped him short.

"When can we get my sister?"

CHAPTER 4

NATE DID NOT WANT to discuss Susannah's sister.

"Well? When can we get her?" She pulled her hands from his, clasping them tightly in her lap, her lips drawn.

Sighing, Nate moved to the opposite seat so he could face her and, meeting her eyes, took her hands in his and kissed her gloved knuckles, silently bemoaning the fact that her soft skin was covered. He smiled at her, but she did not return it. In fact, she looked ready to do battle, and Nate groaned inwardly.

So much for quality romantic time with his betrothed.

He released her hands and leaned back against the velvet squab. "Susannah, she's married. There is no 'getting.' Only visiting."

She frowned, her fingers playing with the wrist strap of her reticule. "Surely her husband does not love her? What does he care where she is?"

"Your sister is married to an unpleasant man. He was the reason your brother and uncle had a falling out." Nate looked out across the park, not really seeing the people who drove by. He wasn't sure he should reveal what he knew, but perhaps more information about her sister would appease her. "Your sister is living in Jamaica, near Falmouth." He leaned forward, cupping her cheek with his gloved hand to get her attention. "I had no idea your uncle was keeping news about Isabela from you, or I would have figured out a way to get word to you." His eyes traced every feature of her face, and without really knowing what he was doing, his thumb grazed her lip. Lord, he wanted to kiss her.

She cleared her throat, pushing his hand away. "Forgive me if I don't believe you, but given your propensity to withhold information, I highly doubt that." She crossed her arms. "I know from stories in the papers and other tidbits I've managed to discover that the tropical climate can be deadly, particularly for Englishmen. You said yourself it doesn't suit her. I would like Isabela returned to native soil as quickly as possible, especially if she will soon have a baby. Can it be arranged?"

Nate sat back on the squab, then ran his hand over his face. Good lord, anything could be arranged if the right amount of money were offered up. Look at him, engaged to Susannah for the price of ten thousand pounds. He'd pay that a hundred times over if he had to. Nate cleared his throat. "Perhaps, if offered the right incentive, Isabela's husband might let her return to England."

"But what about her child? Will she be able to bring her child with her?"

"That I cannot say. If she has a daughter, perhaps. If she has a son?" He shrugged. "I would think the child's father would not allow him to leave."

Susannah huffed. "When can we leave for Jamaica? You said we'd be married in three weeks. So after Easter?"

"It's not that simple. We may not be able to leave for

some time. Until then, you may write her and let her know you will soon be visiting."

"But my uncle withholds letters from us." She rubbed her clenched hands back and forth on her thighs. "And what does that mean? 'For some time'?"

"I will ensure any letters you write get delivered. As for the delay, I have a very important piece of business that I cannot leave to dangle." He removed his hat, scratched his forehead, then set it on his head again. "It shouldn't take long after we're married for it all to be settled, but until then, I have to make it my priority above all else."

"But you said after we're married—"

"Yes, I did. But I didn't say the day after we married." He put up a hand to stem any subsequent protests. "Don't press me on this." Nate leaned forward on the squab, forcing Susannah backwards. "It is not negotiable. I will take you to your sister. But only when my business is concluded."

"It has something to do with my uncle, doesn't it?"

Of course it did, but she couldn't know that. In fact, the less Susannah knew about his scheme with Cressingham, the better. He had to distract her. Taking her hands in his, he said, "I did not come out here to talk about your uncle. I'd much rather kiss you silly."

Susannah's eyes bulged, and Nate burst out laughing. "Oh, for heaven's sake, if the thought of kissing me scares you that much, I'll leave you alone." His face grew serious again. "Although we *are* going to marry. I'd rather the next time we kiss *not* be on our wedding night."

Her face flamed, and a ripple of desire coursed through Nate. *Soon, soon*. He had to focus on Cressingham first.

"I have one more request."

Nate didn't want to talk any more. He *really* wanted to

kiss her. But the set of her jaw, her hands hard like stone in his? It would be...unadvisable. Not to mention they were in the middle of Hyde Park. He sighed and, releasing her hands, sat back once more. "Yes, my dear? What might that be?"

"When she returns, I wish to live with her. Not with you."

Nate chuckled, then shook his head. Did she have any idea how ridiculous her request was? As if he'd let her spend even a single night away from him. He leaned forward and put his hand on her knee. A terrible mistake, for he instantly felt the heat from beneath her gown radiate up his arm, even through his gloves. She tried to move her knee away, but he did not let go. He couldn't.

"I don't think you understand the nature of this marriage, Susannah. It is not a union in name only." He leaned closer, reducing the distance between them by half, and gazed into her chocolate-brown eyes. "I expect you to produce an heir. My heir." Just saying that sent a shot of heat through him.

Susannah licked her lips, and Nate had to hold himself back from sucking on them. Lord, she was tempting. In every sense of the word. He reached out and stroked her cheek, and Susannah bit her tongue, a sour expression on her face.

He tsked. "I think it's time we discuss the details of our agreement."

"You said last night that we will pretend it is a love match."

"Precisely. Giving me a sour face when I stroke your cheek will not convince anyone that we're in love." He looked at her shoulders, hard and drawn in. "Neither will your body language."

"But—"

"You must willingly, convincingly, and earnestly give and receive compliments, kind words, and, most importantly, affection."

"Only in front of others," she said through clenched teeth.

With one arm, Nate gestured to the park and the people promenading around them. "We're surrounded by others." He looked around to prove his point, taking in the pedestrians on foot, spirited and laughing passengers in carriages, and ladies and gentlemen on horseback. All of these people bearing witness to the "love match" with Susannah. His gaze slowly turned towards his fiancée. "But that wasn't the condition. In public *and* private."

Her mouth still formed a frown.

"Poppet," he said in a tone of warning.

Like the lighting of a candle, her expression suddenly changed, her eyes becoming doe-like, her head tilted appreciatively, and her smile so contrived, Nate wanted to laugh.

"Is this better?" she asked.

Nate shook his head in resignation, then sighed. He'd give her a little bit of time—at least when they weren't in the direct company of other people—to come around.

Schooling her features a bit, Susannah said, "I think Minnie is right. Castlereagh does not like you aligning yourself with my family."

"No." Nate frowned. "He does not."

Susannah opened her mouth as if to say something, then closed it and crossed her arms, looking out the side of the carriage.

"What is it?" Nate asked.

"I…" She huffed. "Oh, never mind. You won't tell me the truth anyway."

Nate sighed. He wanted to. It would make this

damned outing far more enjoyable. Not to mention their forthcoming nuptials. He let silence reign, not sure there was anything more he could say or do at this point to get her to soften towards him. In his heart, he knew she needed time. Time and truth. But he didn't have the luxury of either.

"Rainsford," said a deep, booming voice.

Nate turned to see a well-heeled gentleman riding up on horseback, and he groaned inwardly. Lord Harton, a Whig and Napoleonic sympathizer. One of Cressingham's "fine friends" and a bloody idiot who didn't know when to keep his mouth shut.

Harton rode right up to the side of the carriage and extended his hand. "Good afternoon to you, sir."

Rising, Nate reached out and shook it. "And you." Gesturing to Susannah, he said, "My dear, may I present Henry Tewksbury, Viscount Harton. Harton, my fiancée, Miss Susannah Cressingham."

"Ah, fiancée, eh? I wondered if I'd read that correctly this morning." Harton nodded to Susannah. "A pleasure, miss. Congratulations." He turned to Nate again. "Very happy to hear about you aligning yourself with Cressingham. Quite a splendid match there, eh? And about time, I daresay, that you heed the parson's call."

"Yes, well, we have been family friends for quite some time." Nate glanced at Susannah, and her eyes narrowed with suspicion. "It was natural that we discovered an affection for each other."

"Oh, more than that, sir, more than that." Harton gave Nate an exaggerated wink, then leaned towards him, his hand half-covering his mouth. "Things are happening, Rainsford. Quickly." If the man was trying to be secretive, his loudness completely defeated the purpose. "Why, I've heard from Ebrington that—"

"Harton," Nate said, flicking his eyes to Susannah and back in a be-quiet warning.

The man glanced over at her, his face conveying surprise. "But she's you're betrothed."

"Yes, I am," Susannah said, smiling sweetly at Harton. "Pray continue, sir. I assure you, I will recall nothing. I am, after all, merely a female."

Nate returned a droll look to her inane comment. Addressing Harton, he said, "I think it's best if we have this discussion privately." He called up to John Coachman. "Hold them here, if you please, John."

"Yes, my lord."

To Susannah, he said, "I'll return in a moment, my sweet."

She nodded and frowned, but said nothing.

Nate opened the door of the carriage and stepped down, gesturing for Harton to follow him in the direction of a copse of trees.

Harton dismounted and pulled his hack behind him.

Once they were far enough away that Susannah could not overhear, Nate turned to the idiot beside him. "Really, Harton. Watch your words around her. She might be Cressingham's niece, but she knows nothing of what is going on."

Harton looked over his shoulder. "She's a devilishly pretty thing. I can't believe your rotting good luck, Rainsford." He sighed and crossed his arms. "Cressingham offered her to Ebrington, you know, but he's so monstrously in the wind, he couldn't possibly have given up her dowry."

Nate blinked twice, unsure he'd heard the man correctly. "He offered her to Ebrington?"

"Yes." Harton turned to face Nate once more. "Months ago. Why, must have been November or so.

Seemed damned excited about it, too. You should thank me, Rainsford." He punctuated his remark by poking Nate in the chest. "Cressingham asked me what I thought of having you offer for her. Said you two had fallen out of contact, but I assured him you were up to the mark." He winked at Nate. "And was I not right? You clearly have the blunt to give Cressingham what he needs."

Tension tightened every muscle in Nate's body. *Months ago?* But Cressingham had only approached him a few weeks ago about marrying Susannah. What had the bastard been doing all this time? Or, God forbid, *planning*.

"I say, are you well, Rainsford? You look as if you've swallowed a bug." Harton laughed at his own joke.

Forcing a smile, Nate clapped Harton on the arm. "Quite well. Just…thinking about my good fortune."

"Yes, bloody good fortune." Turning around, he looked at the carriage. "Speaking of your betrothed, I think she's getting a bit jealous."

Nate peered over Harton's shoulder. Susannah's eyes were fastened on the two of them, her mouth set in a straight line. Wonderful. Now he'd have to work even harder to convince her that he was not her uncle's toady.

"I think I better rejoin my fiancée." He held out his gloved hand. "I hope we shall meet again soon."

"Oh, I don't doubt that." Harton shook Nate's hand roughly, then climbed atop his horse. "Enjoy the rest of your afternoon, Rainsford." He doffed his hat. "And take care of that lovely little piece I dropped in your lap." He winked, then turned his horse and trotted away.

Nate clenched his teeth, Harton's last comment irking him. *Lovely little piece indeed*. He walked towards the landau, his quick, heavy stride crunching the gravel beneath his feet. Nate had to get word to the Home Office about what he'd learned. If Cressingham had been planning for months to get his hands on a large sum of money, it meant something significant was poised to happen. Something that likely involved Napoleon.

When he reached the carriage, he called out to the driver, "Find the girls, John. We need to leave." Nate settled into the seat across from Susannah but avoided looking at her.

"Very good, my lord." A few moments later, the carriage trundled into motion.

Susannah hadn't taken her steely gaze off Nate since he returned to the carriage, but she said nothing. She didn't need to. Nate knew the one-sided conversation she was having inside her mind, and it involved the words treason, liar, and traitor. He wasn't sure how to correct her incorrect assumptions without revealing everything, either. Regardless, he first needed to speak with his superiors at the Home Office.

The carriage pulled up beside another, in which sat his sisters and one of their friends. After a brief exchange of pleasantries, Nate said, "I'm afraid we need to leave, girls. An appointment that slipped my mind."

His sisters didn't look bothered in the least, but Susannah looked suspicious, as he expected.

The girls said their goodbyes as Nate stepped out of the carriage. He waved off Thomas, then assisted his sisters into the landau. Once the girls were settled, Nate closed the door, still standing outside, and said, "Can I trust you girls to take Susannah directly home?"

"Of course, brother, but after tea." Anna adjusted her bonnet and smiled kindly at Susannah. "I'm sure Mama would be delighted to see you again. You should have seen how excited she was this morning when we read her the announcement in *The Times*. Why, Natey hadn't even told her." She giggled.

Nate could see Susannah stiffen, her face growing ashen. "Perhaps you should just take her home, Anna." Tea was a terrible idea. Susannah was angry and mistrustful, and he was sure that sentiment extended to his entire family, not just him.

"Oh, pish-posh. We won't let Mama eat her, brother," Anna said with a dismissive wave of her hand.

"Don't worry, Nate," said Minnie. "We will take good care of her, I promise."

"As if we wouldn't. What do you take us for, brother?" Juliana asked, her eyes sparkling.

Nate didn't like it, but the sooner he spoke with the Home Office, the better. Besides, his sisters had demonstrated a show of solidarity earlier.

John Coachman made the decision for him as the landau sprung into motion. Juliana leaned over the side of the carriage. "Go, Natey. Do whatever it is you have to do. Like Minnie said, we'll take good care of Susannah."

Nate walked beside the carriage, looking up at Susannah. "I will see you later this evening. I assume your uncle has told you about the card party at Sherry's. I imagine news will have spread about our engagement, so be prepared for good wishes." The carriage picked up speed, and the distance between them grew. "I'll pick you up at nine," he called out.

The hard stare she returned told him that she was not happy with all he'd implied. Lord, he hoped Susannah didn't say anything to his sisters. They just might take up her cause, and instead of spending an evening playing cards, he'd spend it in gaol.

CHAPTER 5

NATE STRODE DOWN PICCADILLY, deftly dodging domestics on errands and rowdy young gentlemen no doubt on their way to the clubs on St. James's. The sky had begun to darken with threatening clouds, casting grey shadows that loomed like a shroud, and Nate hoped his sisters—or at the very least his coachman—had enough sense to return to the house before the sky opened up.

Turning left on Half-moon Street, Nate wound his way to the small homes scattered about the courts off Curzon Street. Keeping his head down, he made a straightaway for number 23 Carrington Court. As he approached the door, it opened as if by magic, and Nate entered the small, dimly lit hallway. The brawny, dark-skinned man who opened the door shut it as soon as Nate cleared the threshold.

"*Bonjour*, Toussaint." Nate nodded politely. "Très occupé aujourd'hui?"

"Oui, monsieur." Toussaint's deep, warm bass echoed in the hall. "Beaucoup d'hommes vont et viennent."

"Bien. Merci." Nate dipped his head in thanks.

Toussaint, a *gens de couleur libre* who had helped the

British during the Royal Navy's blockade of Saint-Domingue, returned to his post by the door. No one got past Toussaint, which is why Sidmouth had brought him on staff.

Nate proceeded into the building and, just before the stairs, entered a small priest's hole, closing the secret panel behind him, then continued through the small space to a door on the opposite wall, which led to a short passageway. At the far end was a windowless anteroom lit by candles. Small, square, and filled with bookcases stacked with piles of paper, maps, and cartons of correspondence, it was guarded by a uniformed man sitting at a writing desk. When Nate entered, the man looked up.

"My lord." He stood, his dark grey eyes guarded. "This is unexpected. How might I help you?" He came around the desk.

"I need to speak with Sidmouth immediately."

The man—Neville, Nate recalled—clasped his hands in front of him. "I am sorry, my lord, but he is not available at this time."

"He's here, though, isn't he?" Sidmouth changed his location frequently to "keep the enemy on their toes," as he put it.

Neville didn't answer.

"Listen to me." Nate clenched his hands, frustrated because he got the same demur every time he came to report his progress, and today, the stakes were higher. "I've just learned some very disturbing news, and it's vital that he know. If he isn't here, then tell me where I can find him."

Neville inspected Nate from head to toe, as if trying to determine whether he was being told the truth. Nate must have seemed earnest, because after a moment, he said, "Sidmouth is here. I'll inquire as to whether he'll see you."

"Thank you." Nate's shoulders relaxed a little.

"Do be seated, my lord. I'll return shortly." Neville gestured to the lone chair placed next to his writing desk.

"I'd rather stand."

"As you wish, my lord." Neville disappeared through a heavy, paneled door behind his desk.

Sidmouth had better see him. Nate would jump over the desk and break down the door if he had to. He had a feeling that Cressingham was involved in something imminent.

Neville stepped into the room again and held the door open. "The Secretary will see you now, my lord."

"Excellent, thank you." Nate walked around the desk and through the door, and Neville closed it behind him. "Sir, I beg your pardon, but—"

"Dammit, Rainsford." Viscount Sidmouth, Lord Secretary of the Home Office, slammed his bony hand on his desk like a gavel. "This had better be important." Tall and balding with muttonchops sideburns, Sidmouth may have had a bark like an angry dog, but he was gentle as a newborn kitten.

"Yes, sir." Nate stopped short and gave him his best "this isn't my fault" look. He glanced around the wood-paneled room, a former study in this row house-turned-meeting house, complete with built-in bookcases, a large marble mantel and fireplace, and shelf after shelf of books. Heavy, brocade curtains blocked out all daylight—and prying eyes—from the large windows behind Sidmouth. Two branches of candles stood on the desk, burning furiously, yet giving off weak light. Just enough to illuminate Sidmouth's face and that of the man sitting opposite him. Nate relaxed a bit when he recognized his good friend Sir Philip Tradwick.

Sidmouth rubbed his hand over his face, releasing a

deep sigh. "Very well then. Come in. Sit down." He leaned back into the dark leather chair, crossed one Hoby'd boot over his knee, then gestured to Tradwick. "He was just finishing his report. Should he stay and listen to yours?"

"Yes."

"Pleasure to see you again, Rain." Tradwick stood, his tall, lanky frame unfolding like a wooden marionette pulled up by its strings. His blue eyes hid behind a shock of straight, dark hair, which fell unfashionably thick over his forehead. He shook Nate's hand, then both men took the seats opposite Sidmouth.

Aside from being a friend, Sir Philip Tradwick was a fellow member of the Beggars Club, a tongue-in-cheek reference to the friendship formed by Nate and five of his mates from Eton, including Susannah's brother, Ben. Like Nate, Tradwick had served during the war, carrying out clandestine operations. When Nate was at his lowest, Tradwick and Ben enlisted him with the Home Office. Not only did that rescue Nate from the nasty world of drunkenness he'd found for himself since his brother's death, but Nate was able to get close to Cressingham, something neither Tradwick nor Ben had been able to do.

As a temporary member, Nate was only called into service when the need arose. But to make sure Cressingham always regarded Nate as an ally, Nate and Tradwick had been required from the beginning to play enemies in the public eye. Tricky, to be sure, and it made communicating with each other deuced difficult, but it was a necessary evil and had been for years. When they did meet, it was at one of a dozen safe places Sidmouth had established—this inconspicuous row house being one of them—that they rotated through.

Tradwick pulled his watch from the fob pocket of his breeches and studied the gold face. "I have ten minutes before I must leave for another appointment." He tap, tap, tapped the watch on the desk, a single eyebrow forming an inquisitive arch. "What has happened?"

Nate took a deep breath, trying to collect his racing thoughts. "I ran into Harton just now while taking a turn about Hyde Park. It seems that Cressingham offered his niece to Ebrington in November of last year. Same sort of arrangement, except Ebrington needed her dowry. He wouldn't have been able to turn it over to Cressingham, having his own debts to pay. When he declined, Cressingham asked Harton about me, and Harton assured the captain I was 'up to the mark.'" Nate rose and began pacing the small room, his hand worrying his forehead.

Tradwick turned his head slightly and squinted an eye. "I'm not sure I understand the problem. We want you to be in Cressingham's good graces."

"And I am. But it's the timing." Nate came to a stop before Sidmouth's desk. He looked between both men. "Cressingham approached me only a few weeks ago about this arrangement with Susannah, which, of course, I brought right to you. However, he originally intended to marry Miss Cressingham off six months ago." He held out his hands expectantly. "You understand the implication here, I hope?"

"Yes, of course." Sidmouth leaned back in his chair and crossed his arms. "Cressingham has been planning this little financial arrangement for a long time."

"But it's more than that." Nate put his hands on his hips, shaking his head. "It could mean that Boney's return is imminent."

Tradwick frowned. "Explain."

"When I met with Cressingham last night, he talked about an *eventual* return of Napoleon. We've assumed that the dowry money is required *before* any of that can happen.

But what if that's not the case? What if it's merely more copper for the pot?"

"I think Boney making a play for the Continent at this time is unlikely." Sidmouth scratched a muttonchops side-burn. "How would he escape? It would have to be by ship, but we have surveillance on Elba constantly. And where would he land?" He shuffled through a stack of papers and pulled out a map of France, unfolding it on his desk. Both Nate and Tradwick leaned over it.

"There." Sidmouth pointed to the map. "It would have to be somewhere on the Mediterranean coast. A place that would put him on the closest path to Paris, for I don't see him out-sailing His Majesty's Navy were he to try to go around Gibraltar for the western coast. That would be suicide. However, a landing on the southern coast would mean crossing the Alps, which would be virtually impossible to do at this time of year." He shook his head. "No, if he's going to do it, it will be in April or May. Still," he said, folding the map and setting it aside, "it would not hurt to put the admiralty on alert."

Nate gave Tradwick a beseeching look. "This doesn't concern you at all?"

Tradwick shrugged. "It's certainly nothing good. But I have to agree with Sidmouth. It would be devilishly hard for Boney to leave Elba, first of all, then land and not encounter resistance." He shook his head. "He has few supporters, and most of them lay north of Dauphiné or east of Bretagne or Poitou."

Nate fell back into his chair, stunned. Napoleon could be on the move, and Sidmouth and Tradwick acted as unconcerned as if his great aunt were coming to town. He didn't understand that at all. Then again, he didn't under-stand much of what went on in the Home Office. The only thing he could do was report what he'd learned and hope they had a plan to deal with it.

"What else have you to report, Rainsford?" Sidmouth asked. "You met with Cressingham last night? Did you make any progress on the settlements?"

Shaking his head to clear it, Nate blinked a few times, then nodded. "Yes. Cressingham signed them."

"Well done, Rainsford," Sidmouth said in a plain tone.

"Yes, indeed." Tradwick gave him the barest smile. "My felicitations."

Nate looked back and forth between the two men. "Your enthusiasm astounds me." There was no mistaking his sarcasm.

His friend upped the smile parlay, but it was still fabricated. "I *am* pleased for you. It is a…significant accomplishment."

"However…"

"However, I still cannot believe you're willing to take this vengeance with Cressingham all the way to the altar."

"It's not vengeance and it's not just Cressingham. Don't pretend ignorance, Tradwick. I made a promise to Ben and I will honor it." He leaned back, tapping his fingers on the desk. "What should I have done? Let Cressingham marry her off to any coxcomb?" *Like he did Isabela?*

Tradwick shrugged. "No, certainly not. But you could do as we originally discussed and pretend to marry her."

Nate shook his head. "And what happens if Cressingham were to discover the marriage was not legitimate? He'd find another warm body and use him as a groom instead." Nate had never intended to make the marriage anything *but* real. It was the least he could do for Ben. And now that he'd actually *seen* Susannah? There was no way he'd let anyone else have her.

"Gentlemen," Sidmouth interrupted. "What's done is

done. Tradwick, it's none of your business why Rainsford is doing what he's doing, except it plays into our ploy to catch Cressingham. You heard him when he brought this to us. If he wants to be leg-shackled to the girl for the rest of his life, that's his business." He gave them both a pointed look. "Keep your eye on the prize."

"Of course, sir." Tradwick nodded.

"Yes, sir." Nate cleared his throat. "I, uh...I might have made things more complicated."

Sidmouth's eyebrows shot up in question.

"I'm afraid I made a rather rash decision last night."

"What prompted this 'rash decision'?" Sidmouth asked.

Nate's face heated up. The mental image of Susannah sent a rush of liquid warmth throughout his entire body. He couldn't believe he had acted without thinking. Marriage to Susannah was a promise, yes, but it was also a business transaction. One aimed at sinking Cressingham. It was certainly not for love.

"Well, friend?" Tradwick prompted. "What did you do?"

Sighing, Nate said, "I made a bargain with Susannah. She and I will pretend our match is for love, and in exchange, after we're married, I will take her to see her sister."

"You did what?" both men asked in unison.

Nate ignored their question. "Tradwick," he said, looking at his friend, "she's..." He couldn't find the right words

Tradwick's lips curled in a slow smile. "Shot by Cupid's arrow, were you?"

"Something like that."

Sidmouth leaned into the desk slightly so he could rest an elbow on it, his mouth forming a frown. "This is not a good time for love, Rainsford. In fact, it complicates things significantly. I can't have you forming a *tendre* for the girl you're marrying, at least not now. It makes you vulnerable."

Nate sat forward in his chair, his pulse pattering. "I've already sent a notice to *The Times*. If I cry off, not only will her reputation be in tatters, but Cressingham will give her to someone else. You *know* what sort of man he'll give her to, Tradwick."

"Careful, friend." Tradwick narrowed his eyes. "You're letting your personal vendetta against Cressingham get in the way of doing your job. Leave Ben and the girls out of this. You owe them nothing."

Nate felt a pang in his chest, as if he'd been struck. Owe them nothing? Nate owed them *everything*. He'd been damn near helpless when Cressingham had pursued Ben. The best he could do was get Ben out of the country. And poor, sweet Isabela...by the time Nate was able to assist her, Cressingham had already arranged her marriage to a dissolute landowner in Jamaica who owed him money.

Nate stood and whirled around, facing the small door, his hands on his hips. He took deep breaths to calm his ragged breathing. For too long had Nate put off fulfilling his obligation to Ben. If he let Susannah go now, he would lose her—and likely Cressingham—forever, to say nothing of not keeping his promise to Ben to protect her.

Nate could not, in good conscience, do that.

He turned back around to face his colleagues, his hand sweeping out in front of him apologetically. "I'm sorry, gentlemen, but when you make a promise to a dying man, you keep it." He eyed them both. "I think you know me well enough to get the job done."

"Well..." Sidmouth shook his head and exhaled. "This marriage to Miss Cressingham will certainly keep you close to the captain." He tossed the quill he'd been holding onto the desk and leaned forward. "I want you to prepare the bank. If Cressingham is going to use his niece's dowry, I want to make sure we have a man on the inside."

"I have not had a chance to speak to Rothschild lately. Last time we met, he was noncommittal."

"Then fix it, Rainsford." Sidmouth turned to Tradwick. "I need you to examine every possible communication path. We've never been able to trace Cressingham's network with confidence. We need that now more than ever."

Tradwick stood. "I will get on it straight away."

Nate rose, as well. "As soon as I know anything, I will advise you." He bowed to Sidmouth. "Sir."

"Oh, get out of here, both of you." Sidmouth shooed them out with an impatient wave of his hand.

The men did as he bid.

In the hallway outside the priest's hole, Tradwick clapped Nate on the shoulder. "Let me know what you find out." With a Tradwick-esque arch of his brow, he asked, "So when do I get to *see* the famous Miss Cressingham?"

"We'll be at Sherry's card party tonight. Naturally, you can't be too friendly to her—or me—of course, but if you want to catch a glimpse of her..." Nate shrugged. "However, be warned that Cressingham will likely be there, too." Nate adjusted the cuffs of his shirtsleeves and pulled out his watch. "I'm late for my fiancée."

"Are you now?"

"Well, she was with me in Hyde Park, but so were my sisters. They've dragged her back to Rainsford House to see my mother. I have to make sure she survived." Nate glanced at the door, then back at his friend. "So you'll be at Sherry's tonight?"

"Indubitably." Tradwick withheld a smile.

Nate held out his hand and Tradwick grasped it. Nate shook his hand, but didn't release it. A wellspring of emotion rose within him, but it took a few seconds for the words to come. "Thank you for peeling me off that tavern floor all those years ago." Nate looked him in the eye. "I don't think I ever properly expressed my appreciation to you for that."

Tradwick squeezed Nate's still-clasped hand, and with his other, slapped Nate on his arm. "You don't have to. That's what Beggars are for. But I appreciate it all the same." His eyes softened, then crinkled with a rarely seen smile. "Who knows, someday you may be doing that for me."

Nate shook Tradwick's hand again, then released it. "Until tonight, then, and keep your distance."

"But that's no fun."

Nate walked out the door, nodding to Toussaint, Tradwick's rare laughter following him. He made his way back towards Piccadilly, chewing his lip in consternation over the doubt expressed by Sidmouth and Tradwick regarding an imminent move by Boney. It sat like a yoke on his neck, rife and heavy. Add to that the questions about exactly who Cressingham was communicating with, as well as Nate's undeniable desire for Susannah and her clear hatred of him, and he felt the pressure keenly. He needed to be prepared.

Prepared to stop a traitor.

Prepared to fulfill a promise.

And prepared for life "till death he did part" with a woman who would no doubt like to usher him into the grave.

CHAPTER 6

"Susannah, I can't say enough how delighted I am that you're going to be my sister."

Juliana spoke up before Susannah could respond. "Yes, Anna. We know. Again." She rolled her eyes. "You can be so tiresome."

"I will tell her that as often as I like." Anna had positioned herself next to Susannah after Nate left. "After all those years playing dolls together while our parents socialized." Her expression grew somber. "I am very sorry for your losses. Ben always was a fun and witty friend to our brother. And your parents were exceptional. We never did properly express that after…well, after."

Minnie and Juliana quickly echoed Anna's sentiment.

But Susannah prickled at their sympathy. They were telling her this now? Where were they when her parents died? When Ben left? When Isabela left for Jamaica? Why had they said nothing—absolutely nothing—while they were at school? She looked at her hands, unable to speak, for anything she did say—"Thank you" or "You're too kind"—would be a lie.

After a gentle pat on her hand, Anna began a one-sided conversation about the deplorable number of stray animals that roamed the streets. Juliana sighed and looked out the carriage.

Susannah half-listened to Anna's chatter, occupied with her own thoughts. Nate was not what she expected. Almost paradoxical. She wasn't sure what sort of meeting he had to go to that prompted him to abandon her to his sisters, but she couldn't deny the girls had given her a warm welcome to the family.

A surprisingly warm welcome, for after her parents died, the visits between the families slowed. When Ben died, they stopped. Susannah might have shared a head-mistress with the girls, but there were no more holidays with the Rainsfords. No get-togethers. No calls. No letters. No condolences. Simply…nothing. Their callous avoid-ance had hollowed out her heart as much as the passing of her parents and brother. It was like losing a second family.

And yet, here they were, as friendly as if nothing had happened and no time had passed. To her surprise, Susannah had enjoyed her time with them at the park. However, Nate might have asked his sisters to be kind to her. Likely they were playing a role, just as Nate was. That had to be it, for they'd all been exceptional so far. Susannah wondered if she'd get the same sort of overly friendly welcome from Nate's mother.

Slowly, she tried to distance herself from Anna, needing space from all of them, for she saw no future with the Rainsford family except heartbreak.

Instead of letting Susannah move away, Anna grasped her hand. She glanced at Susannah, winked, and said, "We shall need to visit the shops. The four of us. And Mama, of course. Nate will want you to be dressed in the finest gowns, the best lace, the softest furs, for it is still chilly enough for furs."

Susannah's forehead wrinkled. She looked down at her peach-colored gown and matching pelisse, made from the finest cambric, and newly purchased by her uncle upon her return to London. Were the girls trying to tell her something? That she was too unfashionable to be seen with them? And their brother in particular?

"Not that your gown and pelisse isn't lovely," said Minnie, as if reading her mind. She leaned over to pat Susannah on the knee. "That shade of pink is absolutely divine on you."

"Shows what you know, Brainy." Juliana scoffed, waving her hand in dismissal. "It isn't pink."

Minnie frowned. "Yes, it is."

"No, it's not," said Anna.

"It is." Minnie looked at Susannah. "Isn't it?"

Susannah shook her head, trying not to smile. Minnie had never been one for fashion. "It is more of a peach color, to be honest."

"Peach." Minnie crossed her arms and rolled her eyes. "Fine. It's a lovely *peach* gown you have on." She gave Juliana and Anna a hard look.

Juliana cleared her throat to get everyone's attention. "Please don't read anything into our suggestion for shopping, Susannah. We're always looking for an excuse to go, and it will be so much fun with you. Why, I can't recall the last time we went."

Susannah could recall, and her heart clenched. *One week before Mama and Papa died.* Clearly, the girls had forgotten. For her, though, every last memory with the Rainsfords had been etched in her mind.

Anna gave Juliana a swift kick in the leg, whispering furiously, "Keep your mouth shut, you dolt." At the same time, Minnie elbowed Juliana in the side, saying, "Really, Jules? Must you remind her?"

Perhaps they hadn't forgotten after all.

"Let's change the subject," Juliana said. "I know something we can talk about, but we have to be quiet." She lowered her voice and leaned in, smiling slyly. "Susannah is going to be the very first of us to find out what it's like to be married."

Susannah frowned. She didn't like the reminder. And besides, why was that significant?

Both Anna and Minnie's cheeks turned bright red, and they covered their mouths with their hands, giggling.

Suddenly, Susannah understood what Juliana meant, and her own cheeks flamed. She looked away, wishing she could drop through the floor of the carriage. It was bad enough Susannah had to wrestle with her own conflicting feelings about Nate, but to have the girls allude to consummating their marriage was almost more than she could bear.

Juliana was also giggling. "Do you remember those tawdry books we sneaked behind the headmistress's back?"

"Oh, they were horrible," said Anna, still laughing. "Especially the one about the celebrated author...what was his name?"

"Peter Aretin." Susannah couldn't stop the little curve that formed in the corner of her mouth. The story had indeed been horrendous, but the scenes between the lovers had been quite explicit. Since her mother had not given her any education on the responsibilities of a wife, those books had formed the foundation of what little she knew about being intimate with a man. And every time she'd read them, she couldn't help but picture Nate doing those things to her, even though she had already blackened her heart towards him. Just the thought made her flush.

"I'm not even sure where we got them," Anna mused.

"From the citesses," Minnie replied. "Their tradesman fathers might have sent them to school to be proper ladies, but they still brought the gutter with them."

"That's a terrible thing to say." Anna sobered. "Those girls were nice."

"Of course they were," Minnie said, "but they still weren't the daughters of gentlemen."

"Well, we are, and we still read those books." Juliana waved her hand dismissively. "Oh well, that's no matter." She eyed Susannah. "Are you nervous?"

"I...um..." Susannah's cheeks grew hotter. What on earth was she supposed to say? Of course she was nervous. She had no experience being intimate with a man, and she certainly wasn't going to talk about it with Nate's *sisters*.

Minnie must have taken pity on her, for she gave Juliana a shove and a pointed stare. "Really, Jules. I think it's one thing to discuss that abstractedly, but clearly another when it's our own brother. And future sister-in-law." She turned to Susannah. "Jules shouldn't have brought it up."

"You're right," Juliana said with contrition. "I'm sorry, Susannah. I should have seen how this conversation would put you in an awkward position." Juliana pressed her hands around Susannah's apologetically.

"It's all right." In reality, it wasn't. Nate had made it clear to her just a few minutes ago that theirs would not be a marriage in name only. She hadn't yet thought explicitly about what that meant, but the more she did, the more she realized that engaging in a physical relationship with Nate would be disastrous. Every time they touched, her body acted as a traitor to her mind.

The carriage slowed, then came to a stop. Susannah looked up at the residence on Cavendish Square where

Nate and his family lived when in London, and her stomach knotted up.

Rainsford House.

Instant flashbacks, short, fast, and brilliant, pierced her mental vision, and her breath hitched. Happy memories flooded her mind. Michaelmas celebrations. Her mother and Lady Rainsford giggling like schoolchildren after too much sherry. The deep, warm laughter of her father and Old Lord Rainsford ribbing each other over a game of billiards. Dancing in the ballroom. Playing dolls in the nursery with Nate's sisters. Running joyfully through the house as Nate and Ben chased the girls, threatening them with tickles.

My first kiss with Nate.

Susannah flushed at that particular memory, then steeled herself. She'd made a deal with Nate to play the loving fiancée. Anything for her sister. But she had to keep the feelings behind her actions hollow.

Thomas hopped down and opened the carriage door, put the step down, and held out his hand for Susannah.

Taking a deep breath to collect her wits, she gathered her skirts together in one hand and exited the carriage, standing to the side to wait for the girls.

"Shall we see what Cook has made for tea this afternoon?" Anna locked arms with her and led the way up the front steps, Juliana and Minnie following behind.

"Yes, of course." Susannah glanced idly at the flower boxes on either side of the entrance, and the corner of her mouth unexpectedly turned upward. Pansies. Her mother had loved pansies. The bright, colorful flowers reminded her of the front door to her childhood home, which Mama had always made pretty with flowers and box trees. Now that her uncle had taken up residence there, the entrance was plain and uninviting, the marble chipped, the ironwork rusted. Susannah had nearly burst into tears when she'd seen the state of her family's former home. It was nothing like she remembered. Every vestige of her past life was slowly being erased.

In a matter of moments, the door opened, and the butler ushered them all into the house.

Susannah stepped over the threshold and stopped short, gaping in wonder. This was not the Rainsford House of her youth. It must have been renovated since she was last here. The now two-story entryway was immense, boasting an ornate, bifurcated staircase that led to the upper floors. A large crystal chandelier, which could easily hold fifty candles, hung from the ceiling, and an assemblage of semi-naked Grecian statues stood like sentinels in the hall. Susannah looked down at the shiny black and white marble floor and could have sworn she saw her reflection. From the street, the house had seemed unchanged, but clearly the façade hid all manner of surprises inside.

The butler stepped forward to take the ladies' bonnets and gloves. "Ladies, welcome home. Is my lord not with you?"

Anna waved her hand. "He had some urgent business to attend." She turned to Susannah. "You remember our beloved butler Crimson?" She removed her bonnet and gloves and handed them to him. "Crimson, surely you remember Miss Cressingham." She paused dramatically, a huge grin on her face. "Nate's fiancée."

The conspiratorial wink she gave Crimson made Susannah want to melt through the floor.

"Anna, don't embarrass her like that." Minnie handed her things over to Crimson.

"Of course I remember," he said, seeming eager to put Susannah at ease. "It is a pleasure to see you again, miss.

And may I please wish you my congratulations on your forthcoming nuptials?"

Susannah bowed her head quickly, not wanting to discuss her "forthcoming nuptials" any more than she had to. "Thank you very much, Crimson."

"If you will give me your bonnet and gloves, miss, I will tell her ladyship that you have all arrived home."

Susannah quickly removed her articles and gave them to Crimson, who left at once, his quick, smart footsteps echoing down the hallway.

Anna roped her arm through Susannah's again. "Let's go find Mama."

The girls started towards the stairs, passing a large, marble-topped console table in the entry, centered below the chandelier. Susannah glanced down, then stopped short. There, situated where everyone could see, were five tiny miniatures. Isabela. Mama. Papa. Ben. Even her as a child. Susannah pulled her arm from Anna's as tears sprung to her eyes. She choked back a sob, fisting her hands at her sides, struggling for control.

"What's wrong?" Juliana asked, a perplexed expression marring her face.

Susannah couldn't speak. She was trying so hard not to break down. She could only shake her head and point at the miniatures.

The girls looked down at them, and Juliana's expression softened. "Oh, no, don't cry." Juliana's eyebrows knitted together, and she took Susannah's hand, squeezing it tightly. "We thought you'd like to see them. We didn't mean to make you sad."

Minnie huffed. "I told Mama we shouldn't have brought those out. That they would surely upset her." She gestured to Susannah. "And look."

"Oh Min, must you?" Anna took Susannah's other

hand between her own in a motherly fashion. "We really didn't mean to upset you, Susannah."

"I...I have no pictures of them," Susannah said through quivering lips. How she hated showing them her vulnerability, her pain. But she couldn't help it. The words would not be held back. "Uncle removed them all. Every picture and portrait of my family, except for one of Ben that I only found last night." She'd had to remember her family in her mind's eye, and as time had passed, those images had begun to fade.

Yet here, before her, the memories of them—her father's mischievous gleam, her mother's delicate smile, her sister's bright blue eyes, Ben's innate confidence—suddenly returned. And with them, more happy memories from her childhood with the Rainsfords.

Susannah pulled her hands away from Juliana and Anna. Her mind whirled. They all seemed so sincere in their regard for her. Of course, the true test would be Nate's mother, but hadn't Juliana just said she was the one who'd insisted on putting out the miniatures to make Susannah feel welcome?

"Susannah?" Minnie's voice, followed by a polite cough at the other end of the hall, interrupted her thoughts. Nate's sisters stared at her with troubled, concerned expressions on their faces. Crimson stood further away, trying to get their attention.

"You should have them." Anna gestured to the miniatures.

"Anna," Juliana scolded, "you can't give them away without Mama's blessing."

"Jules, do be serious. They are her *family*. It's all she has. Let her have them. It's the least we can do." Anna's cheeks were pink with passion.

Crimson coughed again, coming further into the entry. "Ladies, your mother is awaiting you upstairs."

"Let's bring it up with Mama," Minnie suggested, ever the diplomat. "Susannah, can we take you to her? Or do you need some time to freshen up?" She held out a handkerchief.

Susannah accepted it with thanks and quickly wiped the wetness from her cheeks. There was no sense in putting off the inevitable. "I will see her." But she had no idea what she was going to say to her.

Crimson led them up the main staircase and off to the right. Anna excused herself to drop something off in her room.

When Susannah looked at Minnie inquisitively, the middle triplet just shook her head and said, "Don't ask."

The butler continued to lead them down a short hall and into a large, ivory-colored parlor. He stood just inside the door, facing the room. "Miss Cressingham, my lady." He stood back for them to enter, and after they did so, he exited, closing the door behind him.

Juliana and Minnie went further into the room, leaving Susannah to stand at the door. She faced her mother's one-time best friend.

Lady Rainsford rose from a small settee and came towards them. She was dressed in the latest mode, wearing a delicate pink day dress with a large cream-colored shawl wrapped around her shoulders. Her mob cap, made of the finest lace, complemented a pearl choker clasped around her neck. Bright cheeks and sparkling eyes reminded Susannah of the conspiratorial laughs her mother had shared with this woman, and a lump the size of her mother's gravestone formed in her throat. *Mama.* Susannah's cheeks flushed as a flash of anger and resentment towards her ladyship charged through her.

Lady Rainsford smiled brightly at Susannah. "You, my dear, have grown up since last we met." She held out her hands.

But Susannah didn't take them. She couldn't take them. This woman had abandoned her, just as Nate had. Hadn't she? How could she possibly expect Susannah to be happy to see her?

Lady Rainsford's smile faltered.

Susannah felt an uncomfortable pang, almost like guilt. *Except she abandoned us.* Oh, her emotions were in such a stir. Mindful of her manners, if nothing else, Susannah propelled herself forward to greet Lady Rainsford, blinking rapidly to prevent tears from running down her cheeks. But instead of taking her hands, she bobbed a curtsey, keeping her head lowered so she didn't look Lady Rainsford in the eye. "My lady."

Her ladyship lowered her hands. "Well. I daresay quite a bit of time has gone by." There was no mistaking the pained note in Lady Rainsford's voice. "I understand that you and Nathaniel are to be married," she said, her tone brightening. "Although I do wish I had heard it from my son's own mouth, rather than from my daughters reading a notice in the paper. I'm so delighted you will be joining our family."

Susannah's head came up, mouth practically agog. *Delighted?* Blinking her confusion away, she said, "Thank you, my lady."

"We must talk about the wedding plans." She clasped her hands together, eyes sparkling. "Oh, this is something I've dreamed of for Nathaniel for so very long. There's the breakfast, of course, and we must get you a trousseau." She began enumerating the list on her fingers. "And a gown for the service. It should be elegant, which fits your new status, but delicate and beautiful. I'm thinking Brussels lace, mayhap some pearls, but nothing too ostentatious. Then there are flowers to arrange, and—"

"We've already told her we need to visit the shops, Mama," volunteered Anna, who had just entered the room. She scooped up a grey cat missing its tail that had wandered in behind her, took a seat near her sisters, and began snuggling the furry creature.

"Thank you, Anna." Lady Rainsford turned to Susannah once more. "Have you thought at all about what you might like to wear for the wedding? Or what sort of menu—"

"Menu?" Susannah shook her head, trying to comprehend everything her ladyship said. This engagement had been foisted on Susannah only last night. Lady Rainsford may have dreamt of this wedding for years, but Susannah had not. As far as she was concerned, she'd be well-suited with a private service in a local church, followed not by a breakfast but by a swift departure for the docks.

She closed her mouth again, remembering the agreement she'd made with Nate. Love and affection to him—and his entire family. With as much warmth as she could muster, she said, "My lady, I beg your pardon, but I haven't had a chance to think of any of that. I only returned to town recently, and your son only *asked* me"—she choked on the words—"last evening."

Lady Rainsford stood before Susannah, hands clasped at her waist in the way of women in the *ton*. "Of course. Well, we have plenty of time."

"Actually, we have only three weeks and four days," said Minnie.

Juliana elbowed her sister. "Do quit being so precise. It's unnerving."

"I don't require a large wedding, my lady." Susannah

looked down at her gloves and fiddled with the buttons, trying to avoid their direct stares.

Anna gasped, squeezing the cat so hard it meowed. "But Susannah, this is your wedding. A love match. Of course you want it to be special."

No, she didn't. Not at all.

"Not everyone thinks like you," said Minnie, coming to Susannah's rescue. "You may have a large wedding if you want one. Susannah might want to marry in the local parish with just us as guests."

Susannah's eyes flicked up to Lady Rainsford's shocked face. She seemed aghast at the notion of a small, private wedding, but she quickly schooled her features. "Susannah may have whatever sort of wedding she would like. I'll not stand in her way."

Curtseying, Susannah said, "Thank you, my lady." She looked up again at her ladyship to find the woman inspecting her pointedly, almost as if she were untangling a problem in her head.

Unexpectedly, Lady Rainsford turned to her daughters. "Girls, will you please excuse Miss Cressingham and me for a moment?"

"But what about tea?" Anna asked.

"Have Crimson lay it out in the Green Salon. We will join you presently."

The girls all nodded. They quickly got up and walked to the door without saying anything and without looking back.

As soon as the door closed, Lady Rainsford turned to Susannah, her expression a mix of sympathy and confusion. "You needn't hide it from me, child. I can see clearly that, despite what my son has told me, this is no love match."

A surge of anxiety came over her. "My lady…" Her

voice trailed off, unsure of what to say. Of how to explain her situation, if she even could. She groaned inwardly. Lord, what about Nate? What would he think when he learned she hadn't kept up the ruse? Would he renege on his agreement to take her to Jamaica?

"Don't get yourself in a pucker, my dear." Lady Rainsford waved her hand in the air, dismissing Susannah's apprehension. "I don't know why you're marrying, nor is it any of my business, but I am still glad for it. I want you to know, Susannah, that regardless of the circumstances, you have my support. And my love."

Susannah was taken aback. *Her love?* Nate's mother had abandoned her and her sister when they'd needed her most. And now she's professing her love? Susannah swallowed hard. "Thank you, my lady. I..." She chewed her lip. What could she possibly say? "We...that is—"

"No, child. You don't need to explain. I'm sure Nathaniel has his reasons, as well." Her expression was all kindness, but she sighed heavily, knotting her hands together before her. "I do wish you would tell me one thing, please, because I have wondered for years."

Susannah pursed her lips, afraid of where her ladyship was going with this line of questioning. She tried to keep her voice from trembling. "What is it you wish to know, my lady?"

"My dear, why didn't you and Isabela want to live with us after your parents died?"

A wave of dizziness overcame her, and she instinctively reached out for a nearby chair, gripping it hard.

"Oh, my child." Lady Rainsford came to Susannah, putting her arm around her. "Here, my dear, sit down." She guided Susannah to the seat of the chair, her eyes soft and her smile warm and encouraging. "Didn't you know,

my sweet?" She squeezed Susannah's hand. "Oh my goodness. You must have many questions."

Many questions? No, she didn't have many. She only
had one.

"You wanted…me?"

CHAPTER 7

SUSANNAH SAT IN OPEN-MOUTHED SHOCK. Lady Rainsford had wanted *her*?

Her ladyship's smile changed. Instead of warmth and compassion, Susannah now saw pity. Her ladyship heaved a sigh. "Yes, my dear. I wanted you. Of course I wanted you. And Isabela. Did you think otherwise?"

A flash of anger shot through her, and her cheeks flamed. "Of course I did. What else was I to assume? We were…left. With *him*." Her gaze fixed on the kaleidoscope of colors in the carpet under her feet and she took deep breaths to calm her raging emotions. "No one called on us. Asked for us. Wrote to us." She paused, then caught Lady Rainsford's eye. "No one *wanted* us, my lady."

Her ladyship tightened the hold on Susannah's hand, and Susannah was surprised by the martial gleam in her eyes. "I don't want you to ever think that I didn't want you. That I didn't ask for you, *beg* for you to live with us." Her hands shook Susannah's as she spoke, putting power behind her words. "The very moment after your parents' funeral, I petitioned your uncle to allow you and your sister to live under our roof, under our protection. Over and over again, I asked him."

"But I never once saw you at our house. Not a single time did you knock on our door."

"I know it seems that way, my dear—"

"It didn't 'seem' that way." Susannah could barely get the words out civilly. "It *was* that way. How many times did you knock on our door?"

"Susannah, you must understand—"

"How many times, my lady?" Her voice rose in agitation.

With a guilty look, Lady Rainsford said, "I did not meet your uncle face-to-face."

"As I thought." She tried to pull her hands free from her ladyship's grasp, but the woman would not let go.

"I made repeated entreaties to your uncle, Susannah. Especially after Ben left. I even asked Nathaniel to beg him on my behalf, for he seemed to have a connection with the captain that I did not. Then your uncle married your sister off to that unscrupulous landowner in the West Indies, and I petitioned even harder for you."

"But you never did in person." Tears—those dratted, weak-of-character tears—fell down Susannah's cheeks, and she hated herself for it.

"Your uncle warned me to stay away," she said with exasperation.

Susannah ignored her excuse, the anger flaring up inside her like a newly kindled fire. She pulled herself free of Lady Rainsford and came to her feet, taking a few steps away, needing to distance herself. She turned to face her ladyship. "Do you have any idea how *empty* the last three years have been?" Susannah pressed her hand to her heart, as if trying to protect it. "I may have attended school with your daughters, but during that time, they were distant, as if they'd been told not to get too close." She took a deep breath to control her frustration. "Imagine my surprise when I saw them at Miss Glover's, thinking that, at last, I would have around me people who loved me, and whom I loved."

"Susannah—" Her ladyship's voice was pleading.

"Then image how hard it was to endure their frigid politeness? The warmest friendship between us before my parents died, then the coldest civility after. Oh, there were moments, certainly, that we were quite chummy. But not nearly enough of them. And when school finished? I suppose I can be thankful that I didn't have to return to London, but the alternative was not much better. Living with a dowdy old woman in the far reaches of England. No family. No friends. No society. Simply…nothing." Susannah spread her hands wide, then let them fall to her sides, but she held Lady Rainsford's eye, making sure that woman saw the pain she knew was in her own.

Lady Rainsford rose and came to her. Shaking her head and sighing hotly, her ladyship gripped Susannah's hands, her eyes displaying a fierceness Susannah had never seen before. "My child, you must believe me that I would never abandon you or your sister." She released one of Susannah's hands, her expression softening, and stroked her cheek. "Your mama was such a dear and wonderful friend to me, particularly after the two men in my life died."

Lady Rainsford's lips trembled as her own tears formed. She quickly pulled a handkerchief from her sleeve and dabbed her eyes, then returned it to its rightful place. Sandwiching Susannah's hands between her own, she rubbed them comfortingly. "I would never have made it through that time without your mama. The loss of my son John and my dear Charles—first learning about John's fate in Spain, then Charles dying from the shock two days later—left me utterly broken and empty, completely rudderless, and unsure of everything. Nathaniel blamed himself. He would not even talk to me, leaving me so, so alone. But your mother's steady words of comfort, her constant friendship, her love and support? My dear, she helped me navigate that horrible time in my life. I would not have made it through without her." Her grip tightened. "She would never forgive me for not looking after the two of you, and I let her down—"

Her ladyship broke off in tears, pulling her own and Susannah's hands to her forehead, eyes closed, as if praying to the Lord God himself for forgiveness. Sobbing, she said, "I let your mama down so terribly by not being there soon enough to protect Isabela. And by not pushing hard enough for you."

A pang of remorse for Lady Rainsford pushed its way into Susannah's heart. This wasn't what she expected to hear, and it had an unintended effect. While her tears continued to flow, a warm tingle began to spread throughout her. It started in her head, filling her body, her limbs, her heart. She was wanted. Someone had *wanted* her. Just hearing that made Susannah's heart swell with the beginnings of something it had been missing for so very long.

Love.

Her ladyship lowered their still-joined hands. Her eyes lost some of their light, and her mouth turned down. "I didn't push hard enough, though. Not hard enough. I should have stormed the captain's door. Taken it up with his solicitor. Pursued it with family acquaintances who had leverage. Anything to make myself a thorn in his side until he relented. But Nathaniel told me abandon my claim on you and to leave you well enough alone."

Susannah stiffened, her chin dropping in surprise. "He did *what*?" The warmth that had spread through Susannah began to cool, quickly. She tried to pull her hands free, but her ladyship would not release them.

Lady Rainsford looked Susannah in the eye once more, only this time, Susannah could easily read the guilt there. "I know it sounds terrible."

"Sounds terrible? It was terrible." How could she think otherwise?

"I should have ignored him. I should have kept pressing my suit, but Nathaniel made it very clear that it would be in your best interest if I let you alone. He said he had taken care of everything and instructed me not to reach out to you or your uncle again."

"What did he take care of?" Susannah wrenched her hands free, pushing past Lady Rainsford to stand in front of the window. She wrapped her arms about her, fingering the fabric on the sleeve of her gown, trying to calm her racing breath, but it was difficult. In a venomous tone, Susannah said, "You could have made our lives very different if you had made an effort worthy of my mother's memory, my lady."

Her ladyship inhaled sharply, and Susannah felt a momentary contrition at her harsh words, but she pushed it aside. Lady Rainsford should feel bad for what she'd done...or hadn't done, as the case were.

"I regret my decision to this day, Susannah, but I did as Nathaniel asked."

Susannah whirled around. "Did you not press him about why he was forcing you to do this? Why he, of all people, was asking you to leave me and my sister to my uncle's devices?" She strode to her ladyship, angry hands fisted at her sides. "Did it not strike you as strange that your son was befriending someone so wholly unkind to every other member of my family?"

Lady Rainsford took a step backward. "Of course I did. But Nathaniel told me there was more than what was on the surface. He assured me he had your best interests in mind. I took him at his word. He has never lied to me."

Well, wasn't she the lucky one? Because Nate had certainly lied to her. "He may not have told you an untruth, but he certainly lied by omission." Susannah's tears had stopped, and that angry heat began to grow within her once more.

Taking Susannah's hands again, she said, "I am more sorry than you can know for not following through on my promise to your dear mother. But I will make it up to you, I assure you. I will be the mother you haven't had for the last three years."

At those words, something clicked inside Susannah, and her entire body went stone cold. *She doesn't want to help me. She wants absolution from guilt.* Pulling free from Lady Rainsford's grasp, Susannah turned away, striding to the window across the room.

"My dear, what is it? What did I say?"

Susannah ignored her, the anger within rising up like boiling water, the burning heat flowing to the point of every finger, the tip of every toe. She stared down at the square, blindly watching the pedestrian traffic, trying hard to regulate her breathing. How *dare* she? No one could or would replace her mother, least of all someone who couldn't fulfill a simple promise to her.

To Susannah's chagrin, her ire was directed not only at her ladyship and Nate, but also herself. Susannah wanted to kick her own derrière for falling for such pathetic stories told by people who claimed to care, but obviously did not, for if they had, they would have figured out a way long ago to remove Susannah and her sister from her uncle's custody. Was she that desperate to trust people? To be loved? Hadn't she already learned—painfully, so painfully—that she could trust no one? Lady Rainsford was clearly spinning this Canterbury tale to make herself feel better about abandoning her best friend's daughters.

And Nate. How could Susannah think that Nate wouldn't have something to do with her misery? Of course he did. She didn't doubt that before Ben left, Nate was already chummy with her uncle. She remembered exactly what Nate had done, too, making that promise to her uncle about her brother to "get him out." In fact, Susannah wouldn't put it past Nate to have had a hand in arranging Isabela's marriage to that landowner.

"Susannah?"

She had to leave. This was never going to work. She refused to be part of a family that had ignored her when she needed them most. Turning away from the window, she rushed past Lady Rainsford, who had come up behind her, and headed to the door, nearly blinded by her rage and resentment. She'd walk home if she had to, propriety be damned. But she wouldn't spend another second under the same roof of such lying, dishonest people.

Susannah opened the door and rushed out of the drawing room, leaving her ladyship calling after her in vain.

CHAPTER 8

Shortly after nine that evening, Nate stood in an alley near the home of his friend, Sherry, arms crossed as he analyzed the merits and drawbacks of the street's accessibility. Would his carriage have enough navigable space to get out if another were in the street? Was the corner down there too tight? Nate had been reminded to do this after reporting for duty to the Home Office a few weeks ago. He was sure he looked ridiculous, standing there in the open street, but he would rather be prepared should things go sour.

After another glance at the alley where John Coachman had pulled the carriage to a stop, Nate was satisfied. There was enough room for John to walk the horses, if necessary, although it wasn't that cold. He looked up at John, perched on the box. "See you in a few hours?"

"Yes, my lord." He tipped his hat.

Nate patted the side of the horse and nodded before walking briskly back to Sherry's large townhouse on Upper Grosvenor Street. He *should* be arriving with his new fiancée, but when Nate had returned home that afternoon, he'd found Susannah gone and a note awaiting him.

My lord,

I will join you at Sherrington's home this evening because Uncle Alastair is forcing me, but I will arrive—and leave—with my uncle.

Miss Cressingham

The second he'd read it, he'd crumbled it, swearing, then tossed it into the fire. Arriving stag was not how he'd intended to make his engagement public. Taking the steps two at a time, he bounded through the doorway of Sherry's massive townhouse, immediately scanning the front hall for any sign of Susannah or her uncle.

But Sherry, wearing formal black evening wear and greeting guests, stopped him on the way in. "Rain, ol' friend. Haven't seen you for an age." He slurred his words, his thin frame swaying ever so much. Sherry's raven-colored hair was slightly disheveled, as if he—or a lady friend—had run their hands through it, and he looked at Nate with piercing blue eyes that were glassy, bright, and slanted to make him look like the very devil.

"Hello, Sherry." Nate could smell the spirits coming off Sherry's breath. Hugh Norford, Viscount Sherrington, was another member of the Beggars Club. Unlike the others, Sherry's membership came about out of sympathy when his older brother, an original Beggars Club member, died, leaving Sherry the title. *Just like me*, Nate thought wryly. Except Sherry hadn't done much in the way of keeping up with his responsibilities. Instead, he gambled and drank his life away. Then again, that had been the direction Nate was headed before Tradwick and Ben had peeled him off the floor of the local tavern. However, Sherry's trajectory seemed to be taking a serious wrong turn lately. Nate made a mental note to speak to the other Beggars about their friend. Perhaps a similar intervention was necessary before any further trouble developed.

"Met your fiancée this evening." Sherry waggled his eyebrows suggestively. "Thought you two would arrive together, instead of her on the arm of her prosy uncle." He put a hand on Nate's shoulder and leaned in close, his alcohol-tinged breath hot on Nate's face. "She's devilish pretty, you know. Lovely figure. And her eyes——"

"Yes, thank you." An uncomfortable agitation made Nate clench his fists. To his surprise, he didn't like anyone speaking about Susannah like that, but he kept his countenance. "Can you perhaps tell me where she is?"

Sherry waved his hand, stumbling slightly into Nate, his unfocused gaze darting about the hall. "Off in the ballroom, I imagine. With your sisters?"

A lady guest arrived at the door, and Sherry shoved off from Nate, extending his hand as she tittered. "Well, hello, my lady," he said seductively. "So glad you could make it."

Nate shook his head, promising to himself that once this business with Cressingham was finished, he would devote his attention to Sherry. *After I marry Susannah and take her to her sister.* Nate's pulse kicked up a notch at the thought of marrying Susannah. He wanted to find her. Now.

Nate entered the ballroom, a large, tall space that ran the entire width of the house. Mirrors filled almost the whole of the interior wall, making the room seem twice as large—and twice as crowded. The ballroom had been converted to a gaming den. About a dozen tables were set up, each covered in green baize, some staffed by croupiers, while a buffet of cold meats, cheeses, and various side dishes lay on sideboards around the perimeter. Footmen in formal wear circulated throughout space, offering flutes of champagne or glasses of wine. And all around him stood throngs of guests casually drinking, talking, and laughing.

"Rainsford, you scoundrel, get over here." Someone grabbed him by the elbow and pulled him into a crowd of men.

"There he is, the latest victim," said a deep voice, also slurred by drink. Mr. Jackson Trent, Sherry's classmate at Eton. Nate should have known he'd be here. He'd been a bad influence on Sherry since his brother had died.

"Saw the announcement in *The Times*. Can't believe you've come up to scratch." Nigel Peterson, future Earl of Sloan, clapped him on the back rather hard.

"Yes," said another, laughing. "You're the last person we thought would take the bait."

Nate had expected this sort of congenial ribbing once news got out, but it irritated him like a rock in his boot. His marriage—and Susannah—was none of their business, even though publishing such news in the papers certainly made it fodder for public gossip. Taking a deep breath to calm his annoyance, he said, "Well, as you can see, I did, and if you'll excuse me, I'd like very much to find my intended." He bowed deeply. "Good evening, sirs."

Nate turned away amid a chorus of cat calls and saucy remarks, but quickly put his school chums out of his thoughts. He scanned the room, and in the far corner, at a small table, sat his fiancée, Minnie, Tradwick, and a casual acquaintance, Captain Lord Whitsell, heir to the Earl of Granston.

Tradwick, who faced the room, spied Nate first, nodding almost imperceptibly. Slowly, Nate weaved his way to the table, mentally reminding himself to keep up the unfriendly façade he had to maintain with Tradwick when in public. He forced his mouth to frown, narrowing his eyes in what he hoped was a stern, disapproving look.

Fortunately, Susannah sat opposite Tradwick, her back to the room, so she likely had no idea he was approaching. Nate didn't doubt that if she had seen him coming, she would have made an excuse to visit the retiring room for the remainder of the night.

Nate had returned home after meeting with Sidmouth and Tradwick hoping to find his betrothed in happy conversation with his mother and sisters while sharing a cup of tea. Instead, he'd learned that she'd left in anger—and when he'd heard an accounting of the conversation she'd had with his mother, he'd been livid at his mother's gross impropriety for telling Susannah damn near *everything*.

His sister, on Tradwick's left, saw him approach. Wearing a modest ivory gown, she cocked one eyebrow at him, glanced quickly at Tradwick, then back to him again, a coy smile forming. She knew he and Tradwick weren't friendly. Was she goading him, hoping for sparks between him and Tradwick? Had she seated herself—and presumably Susannah—at Tradwick's table on purpose? He put the thought out of his mind for now. Sometimes he didn't understand how Minnie's mind worked.

Nate bowed his head in greeting. "Good evening." He put his hands on Susannah's almost-bare shoulders, just above her golden silk gown, and a flare of heat singed his hands. She stiffened at his touch. *Damn.* Squeezing her gently to remind her to play the part, he leaned down and half-whispered, "Hello, poppet. Are you having fun?"

Susannah turned her head slightly, her hot-as-Hades eyes meeting his, and gave him a forced smile. "The most a lady could wish for."

Oh, she was angry all right. Nate straightened, but kept

his hands on her shoulders, even though she twitched and moved in an unspoken signal to unhand her.

As if he would.

"Well, it's about time you arrived, brother." Minnie held a hand of cards above a large pile of betting chips. "Do join us. You know Sir Philip, of course."

Nate glanced across the table at his friend, then to his sister, giving Tradwick the cut indirect to keep up their pretense of discord.

Whitsell looked back and forth between Nate and Tradwick, his expression unsure.

Minnie rolled her eyes at Nate. "Fine. Ignore him." Huffing in exasperation, she gestured to the man sitting across from her, then smiled at him. "I believe you've met Captain Lord Whitsell, have you not?"

Nate turned to Whitsell, dressed smartly in his dark blue naval uniform, and bowed. "Of course." He extended his hand. "How are you, Captain?"

Whitsell, after another quick glance at Tradwick, rose, his excessively tall frame forcing Nate to look up to meet his bright blue eyes. "I'm doing very well, thank you, Rainsford." They shook hands, then Whitsell gestured to Minnie with his thumb, giving a nervous laugh. "Except we are all getting kicked in the tail by your sister here." He indicated to his meager pile of chips on the table. "I'm afraid I'll be signing vowels to her if I don't quit while I'm ahead."

"Nonsense, Captain." His sister blushed. "You're doing very well, all things considered."

Minnie? Blushing? Nate mentally scratched his head at that. She *never* blushed. "I do hope you are not going to insult the man, sister."

Minnie put her cards face down on the table and

paused, biting her lip. Her face turned even more red, but this time, Nate suspected it was because of embarrassment.

"I'm not terribly good at remembering which cards have been played." Whitsell looked at Minnie with softness. "Lady Minerva seems to have quite an excellent memory."

"That she does." Tradwick set down his own cards. He directed his penetrating gaze on Minnie. "She has an exceptional mind."

"Gentlemen," his sister said, her face redder than ever. "Do stop. You're both very good card players. I'm just having a bit of luck tonight."

Nate was surprised by her diplomatic comment. She was usually very forthright and honest, oftentimes at the expense of one's feelings, and Nate knew from personal experience that she was ruthless at cards.

"If luck is on your side in addition to your excellent playing skills, Lady Minerva," Tradwick said, "we ought to find another table."

"That sounds like an excellent idea—for you, Tradwick." Nate hoped the barb sounded genuine. "I would be happy to take your place."

Tradwick frowned. "I'm sure you would, my lord. But we have not yet finished our play."

Minnie placed her hands on the table, her gaze switching back and forth between both men. With a look that Nate knew spelled trouble, she said, "I do declare, I don't understand the animosity between you two. What happened? You used to be friends, and now you're not."

Nate looked at his sister. "Things change, Minnie."

"That seems like a—"

"I understand congratulations are in order, Rainsford," Whitsell said. "Your delightful sister has been telling us about your whirlwind romance to Miss Cressingham."

Nate quickly took the bait. "Yes, it was indeed a whirlwind, wasn't it, my dear?" He looked down at Susannah just as she looked up, her dark eyes blazing.

"Indeed," Susannah bit out. "A whirlwind." She looked around at the others and smiled, then straightened her shoulders in what Nate interpreted as yet another silent communication to unhand her. "Well, shall we finish our game? I doubt I'm in a position to win, but I would like to see if Minnie can keep up her streak."

"Pooh," said Minnie, glancing at Tradwick. "Sir Philip is holding his own against me." She then gazed up at Whitsell, a playful little smirk on her face. "But I am afraid perhaps luck is not on your side tonight, Captain."

Whitsell met Minnie's gaze, and Nate could have sworn there were sparks flying between the two of them. "The only luck I've had this evening is the privilege to play against you."

Minnie blushed again.

"If you're done flirting, Whitsell," Tradwick said, taking up his cards and gesturing to the small pile of chips in the center of the table, "do get on with it. I believe it's your play."

The captain's face turned beet-red. "Indeed, it is." He dragged his eyes away from Minnie, murmuring apologies to Susannah. Resuming his seat, he consulted his cards, then made his selection and placed it on the table. "There. Beat that, Lady Minerva."

"Handily." Minnie smiled broadly and placed her own card on the table, and both Tradwick and Whitsell groaned. With a laugh, she pulled the pile of chips towards her as the gentlemen threw their cards on the table with feigned disgust.

"Well done, Minnie," Nate said. "Now that you've finished your game, perhaps you're ready for some refreshment. Come, Susannah." Nate stepped back in order to pull out Susannah's chair. "Minnie, do join us."

"But I'm in the middle of a winning str—"

"Minnie." Nate cut her off, his voice full of warning.

"I'd be happy to escort you, Lady Minerva," said Whitsell, rising. "You don't mind, Tradwick, that we abandon you?"

"No, not at all." Tradwick stood and straightened his coat. "Thank you for the game, ladies. Whitsell, a pleasure." He bowed before them, pointedly ignoring Nate, then strode off.

Whitsell came around to Minnie and pulled out her chair. She gathered up her winnings, a few of her chips falling onto the table.

"Oh, do let me help you, my lady." Whitsell picked the errant chips up off the table. "I'll hold them for you in my coat pocket, separate from my own, of course."

"Thank you, that's very kind." She smiled up at the captain.

Nate helped Susannah out of her chair, then folded her arm into the crook of his elbow. Giving his sister a look, he said, "Don't run anyone else into debt, Minnie."

"No, of course she won't." Whitsell grinned. "If you are agreeable, Rainsford, I'll take your sister to the dining room."

The protective instinct within Nate kicked in, and he thought about telling Whitsell to jump off a ship and leave his sister alone, but Nate needed a moment of privacy with Susannah to talk about the conversation she'd had with his mother.

"Very well."

As Whitsell led a smiling Minnie to the dining room, Nate guided Susannah through the crowds in the opposite direction towards the tables along the side of the room.

Nate held Susannah's gloved hand in his own, her heat seeping up his arm and warming his chest, but Susannah's stiff posture and semi-forced smile wasn't lost on him. She might be angry with him, but she had made a bargain to pretend to love him. Besides, he wanted her to look upon him with adoration, not contempt, regardless if it were forced.

Leaning down, he whispered, "You look like I'm taking you to the gallows."

Without a word, she softened her countenance, even smiled warmly, but it didn't reach her eyes.

As they progressed, they were stopped repeatedly by well-wishers offering their felicitations. Nate accepted them, and to his surprise, Susannah did, too, even going so far as to sound genuine. Yet when they finally made it to the refreshment tables, Susannah pulled her arm from his. "Excuse me, I must…I must leave."

As he had at her uncle's house, Nate anticipated her hasty exit. He grabbed Susannah by the elbow, reeled her in, and rethreaded her arm through his. "We have to talk first."

Susannah tried to pull away once more. "I do not wish—"

Nate bent his head to whisper in her ear. "I know what my mother said to you, and I know what you must feel right now." He straightened, taking her hand and guiding her unwilling body towards the door. Once in the hall, he steered her down a long corridor and into a small, elegant salon decorated in shades of teal and ivory, lit only with a few branches of candles.

But as soon as he entered, he heard an unmistakably deep voice behind him. "Rainsford."

Hell and damn. Cressingham. What bloody rotten timing.

The captain limped into the room and, seeing Susannah and Nate together, smiled lecherously. "Getting away from the party for some quiet time, are you?"

"Certainly not." Susannah pulled away and turned her back on both men.

"Get out of here, chit." He motioned to the door with his cane, his hands fidgety, his eyes bright with mischief. "I need to speak with your betrothed."

Susannah whirled around. "Gladly, Uncle." She marched to the exit.

But Nate came up quickly behind her. He reached out and took her by the arm, stopping her before she could leave. Leaning his head down, he said, "I will find you, and we will speak about this." With his other hand, he tipped up her chin so she'd meet his eyes. "Do not leave Sherry's house," he whispered, raising his eyebrows in challenge. "Go find my sisters and stay with them until I come for you."

She held his gaze, sparks and flames shooting from her eyes, but she nodded. Pulling herself free, she left the room.

Nate took a girding breath. He had no patience for Cressingham right now.

"Go on." Cressingham waved an irritable hand at Nate. "Close the door and lock it."

Nate did as instructed, then stepped into the center of the room, keeping his gaze on the captain, whose proud look and puffed up chest reminded Nate of a peacock. A shot of apprehension coursed through Nate's veins like liquid lightning, but he forcibly relaxed his body in an effort to look unaffected. "You wish to discuss something?"

Cressingham set down on a nearby table the glass of wine he'd brought with him and pointed the marbled end of his cane at Nate, his eyes ablaze. "It's done. Done! His

Highness, our beloved L'Empereur, the magnificent Napoleon Bonaparte has, by the grace of God"—Cressingham spread his arms wide, his smile broad—"escaped Elba." There was no mistaking the triumphant tone in his voice.

Hell. And. Damn. Nate's stomach sank to his knees.

CHAPTER 9

NATE, praying Cressingham could not read his mind, feigned a broad smile and gave a vigorous nod of his head, rolling back on his heels and clapping his hands together. "So soon? I didn't expect this until much later in the season."

"Neither did I, frankly. However, I received word this morning." Cressingham's exuberance was hard to hide as he limped from one side of the small room to the other, fidgety and restless like champagne bubbles after the bottle had been shaken.

Nate's stomach also felt like it had been shaken, and he broke out into a sweat. *Napoleon. Escaped.* Everyone at the Home Office had suspected that, at some point, Napoleon would outgrow his little island paradise, but for it to happen now? The timing was most inconvenient, and the implications of a return of Napoleon were huge. England had only been at peace for a year. Castlereagh and his cronies in Vienna had nearly worked out a permanent peace in Europe. But Nate had to keep up appearances. Perpetuating his smile, he asked, "When did he leave?"

"On the 28th of February. I received an express. His sister, Pauline, and his *maman*, blessed creatures, assisted him, throwing a party that evening as a distraction. He landed in Gulf de Juan, near Nice, with horses, gold, and a small complement of soldiers and is already making his way to Paris."

"Nice to Paris? Surely, he will meet with resistance," Nate said, pursing his lips. "Louis will not take his arrival laying down."

"Bah," Cressingham spat out. His expression turned cross. "The only thing that corpulent king can do is lie down. He's not fit to rule."

"Perhaps, but I can tell you that no one else in Europe will welcome L'Empereur. Wellington and Talleyrand are in Vienna as we speak. In fact, they likely already know of Bonaparte's landing."

Cressingham continued to pace, his cane tapping the floor. He waved his hand to brush Nate's comments aside. "The *citoyens* are loyal. They will rally."

"Don't be so sure. The people of France have endured much hardship under Napoleon."

The captain stopped and turned to face Nate, his eyes narrowed, and he frowned. "What the devil side are you on, Rainsford?"

Nate crossed his arms, puffing out his chest to make himself look formidable. "Are you questioning my allegiance?"

"Perhaps," Cressingham said, his voice hard. "You seem quite determined that Bonaparte will not succeed. And awful bloody suspicious, doubting the people's loyalty to their emperor."

Nate took two steps towards Cressingham, pummeling him with his gaze. He didn't get this far to have Cressingham pull the rug from under him. "You know precisely where my allegiance lies. Have I not promised to you all of your niece's dowry in support of Bonaparte's return?"

"You have." Cressingham's expression didn't relax. "But—"

"But nothing. Of course I'm suspicious of the people, of Napoleon's plan, of the rest of Europe." Nate pointed his finger at the captain. "You should be, too. If Napoleon enters France expecting a warm welcome and it's not given, then what? What are our next steps? What will he do? Where will he go? Or do we wait for the German and Russian armed forces to surround him?"

Cressingham didn't answer.

"Well?" Nate pressed, his voice rising. "What do we do then, Captain? I, for one, would like to make sure we have a fool-proof plan, rather than going into this on the faith of my consequence, the few men I have with me, and the grace of God, as I'm sure Napoleon has done."

"Stand down, Rainsford," Cressingham growled. "You needn't be so…contrary."

Nate took a deep breath. "I'm quite calm, as you see." He strode over to a nearby table, well-stocked with various decanters of amber-colored liquid. Lifting the lid off one, he sniffed it, then capped it and set it down again, repeating the process with another. *Brandy.* That's what he needed. And he needed Cressingham to reveal a little more information.

Over his shoulder, he asked, "How do we know this news is accurate?" He poured a finger of the French liquor into a snifter, swirled it, then turned to face Cressingham. "What if we're receiving misinformation?"

Cressingham snorted again. "Not possible. It comes from a very good, *very* reliable source."

Nate sipped his brandy. "So you say." *Just tell me who he is.*

Fisting his cane, Cressingham marched over to Nate, his eyes blazing. "Yes, I do." He held up a warning finger. "You've been downright strange, Rainsford. Ever since clapping eyes on my niece." He sneered. "Could it be that your loyalty has suddenly shifted from Napoleon to a wench with brown eyes and soft thighs?"

Nate bristled at Cressingham's deliberate barb, but he refused to let this man get the best of him. Instead, he played right into him. "You noticed? I thought it would be a nice distraction from L'Empereur." He held up his brandy snifter, offering silent cheers to his adversary.

Cressingham frowned. "What are you talking about? What distraction?"

"Why, playing the lovebirds, of course." He sipped his brandy. "I made a…deal, a little arrangement, with your niece. In exchange for something trivial she wants, she promises to pretend this is a love match. Old acquaintances reunited and all that. It's no secret you sympathize with Napoleon, Captain. This gives the matchmaking mamas— and the gossip rags—something to talk about. It makes her less of a pain in my arse, as well. But most importantly, it takes the focus off the fact that our two families are coming together for any reason besides true love." Nate took a few steps backwards, leaning against the back of the green settee in the middle of the room, and downed the amber liquid.

"Well, I…" Cressingham's expression relaxed a bit, but a hint of suspicion lurked in his eyes. "If you say so, Rainsford."

"I do." He crossed his arms. "We have the same goal, Captain."

There was a long pause, a scrutinizing gaze, a somewhat disgruntled curl of the lips, then Cressingham's expression became complacent. "Yes…we do."

Nate gave a mental sigh of relief. At least he would not have to treat Susannah poorly to prove his allegiance. To make his point, he said, "I'm as pleased as any loyal subject that Bonaparte has finally returned to take back France from the royalists. One only hopes he can sustain a return that will allow him to conquer all of Europe."

"I believe he can." Cressingham ambled over to the table, picked up his wine glass, and took a long swallow, then set it back down. "With men like us supporting him." He began to pace again, peering at Nate every moment or so, and a prickling sensation skittered down Nate's spine. The man was after something else.

Nate moved to refill his brandy. He definitely needed another. "Clearly there's something else, Captain. You may as well tell me."

Stopping by the fireplace, his face in shadow, Cressingham said, "You're very perceptive. One of the things I like about you, Rainsford."

Nate uncapped the decanter. "Well? What is it?"

The captain didn't even pause. "I need all of Susannah's dowry. Now."

Nate's pulse tick-tocked, and he nearly spilled brandy onto the table. "I beg your pardon?" He quickly righted the decanter and set it down, then scooped up his snifter and turned around to face the captain.

A devilish smile curved on Cressingham's lips, enhanced by the dim light of the candles. "All ten thousand pounds. By Friday."

"What's happened?" Nate didn't even try to hide the suspicion in his voice.

Clasping his cane behind his back, Cressingham said, "According to my source, Napoleon experienced some trouble immediately after landing in France. He finds himself short of the gold he brought with him."

"I don't understand." Nate picked up his snifter and joined Cressingham near the mantel. "You just learned that he escaped. Did he come under attack? Or, God forbid, did he depart unprepared?"

Cressingham frowned. "No, blast it. Wretched timing crossing the Alps in winter. I had cautioned him about the weather. Told to take a different route, yet he didn't heed my advice. He began his march north when one of the damn donkeys carting a case of gold coin fell down a crevasse."

Nate clenched his snifter. The captain was advising Napoleon directly? Good God, how was he doing that? Nate couldn't believe the Home Office hadn't yet discovered his communication channel. "How much did he lose?"

"The equivalent of ten thousand pounds, money he would use to pay his soldiers."

Well, that explained why Cressingham wanted Susannah's dowry. The captain's expression had darkened throughout their conversation, and Nate wondered briefly whether he should continue to prod the pig, but if Cressingham expected Nate to hand over all of Susannah's money before they married, he was about to be disappointed. "If Bonaparte is progressing as quickly as you say he is, I don't understand why there is a rush to replenish his coffers."

Cressingham kicked the metal grate of the fireplace, his expression hard. In a rush, he said, "Dammit, Rainsford, I have waited years to be part of Bonaparte's inner circle, and if there's one way to prove my dedication to him and his beautiful sister, it's by providing him the money he desperately needs."

Nate's gut churned, then fell, sinking deep like a ship going down. *Good God, his contact is Pauline Bonaparte.* Nate's mind worked quickly. Pauline was a harlot who fornicated with any man who would give her what she wanted, be it money, title, power, or information. She was also her brother's most ardent supporter, willing to do anything to serve him. Didn't Cressingham just say she and Boney's *maman* had thrown a diversionary fête so he could escape unnoticed? Nate didn't doubt Pauline had lured Cressingham fully over to her brother's side.

In a smug, conspiratorial way, Nate said, "So, the beautiful Princess Borghese is your contact." It was a statement, not a question.

The captain said nothing for a moment. But when Nate raised his eyebrows expectantly, Cressingham mirrored his expression. "Yes. She is."

That confirmation, while expected, still jolted Nate like he'd been shocked. Things were moving too fast. He had to slow it all down…significantly. He'd not even had a chance to meet with the head of the bank to make sure he could track the flow of funds, to say nothing of telling Sidmouth that Napoleon had escaped. "Captain, I understand your desire to demonstrate your loyalty, but I'm not sure I will be able to secure those funds from her accounts without us actually being married."

Cressingham's sinister laugh filled the room. "Exactly, my boy." He reached into the breast pocket of his coat and handed Nate a folded packet.

Nate took it, and as soon as he saw the seal, he mentally swore. A special license. Another quake of nerves crashed through Nate's body.

"I want you to marry as soon as possible. I cannot afford to wait three weeks until the banns are read. That simply will not do. Not while L'Empereur is on the march." Cressingham set down his glass, his dark eyes glittering in challenge. "There's a parson who serves out of St.

Mary Woolnoth at Lombard Street. He will officiate when-ever I give the word."

Nate would never get everything lined up in time. The entire plan was running away from him like a bolting horse, leaving Nate clutching the tail and hanging on for dear life. How long could he put this off? "You needn't ask him. I will write to the rector of my church at Langley Park to come to London at once and officiate."

Cressingham scoffed. "I don't think you understand, Rainsford. I need you to marry immediately. Napoleon will wait for no one, and I don't mean to make him wait for me."

Nate's grip on the special license tightened, wrinkling the paper. He hated being forced into a corner, especially by this man.

The captain stole up to Nate, his mouth a sneer, his bushy eyebrows nearly touching above his hawk-like nose. "Let me be clear. You will marry Susannah by Thursday—two days hence—and the money gets transferred on Friday. No exceptions." He headed for the door, unlocking it. "Now, if you'll excuse me, I have another engagement else-where." He looked back at Nate. "As for my niece," he said, shrugging, "keep her. Return her to my house. I don't care what you do with her." His eyes narrowed. "So long as you marry her." With that, the captain turned on his heel and limped out of the room, slamming the door closed behind him.

Damn that man. Damn him to hell. Cressingham was putting him in a corner, one where he was not in control. Nate issued a grunt of rage, his jaw nearly cracking, he clenched it so hard.

He stuffed the special license into the pocket of his waistcoat, downed the contents of the snifter, and set it on a small side table with a thump. Wrenching open the door, he stepped into the hallway and froze.

His ashen-faced fiancée stood before him, mouth agape, eyes wide, and Nate could read every word of condemnation in her expression.

Hell.

CHAPTER 10

SUSANNAH STOOD ROOTED to the wooden floor of the hallway, unable to look anywhere but at her betrothed.

She'd just barely escaped being noticed by her uncle as he came storming out of the salon. When he had ordered her to leave, Susannah had resolved to find out once and for all what was going on between her uncle and Nate. She'd crouched by the door handle, listening through the keyhole, just as she'd done the day Nate took Ben away, and what she'd heard nearly made her retch.

They were Bonapartists. Conspirators against the Crown. *Traitors.*

She knew it. Had suspected it all along. But she hadn't been prepared for the impact of the truth…for each beat of her heart to pound her soul with the betrayal of Nate's earlier words.

Trust me. Trust me. Trust me.

A physical ache flowed through her body, for in her heart of hearts, she'd wanted to love him again as she'd done in her youth. Moon to night, sun to day, moth to flame…the analogy of her attraction didn't signify.

Susannah was magnetically drawn to Nate, despite his high-handedness, his gross mistreatment of her brother, his blatant neglect of her and her sister. But she couldn't. She dare not let herself love a man she couldn't trust.

"What are you doing here?" His expression immediately darkened. He knew that she knew.

Susannah straightened her shoulders, refusing to be cowed by him. "Looking for the retiring room." If he could lie, so could she. She stepped around Nate and walked down the hall, her slippers tapping rapidly on the hardwood. The further away she could get from him and his family, the better.

"That can wait," Nate said, taking her by the arm, "until after we talk. There are a few things we need to clear up. Into the salon."

"Natey, there you are," said a voice from down the hall. Susannah peered over Nate's shoulder to see Anna and Minnie, arms locked, making their way towards them. They were the last people Susannah wanted to see. She wondered briefly if they were caught up in Nate's deceptions, then dismissed the idea. Anna was far too innocent, and Minnie was too bookish and studious. But that didn't mean she wanted to spend any more time with them. For even though she knew Nate had dictated the interactions his family would have with Susannah and her sister after Ben died, she felt the girls should have tried harder to engage her.

Nate turned towards his sisters, a tight smile on his face, Susannah's hand forcibly threaded through his elbow. He gripped her fingers hard, giving her no opportunity to get away. "Hello, sisters. What is it?"

The girls stopped before the two of them, Anna's expression joyous and Minnie's cautiously curious. "Sherry is starting a dance in the ballroom," said Minnie. "I suppose he's decided cards are not enough. He's arranged to move some of the tables to another room, and they're rolling up the rugs right now."

"We want to dance and thought Susannah might, too." Anna looked expectantly at her.

Susannah hadn't the slightest desire to dance, but if it meant extracting herself from her betrothed, she would take part in every set.

Minnie must have read the expression on Nate's face, because she said, "I don't think he wants her to." Then she leaned closer to Anna and whispered, "I told you we should leave them alone."

"Oh nonsense. Natey doesn't care, do you?" Anna disengaged herself from Minnie and threaded her arm through Susannah's free one. "Come. It will be such fun. I'm sure we'll have no trouble finding you a dance partner."

"Neither Susannah nor I are in the mood for dancing right now," Nate said. "We have some things to discuss." His stern tone made it clear his position on the matter.

But for Susannah, it was an escape from a conversation she didn't want to have, and an easy one at that, for it was well-known that Nate didn't dance. At least he never did when they were younger and pretended to have balls of their own in the children's wing of his family's home.

Directing her gaze to Anna, Susannah said in overly exuberant voice, "I would very much like to dance." She smiled at Anna and tried to pull her hand free from Nate, but he wouldn't let go. Frowning at him, she said, "You heard your sister. It will be great fun, and I'm sure to find a partner. Besides, you likely have more *business* to discuss with my uncle."

Nate gave her a darkling look that nearly froze the

blood in her veins. "Very well then, *my dear*." He addressed his sisters. "We shall dance. All of us."

All? Susannah's surprise was quickly replaced by dread, weighing down her limbs like liquid lead.

"Come, my dear," said Nate, putting emphasis on his endearment to her. "I believe they're starting up a set right now."

"Splendid. This will be such fun," Anna said brightly. She turned to lead the group towards the ballroom, chatting like a magpie the entire way.

Susannah tuned her out. She didn't want to dance, most certainly not with Nate, for it required touching him. She couldn't bear to feel the light pressure of his hand pressed against the small of her back, or his hand sending heat through the fabric of her glove. How could she avoid looking at the man when he would be everywhere, all around her, all the time? His nearness made her lose all capacity for rational thought.

As they entered the ballroom, Anna said over her shoulder, "Sherry has asked me for the first dance, so we'll have to find a partner for you, Minnie."

"I would be honored if Lady Minerva would give me the first dance," said a voice on their left.

All heads turned to see Whitsell's tall frame bent over in a polite bow, his hand extended towards Minnie. He raised his head, smiling at her.

Her cheeks flushed, her expression demure, and she put her hand in his. "Of course, Captain."

"I'm not sure—" Nate started.

"The captain will not do anything untoward, will you, sir?" Minnie looked up at him, a twinkle in her eye.

Whitsell stood straight and nodded to Nate. "Don't worry, Rainsford. She'll be safe with me."

"Of course," Nate said, but Susannah could feel his

arm tense beneath his coat. Why was he worried about Minnie? Captain Whitsell seemed to be an exceptionally polite young man, even if he was a friend of Nate's.

Anna curtsied. "If you'll excuse me, I'm going to find Sherry." She darted off through the doors of the ballroom that led to the hall.

Setting her mind back to her own problems, Susannah wracked her brain for an excuse to avoid dancing with—and touching—Nate. Pretending to yawn, she said, "I don't think I'm quite up for dancing after all. Perhaps I should retire for the evening." She tried to pull away, gesturing to the door. "I'm sure uncle is ready to leave. If you'll excuse me—"

"He's gone, Susannah," Nate said, looking down at her, all teeth. "He asked me to see you home."

Drat. Her shoulders slumped, and she clenched her jaw, resigned to dancing with a traitor. A traitor who stirred her blood.

"Come, it's not that bad," Nate said with a touch of asperity. "After all—"

A loud, grinding noise that sounded outside the doors of the ballroom, followed by men's shouts. They all turned their heads and peered towards the glass-paned doors that led to the terrace, leaning forward and back, left and right, trying to see where the noise originated. The other guests milling around them hushed for a moment, craning their necks to see more. Soon, the crowd around them began moving *en masse* towards the doors, ladies poking gentlemen with their fans to make way, the tone of their chatter turning serious and questioning. Susannah, Nate, Minnie, and Whitsell found themselves swept along with the group.

"It must be the riots," Minnie said. "They've been intensifying in advance of Parliament's vote on the Corn Laws on Friday. If it's approved, it will make the cost of grain exceedingly high for the masses. Oh, I do hope the rioters don't spill over into Sherry's house."

A tall, elderly, yet graceful lady leaned towards them. "They've come from Grosvenor Square and entered Lord Erskine's home. My husband has gone to fetch the carriage. He feels it's unsafe for us to remain here any longer."

Susannah saw Whitsell and Nate exchange a quick glance even as Minnie pulled her away from Nate and towards the now-open doors. She silently thanked Minnie for the unintended rescue.

Several guests had spilled out onto the terrace. The garden was dark, save for a few torches scattered about. Susannah realized that the noises they heard were coming from the street, the sounds bouncing through the alleys and mews and off the back wall of the garden.

"I'm not sure we should stay here." Susannah fingered the gold tassel of the swag that framed the door. She was only slightly worried about the rioters, her interest more heavily drawn to any excuse she could find to escape Nate.

"It will be fine." Minnie patted her arm reassuringly. "They've not done any looting, except for Lord Harrowby's home; however, he has been a most ardent supporter of the Corn Laws. Quite a provoking gentleman, as I understand."

"We will be safe," Nate whispered in her ear, his breath hot on her neck.

A thrilling trill of shivers ran up Susannah's spine, for she hadn't known he was behind her. She silently cursed herself for her involuntary reaction.

"Come, we're dancing." He held out his hand from behind her. "No matter how tired you are."

"Yes, let's," said Minnie, who had already turned back

towards the ballroom. "The caller is asking us to take our places."

Susannah stiffened, determined to remain rooted to her spot, but Nate pulled her towards the center of the floor where other guests were setting up for the quadrille. He looked over at her, his brow questioning. "Do you know this dance?"

For a brief second, she thought to answer no. But her hesitation must have also revealed the truth, for Nate's face relaxed and he said in a decided tone, "Of course you do."

"Places, please," the caller announced, and the musicians struck a chord.

The rioters momentarily forgotten, Nate situated Susannah next to him, perpendicular to two other couples who faced each other, one of them being Minnie and Whitsell. Nate and Susannah were the firsts, but the spots across from them were empty. Susannah closed her eyes, silently wishing no one would step forward to fill it. Then they would not be able to dance. The simple act of standing next to him made her feel the heat emanating off his body, as his unique scent tickled her nose, and her breath caught. Why did she have to be so cursed attracted to the man?

The music started. Susannah opened her eyes and her spirits fell, but quickly rose again. Another couple stood in formation, so she would have to dance, but opposite her was Sir Philip and a beautiful, buxom blonde whose repeated titters reminded Susannah of a brainless pigeon. He offered her the slightest nod, but said nothing. Suddenly, Susannah knew who she could speak to about Nate's treasonous plans, and her heart pattered anxiously in her chest.

She looked around at the other dancers. To her right

was Whitsell and Minnie, and to Nate's left, an elderly couple she did not know.

The dance caller, standing in the minute gallery above the ballroom, shouted, "My lords, my ladies," bringing the dancers to order. The musicians, playing a few strings and woodwinds, sounded the opening bars, and the caller spoke above the crowd. "Dancers, salute your partners."

Susannah angled left towards Nate and gave him a stiff curtsey. She riveted her gaze to the floor, unwilling to be swayed by attraction, for there was nothing good about a traitor.

"Salute your corners."

Susannah turned to her right and curtsied to Captain Lord Whitsell, willing her jaw to relax.

His eyes crinkled with a smile. "I hope you enjoy the dance, Miss Cressingham."

"Likewise, Captain." Susannah kept her eyes mostly averted, torn by civility and not wanting to befriend any friend of Nate's.

The music continued, various couples around them clapping in time, and the caller began. "First couples, vis-à-vis."

Susannah stepped forward into the middle of the square. Sir Philip did the same. Their eyes met and locked, and he gave a slight nod. She returned the gesture, determination making her pulse gallop like a runaway mare. He was the man in whom she needed to confide. But how?

He spoke in low tones. "Hello again, Miss Cressingham. Are you enjoying yourself this evening?" His eyes flicked to Nate for a brief second, then he smirked.

The caller continued. "*À droite, à gauche.*" They each performed a step-hop to their right, then their left, their shoes tapping on the wood floor.

As quietly as she could while still being heard above the

din, she said, "I need to speak with you in private after this set."

"Together, then turn." The caller's booming voice echoed off the walls of the ballroom in time to the music.

She and Sir Philip stepped towards each other, hands extended. He took them gently in his own, his expression curious, and led her in a small circle, his head close to hers. "About what, might I ask?"

"It involves—"

"And back. Now, through and through," said the caller.

Susannah frowned as Sir Philip released her hands and they stepped back to their spots.

With a protective look, Nate took Susannah's hand, his fingers pressing hers tight. His thumb rubbed a circle on the back of her hand, and a hot shiver shimmied up her arm, exploding in her chest. She closed her eyes for a brief moment, hating her body's reaction to him. They walked forward, as did Sir Philip and the blonde, with Nate and Susannah passing in between the pair.

"We need to talk," Nate said to her in low but urgent tones.

Susannah turned to look at him.

He stared down at her, eyes dark and dangerous, his dratted lips soft and kissable. "I suppose we'll have to do it now." His last words a seductive whisper even as he rubbed soft circles on the back of her hand.

The couples turned and thankfully, Nate was forced to let go. Susannah immediately massaged the traitorous burn off the back of her hand. Sir Philip and the blonde now held hands and passed through Susannah and Nate, then the couples returned to their original places in the square.

"Gentlemen, left-hand star, ladies out."

The men came together, their left hands extended towards the center of the square. The ladies stepped to their right side, grasping the men's right hands with their left, facing their partner, offset. Nate took up her hand once more, and Susannah felt the sensual burn, amplified by his direct gaze.

She dropped her eyes to the floor.

The caller continued. "Two sets." Susannah, as if pulled by gravity, skip-hopped to Nate, as the ladies did to the other gentlemen.

Nate lowered his chin as she drew near. "I think you overheard something…" Nate was cut off when Susannah skip-hopped away, but when she came to him again for the second set, he continued. "…that you don't fully understand."

Susannah frowned, a chill coming over her. "Oh no, my lord. I understood perfectly."

"*Chassé*, then round and round."

Susannah longed to dash off the dance floor. But she *chasséd* to the center as the other ladies did, passing in front of Nate, and took up hands with the other ladies, forming a circle. The gentlemen, on the outside, walked clockwise, the ladies counter-clockwise, their gowns swishing like leaves in the wind. Minnie, who stood across from Susannah, leaned her head in a bit. "Is everything all right, Susannah? You don't look well." Her voice was low, barely heard above the music.

Susannah shrugged her shoulders. She hardly knew anymore.

"Return, and turn." The couples, now back where they started, clasped hands with their partners and turned counter-clockwise in place.

"I am not like your uncle."

Susannah dismissed his comment. Of course he would say that. Nate's grip was firm, and Susannah felt a perfidious arc of pleasure at his touch. She tried to pull her hands away, but he wouldn't release her until they had returned to their original positions in the square.

"Seconds, vis-à-vis." The caller raised his voice in a battle to be heard over the increased noise coming from the rioters in the street.

Nate and the blonde, who smiled suggestively at him, moved to the center of the square, following the steps of the caller. Susannah, to her chagrin, found herself throwing mental daggers at the woman, even as she herself could not take her eyes off Nate. She noticed everything about him...how well he moved to the music, how dashing he looked in his black coat and breeches, his distinctive scent as he passed by her. *Drat him and his perfection.*

As if he knew she was watching, Nate met Susannah's gaze as he took the blonde's hands and turned.

"And back. Now, through and through."

Nate and Susannah maintained eye contact as the couples walked towards each other, but this time Sir Philip and the blonde passed through Nate and Susannah first. They turned, switched places, and passed through again, their gazes never wavering.

How did he have such control over her? Why could she not feel the same blatant disgust for him as she did her uncle?

Because you were never in love with your uncle, you ninny.

The dance continued, the men formed the left-hand star, and as Susannah set, she dropped her head, deciding the floor was a much safer view. Nate leaned towards her, whispering in soft tones, "I know it doesn't seem like it, but I am not playing your uncle's game. You must trust me on that, poppet."

Susannah looked up. Again, that word. *Trust.* The ladies *chasséd*, took each other's hands, and turned a circle.

When everyone returned to their original places in the

square and the couples on either side performed vis-à-vis, Nate continued. "And you must trust that no matter how bad things look, I have your best interests at heart."

She glanced over at him, a strange bristling poking under her skin. "*Trust* you." Her words crackled with newfound anger. "Trust *you*."

Nate nodded, his expression neither mocking nor angry. He looked…serious. "I need to tell you…your uncle has said…" He frowned. "He gave me a special license."

She stood there, holding Nate's hand, her mouth gaping, the blood draining from her face. Special license? Did her uncle intend that they marry sooner? But…she could not. Not an hour ago, she learned that Nate was a traitor in league with her uncle. It was a *fait accompli* that marriage wouldn't happen.

Yet he seemed to be implying that it would, and soon. This made telling Sir Philip what Nate and her uncle were doing even more urgent. It was the only way she could ensure the pair were arrested. Only after that happened would she be able to gain control of her fortune and seek out her sister on her own.

"Susannah, are you all right?"

Nate's words quick-started her brain. The ladies had already *chasséd* to the center, but Susannah had missed the count. She hurried to them, grasping the hands of the ladies on either side. Minnie leaned forward. "You're pale. Are you sure you're well? What did he say to you?"

Susannah could barely register Minnie's question, much less answer. The sounds in the room—music, conversation, laughter, dancing—melded together to become a dull roar. A roar that ate away at her brain, leaving her edgy and anxious.

She looked over her shoulder, searching out Sir Philip, but he passed by her and she caught Nate's eye instead.

The ladies circled, then the couples all returned to their starting points. Susannah performed the moves in a daze. Minnie and the older gentleman began their vis-à-vis.

Susannah couldn't wait. She had to tell Sir Philip the truth about Nate now. Catching his eye, she opened her mouth to speak, but was cut off by the sound of breaking glass and screams and shouts coming from outside the ballroom.

The music came to a crumbling halt as everyone stopped moving. Stopped laughing. Stopped talking. They all turned to the door, and Minnie said in a small, surprised voice, "The rioters are here."

CHAPTER 11

NATE'S HEART fired in successive, rapid bursts, and for a brief moment, he thought it would explode from his chest. He looked at the doorway where the sounds originated, momentarily frozen, then suddenly overcome with vivid memories of cannon fire and the wails of dying men, his brother lying on the ground, soaked with rain and half his head scattered about in bloody, boney bits. Nate began to shake, the familiar nightmare of Albuera coming back to him, as well as other feelings he'd not been able to bury with his brother.

Fear. Anguish. Self-loathing.

"Nate? Natey, answer me."

A voice was yelling at him. Calling to him. *Smack.* Something hard cracked against his cheek, and he blinked.

"Nate Kinlan, come back to us. That's an order." Minnie's words startled Nate and he looked down at her, her hand raised, her palm pink from slapping him in the face.

It took mere seconds to realize where he was...or rather, where he wasn't. This wasn't Albuera. These weren't dying men. And he wasn't the same man anymore. Back then, he had let down his brother, his father, indeed his entire family, and he'd sworn he'd never shirk his duty again. He would protect that which was his...to the death, if necessary. Nate felt a sense of calm and control come over him, as if his brother John were standing there reassuring him. He could do this. He *would* do this.

He squeezed Minnie's hand in thanks. Then he turned to Susannah, her expression confused and scared and distant, and his heart skipped a beat. Someday, he would need to explain Albuera to her, along with everything else. But first, he had to get everyone out of the house safely.

Nate scanned the room, looking for his other sisters. Anna was standing with Sherry, who had a confused expression on his face. That didn't sit well with Nate. Damned man may be too drunk for anyone's good. He surveyed the room again, but he couldn't locate Juliana anywhere. Looking at Tradwick, he mouthed her name.

His friend raised a dubious eyebrow, wordlessly questioning Nate's mental fitness.

Nate gave a slight dip of his head to indicate he was fine.

Tradwick nodded. Taking Minnie by one hand and the blonde by the other, he propelled them towards Susannah. "I think you best stay with Miss Cressingham, ladies. I'll send Lady Anna and Lady Juliana this way, and Sherry and I will see what this riffraff is about."

But Sherry had already brought Anna to them. "C'mon Tradwick," he said with alcohol-induced bravado. "Let's see what these jackanapes are up to."

"First, we find Lady Juliana." Tradwick dipped his chin, his face serious.

"Of course, of course." Sherry pulled Tradwick by the arm towards the door.

"I'll join you," Whitsell said, following them.

Tradwick looked over his shoulder at Nate and mouthed, "I'll find her."

Nate nodded, then looked around. Barely thirty seconds had passed since the first sound of glass breaking, and people in the ballroom had begun to scatter, husbands collecting wives and exiting, other men talking loudly, escorting ladies to one corner of the room in a rush, knocking down chairs and tables in their wake. The musicians had abandoned their post at the first sound of trouble, and Nate watched them dart out the back door towards the terrace and gardens. *Cowards.*

Nate's protective instinct hit a high. No doubt John Coachman knew what was going on and would have the carriage ready. Nate could not let anything happen to his sisters, and he certainly could let nothing befall Susannah, no matter what her feelings were toward him. Staring intently at the girls, he gestured for them to come closer, so he could be heard over the chaos. After they'd all leaned in, he said in a loud voice, "Whatever is happening, you do as I instruct."

The frightened look on Susannah's face gave Nate a start, like someone had reached into his chest and clamped a fist around his lungs. Anna and Minnie had their hands clasped together, their expressions mirroring Susannah's, their heads darting about the room as they took in what was happening.

He motioned to the corner of the ballroom. "Stand with the other ladies there." He gave them all reassuring smile. "No doubt it's just a handful of rowdy men, stirred up by the riots. They can't get over the wall into the garden, and we won't let them into the house." He stared at Susannah until she met his eyes. "I will come back for you, do you understand? Do not leave this room."

She nodded, and Anna reached out and took her hand, squeezing it tightly.

Nate felt a momentary relief at his sister's kind gesture. God bless Anna's protective, caring instinct. He had a moment's hesitation, though, as his gut told him he should not abandon the girls, but logic overruled. He had to find a safe exit from Sherry's house. The sooner he could get the girls out, the better, for as the night went on, and the rioters continued to drink and carouse, the worse it could become.

He made for the doorway that led to the hall, looking over his shoulder one last time. The girls had all formed a cocoon, standing amidst other female guests. They'd intertwined their hands, eyes constantly scanning the room. His sisters had good sense, Minnie in particular, and he had to hope in the few minutes it took Nate to find a suitable exit, nothing would befall them. Yet pangs of doubt reverberated through his chest like bullet fire.

Steeling himself to what was surely a natural instinct, he left the ballroom and nearly collided with Juliana. "Jules," he said in a breath of relief. He grabbed her by the shoulders and squeezed. "I'm so glad you're safe."

"I'm fine, but where are my sisters?"

"In the ballroom. Go with them and stay there until I come for you."

She nodded, looking up at him with scared eyes. "There are so many of them. I saw them on the street from the window. Mobs and mobs. They have torches and clubs, axes…"

Nate felt yet another press of anxiety. Jules almost never showed fear.

"You'll get us out of here?" she asked.

He smiled, hoping it conveyed confidence. "Of course I will. Now go inside and wait. I'll be there soon."

Nate proceeded down the hall. The sounds of the rioters grew louder. Surely they weren't in the house?

He came to the stairs, stopping short at the top step. Two skeleton-thin men in dirty, hole-ridden rags were coming up. One wielded a makeshift club, the other a flaming torch, and both looked eager to make trouble.

Behind Nate, someone growled low and deep. He flicked a glance over his shoulder.

Whitsell had removed his uniform coat and was rolling up the sleeves of his shirt. His hard, slanted eyes and strong, powerful fists made him look like a professional boxer. "Get the hell out of this house," he snarled at the men.

They paused for only a moment. Ribbing each other with their elbows, they grinned, showing their stained and missing teeth. "Look, it's a nob," said the one, gesturing with his club.

"We came fer the party, yer grace." The torch-bearer gave an exaggerated bow, swinging the smoky flame wide.

Nate's blood began to boil. "You're not invited." He inclined his head to the man holding the torch. "I've got that one, Whitsell."

"Perfect."

Both men started down the steps.

The ruffians, their faces darkening, raced up the stairs waving their weapons and yelling.

"Bloody curs." Nate met his adversary on the landing and reached for the torch, while Whitsell engaged with the other man.

The rioter swung the flaming end at Nate's head, grunting with effort.

Nate ducked, the fire almost singeing him, and quickly plowed his fist into the brute's side.

The man groaned, ashes falling from the torch, but came at Nate again, flame-first. "Ye'll get yers—"

Nate deflected the attack with his arm and managed to grab the torch. They both held it, fighting, straining, struggling for control as they tried to keep their balance on the stairs.

The thug angled the torch towards the wall while his free hand shoved Nate's chin upwards.

"Sturdy...beggar," Nate gasped. He grabbed at the man's hand near his throat and turned his head side to side, trying to dislodge it.

Thwack. Nate heard skin connect with skin. It was Whitsell and the other thug. Groans and curses filled the stairwell, mixing with the *kshhhh* of breaking glass and cries from shouting men.

Nate grunted, pushing the torch away from the wall. "You're...going to...die," he ground out. Releasing the hand holding his chin, Nate thrust his arm upward, knocking the thug's hand away. Quickly, Nate angled his body, going for the man's neck. He clenched it hard and dug his fingers deep, wanting to crush the cur's bones.

The skeleton man bucked, freeing himself from Nate's grasp on his throat. He spat a greenish wad of phlegm that hit Nate in the corner of his eye.

As repulsed as he was shocked, Nate's grip loosened on both the man and the torch.

It was enough for the cur to wrest it from him and step aside. He pushed the fiery end into Nate's chest, half-laughing, half-coughing.

Nate cried out, then leaned back and knocked the torch away. Searing pain scorched his chest as smoke burned his nose. He quickly stepped away from the man and patted himself down, trying to extinguish his smoldering shirt and waistcoat.

The bastard took another swing at Nate. "Yer gonna burn in 'ell, ye flash cove."

Nate stepped back in retreat, but his boot caught the stair and he fell on his arse with a bone-jarring thump.

The ruffian leaped over him. "Stupid nob."

Nate lunged for him, managing to grab a foot.

The rioter fell forward and dropped the torch. It rolled down two steps, coming to rest next to the wall.

Pulling on the man's leg, Nate tried to get leverage, but he squirmed violently. *Ooof!* The bastard's boot connected with Nate's mouth and shoulder as he struggled for freedom, and Nate's hold loosened.

Nate tasted the salty, metallic tang of blood in his mouth. "Damn you!" Ladies' screams and the crashes of breaking glass in the ballroom above echoed in Nate's ears. Flames were licking their way up the wall and across the carpeted stair. Nate's eyes watered from the smoke.

He was done with this bastard. Launching himself up the staircase, Nate clutched at the cur's threadbare pants, coat, anything. He landed on the man with a groan.

The rioter wriggled like an eel, his strong arms trying to push Nate away. *Not this time.* Kneeling above him, Nate clenched the man's collar with one fist and raised the other.

Eyes gleaming, the ruffian raised his knee towards Nate's groin. But before he could connect, Nate drove his fist into the bastard's face, cutting his cheek. The force slammed his head against the step, knocking him out.

Panting, Nate pushed aside the prone body just in time to witness Whitsell whack the other brigand in the side of the head with the makeshift club, sending the man rolling down the stairs. He landed in a crumpled heap, unmoving.

"The fire." Nate struggled for breath in the smoky stairwell. He shucked his coat and began beating the flames. Whitsell, his face bloody, raced up the stairs to grab his coat, then joined Nate.

More chaotic sounds echoed from the rooms above them.

"Go," Whitsell said, breathing heavily as he beat the nearly extinguished fire. "Take care of yours."

With a nod, Nate scrabbled to the landing and down the hall, stopping short at the entrance to the ballroom. *Good God.* A corner of the room was on fire, billows of smoke obscuring half of it from view. What he could see looked like it had been shelled. His stomach sank to his knees, and the helpless feeling he'd experienced when his brother had been shot coursed through his body. He pushed that aside. Over his shoulder, Nate shouted down to Whitsell. "Fire! There's fire. Send men up with buckets."

He could hear screams, but they sounded far off. Surely the girls weren't still in the ballroom? He had to be certain. Quickly untying his cravat, he balled it up and put it over his mouth, then dashed into the room. Only half the ball-room had been opened up for dancing, forcing Nate to step around overturned chairs and broken gaming tables. His boots crunched the shattered crystal glasses beneath him. Two candelabras, which had lined the perimeter of the room, lay on their sides, the lit ends pointed into the floor-to-ceiling curtains. Flames slowly ate their way up the fabric as smoke clouded the two-story ceiling from view. It was like looking through a thick London fog. Thank God the curtains were silk and not brocade, for they would burn slowly, giving the men time to extinguish the flames.

"Susannah," Nate called. His eyes burned, and he could hear men yelling downstairs and then, the loud *pop* of a pistol. Through patches of smoke, Nate saw destruction, but no people. What if someone had been trampled, unable to get up, perhaps laying under a table?

"Susannah!" Nate threaded his way through the room, his pulse quickening with each step, his heart pounding in his ears with each crunch of crystal. With one hand still covering his mouth, he moved the broken pieces of furniture to reveal what lay underneath. Fortunately, there were only scattered cards, piles of food, shattered glass. The room was empty of guests.

He breathed a sigh of relief. They'd gotten out, and likely to safety.

"Rainsford." A loud but muffled voice sounded behind him.

Nate turned to see Tradwick heading towards him, his mouth also covered with fabric. "Tradwick, where is everyone? Where's Susannah?"

"Most of the ladies have been escorted out of the house and into carriages." He motioned towards a side door, which led to a parlor off the ballroom. The two men ran through the door even as footsteps, shouts, and sloshing water sounded behind them.

Nate looked over his shoulder at the servants and other gentlemen forming a bucket brigade and throwing water on the fire. Satisfied they could bring it under control, he tossed his smoky neckcloth onto the floor. "You have Susannah and my sisters?"

Tradwick lowered his hand and met Nate's eyes, a guarded expression on his face.

A flare of worry ignited in Nate's chest. "Who's missing? Is it one of my sisters?"

"Your sisters are fine. They are on their way back to Rainsford House even as I speak. I instructed my coachman to take a circuitous route to avoid any further danger."

Nate exhaled with relief. "And Susannah? She is with them?"

"No, Rain." Tradwick's expression changed, becoming darker. The man who never showed any emotion suddenly looked guilty. "She wasn't with them."

Nate's body stiffened with rage, and he clenched his fists. "You *left* her?" This couldn't be happening. He'd just found her again. He couldn't lose her now.

Tradwick huffed. "Of course I did not *leave* her, you ass. What do you take me for?" He glared at Nate. "Susannah became separated from us. She'd been with us all along, until the last crush of people escaping out the door that leads to the servants' hallway. That's when I discovered she wasn't there."

"You left her." Nate's menacing tone matched his mood. He *would* kill his friend.

"Focus, you idiot." Tradwick straightened his shoulders indignantly. "You can take out your rage on me another time. For now, we need to find her. I suggest we split up and search the house before it turns into a pile of ash. Once we're sure she's not in the house, we can look elsewhere. But it behooves us to make sure she got out and then track down where she might have gone."

Nate took a deep, clarifying breath, allowing logic to take over. Whatever happened wasn't Tradwick's fault.

"Come, Rain. I will scour the rooms upstairs. You're sure she's not in the ballroom?"

Nate shook his head. "It was empty."

"Very well, then. Head downstairs. Use the servant staircase, as she might have gone that way and gotten waylaid."

Nate thought briefly about sharing the intelligence Cressingham had revealed to him, then brushed it aside. First, he had to find Susannah, then he could report what he'd learned. He left the room and quickly made his way down the servant staircase. He ended up in the kitchen, the room cloudy with smoke and reeking of burnt bacon. Not surprising when Nate saw the unattended pig on the spit, one half of it blackened and charred. Staff and gentlemen ran to and fro carrying sloshing buckets of water, stepping on and around overturned trays, serving dishes, amalgamated piles of food, and puddles of who-knew-what. Nate scanned the room, but caught no sight of Susannah. He quickly descended into the basement to make sure she wasn't there, perhaps hiding from all the chaos above.

Satisfied she wasn't in the basement or any of the storage rooms off the kitchen, he went down the servant hall, opening the doors to the various rooms he passed. She wasn't in any of them, and an uncomfortable tingle weaved its way through his limbs. Every moment that passed was another moment of not having Susannah safely in his arms. *Dammit.* He never should have left the girls alone.

The third door he opened led into the conservatory on the back of the house. It was dark, with no candles or lamps lit, and the commotion from the rioters outside the house permeated the glass, creating a muffled sound within. The leaves of the plants and trees that he could see from the dimly lit hallway didn't move at all, and Nate was about to close the door, when he heard a sharp intake of breath.

He stopped, every muscle in his body going taut, his mouth turning dry as sawdust. Stepping into the room, he bemoaned the crunch of gravel beneath his feet. He closed the door behind him and waited a moment for his eyes to adjust. The moon played hide and seek with the clouds, creating a bit of light every now and then through the glass ceiling, but when obscured, Nate could hardly see his own hand before him. Tuning his senses, he listened for crunching gravel, breathing, movement...anything. Was that a sound off to the right? He slowly made his way towards the trees that lined the far wall, scouring his memory for a mental map of Sherry's conservatory. He'd been in it a handful of times over the years, but not lately. He seemed to recall a line of trees against one wall, then flowers, smaller fruits, and other plants closer to the large, paned windows on the left.

With his hands extended, he reached out, feeling past pots, plants, and trees. Hearing another breath, he stopped, focusing on the sound. It was just ahead of him and to the left. He took two steps towards the noise when a man's voice suddenly broke the silence.

"Yeow! Bleedin' witch, ye bit me." Nate heard the crack of palm against cheek.

"Let go of me, oaf!" Susannah's voice rang out, and Nate's chest nearly burst with relief, followed quickly by a flash of anger.

"Susannah, where are you?"

"By…the…ow! By the windows," she managed to get out through shouts of pain.

"Shut up, wench," said the man.

The scramble of feet against gravel mingled with Susannah's cries helped Nate hone in on her. He turned the corner just as the moon revealed itself. Against the glass stood a tall, raggedy-looking man leaning against it with one arm slung over Susannah, holding her against him, her back to his front. His free hand held a knife near the underside of her neck, the dull metal barely glistening in the moonlight. His other hand cupped her breast over her dress, which seemed to be partially torn down the front.

A fury unlike anything Nate had ever known consumed him from the inside out, burning under his skin like the hottest coals. His hands twitched with the desire to tear the man apart limb by limb, and it was only because of Susannah that he did not charge straight ahead and plow the man through the massive window. "Get your hands off my fiancée," Nate growled.

The man cackled. "She's yer luv, eh? Pretty thing she is. We's havin' some fun before ye came along."

Even from a few feet away, Nate could smell the liquor on the man's breath. *This man is going to die.* Nate had only to get Susannah out of the way, and he'd take the bastard's knife and plunge it into his heart. Slowly.

Susannah clenched the man's arm, trying to keep the blade away from her neck. The moon ducked behind the clouds, obscuring her from view, but when it shone again, it illuminated her face, and Nate's chest swelled with pride.

She was livid. As livid as he'd seen her with him, and for a brief second, Nate pitied the man who held her.

As if on cue, Susannah jerked hard at the man's arm, then ducked her chin and bit him again, startling him into yelling and looking down at her.

As soon as the man dropped his gaze, Nate charged, his fist ready. The man barely saw what was coming before Nate grabbed the knife with one hand and plowed a hammer-like fist into the man's cheek with the other. Susannah sank to the ground and scuttled out of the way on her knees as the two men fought.

Nate surrendered to the rage that had built inside him. Rage that stemmed from Susannah's coldness to the special license to Napoleon's escape to Cressing-ham's secret informer and the wild, riotous events of the evening. He blindly threw punch after punch, easily knocking the knife out of the man's hand, turning his face into a bloody puree of swollen lips and eyes. And yet Nate continued, delivering punches to the man's ribs, his stomach, his kidneys. Anywhere he thought the bastard would feel it. He wanted this thug to suffer every bit of pain that Nate could deliver.

"Rain."

Another punch. And another. This sorry excuse for a human would pay for touching his beautiful betrothed.

"Rain." The voice—Susannah's?—was louder and more insistent, and it cut through to Nate's brain. He stopped mid-punch, his hand poised above the now-unconscious man's face. He sat back on his heels, slightly stupefied.

A hand clasped his shoulder, and he turned. Behind him, Susannah looked down upon him, her face full of fright. "Enough. Please."

Nate rose quickly, too quickly, and he swayed slightly as the blood drained from his head. Susannah reached out to steady him, but he found his own footing.

"Are you all right?" he asked, his voice hoarse. He scanned her face in the moonlight, searching for any cuts or abrasions.

She nodded, her eyes riveted to his.

He could see the quick, shallow rise and fall of her breathing, and something primitive and passionate inside Nate came alive. But he reeled it in, tempering it, although it left him shaking like a newborn foal. He'd almost lost her, was nearly too late to prevent that bastard from violating her.

With trembling hands, his fingers hovered over the delicate curves of her face, close enough to feel the heat from her skin. Lord, he wanted to touch her, but he would not. It was the last thing she likely wanted. To have another man—especially one she despised—putting his hands on her? Nate swallowed hard, fisting his hands by his side, willing his ragged breath to slow down.

"I almost lost you, poppet." His voice cracked with emotion.

Susannah shook her head. "You came. It's over." She cast her eyes downward, her cheeks turning pink. "My gown..." Quickly, she placed her hand over the gaping tear in her bodice.

"Take my waistcoat." Nate quickly unbuttoned the garment and draped it over her shoulders, holding it closed. He frowned, for it was so large, it hardly covered her.

"I...thank you." Susannah grasped the edges of it with her fingertips from underneath.

Nate quickly pulled his hands away so she wouldn't have to touch him, even though the very action sent a reverberating pang of regret through his body.

"Your eye. Your mouth." She inspected his face. "They're bleeding."

His heart thumped at her concern, but he shrugged. "It's nothing."

Susannah looked up at him again, her forehead lined with an emotion he couldn't discern. The faint moonlight illuminated her like a halo from heaven above. He watched her pulse thump in her neck, *ba-dum, ba-dum,* quick and fast and so very alive. Nate could have sworn his heartbeat matched hers, and passion flooded his body like the first hit of brandy in one's blood. His gaze was drawn to her lips. Those beautiful, beguiling lips. When they parted, Nate felt as if she were extending a personal invitation to be tasted.

God, he wanted to kiss her.

Their gazes never wavered. Everything around them faded to black, the silence in the conservatory broken only by their rapid breaths. Slowly, Nate leaned towards her, feeling her pull. She was his lodestone, drawing him in, luring him closer and closer, and he was helpless to resist.

Susannah did not move away. On the contrary, she leaned in, as well, as if she, too, felt the attraction.

Inches apart, her heat washed over him, and another wave of desire swept through every limb. His brought his hand up, slowly, deliberately, not wanting to scare her, but so desperate to touch her. To reassure her. To show her what a man's touch could really be. With the gentlest caress, he slid his fingertips along the curve of her reddened cheek, and Susannah leaned into him like a kitten begging for affection.

"Poppet, I—"

"Rainsford? Are you in here?" Whitsell's deep voice sounded from the entrance.

Susannah stiffened, inhaling sharply, and like a flame doused by water, the moment ended.

Nate closed his eyes, cursed under his breath, and let his hand drop, taking a step backwards. He glanced up at Susannah. The moonlight now cast a grey pallor upon her skin. He watched as like water freezing, her expression hardened, her sudden, cold demeanor chilling Nate to his bones.

His icy, angry betrothed was back.

CHAPTER 12

A FEW STREETS from Sherrington's townhome, and thankfully in the opposite direction of the rioters, Susannah climbed into Nate's waiting carriage with his assistance.

"I need to speak to John a moment, then we'll be on our way." He snapped the door shut.

Susannah fell back onto the squab, grateful for the moment alone. Her pulse still pounded in her ears from the frightening events of the evening. *Poppycock*. She was fooling herself if she thought her heart wasn't also racing because of Nate. *Good Lord*. He'd wanted to kiss her. She knew it, felt it to the depths of her soul. And worse, she'd wanted him to.

That horrible man who had touched her, almost defiled her, had frightened her terribly. Susannah shuddered just thinking about it. She'd never been so relieved than when Nate had arrived. His soft voice, kind words, and gentle touch, so different from the other man's painful groping, had comforted her like a balm. How could one man make her feel so protected and safe?

She put an ungloved hand to her face, her fingertips

barely peeking out of the sleeves of the footman's coat that Nate had borrowed for her. Slowly, she touched her cheek just as Nate had, remembering in vivid detail the shocking feel of his bare fingers on her skin. His touch had comforted her, to be sure, but it had also stirred her passion. She was mortified by her reaction to him, and her face flamed at the thought of how she'd leaned into his touch. He had much more power over her than she had previously thought.

Power to crush her heart.

Because if she were honest with herself, she was still attracted to the man. Despite his lies. Despite his hand in her brother's death. Despite his collusion with her uncle. He was like a spider web...sticky, difficult to remove oneself from, yet beautiful, all at the same time.

The carriage door opened, and Susannah gave a start. Nate climbed in, sat on the seat opposite her, and immediately drew her hands into his, pressing them gently as he rubbed his thumbs in circles over the backs. A delicious heat ran up her arms, spreading throughout her chest, and she silently cursed to herself. The dim light from the carriage lamps flickered in his dark, intense eyes, and she wished she could look away.

Giving her hands a tight squeeze, he said, "Poppet, whatever you heard between your uncle and me, it's not what you think."

Well, if anything could convince her wretched body that she shouldn't be attracted to him, a reminder of his treasonous activities would certainly do it.

Stiffening, she pulled her hands out of his, clenching them on her lap. "Then what are you doing?" she asked defiantly.

He reached for her again, but she evaded him. Touching him was the last thing she should do right now.

"I'm sorry, I can't tell you. It's—"

"This is precisely why I don't trust you, my lord. You can't possibly expect me to take your word on faith alone."

He leaned forward, forcibly taking up her hands and held them tight. "That is precisely what I expect," he said earnestly. "What I'm *asking* you to do."

She looked away, willing herself to be strong. "I cannot."

"Susannah, what is happening…it involves more than me, and I've sworn to stay mum."

"Sworn to whom?"

He hesitated. "I can't say. But—"

Susannah cried out in frustration, pulling her hands free and folding her arms under her chest. She turned towards the window, not caring that her actions were childish or petty. Until he was willing to be completely forthright with her, she wouldn't listen to his lies.

He sat back on the squab and sighed, running his hand through his hair. Susannah stole a glance at him and was unnerved to find him staring intently at her. Something about the way he looked at her plucked at her heartstrings. His eyes did not match the man she thought he was. They weren't deceitful or hard like her uncle's, but caring and compassionate. She'd seen it clear as day as he'd helped her out of Sherrington's house. Her belly churned with turmoil. How could a man so embroiled in treachery and dishonor be so kindhearted at the same time?

"About what happened in the conservatory…" He trailed off, then leaned towards her again.

Goodness, now he was bringing up the almost-kiss? She turned towards the window even more, definitely not in the proper state of mind to rehash that.

"Susannah, look at me. Please."

Was he jesting? She wasn't sure whether she wanted to

pound the life out of him, burst into tears, or beg him to kiss her. None of them was a viable option, so instead, she gave a swift shake of her head.

"Very well, then." He sighed. "I want to apologize. I should not have lost control." He drew in a breath, held it for a moment, then let it out. "It was wrong of me to thrash that man right before you. I'm sorry you had to witness that. But I couldn't help it. He...he *touched* you, poppet, and I nearly lost my mind."

Some of the tension coiled within Susannah eased. She opened her eyes, unthreading her arms, and cast him a quick, sidelong glance. In a near-whisper, she said, "You did what you had to do."

"Everything I do is for you."

She opened her mouth to protest, but he put up a hand. "No, I need to say this. And you need to *hear* it." He paused. "I know what you overheard tonight between myself and your uncle. That you think I'm colluding with him. I assure you I am not."

"But you won't tell me what you are doing."

He huffed. "I can't."

"Very well then." Susannah looked away.

Nate took up her hands, his grip on them tight. "Look at me, Susannah."

With trepidation, mostly over her own dratted feelings towards him than any thought that he might actually be honest with her, she braved a look.

His eyes met hers, and as before, they showed compassion and empathy. "My responsibility is to protect you." He dropped his head, shaking it. "Good God, it was the one promise I made to your brother, but...never mind that." Returning his gaze to her, he squeezed her hands. "Someday, I will be able to tell you everything."

Susannah angled towards Nate, her pulse skipping

under her skin. "Wait one moment. What promise? What are you talking about?"

He kissed both knuckles. "I promised Ben I'd protect you and Isabela."

She frowned. What the devil was he talking about? If he'd made such a promise, then why was he working with her uncle? Of course she didn't believe anything he told her. She couldn't. Not without proof. But if he was supposedly protecting her, then why was he marrying her? Why didn't he simply let her go to her sister? And why had he kept his family from her when she'd needed them most?

"I can see the confusion on your face."

She opened her mouth to speak, but the carriage came to a halt. She peered out the window, not quite recognizing where she was. Then realization dawned. They'd arrived at Rainsford House.

She narrowed her eyes. "Why have you brought me here?"

"You will stay here for the time being. It's safer, and I daresay more comfortable, than your uncle's accommodations."

She doubted that. Living at Rainsford House was a bad idea. It would be exceedingly difficult for her to maintain a hardened heart around him, and his family, regardless of her past and present interactions with them.

"I can tell this whole ordeal is bothering you."

Of course it was! There were too many things bothering her. Too many conflicting feelings. She mumbled a response, averting her eyes. Drat him. If he hadn't mentioned her brother, and hadn't made her feel that cursed attraction to him while in the conservatory, she would no doubt be dressing him down right now over what she'd overheard. *Focus on what you know he's doing, not what he's saying.* He's a traitor. She had to tell Sir Philip that.

Didn't she?

Nate wasn't making this easy. Something deep inside her told her he was a good man. Yet if she went by his actions, he clearly was not. If she could keep her mind on that, perhaps she could silence her qualms—and not relive every delicious moment of their lips nearly coming together.

Someone let the steps down, then the carriage door opened. Thomas the footman stood at attention.

Before Susannah could move, Nate said sternly, "Close it and step away."

"Yes, milord." Thomas quickly closed the door.

"But—"

Nate cut Susannah off, tugging on her hands until she looked at him, and she steeled herself from getting lost in his warm, brown eyes.

"We have to talk about the special license."

"There's nothing to talk about. And as for getting married, I don't think—"

The door to the carriage opened again, and Susannah gasped with surprise.

Nate growled. "Thomas—"

Lady Rainsford stuck her head in. "Oh, thank heavens the two of you are all right."

With a stern voice, Nate said, "Mama, shut the door. We're not done talking."

"There's nothing more for us to say." Susannah gathered her skirts and slid towards the door.

Nate put his hand up on the doorframe to block her in, but she turned a hard gaze on him. "Excuse me, my lord."

"Nathaniel, let her out of this carriage at once," commanded Lady Rainsford from the pavement. "The poor child. What a frightful evening you must have had. Come, dearest, let's get you settled in the house."

Susannah glared at Nate, raising an I-dare-you eyebrow in challenge.

His jaw ticked, then with a frustrated sigh, he lowered his arms.

Thomas helped Susannah out of the carriage. Lady Rainsford escorted her up the front steps, offering consoling murmurs the entire way. At the top step, Susannah glanced over her shoulder to see Nate still in the carriage, his body hidden except for one foot that hung halfway out the door. A small pang of regret echoed through her. She pushed it aside, though. Nate had had every opportunity to explain himself, and he did not. Not in a way that would satisfy her. He was probably conjuring up another untruth so he could convince her he wasn't working with her uncle.

The large front door opened wider, and Crimson stood back so Lady Rainsford and Susannah could enter. His bland expression gave no indication of his surprise to see her. "Miss Cressingham. My lord. We're so glad to see you safe."

My lord? Susannah turned quickly and found Nate standing behind her, an angry scowl on his face, and her heart skipped a beat. Goodness, she hadn't even heard him come up the steps.

Lady Rainsford drew Susannah further into the entry, her flowing silk dressing gown swishing on the marble floor. "Come, my dear." She patted Susannah's hand reassuringly.

"I assume the girls are home?" Nate asked Crimson.

"Yes, my lord. They are settled in for the evening, none worse for the wear."

"Thank you." He strode into the hall. "Miss Cressingham will be staying with us indefinitely. She will use the countess suite. Please have a light meal and bathwater brought up. Send a footman over for her belongings, but only after I have penned a note to her uncle. Summon Dr. Martin at once, and tell Fernsby to lay out a new set of clothes for me. I have an errand to run."

"Very good, my lord."

"I don't need a doctor," Susannah protested.

Both men ignored her.

"Miss Cressingham, shall I have Mrs. Friars prepare a pot of tea?" Crimson looked expectantly at Susannah.

She opened her mouth to answer, but Nate, in his high-handed way, cut her off. "Yes. Bring it to the suite."

Crimson nodded respectfully, then left.

Nate took Susannah's hand in his own and, without breaking his gaze, kissed it. "I have much I must do right now, but I'll be home later. Let Mama take care of you. You're safe now."

Lady Rainsford put an affected hand over her heart. "Good gracious, what has she been through?"

"Too much," Nate said. "Far too much." Nate released her hand and headed for his study.

Susannah watched his retreating form, her breath catching just slightly. She knew what he was going to do, yet she was captivated by his aggressive stride, which only emphasized his power and strength. Hadn't she bore witness to it that very evening? And he'd done it on her behalf. It annoyed her, but she *did* feel safer with him. *Stop, you ninny.* She gave a slight shake of her head to break whatever spell he'd cast over her. She was glad to see him go. Yes. Very glad. It was too easy to capitulate to her emotions when he was near.

"Oh, Susannah, you poor dear."

Susannah turned to Lady Rainsford. The woman's face was an open book, and Susannah could easily read the compassion in her ladyship's creased lines, furrowed brow, and taut mouth. A swell of warmth burst forth in Susannah's heart, and she admonished herself. *Goodness, can't I be mad at anyone?* This woman had lied to her. Was likely lying to her now, feigning her concern. But when Susannah regarded her ladyship's distressed face once more, she could see very plainly in the woman's eyes that her feelings were sincere.

Taking Susannah by the arm, Lady Rainsford led her up the stairs. "These rioters," she said, shaking her head. "Why must they make such chaos of the city?"

"Because they're starving, Mama." Anna's answer took everyone by surprise. She stood at the top of the stairs, holding a single candle as a scrawny cat threaded itself around her legs, meowing.

"Good God, girl, what are you doing up? Go back to bed," said her ladyship. "And take that bedraggled creature with you."

Anna ignored her. "Susannah, are you well?"

"I'm fine, Anna." Couldn't everyone simply leave her alone? And stop caring? They were starting to make Susannah forget that she was supposed to distrust them.

"What is she doing here?" Anna looked quizzically at her mother. "Is she staying here?"

"Yes, my dear."

"For how long?" Anna asked.

"I have no idea, but Nathaniel has asked that her things be brought over."

"Until they're married, then," said Anna decisively.

But they wouldn't be getting married once Susannah told Sir Philip what she'd learned. She paused, intending to refute Anna, but Lady Rainsford propelled her up the last few steps. She led Susannah down the hall and into the first room on the left, pushing the half-closed door open and gesturing for Susannah to enter. "This will be yours, my dear."

Susannah entered the suite, which contained a small sitting room complete with a chaise and a delicate wooden writing desk near the window. A shaft of light from the sconce in the hallway illuminated a path to a door on the far side.

Anna followed her in, then raced ahead, her candle lighting the way. She opened the other door. "This way, Susannah." She led her into an elegantly appointed bedchamber with a large bed on the opposite wall. Behind them, a servant entered carrying a branch of candles, which she placed on the bedside table.

Lady Rainsford and Anna buzzed around Susannah. "Now then, my dear, why don't you give me that horrid coat and we will get you settled." Without waiting for a reply, she began to remove the footman's uniformed coat and Nate's waistcoat.

"My goodness, Susannah, what happened to your dress?" asked Anna, her eyes agog.

Susannah's hands flew up to cover her torn gown. "It's nothing. I...I caught myself on something is all."

Her ladyship frowned. She turned to Anna. "Do you have a dressing gown, my dear, that Susannah can use until her things arrive?"

Anna smiled. "Of course. I'll get it right away." She picked up a candle and left the room, quietly closing the door behind her.

Lady Rainsford made herself busy arranging pillows, moving blankets, and guiding Susannah to the bed. Mrs. Friars entered the room with a tea tray, and Crimson followed with more candles, towels, and a small vial.

"Here's some hot tea for the miss, which will surely set

her to rights." Mrs. Friars set the tray down on the table next to the bed and clucked over the cleanliness of the suite, the arrangement of the bedclothes, the fire in the grate, and anything else that seemingly fell under her domain.

"We'll have a small meal for her shortly, my lady," Crimson said, with a bow.

That suited Susannah just fine.

"Excellent." Lady Rainsford gave Crimson the footman's coat and Nate's burnt waistcoat. "Mrs. Friars and I can help her with her bath before the doctor arrives."

That did not suit Susannah at all. "Thank you, my lady, but I don't want to trouble you, nor do I need a doctor."

Lady Rainsford leaned down, tucked the blanket around Susannah, and caressed her face with her hand. "I told you I would make up for my past sins, dear. I mean that." She smiled once more, warm and genuine. "Your mother would have it so."

To Susannah's surprise, a comfortable, relaxing sense of peace came over her. She almost felt...cherished. Perhaps Lady Rainsford *was* being sincere in her desire to help her.

Her ladyship stood and addressed the room. "Now, out with all of you except Mrs. Friars. Crimson, I expect the hot water will arrive soon?"

"Yes, my lady. At once." He and the other servant left the room, closing the outer door behind him.

Susannah, suddenly overcome with exhaustion, was glad Nate hadn't followed her up here. He'd been excessively dramatic in her view. She wasn't in the right frame of mind to have any sort of conversation with him. At all. Of course, she wasn't in the mood to talk to her ladyship, either, but she didn't have to worry about wanting to kiss Lady Rainsford.

"Now then," said her ladyship. "Let's get you out of these clothes and into a wrapper. I'm sure you'll be much more comfortable until the bathwater is brought up."

Susannah endured the ministrations as the two ladies helped her into the garment Anna had left in the other room.

After being escorted back to bed, Lady Rainsford gently but firmly put a cup and saucer in Susannah's hands. "Drink this. It will help calm you."

"I can manage just fine, my lady."

She smiled down at Susannah. "I know you can."

THE DOCTOR STAYED ONLY a short while, pronouncing her healthy, except for some small abrasions on her arms and a slightly turned ankle. Fortunately, he prescribed nothing more than a salve for her arms and tight binding for her ankle. He left a tincture for her to take if she found she couldn't sleep.

As promised, Lady Rainsford and Mrs. Friars helped her bathe, chattering and laughing the entire time, no doubt in an effort to distract her from her own thoughts. It had worked, too, for although she was tired, Susannah had gotten caught up in their good-natured conversation. Ever since she'd arrived at Rainsford House that evening, Susannah had felt her heart softening towards Lady Rainsford. The woman might have been misguided by Nate in the past, but Susannah could tell she was a good and kind person. After all, isn't that what her mama had always said about her?

By the time Susannah had finished her bath and a light meal, she was ready to sleep. However, she could not rest until she addressed the issue of Nate's treachery.

Susannah sat at the small writing desk, a candle burning brightly on the corner. Her hand, poised above a blank sheet of paper, clasped a now-dry quill as tears streamed down her face. At least a dozen crumpled sheets of paper littered the floor by her feet. Writing this letter should have been easy, but Susannah was finding it exceedingly difficult. Her heart was at war with her mind, waging an internal battle between her perception of Nate's inherit goodness against what she'd so blatantly overheard this evening.

He's not telling you the truth. You must confess what you know.
Gritting her teeth, she dipped the quill in the ink.

Dear Sir Philip,
   I have learned the most shocking news this evening, which I must share

Frowning, Susannah dropped the quill and crumpled the paper, tossing it onto the floor with the rest. Why did *she* feel like a traitor for wanting to reveal Nate's misdeeds? She sighed heavily. She had to put this into perspective. What she'd learned was much bigger than her. She thought briefly of her brother, killed in battle by Napoleon's forces, and her eyes filled with more tears. If Bonaparte were to come to power again, countless more lives could be lost.

She straightened in her chair, resolute that, if nothing else, she would do whatever she could to prevent other women from losing a brother, husband, or father.

Pulling another blank sheet from the drawer, she chewed her lip in thought. Then she inked her quill and quickly scratched out her missive. When she was done, she sat back and surveyed her work.

Dear Sir,

I beg you will grant me an audience on Wednesday before the start of the fashionable hour in Hyde Park. I will place myself near Grosvenor-Gate between two and half-past in the afternoon. I have learned something of great import which I must convey to you. Indeed, the safety of our country depends upon it. I beseech you, in memory of my dear brother, Ben, to fulfill this engagement.

Most respectfully,

Miss Susannah Cressingham

She folded the note and sealed it. Then she rang for the lady's maid that had been assigned to her for the evening. While she waited, she wiped her cheeks dry and disposed of the crumpled letters into the fireplace.

A knock sounded on the door.

"Enter."

A short, scrawny girl with mousy brown hair done up neatly in a cap came into the room, closing the door behind her. "Yes, miss? Can I help you? Are you ready for bed?" She held her hands before her, wringing her fingers. According to her ladyship, she'd been elevated to the title of "lady's maid" upon Susannah's arrival at Rainsford House.

"Lucy, is it?"

"Yes, miss." Lucy smiled nervously.

"Oh good, I remembered." Susannah willed herself to look calm. "I would like for you to deliver a message. It's very important that it be done this evening. Are you comfortable with that? Or should I ask someone else?"

Lucy shook her head. "Oh no, miss. I'd be happy to do it for you."

"Now, I don't want you to balk, but I'm asking you to deliver this to Sir Philip Tradwick." Susannah didn't doubt for a second that every member of the staff was aware that Nate and Sir Philip were not on friendly terms.

Lucy's eyebrows went up, and Susannah's suspicions were confirmed. But she tried to maintain an aura of calm. If Lucy suspected for a second that Susannah had ulterior motives against the Rainsford family, she'd confess all to Nate faster than a racehorse crossing the finish line at Ascot. With a benevolent smile, Susannah handed the note to the girl. "It's simply a thank you for everything he did for me this evening to make sure his lordship's sisters and I stayed safe. I know that Rainsford and Sir Philip are not friendly, but Sir Philip and my brother Ben, now deceased, were once schoolmates, you see. So it's my dearest wish that I be able to express my gratitude."

That seemed to mollify Lucy, for she stepped forward and took the note from Susannah, yet her wrinkled forehead expressed lingering doubt. "It's just a thank you?"

Susannah nodded, then extended her hands apologetically. "I'm sorry to make you seek him out this evening, but he's such a busy man, and I'm afraid her ladyship will keep you occupied tomorrow with your new responsibilities as my lady's maid." Hopefully, the reminder about Lucy's good fortune would be the impetus she needed to seek out Sir Philip this evening.

The maid's eyes widened, and she nodded her head vigorously. "Oh yes, miss. Of course, miss." Lucy put the note in the oversized pocket of her apron and patted it with her hand. "I'll deliver this right away."

Susannah put her hands together in front of her chest as if saying a prayer of thanks. "Oh, I'm so relieved. You are so good, Lucy. Be sure to take a footman with you."

The maid beamed. "Yes, of course, miss. Is there anything I can get you before I leave?" she asked, a frown of concern marring her freckled face.

"Thank you, no. I'm going to read for a spell, then prepare for bed."

"Oh, I should help you." She moved towards Susannah.

A ripple of apprehension made her tense. Lucy *had* to deliver the note this evening, so she waved her off. "Don't worry, Lucy, I'm fine, nearly back to rights. I'm more concerned that my note of thanks makes it into Sir Philip's hands, for I am *so* grateful. I won't call for anything until morning, I promise." She turned to pick up a book that had been lying on the edge of the writing table and held it up. "This will keep me quite occupied."

With a nod and a curtsey, Lucy left the room and closed the door behind her. Susannah slumped against the high-backed chair near the desk.

She hoped Tradwick got her message in time, for if he didn't meet her at the park tomorrow, she just might have to pound on the man's door herself.

CHAPTER 13

DESPITE THE WEE HOURS—OR because of it—Nate pounded on Viscount Sidmouth's front door. "Dammit," he mumbled to himself. The man better be at home. He raised his fist to strike once more when the lock tumbled and the door opened.

Sidmouth's butler held a lamp, his slightly disheveled appearance indicating he'd dressed in haste. "What can I do for you, sir?" He looked down his long nose at Nate.

"I need to speak to the Lord Secretary. It's urgent. Tell him Rainsford is here to see him."

The butler twitched his lips but didn't answer. After a pause, he stepped back, allowing Nate to enter. "I'll see if he's available."

"Thank you." Nate removed his gloves and hat.

Sidmouth's butler set the lamp down on a nearby table, took Nate's things, then picked up the lamp again. "This way, if you please, my lord." He led Nate to a small salon just off the main hall, set the lamp on a delicate wooden table, and left, closing the door behind him.

Nate sat down on the edge of a chaise, then jumped up again, far too agitated to remain still. He paced back and forth in front of the unlit fireplace, turning over in his mind the mental list of things he still had to accomplish. The minutes dragged. What the devil was Sidmouth doing? After what felt like an age, he pulled his watch from the fob pocket of his waistcoat and snapped it open. One-thirty in the morning. Hardly late by *ton* standards. Sidmouth had to be home, or his butler would have turned him away. Did the man really retire this early?

He returned his watch to its rightful place and continued pacing, each one of his senses grossly magnified. His footsteps on the Persian rug pounded like drum beats. The banked coals in the grate made the room hotter than Hades. His finely tailored clothes rubbed against his skin like flour sacks. His every breath, every heartbeat echoed in his ears.

Slipping his hand into the pocket of his coat, he pulled out his talisman. The one thing that grounded him and reminded him of his purpose. The metal button from his dead brother's uniform was cold to the touch, but warmed quickly as Nate turned it over and over between his fingers. Soon, the familiar sense of calm came over him. He took a deep, fortifying breath, touched the button to his lips, then dropped it back into his pocket.

The door handle creaked, and Nate turned quickly to see Sidmouth's butler, his appearance now more dignified, standing at the entrance.

"Well? Will he see me?"

Nodding gravely, the butler gestured to the hallway. "This way if you please, my lord."

Nate followed the man into Sidmouth's study. It was a small, cozy, book-lined room with most of the space taken up by a very large and intricately carved mahogany desk. Above the mantel was a large painting of a hunting scene, while below, a fire roared in the hearth, casting an orange glow everywhere, despite the numerous candles. His lordship, wearing a dark blue banyan and looking as unkempt as his butler had earlier, glanced up when Nate came in and pushed aside the numerous papers on his desk, which were interspersed with various quills, pots of ink, and an empty brandy snifter.

"This better be good, Rainsford." He gestured to his butler. "Grayson, get this man a glass of brandy and refill mine." He handed over his empty glass.

"Yes, my lord." Grayson set about following his master's orders.

"Have a seat." Sidmouth waved Nate to the two Chippendale chairs on the other side of the desk, then raised a single eyebrow. "Well?"

Instead of sitting, Nate looked over his shoulder at Grayson, still pouring brandy at the sideboard on the far side of the room.

"Don't worry about him," Sidmouth scoffed. "Used to work for the Home Office. He hears everything, but says nothing."

Nate shook his head. "I'm not sure you want him to hear this, sir," he said quietly.

Sidmouth sat back, threading his fingers together and resting them on his midsection. He looked at Nate long and hard. "Very well then."

The two men stared at each other, saying nothing, while the butler finished his task. After what seemed an interminable amount of time, Grayson set the two glasses on the desk, then bowed. "Will there be anything else, my lord?"

"No. Off to bed with you. I'll show Rainsford out." Sidmouth flung a hand towards the door.

"Thank you, sir." Bowing stiffly, Grayson quickly departed, shutting the door quietly behind him.

Nate stood before the desk, picked up a quill that lay near the edge and spun it, then ran the feathered end over the fingers of his other hand. He should just blurt out what he knew, but he hesitated, for he knew that once he revealed his intelligence, everything—*everything*—would change.

Sidmouth sighed. "Out with it, Rainsford. I can't stand the suspense."

Nate pursed his lips, his gaze meeting Sidmouth's. "We have a problem."

"Yes, I figured as much." Sidmouth sat forward, took hold of his glass, and swirled the dark liquid. "'We' who?"

"England."

"Well?" He looked expectantly at Nate. "What is it?" His lordship took a large sip of brandy.

Nate dropped the quill on the desk, inhaled deeply, then let it out with a *whoosh*. "Napoleon has escaped Elba. In fact, he's already in France."

Sidmouth eyed Nate, then tossed back the remaining contents of his glass, seemingly unperturbed.

"Did you hear me?" Nate pushed his brandy aside and leaned his hands on the edge of the desk.

Thumping the glass down, Sidmouth said, "Yes, I heard you. Where did you learn this?"

"Cressingham cornered me at Sherry's this evening to tell me his 'exciting news.'"

Sidmouth said nothing, just sat back in his chair, eyes fixated on the fireplace across the room.

Nate cleared his throat. "I beg your pardon, sir, but are you not concerned?"

His lordship flicked his gaze to Nate, his expression dumfounded. "What do you think?"

"I don't know what to think, quite honestly." Nate's voice rose. "You seem so...unaffected by my intelligence."

"I already know," he said with a droll look.

Nate straightened. "What? How?"

Sidmouth shrugged and shuffled some of the papers around on his desk. "I received the intelligence this evening. He escaped at the end of February, has landed in Gulf de Juan, and is making his way to Paris."

"Yes." Nate nodded. "That is what I learned." He picked up his snifter of brandy and took a healthy sip.

"Is that all you have to report?"

Shaking his head, Nate set his glass down. "I also learned who Cressingham's source is."

Sidmouth showed no reaction, but when Nate didn't say anything, his lordship leaned forward and rested his elbows on the edge of his desk. "Well? Are you going to tell me who the bastard is, or do I have to beat it out of you?"

Nate spun his glass in slow circles on the desk. In a deceptively quiet voice, he said, "Not a bastard. A harlot. The infamous Princess Borghese."

Sidmouth scoffed loudly and threw himself back in his chair, eyes wide as saucers. He looked away, then back at Nate and slapped a hand on his desk. "You're hoaxing me."

"I am not. Apparently, the captain fancies himself in love with Pauline Bonaparte. Says he wishes to be part of Boney's inner circle." Nate dropped into the chair opposite Sidmouth and scrubbed his face with his hands. "If I had to guess, I'd say he's planning to leave for France. Soon. And he wants Susannah's money, too."

Nate relayed to Sidmouth the story of Boney losing his

gold and Cressingham's "request" for Susannah's dowry. "It puts the emperor at a slight disadvantage, because if he can't pay his men, he won't get very far."

Sidmouth sat slumped in his chair, one arm crossed over the other, the fingers of his right hand drumming his forearm as he thought. "You're going to give the captain Miss Cressingham's dowry?"

"Well," Nate said, scratching at a scar on the wooden chair arm with his thumb, "I tried to pawn him off, telling him I couldn't gain access to her money without being married. Of course, that would take three weeks." He rested his elbows on the chair, hands clasped together. "I knew he wouldn't be satisfied with that, particularly when he spoke of how much he desired to be part of Boney's 'inner circle.' I expected him to ask me to front the funds myself, but instead, he gave me this." Nate reached into his waistcoat pocket, drew out the special license, and tossed it onto the desk.

Sidmouth's mouth made an *O*. Without preamble, he asked, "When?"

Nate shrugged one shoulder. "Said to marry tomorrow —well, today—but I managed to fob him off until Thursday. Still, that's not much time to get everything organized. I don't think any of us expected Napoleon would leave his little island paradise so soon after winter."

"No, we didn't. And you're right, it's no time at all to prepare." His lordship drew out a small silver snuffbox from the pocket of his banyan. He tapped the side of it two times, flipped open the lid, took a pinch, and inhaled it swiftly. After snapping the lid shut, he returned the snuffbox to its rightful place. "What have you arranged with Nathan Rothschild?"

Shaking his head, Nate said, "Not very much, I'm

afraid. I worry that Cressingham will attempt to use another bank to move the money to France, but short of alerting every bank in England of what might occur and getting our own men planted—"

"No, no. You can't do that. Aside from being a logistical nightmare, someone will surely talk. Rothschild's is Cressingham's bank, of that we know. It's also the easiest, most convenient, and, of tantamount importance to the captain, the most private way to move money throughout Europe."

"Yes, sir."

Sidmouth frowned, scratching a sideburn. "When are you meeting with Rothschild?"

"First thing tomorrow."

His lordship nodded. "What about Cressingham? Where is he?"

Nate shrugged his shoulders. "At the current time, I do not know. He disappeared with all due haste after giving me the license. I would have followed him, except my betrothed eavesdropped on our conversation. She now suspects me of treason, too. Then, of course, the riots—"

"Just a moment, sir," Sidmouth said, holding up his hand. "Cressingham's niece overheard you and now thinks you're a traitor? Did you not explain it to her?" Sidmouth made a waving gesture with his hands. "I mean, what you could explain. Or whatever story you've concocted."

"I tried. But there's a bad history between us, and short of telling her the truth, it's unlikely she'll trust me and let it alone."

Sidmouth narrowed his eyes. "We can't have her compromising you." His voice was as hard as his mahogany desk. "She may be your betrothed, but she's also a pawn. A means to an end. Get her in line. Whether you lock her in a room or gag her, frankly I don't care. But you have to contain her."

Nate opened his mouth to speak, but Sidmouth put his hand up, silencing him. "Miss Cressingham and your forthcoming marriage are the least of my worries, save where it intersects with catching that bastard Cressingham —or her compromising you. The Prime Minister and Castlereagh have already sent me communications about neutralizing this new threat. In fact, Castlereagh is making plans to depart for Vienna. No doubt Wellington is strategizing with the other members of the Coalition the remobilization of the army. That means coordinating men, arms, munitions, and supplies, not to mention thirty-odd other details that all have to be coordinated with the Home Office. I haven't the time to hold you by leading strings on this one."

"Yes, sir." Nate felt like he was being called out by the headmaster for insubordination.

"At your request, I've left this investigation largely to you, but I'm beginning to second-guess my decision. You cock things up, Rainsford, and you're on your own."

The skin on the back of Nate's neck prickled. "Sir, I assure you, I have things under control."

He pointed a finger at Nate, his voice hard and gravelly. "Then prove it." Leaning back in his chair a bit, he said, "I suggest you spend this morning getting assurances from Rothschild, as well as making sure you can line up informants who can track that flow of money, because I don't doubt that even before you consummate your marriage"—Nate's face reddened at the remark—"that bastard is going to ask you for her funds, no matter what he's already told you." Without even looking at Nate, he waved his hand towards the door. "Now then, get out of my house and get busy. Neutralize any threat posed by

Miss Cressingham, get the bank in order, and be ready to circumvent the captain. We have to know where the money goes and we cannot—absolutely can *not*—allow him to continue communicating with Napoleon or any of his ilk. Am I clear?"

Nate rose, plucked the special license off Sidmouth's desk, and tucked it into his pocket. "Yes, sir."

CHAPTER 14

JUST BEFORE NINE O'CLOCK, Nate stood outside the office of Rothschild Bank in St. Swithin's Lane. He clenched and unclenched his hand, angry at himself for…well, a lot of things. Cressingham's confession. Susannah getting hurt. The events at Sherry's house. The bastard who touched his fiancée. Mostly, though, he was angry that Susannah didn't trust him, particularly because that was of his own making.

After returning home from Sidmouth's, he'd holed himself up in his study and consumed far too much brandy. Oh, he'd managed to pen a note to Cressingham's butler to deliver Susannah's things, as well one to his friend and fellow Beggar, Andrew Acland, the rector of the church at his estate, Langley Park, asking him to post up to London with haste. Nate didn't give a damn who Cressingham had available to officiate their wedding…if Nate couldn't get married at Langley Park, then at least his own rector would do it. He'd also sent notes 'round to his men letting them to know that the time had come for the next phase of the plan and instructing them on where and when to meet this morning.

But when he'd concluded his business, he sat. And drank. And remembered. The touch of Susannah. Their almost-kiss. Her delicate hand in his. The heat he always felt from her when she was near. He let his imagination run wild, and by the time he retired for the evening, his own body was on fire. Unfortunately, a few splashes of cold water from the washstand did nothing to douse the flames.

While lying in his big, empty bed, he tossed around in his mind Susannah's eavesdropping. Nate was certain she would attempt to tell someone. The question was whom—and when? He'd left a message for his mother via Crimson that Susannah was not to leave the house, using the previous night's events as the excuse. However, Nate feared in all the wedding excitement, she'd take it as a recommendation rather than a command.

Nate had the feeling he was standing on the edge of a precipice, weaving and tottering, almost going over, then getting blown back by the wind rather indiscriminately. It left a sick sensation in his gut and made him anxious to resolve this business with Cressingham so he could bring everything out into the open.

Or, at the very least, convince Susannah he wasn't the traitor she thought he was.

He sighed. Standing at the threshold wouldn't get him anywhere. Nate entered the office for Rothschild Bank and was welcomed with courteous deference. A clerk silently took his overcoat, which he'd needed against the cold snap that had descended early that morning, as well as his gloves and hat. After directing Nate to a chair inside a large office, he said, "Mr. Rothschild will be with you momentarily. Can I get you a cup of tea or a glass of sherry?"

Nate shook his head. "Thank you, no." He'd best keep his wits about him.

"Very good, sir." He left the room, closing the door behind him.

Nate paced the office, too agitated to sit. He and Cressingham had agreed on Rothschild's because it had already been acting as the financier to pay Wellington's troops during the war. What could arouse less suspicion than using the army's own banker? The Rothschild family banking houses, which were scattered across Europe, would make transferring money easy. And although Nathan Rothschild was a shrewd, calculating, and exacting businessman, he'd been eager to demonstrate his loyalty to the Crown when Nate had approached the man previously.

The door opened, taking Nate by surprise, and Rothschild walked in. Balding and portly with thick hands that had likely touched over a million pounds during the course of his lifetime, he possessed a keen intelligence that shone in his eyes. Nate didn't doubt that, during every conversation Rothschild conducted, his mind was constantly analyzing for the advantage. This conversation would be no different.

"Well, my lord, I certainly didn't expect to see you here today." He spoke with a thick Austrian accent.

Nate dipped his head respectfully. "Good morning, sir. I trust you are well."

Rothschild sat down behind the massive and paperless desk that took up a large corner of the stylish yet understated office. The room was decorated in muted green tones, featuring tasteful artwork of idyllic landscape scenes, floor-to-ceiling silk window treatments, leather chairs near the desk, and a comfortable-looking settee near the fireplace.

Inclining his head, Rothschild said, "I am very well,

thank you." He looked Nate over from head to toe. "As I said, I'm surprised to see you here today."

Nate shrugged. "I can't image why. I solicited your cooperation a week ago."

"Yes, but that was before Bonaparte left Elba."

Nate's jaw dropped open. Even he couldn't hide his surprise. How the devil did Rothschild know about that already?

The man must have anticipated Nate's question, for he said, "Yes, I know much about the political landscape of Europe right now." He smiled slyly. "Information is…profitable. As I'm sure you are well aware."

What was that supposed to mean? What else did he know?

"I'm merely surprised that *you* know about Bonaparte. I was quite certain it would take another day or two for the rest of England to find out." He arched a single eyebrow. "I take it the Home Office knows?"

Nate frowned, suddenly unsure whether he should reveal his hand.

"Never mind." Rothschild waved a hand dismissively. "You clearly weren't surprised by my intelligence— although you were certainly perplexed as to how I knew. But that's neither here nor there." He opened a drawer and drew out a letter, glanced at it, then eyed Nate. "I gather that all efforts will be directed to the defeat of Napoleon?" He let the letter flutter back down to his desk.

Was that letter from Sidmouth? Or was it information Rothschild had gathered from his extensive communications network? Nate wasn't sure, but it was paramount that the banker kept his word. "Of course, we must defeat Napoleon. And apprehending traitors who seek to support him is a part of that effort."

A small, disbelieving laugh escaped Rothschild. "If you insist."

Nate ignored the meaning behind the tone. "Events are happening. Quickly. We have not yet discussed the particular details of what the Home Office needs from you, but that time has come."

Rothschild gestured to the leather chair opposite his desk. "Please. Do sit."

Nate perched on the edge, his pulse racing at a full gallop. "In order to catch the traitor, I need one man in your bank for twenty-four hours on Friday. I'll make sure we're here to conduct business *that day*. He will bear witness, recording the transfer of funds between the accounts in question. Another man will monitor the subsequent deposit to the traitor's account at de Rothschild Frères in Paris. It is your brother James's bank, after all." He paused. "Finally, one of our men will witness the traitor's withdrawal—in gold, of course—from the French account, then I'll follow him to Napoleon."

Rothschild balked. "You didn't tell me you'd require a man in my brother's bank." He tapped his fingers on the top of his desk...slowly. "I will have to discuss that with him. I cannot speak on his behalf."

No one said anything, the silence hanging in the air like a death sentence. Nate wondered what the hell was going on inside the man's head.

Finally, Rothschild broke the quiet. "I would like to help you, Rainsford. I really would." He threaded his fingers together and rested his elbows on the arms of his chair. "But, if you'll recall, I never committed to assisting you. And—"

Nate jumped to his feet. "I beg your pardon? Never committed?" He scoffed, his tone accusing. "You never said no, either."

"Of course not. A good businessman never turns down an opportunity. But this news about Bonaparte's departure from Elba changes things." He steepled his index fingers and tapped them on his lip. "It means we will be very busy in the months—possibly years—to come. And we must prepare for that." The tenor of his voice dropped. "Immediately."

It took a second for Nate to process the man's words, but when he did, his blood went cold. *Bloody hell.* Rothschild *wanted* a war. He *wanted* a fight from Napoleon, for as the official banker to Wellington's army, he profited from it. Greatly.

Nate's throat tightened. How *dare* he angle for profit on the backs of dead men? Dead *Englishmen*. Nate didn't fault Rothschild for playing the army's banker before Napoleon was captured. Truly, the Bank of England couldn't get local currency fast enough to pay His Majesty's soldiers. But to anticipate another war with greed and eagerness made Nate's stomach turn.

His emotions shifted from indignation to rage. Hot, pulsing heat wormed its way through every bone, every organ, every limb in his body. He clasped his hands behind his back, if only not to throttle the man. In the most vitriolic voice he could muster, Nate said, "Indulge me, if you will. Allow me to present you with a hypothetical situation."

Rothschild gestured once more to the chair opposite the desk. "Do be seated then." Excepting a pair of wary eyes, the banker seemed unperturbed at Nate's demeanor.

Nate remained standing and faced Rothschild. "Remember Ulm? 1805? In your brother Salomon's adopted city of Vienna?"

Rothschild stared at Nate, his expression going stony,

his eyes dark with contempt. *Good. He knows where I'm going with this.*

"An agent of Napoleon, Charles Schulmeister, infiltrated Austria's military so convincingly that General Mack made him the Chief of Intelligence." Nate paced back and forth slowly, drawing out the story for effect. "In fact, Mack brought Schulmeister into his personal confidence, introducing him to his social peers, including your brother. And what did Schulmeister do?" Nate raised his eyebrows expectantly.

Rothschild stared at him with dead eyes.

"He appropriated your brother's assets. I'm sure it was a terrible blow to Salomon," Nate said in mock sympathy. "So many of his fine paintings confiscated by Napoleon's agent. Along with jewels. Furniture. Homes." Nate glared at the man. "*Rothschild gold.*"

Still nothing.

"When you have no gold, you have no bank." Nate stared down the man, putting power behind his words. "I'll be frank. Napoleon can wipe out your brother James's bank if he wants to, and I can encourage England to look the other way. Unless we're given a good reason to defend it."

To Nate's surprise, Rothschild sat back in his chair and laughed, his round belly jiggling. He cocked his head, a shrewd smile on his face. "I like you, Rainsford," he said, pointing his fat finger at Nate. "Like you very much. You don't beat about the bushes, do you?"

"Why should I?" Nate stepped back from the desk, straightening the cuffs of his shirt. "I know what I want. And I will get it."

Rothschild's expression turned shrewd. "So will I."

Both men stared each other down, saying nothing. Nate was growing tired of these games. Of trying to convince Rothschild to do the right thing, when really, what choice did he have?

At long last, Nate broke the silence, but his voice was bitterly businesslike. "You said yourself that information has unfathomable value. The traitor in question may have intimate knowledge of the inner workings of our military that could spell doom for the sovereignty of England. You've made quite a comfortable life for yourself here and made quite a profit during the war. But your agreement with the army can be terminated. And, God forbid we fall under French rule, I highly doubt Boney would be so generous with you as Parliament has been."

Rothschild frowned. "What do you want?"

Inwardly, Nate sighed with relief, but he maintained his unbending mien. He leaned forward on Rothschild's desk, his face inches from the banker's. "I want you to uphold our agreement. Help me catch the traitor, including putting a man on the inside at de Rothschild Frères." He stepped back and crossed his arms, looking nonchalant. "I'm sure you don't wish your adopted city to end up like Vienna in 1805. Or your assets to be liquidated like your brother's."

Rothschild rapped his knuckles on the desk. "I don't like being strong-armed."

"I don't blame you. However, the traitor's contacts extend high into Napoleon's upper echelon, giving him too much opportunity to share critical information. I cannot let this man and his money get to Napoleon."

"What do I get for the trouble?"

Nate scoffed. "You want to be *paid* for this?"

"Everything has a price." Rothschild fingered the letter on his desk. "And I don't want gold."

"I don't care what you want." Nate tipped his chin up. "I need your brother's cooperation, and I need you to stand aside and let my men do their job—both here and in France."

"Ridiculous. This is an inconvenience we will have to explain to our workers."

"Are you or your brother in the habit of explaining yourselves to anyone?" Nate asked incredulously.

"No, of course not."

"Then it's none of their business."

Rothschild tapped his fingers on the desk, looking into the fire, saying nothing.

But Nate couldn't sit here all day while the man thought about it. He coughed politely. "What is it you want, Rothschild?"

The man's head swiveled around, his eyes gleaming. "A guarantee that Rothschild is the only bank for the army for the duration of the war, which certainly is coming—"

"Done," Nate said. "Now then—"

"I'm not finished, my lord."

Nate narrowed his eyes. "What else?"

"I want Rothschild to be the bankers to the army—and navy—indefinitely."

Nate's insides quivered with apprehension. He was most definitely not authorized to bargain on the government's behalf. If he made this promise, he'd have some serious explaining to do to Sidmouth and Wellington, not to mention the Board of Admiralty. But if he didn't, Cressingham could slip through his fingers. Nate had to protect England from the threat of secrets spilled to Napoleon. And he had to catch the bastard and punish him for everything he'd brought upon Susannah and her family.

Nate took a deep, fortifying breath. "As I said, done." He would worry about Sidmouth later.

Rothschild smiled as if he'd won a prize. Which, in truth, he had. "Have your man here at seven o'clock Friday morning. I will send a communication to my brother. It will be done."

Nate nodded. "Your cooperation is greatly appreciated." He turned on his heel and strode from the room before Rothschild could change his mind.

Leaving the office, he exited onto the street, his mind in a whirl, his body in a state of gross agitation. Nate stood on the pavement as he shifted anxiously from foot to foot, trying to mentally arrange the rest of his day. He had to quarantine Susannah and speak with Tradwick, as well. No doubt he'd already been informed about Napoleon. Sidmouth had to be notified of the deal he made, which would require Nate to grovel and beg forgiveness. And he'd need to share with his men the plan. Pulling his watch from his fob pocket, he flipped it open. Too little time, and far too much to do.

But one thing would have to take precedence. He could not let his betrothed leak information to the wrong people, or he could forget about marrying her and catching Cressingham.

And he hadn't come this far to let that happen.

CHAPTER 15

NATE TOOK two steps on the pavement, grateful to be done with Rothschild, when someone loudly called out his name.

"Rainsford."

He swiveled around, scanning the pedestrians nearby. About twenty feet away, Captain Cressingham came limping towards him, his cane tapping the pavement. He was not the person Nate wanted to see right now, but he couldn't very well ignore the man he was trying to lasso with the looped end of a hangman's noose.

Nate bowed his head slightly and smiled in greeting, even though the latter action galled him. "Good morning, Captain. I trust you are well? Deuced fortunate you left Sherry's when you did. I'm sure you heard what happened."

Cressingham caught up to Nate. "Yes. Bad business, that. But not my affair." His voice was gruff and unconcerned.

"You'll be happy to know your niece is well."

The captain didn't answer, merely waved his hand to dismiss the subject.

His action perturbed Nate, but he wasn't going to make an issue of it. Instead, Nate changed topics. "What brings you to this side of town?"

"Some business to finalize before my niece marries." He gestured to Rothschild's Bank, his face set in a frown. "That is all."

Nate's muscles tensed, but he willed himself to relax. There could be nothing wrong with Cressingham making sure all was well. As for the wedding… Nate forced himself to grin devilishly. "I sent an express last night to the rector of our family's church at Langley Park, asking him to offi- ciate on Thursday. It's only a few hours' ride by horseback, as you well know. We will have a small, quiet ceremony, but it will suit our purposes."

"I thought I told you there wasn't time for that," the captain said in an ornery voice.

Nate rubbed his nose, quietly thoughtful for a moment. "You did. However, it can't signify. One parson is as good as another, is he not? And once the ceremony is finished, we will leave for our honeymoon." Nate moved his head closer to Cressingham's ear, speaking in *sotto voce*. "To France."

The captain's lips drew into a thin line. "You should have left well enough alone, Rainsford. I met with some men last night. Powerful men. Wealthy men." His eyes took on a strange gleam, almost as if he were gloating. "I've a different scheme in mind now."

Nate drew back and stared at the captain, his gut knot- ting up and hardening like braided leather left in the rain. "I beg your pardon?" He frowned. What did Cressingham mean? Surely, he wasn't reneging on his agreement?

"I intended to seek you out after I finished my business

here." He dropped his chin, his eyes glinting, his mouth turned down in a snarling sneer. "I'm giving Susannah to someone else."

A terrible coldness descended, robbing Nate of air, freezing him to the core. But only for a moment. "I beg your *pardon*? Someone else? Who the bloody hell might that be?" Nate's near-shouts began to attract the attention of passersby.

Cressingham grabbed him by the arm, trying to pull him towards the building, and snapped, "Lower your voice, you fool."

But Nate didn't budge, his boots rooted to the pavement, oblivious to the busy street around him. He brushed Cressingham off. "Might I remind you you've signed settlements, sir?" He couldn't let Cressingham get away. Certainly not with Susannah. Couldn't let him give her to anyone else. His mind turned a thousand times a minute, playing out possible scenarios, wondering who the hell Cressingham had in mind for her to marry.

But the captain scoffed. "Settlements be damned. It wouldn't be the first time a marriage was called off after the document had been formalized. And it won't be the last." He walked in slow circles around Nate, who stood in the middle of the pavement as the rest of London moved around them, eyeing them curiously. "There are a few other men in my acquaintance who are eager to support *our friend* and who enjoy a bit of bedsport, too." Cressingham stole up to Nate, his bushy eyebrows nearly touching above his hawk-like nose. "They're also willing to part with their own personal wealth, in addition to my niece's dowry. Willing to give me more than ten"—poke —"thousand"—poke—"pounds." Cressingham jabbed the marbled end of his cane into Nate's chest repeatedly.

Nate shrugged him off, his temper flaring. His initial

thought was to dash off and find Susannah, but first he had to dissuade Cressingham from this plan. "How much do you want?" he ground out.

Cressingham threw his head back and cackled with laughter. "So, think you can buy your way in? Mayhap before. But now?" He must have read the sincerity in Nate's face, because the captain sobered quickly, his iron-like gaze riveted to him. "Very well, then. I'll name a price. Thirty thousand pounds."

"Done."

"Sixty."

This time, a small pause. "Done." He'd have to beg Sidmouth for financial assistance, but he was confident his lordship would agree.

Then Cressingham's face turned dark, and Nate's heart did a double-beat. In a slow, taunting voice, the captain said, "One hundred thousand."

Nate's blood pounded in his ears, but he held the captain's gaze. Sidmouth would never approve such an audacious amount.

"She's not worth that much, is she?" Cressingham whispered. He shook his head. "No woman is."

"This isn't about your niece. I made a pledge of support."

"Don't lie, Rainsford." Cressingham gave a disappointing shake of his head. "It's unbecoming. I've seen you look at her. You're besotted. And I need money. Immediately. Fortunately, another man has more than you. Unfortunately for him, he'll get a wife to go with it, but at least she won't be my problem anymore. He can *use*"—Cressingham sneered at the word—"her however he pleases."

A flare of disgust ignited and burned in Nate's body, but he cooled himself. "You do realize that I hold the special license, Captain?"

Cressingham laughed, the boastful sound causing the hair to rise on Nate's arm. The captain tightened his gloves. "Clearly, you didn't even look at the document I gave you. It's counterfeit." He turned to face Nate, scrutinizing him, and clapped him on the shoulder. "Did you really think I'd let you marry her? With the history your families shared?" Cressingham shook his head. "The only thing your betrothal, and that silly license, did was force the hand of the man I really wished her to wed"—another clap on Nate's shoulder—"so thank you for that." He took two steps towards the bank, then turned back, a single bushy eyebrow raised. "Obviously, you will return her to my home as quickly as possible. Now then, I have business to conduct."

Nate watched Cressingham thread his way through the crowded pavement and ascend the steps to the bank. A thousand thoughts went through his mind, his stomach churning, his limbs quivering, a cold sweat soaking his shirt. He was filled with rage, fear, dread, the emotions marching through Nate's body like mercenaries on the move, pillaging every fiber of his being in their wake.

Once Cressingham was out of sight, Nate turned, strode down the street, and hailed a hackney.

"Eh, where to, guv?" the dirt-crusted jarvey asked.

"I have several places I need you to take me," Nate said as he climbed in. He stuck his hand through the opening in the roof, near the box, and held out a guinea.

"Yes, milord," the driver said in a jubilant voice, snapping the coin out of Nate's hand. "Anywheres you wishes to go."

Nate sat back against the seat. "I wish to go to Doctor's Commons." He silently prayed that the captain hadn't already sought a real license for Susannah, or their first trip together wouldn't be to Jamaica but to Scotland.

TOO MANY HOURS LATER, a hackney dropped Nate off at Rainsford House. He dashed up the stairs and pounded on the door, waiting for Crimson to unlock it. The butler did, his face showing surprise.

"My lord. We did not expect you back—"

"Never mind that. Where is Miss Cressingham?"

Crimson came forward to help Nate out of his overcoat, hat, gloves, and cane. "She is with Lady Minnie. They—"

"Are they upstairs?" Nate shrugged out of his coat and gave Crimson his other articles. Without waiting for an answer, he raced up the stairs and into the hall. "Susannah? Susannah?"

Juliana stuck her head out the door to her room. "Whatever are you yelling about, brother?"

"Where is Susannah?"

Juliana shrugged. "I don't know. We returned from shopping, but instead of—"

"You went shopping?" Nate's voice boomed in the hallway.

Eyes widening, Juliana drew back behind the doorframe. In a meek voice, she said, "Yes? Mama thought it would be good to get Susannah out of the house to distract her from the events last night."

Nate put his hands on his hips, head down, as he struggled to keep his countenance. He should have known his mother would do this. "Except I expressly instructed that she not leave the house."

"I can't speak to that, brother. I knew nothing about it." She cowered behind the doorframe a bit more.

Good lord, now his sister was afraid of him. Groaning inwardly, Nate gestured for Juliana to come into the hallway. "I'm not going to hurt you, Jules. I am concerned for Susannah's safety is all. Come here."

Juliana did so.

Rubbing her arms in a brotherly way, Nate asked, "Where are Susannah and Minnie now?"

"I don't know. After Mama, Anna, and I exited the carriage, they left for another engagement, I think. I'm not sure where."

"How can you not know? You've managed every aspect of this household since Papa died." He blew out a breath. "I suppose it's too much to ask where Mama might be?"

"Visiting friends," she replied tartly. She held up her hand when Nate opened his mouth. "And before you ask, no, I don't know whom."

Crimson mounted the last step, his posture as straight as an obelisk, despite his pinked cheeks and huffed breath. "My lord, if you would permit me to finish, Lady Minnie and Miss Cressingham went to the park for an early walk."

"Which park?"

"Hyde Park, I believe. At least, that's the direction they were headed."

"And you did not stop them?" Nate crossed his arms, a formidable scowl on his face.

Crimson looked down at his shoes, then met Nate's eyes. "No, my lord. They were quite halfway down the street before her ladyship and the girls knocked on the door."

Nate pulled his watch out of the fob pocket of his breeches. "And when was that?"

"About an hour ago, my lord."

"Did a footman go with them?"

"Yes, my lord. Thomas."

Nate nodded. Well, at least there was that. But if Cressingham meant to marry her to someone else, he would be coming for her. And Nate was going to make sure that when he did, she was already Lady Rainsford. He fixed his gaze on Crimson. "If she returns, I give you permission to lock her in her room. She's not to go out again. Is that clear?"

Crimson bowed. "Of course, my lord."

Nate turned to Juliana. "I want you to summon Anna, and the two of you must go out and find Mama. Tell her to return to the house at once. Trust me, she will want to."

"But I have no earthly idea who she intended—"

Nate scowled. "If Minnie has the carriage, she's gone out on foot, so she can't have gone far. I don't care if you have to visit each one of her friends. Find her." He started for the stairs. At the top, he grasped the handrail, then turned back. "Tell her I'm getting married. Today. That will hasten her return."

Juliana's gasp filled the air as Nate sped down the stairs. Hopefully, his betrothed had kept quiet about what she'd learned the night before, or he might not make it to the altar.

Minutes later and mounted on his gelding, Pernicious, Nate threaded his way through the frustratingly crowded streets until he reached Hyde Park. Several times he had to bite his tongue not to lash out at a sap-skulled rider or jarvey. Despite the chill in the air, Nate could feel his shirt sticking to his back, but he suspected that was from anxiety over finding Susannah. Because he had to find her.

The real special license, tucked safely in the breast pocket of his waistcoat, seemed to burn a hole into his chest. The archbishop's clerks hadn't said anything when Nate arrived to request the document, which signaled to

Nate that Cressingham hadn't yet sought the legitimate license. But if he did, and found out it had already been issued to Nate, there was no doubt he'd be after Nate post haste.

Nate entered through Cumberland Gate, the same one John Coachman used each time he brought the girls or Mama to the park for the fashionable hour, and veered south, setting Perny off at a gallop. He scanned ahead at the carriages, ignoring the calls from other riders and pedestrians to slow down and mind his speed, but Nate's carriage was nowhere to be seen. His heart kept time with Perny's hoofbeats, vibrating loudly in his chest and pushing into his throat. Nate could scarce draw a breath. He switched the reins to one hand and with the other, pulled at his too-tight neckcloth, briefly wondering if that's what men at the gallows felt before the floor dropped out.

He passed another carriage, and another, and still no sign of Susannah. There was a handful of pedestrians near this stretch of the bridle path, but none of them bore any resemblance to his fiancée. His heart was pounding now, his breath coming in loud, gasping pants. Nate had to find her before her uncle did.

Nearing the Corner, he turned his horse north and followed the path along Park Lane, his eyes scanning the trees on his right for Susannah. Ahead of him, Nate's eyes were drawn to a lone female figure walking along the bridle path, with a footman following at a respectful distance. The hair on Nate's neck stood up as he recognized his sister. But where was Susannah? Spurring his horse faster, he called out to her, his voice as hard as flint. "Minerva Georgina Kinlan."

She turned back, eyes squinting against the sun, her mouth curved into a know-it-all grin. "Is that you, brother?"

He raced past Thomas and drew up hard, Perny's hooves skidding on the gravel and causing a cloud of dust. Nate jumped off the gelding before he'd come to a full stop. Throwing the reins at the footman, who'd ran to catch up to them, Nate ordered, "See he gets home."

"Yes, my lord." Thomas quickly drew Perny away and off the path.

"Where's Susannah?" he asked as he marched towards his sister. He wasn't going to waste time on a proper greeting.

"How has your morning been?" She clasped her hands behind her back and rocked on her heels, that damned smile still present. "You left before any of us had even risen."

Nate took her by the arm. "Where is Susannah? I know she's somewhere in this park. But why isn't she with you? What have you done with her?"

Minnie's grin evaporated, her eyes flashing. Wrenching herself from Nate's grasp, she straightened her tilted bonnet. "I haven't done anything with her. She wanted a moment alone to think, so I granted it to her."

"Alone?" Nate pulled off his hat and ran his hand through his hair distractedly, then clapped it on his head again. "You left her alone?"

"Don't be daft. Of course I did not. John Coachman is nearby."

"Where?" The word hit like a hammer to iron.

"Nearby." She folded her arms across her chest.

He clenched her shoulders. "Where is she?" He was dangerously close to shaking the answer out of his sister. Cressingham could be following them at that very moment, and Nate wouldn't put it past the man to abduct his own niece. "Tell me now," he said, loud and threatening. "It's urgent."

"Take your hands off me." She broke free from his hold once more. "She's near Grosvenor Gate. There's a copse of old trees after the reservoir, just before the gate, on the right. John Coachman is parked nearby. And, if you must know, she might not be alone."

Nate's stomach dropped to his knees. Dammit! She was giving Nate up as a traitor. "Who is she meeting with?"

Minnie pursed her lips together, seemingly unwilling to betray Susannah's confidence.

But Nate was done playing games. "Tell me who, Minnie. I'm going to find out anyway."

"Oh, very well. She's meeting with Sir Philip. But it's not—"

Turning from Minnie, he ran towards the gate, his booted feet crunching the gravel as he weaved through a gaggle of riders headed towards him, completely ignoring the entreaties that his sister lobbed his way. He cursed his own stupidity for not seeing Tradwick as the ideal person in whom Susannah could confide her secret. Her brother's old friend and Nate's purported enemy? He was perfect.

Within minutes, he entered the small cluster of trees, but stopped short at the sight that greeted him. It didn't look at all like Susannah was confessing anything. Instead, she and Tradwick were huddled together like lovebirds, her hands clasped in his, their faces nearly touching, their voices barely a whisper.

A blind rage came over Nate. Was his friend intending to marry Susannah in order to protect her? Over his dead body. Nate fisted his hands at his sides, every muscle tensed and quivering, ready to pound the bloody pulp out of his so-called friend. Gesturing wildly at them, he barked, "What the devil is this, Tradwick? Stealing my bride?"

Susannah inhaled sharply, her head turning to face him, and Tradwick took a step back, eyeing Nate with caution. "Hello, Rainsford. Pleasure to see you on this fine afternoon."

Nate took a slow step towards them. "Oh, it's fine all right. I come home to find my betrothed missing, and when I find her, she's in the arms of my so-called enemy. You can forget any plans for a clandestine elopement, *friend*"—he spat out the word—"for I won't let you have her."

Susannah's face lost all its color. Tradwick straightened to his full height, forcefully putting Susannah behind him in a protective way. "Respectfully, I don't *want* her."

"Then what the devil are you doing with her?"

Tradwick looked over his shoulder at Susannah, whose eyes were cast downward, then back at Nate, his always-impassive face revealing nothing. "I'm *listening*."

"Listening?" Nate stopped, forcing his mind to start working again. Yes. Of course. Susannah was telling Tradwick what she had overheard the night before. He cursed himself for thinking otherwise.

Tradwick must have sensed Nate's realization, for he relaxed his stance. "Your fiancée has been busy, Rainsford. As have you."

Nate's racing pulse began to slow…slightly. Quirking his mouth, he asked, "What has she told you?"

"Damn near everything." Tradwick folded his arms across his chest. "Quite a curious little bird you have here, my friend."

Susannah stepped out from behind Tradwick, her brow furrowed in confusion. "But—you two aren't friends."

Nate lowered his head and directed his gaze at his future bride. "I have asked you to trust me, poppet. Someday I will tell you everything, but I can't yet. Right now, I need you to come with me. There is business we must take care of at once."

She frowned. "I'm not going anywhere with you. You're a traitor," she said, the pitch of her voice rising. "You're colluding with my uncle to aid Napoleon, who has escaped Elba." Susannah turned to Tradwick, grabbing his arm with both hands. "Don't you see? He's helping the enemy. You have to stop him," she pleaded.

Unfolding one arm, Tradwick patted her on the hand, his face softening. "I promise you, Miss Cressingham, he is nothing of the sort. You are quite safe with him."

All at once, her eyes grew large, and she released Tradwick, stepping away from him. Her hands covered her mouth as she looked back and forth from Nate to his friend.

Her sudden change in demeanor caused a spiny, prickled sensation under Nate's skin. "Susannah—"

But she cut him off, saying, "You're both traitors. Both working for my uncle." Susannah grabbed her skirts and tried to run between them towards the main bridle path.

"Oh no, you don't." Nate reached out and grabbed her by the waist, then hauled her up against him. He looked down, tipping her chin up with his forefinger. "No one is a traitor, except your uncle."

Susannah struggled against Nate, trying to free herself. "Of course you would say that. What else should I expect from you?"

Nate grabbed her firmly by the chin with one hand as the other cinched tighter about her waist. "Susannah, look at me," he said, forcefully.

She stilled, raising her eyes to his.

"I swear to you on my brother's grave that I am not aiding your uncle." He blew out a frustrated breath. "I shouldn't tell you this. I really shouldn't," he mumbled.

"But you have to, Rain," Tradwick said.

Nate sighed. "Very well then." He looked down at

Susannah, his eyes scanning hers, noting her fear and agitation. "I'm not aiding your uncle. I'm trying to catch him. He's a traitor and we—Tradwick, myself, the Home Office—are trying to prove it. I am not colluding with him, I promise."

Susannah held his gaze for a minute, then looked over at Tradwick, who nodded his assent.

"There's much you don't know, Miss Cressingham, and much we cannot tell you, but that is true." Tradwick raised his right hand. "Rain is worthy of your esteem. You can trust him. I swear to you on your brother's grave."

Susannah nodded, then pushed gently on Nate's arm. "Let me go, please. I won't run."

He eyed her dubiously, but did as she requested.

Straightening her gown, she shot Nate a look that was as hard as it was penetrating. "Prove it."

"Beg pardon?" Nate asked.

She crossed her arms. "Prove to me that you're not traitors. Prove to me that you're working for the Home Office. Prove to me that you are not working with my uncle." She cast both men a doubtful glance. "If you say you're doing these things—or not—then prove it."

Nate and Tradwick shared a glance over Susannah's head. What the devil proof could he give her right now? He had nothing. It wasn't like he could conjure up some sort of document that would attest to what he was doing.

He took her hand in his. "I wish I could. Sincerely, I do. But short of taking you to the Home Secretary's office—"

"Very well then. Introduce me to him. If he says you're not a traitor, I will trust you."

"Miss Cressingham," Tradwick said, "Rain cannot possibly do that. Secretary Lord Sidmouth would not wish to be bothered by this sort of request."

"'This sort of request' is the only way to convince me you both aren't traitors," she said indignantly.

Nate was done with this conversation. He didn't care if he had to tie her and toss her into a trunk, he was not going to engage with her any more. Each minute that passed was another minute Cressingham gained an advantage.

He gripped her hand tighter. "Enough. We don't have time for this. Your uncle has changed his plans, and we must marry at once." Nate began to walk towards the carriage, but Susannah refused to go with him.

"What do you mean, 'marry at once'? What plans has he changed?" She jerked her hand from his and took a step back, frowning. "Even if you are working for the Home Office, there isn't anything in this world that would persuade me to marry the man who killed my brother."

Minnie popped into the clearing, her face aghast. "You think he killed Ben?"

Nate ground his teeth and swore under his breath. "How long have you been standing there eavesdropping?"

"Long enough."

"Lady Minerva," Tradwick said with a frown. "That was unseemly."

She didn't seem the least bit contrite. "Don't worry. I'm very good at keeping secrets." She winked.

Nate was quickly running out of patience. "Please, Minnie. You've caused enough trouble."

"Me? What did I do?"

"Your brought Susannah here," Nate said through clenched teeth. Susannah had inched away from all of them, and Nate was afraid that any talk on the subject would ruin his chance to get Susannah to come with him peaceably.

"She asked me to." Minnie shrugged, then turned back

to Susannah. "But you think Nate killed Ben? Of course he did not. He died at Tordesillas."

"And if his lordship hadn't coerced Ben into joining the army, that never would have happened," Susannah retorted.

"But that's not what I—"

"Minnie," Nate said, "you're not helping."

"It's complicated." Of course Tradwick would try to defuse the situation.

Nate wanted to shout. As much as he appreciated his friend's words, even he didn't know the truth, and he doubted Tradwick's statements would make any traction with Susannah.

"We can discuss this later," Nate said dismissively. He took Susannah by the hand so she couldn't run off, then addressed his friend. "Tradwick, the special license Cressingham gave me yesterday was a forgery. He intends to marry Susannah to someone else for more money. Soon, he'll discover I have the real license. We must marry at once, and I need someone to give Susannah away. Will you?"

Tradwick nodded. "Of course. But I have an appointment at five o'clock."

"We will be quick," Nate said.

"So you two aren't really enemies?" Susannah asked in a frustrated voice, pointing from one man to the other. "I went through all this trouble for nothing."

"Well, not necessarily. At least you know you can rely on Sir Philip," Minnie said. "Of course, I knew all along they weren't really at outs. And I'm not at all surprised to learn that Captain Cressingham is a suspected traitor. I never did like that man."

What? Her comments momentarily distracted Nate. How did Minnie know their rivalry was a hoax? That little busybody. But Nate shook his head. He would have to address that later.

Tradwick must have read Nate's confused expression, because he extended his arm to Minnie, saying, "I always knew you were smart, Lady Minerva. This way to the carriage, if you please. Now, about what you heard…" His friend had better instill in Minnie the importance of secrecy.

Nate followed his friend, dragging Susannah with him. She continued to pull at her hand, trying to free it from Nate's vise-like grip. "Let go of me, you cad."

"Stop fighting me." He was growing frustrated and weary of her protestations. "We have to, or you will regret it."

"The only thing that I regret"—she scratched at Nate's gloved hand, trying to free herself—"is ever meeting you."

Her words stung. However, he had one, singular focus right now, and that was to keep his promise and protect Susannah, whether she wanted it or not. "Have you listened to a word I've said?" Nate practically yelled.

She paused in her struggles and looked up at him, her eyes wide with caution.

"He's doing it, Susannah. He's planning to marry you to someone else. Soon." Nate took the opportunity offered by her stillness to grab her other hand, pulling her close. "You must believe me. Your uncle is…is…*selling* you"— Nate spat out the word—"to the highest bidder. And he doesn't care a whit how you'll be treated or what your future husband will do to you." He furrowed his brow, raising her gloved hands to his, and kissed her knuckles. "The only way I can protect you, poppet, is to give you my name."

Her eyes flashed, then, to Nate's surprise, filled with tears, and she pulled her hands free. "Do you not see how hard it is for me to blindly do as you bid? You have taken everything from me, my lord. Everything."

Her words reached into Nate's chest and squeezed. Softly, he said, "I'm trying to make up for that."

"You can't!" She huffed, swiping at an errant tear. "I would rather take my chances with a man I didn't know than one I do, but do not respect or trust."

Nate scoffed. "Like your sister? Look what happened to her." He lowered his voice. "Do you not care about Isabela? About seeing her again?"

Susannah said nothing, just stared into the trees. "I will take my chances. I'll figure something out. I'll…" Her voice trailed off.

For a moment, Nate's throat clenched, a lump like a boulder settling there, but he swallowed it away. He was anxious for this whole ordeal to be over with, because only then could he tell her the truth, and Susannah wouldn't be satisfied until she had it.

Becoming business-like again, he turned towards the carriage. "I'm sorry to force you like this, but you leave me no choice." Wordlessly, he approached the carriage, towing a very reluctant Susannah behind him. Tradwick and Minnie were already seated inside. After Nate pushed Susannah, protesting loudly, into it, he climbed in, then drove his fist into the roof a few times. "Home, John," he shouted, and in a few seconds, the carriage was in motion.

Susannah glared at Nate, the hate in her expression so palpable and potent, he experienced a twinge of fear. Someday she'd understand his motives. And if she didn't, he wouldn't put it past her to try and kill him.

Nate didn't care. Susannah Cressingham was worth dying for.

CHAPTER 16

JUST OVER AN HOUR LATER, Nate stood at the chancel of St. Marleybone's parish church. He had already endured a tearful tirade from his mother about everything from the impropriety of not marrying in the estate church at Langley Park, where generations of Rainsfords had wed, to the social disgrace of not hosting a wedding breakfast, to the unseemliness of marrying by special license. Nate had called poppycock on every argument save the one about Langley Park, and if his friend Andrew had arrived in time, it he would be him officiating right now. But Andrew wasn't there, and Nate certainly would not use the parson recommended by Cressingham.

Nate looked back towards the entrance, waiting for Susannah, who was outside with Tradwick. He pulled his watch from his fob pocket and checked the time. Surely Cressingham was looking for his niece, especially if he'd tried to get a legitimate license. Nate had instructed Crimson to reveal nothing when the captain came by Rainsford House. He looked at his watch again, then at the doors to the church. What could possibly be taking so long?

He restored his watch to its rightful place and looked around the small, whitewashed church. The interior was simple and no-nonsense, the tall, narrow windows doing little to brighten the wooden-ceilinged space on this cloudy day. Branches of candles scattered about the nave were as ineffective at lightening the gloom as stars in a moonless sky. The darkness caused his heart to clench in apprehension, as if foretelling doom.

In contrast were his sisters, sitting in the nearest pew box, wearing joyous expressions...bright eyes, warm smiles, and engaged in happy conversation. Mama sat with them, much more subdued, but at least she wasn't crying anymore.

The realization of what was about to happen made Nate's breath hitch. Susannah was going to become his wife.

"Is the bride nervous?" asked Reverend Crowther in a deep voice that belied his short stature. "She should be here already, my lord, should she not?"

Nate looked at the balding Reverend Crowther, rail-thin with bony, protruding cheekbones and gnarled, skeleton-like hands, and cursed under his breath. He'd much rather have had Andrew there to officiate. Nate opened his mouth to answer when he heard voices and movement at the other end of the aisle. The large wooden door at the entrance of the church creaked, and all eyes turned in that direction. The light from outside created a silhouette of the two people who entered, but after they took a few steps into the church, Nate could see Tradwick holding Susannah at her elbow.

His breath hitched. The beautiful creature standing on the far end of the nave was going to be *his wife*. His body thrummed with desire and pride and adoration. Her plain violet day dress enhanced her brown hair and light complexion, the straw bonnet she wore framed her face, and the small posy of flowers she carried emphasized her delicate features.

That's when Nate noticed her expression. Her eyes, those beautiful brown orbs that Nate could get lost in, were narrowed and spewing hate. Instead of a smile, her lips were drawn into a thin, disapproving line. Nate took a fortifying breath. She may not be happy with what was happening today, but Nate, for one, had no qualms about the promises they were about to make to each other. The only thing he worried about was getting the ordeal over with before her uncle discovered them.

"If everyone will please stand." Reverend Crowther made a rising motion with his hands, and Nate's mama and sisters quickly rose. Gesturing to Tradwick, he said, "You may come forward."

His friend took Susannah's hand and placed it on his arm, then hastily walked down the aisle, as if he expected Susannah to bolt. When they reached the chancel, Tradwick gave Susannah's hand into Nate's own, winked, then turned to sit in the first pew box on the other side of the aisle from his mama and sisters.

Nate looked down at his intended, wanting to give her an encouraging smile, to tell her with his eyes and his heart that all would be well, but she stared straight ahead, patently ignoring him. He watched as she jutted out her jaw and raised her chin in that damned defiant manner of hers. What if she refused him, despite everything he'd told her thus far? The prospect set his entire body quaking with frustration, and he breathed through his nose a few times to get himself under control.

Reverend Crowther cleared his throat and opened his

prayer book. Holding it with one hand, he raised the other before the couple and addressed the other members of the church. "Dearly beloved, we are gathered here in the sight of God and the face of these witnesses to bring together this man and this woman in holy matrimony." The echo of his deep voice in the cavernous church underscored the solemnity of what was about to take place.

The prayer continued, but Nate didn't hear him. His attention was riveted to Susannah, who looked neither at Reverend Crowther nor at Nate. Her gaze remained fixed to a spot on the wall of the chancel, as if it held all the answers to life's questions.

"My lord," Reverend Crowther whispered.

Nate looked over at the priest. He hadn't heard a thing Crowther had said for the last several minutes.

"It's your turn." The officiant raised his eyebrows expectantly. "Nathaniel Edward Raymond Kinlan, Earl of Rainsford, wilt thou have this woman to thy wedded wife, to live together after God's ordinance in the holy estate of matrimony? Wilt thou love her, comfort her, honor, and keep her in sickness and health; and, forsaking all others, keep thee only unto her, so long as ye both shall live?"

Nate looked at Susannah once more, but she still ignored him. In a firm, resolute voice, Nate answered, "I will."

Reverend Crowther turned to Susannah. Consulting his prayer book, he said, "Susannah Hélène-Marie Cress-ingham, wilt thou have this man to thy wedded husband, to live together after God's ordinance in the holy estate of matrimony? Wilt thou obey him, and serve him, love, honor, and keep him in sickness and in health; and, forsaking all others, keep thee only unto him, so long as ye both shall live?"

Susannah looked at the floor, her forehead wrinkled in concentration.

She had to say yes.

Nate cleared his throat.

She looked over her shoulder at Nate's mama. He did the same, wondering what on earth she could have to say about the whole thing. Clutching a handkerchief and dabbing her misty eyes, his mama smiled encouragingly and made a "go on" motion with her hands at Susannah.

His bride huffed, then looked up at Nate, her anger on full display.

Once again, Nate felt as if he were falling off a cliff, and the only thing saving him from crashing on the rocks below was her answer. He took her hand and pressed it warmly between his, and as he did so, realization dawned.

He loved this woman. This disagreeable, opinionated, stubborn woman. And he wanted her in his life forever.

With renewed fervor, he squeezed her hand again, willing her to feel his love through his touch. *Say yes and let me love you, please.*

"Miss Cressingham, you must answer in the affirmative," interjected Reverend Crowther.

"You can trust him," Tradwick said.

Susannah's eyes flashed, and she inhaled sharply, looking over her shoulder at his friend. Tradwick gave a quick nod of his head as encouragement.

Wrenching her hand from Nate's, she scowled at Reverend Crowther. Straightening her back, she answered, "Very well. I will."

The tension Nate had been withholding in his chest released with a long, expelled breath.

The rest of the service continued. When it came time for the ring, Nate had to pull her hand to him, for she did not offer it willingly. Liquid heat shot up his arms and into his chest, warming his body like a fever. He had no idea if she'd felt it, too, for her body posture was so stiff and cold, she could have doubled for one of the large pillars supporting the galley. But Nate's blood flowed through his veins like molten lava.

He pulled an intricate gold band encrusted with emeralds and diamonds from his waistcoat pocket. The Rainsford ring had been in the family for generations, bestowed on the heir for his new wife, and should have gone to his brother John, had he lived. Nate had expected to feel a twinge of guilt when he'd taken it out of the strongbox, but surprisingly, he had not.

Keeping his eyes riveted to Susannah's face, he slowly slid the band onto her finger, hoping it fit. Each gentle push and turn of the ring confirmed that she belonged with him, bound together for life. When it finally slid into place, fitting her delicate finger perfectly, Nate felt to the depth of his soul that they were destined for each other. Slightly overcome, he covered her hand with his.

She offered no reaction.

Reverend Crowther spoke the final words of the service. "For the husband is the head of the wife, even as Christ is head of the Church; and he is the Savior of the body. Therefore as the Church is subject unto Christ, so let the wives be to their own husbands in every thing. Wives, submit yourselves unto your own husbands, as it is fit in the Lord."

Susannah's head snapped to Nate. With a glaring look, she gave a small shake of her head. Behind him, Nate heard his mama gasp.

Inwardly, Nate sighed. Of course Susannah would take issue with the vows, which required her to obey her husband. After all, she'd been ordered around for years by her uncle, and Nate certainly hadn't given her much choice in regards to wedding him. If only she knew the full reason he was marrying her. The moment he'd clapped eyes on Susannah, he'd made a vow to himself to be with her.

To ensure her safety.

To make her happy.

To *love* her.

"My lord." Reverend Crowther's voice knocked Nate out of his reverie. "If you and your bride will please come with me, and you, sir," he said, motioning to Tradwick, "and you my lady." He gestured to Nate's mama. "We will sign the register."

The five of them crowded into the small vestry off the chancel. With an uncharacteristically broad smile, Tradwick slapped Nate on the back. "Congratulations, Rain. I'm glad to see the first of us has gone the way of the honest man."

The parson, who flitted about the room with seemingly nervous agitation, handed the quill to Nate. "You first, my lord." He pointed to the spot in the register, and Nate signed, then handed the quill off to Susannah.

With a huff, she took it, dipped it in the inkwell, and scribbled her name. As soon as she finished, she dropped the quill on the table, then thrust her small posy of flowers into Nate's hands. "Satisfied?" With a dark look, she turned on her heel and stalked out of the vestry.

Mama opened her mouth, eyes wide with shock, but no sound came out. Even Tradwick arched a disapproving eyebrow. Nate did not stay to witness the other signatures. He quickly followed her into the nave, calling out, "Susannah, where the devil are you going?"

She made a beeline to the doors of the church. Nate's sisters sat in stupefied silence as they watched Susannah's quick retreat. When she reached the door, Susannah wrenched it open and walked out.

Damn her for this. Nate's face flamed, part anger, part embarrassment that she would leave in such an undignified manner. If her brother were here, he'd surely set her straight. Nate dashed down the aisle and out the door. Ahead of him, Susannah walked briskly away from the church. He sprinted to catch up, weaving his way through the scant pedestrian traffic, and grabbed her by the arm. "Where are you going?"

She whirled on him, pulling her arm free. "Away. You got what you wanted, but if you think I'll be your wife in any way save name only, you're quite wrong."

Nate raced around her, blocking her path, and ushered her to the side of the nearest building, where they would be out of earshot of any observers. He was breathing hard, having a difficult time controlling his frustration. Why the devil wouldn't she listen to him? Why did she keep fighting him? He put his hands out on either side of her against the wall, boxing her in. Bending low, his mouth near her ear, he said in a stern whisper, "This marriage is not in name only. It is not a matter of convenience."

Susannah crossed her arms and turned away as best she could, given the tight confines. Over her shoulder, she said, "So you say."

"Did you not hear anything Tradwick and I told you earlier? I'm trying to catch your uncle."

She frowned. "I heard you. But you've shown me no proof." To Nate's surprise, she ducked under his arm and continued marching briskly down the pavement.

He'd had about enough. He might love her, but if he had to, he'd lock this damnable woman in a room for a year. Coming up behind her, he took her by the elbow and turned them around so they were headed back to the church entrance. She tried to pull her arm free, but Nate's grip was hard and firm. He didn't say anything to her as they approached the entrance. His mother and sisters stood on the steps watching them, their mouths forming *O*s. Tradwick was gone, presumably on his way to his appointment.

"Mama, Susannah and I need to clarify a few things. John Coachman?" he asked, looking up at his driver. "Can you see Mama and the girls safely home...in time?"

"Yes, my lord."

Nate turned to Thomas. "Get a hackney."

"Yes, sir," he said, and ran off.

"I will not—" Susannah began, but Nate squeezed her arm to silence her.

"Nathaniel," his mama said indignantly, "you aren't taking *your bride* home in a hack?"

"I am," he replied, then forcibly led a protesting Susannah down the pavement in the direction Thomas had gone.

NEITHER OF THEM said a word on the ride home. Once there, Nate wordlessly escorted Susannah down from the hack, paid the driver, and entered the house as Crimson held the door, the butler's expression changing from happy to confused as he took in their dour expressions while helping them off with their things. Wisely, Crimson said nothing, and as soon as Susannah and Nate were divested of their gloves, bonnet, and hat, he retreated to the back of the house.

Nate stood in the front entry staring at his wife. *Wife.* Lord, he had a wife now. Overwhelmed by the thought, he ran his fingers through his hair, those damn conflicting emotions stirring up his insides like a butter churn. He felt like a firecracker about to explode, and it took every effort to keep his emotions in check. In a careful, controlled voice, he said, "This is your home now. You will have the same suite as you did last night. Until your uncle knows we're married and you're under my protection, you are not to leave the house. I have no doubt he will try to cause you harm. He certainly cannot be trusted."

Susannah suddenly came alive, her eyes flashing. "There's that word again—trust." She looked up at Nate. With a scathing look, she whispered, "Are you ever going to admit you're responsible for Ben's death?"

To Nate, her whisper was a roar.

Quickly grabbing Susannah by the arm, he dragged her towards the stairs. "Come, *wife*. We need to talk. Privately."

"Unhand me." Susannah fought tooth and nail, her fingers scratching at his hands as she dug in her heels.

Nate wasn't about to let her go. He was tired of being blamed for something that wasn't his fault. Nate marched up the stairs, pulling his wife behind him, and pushed the door to her suite open so hard that it banged against the wall and the candles flickered. He shoved Susannah forward into the room, then slammed the door behind him, turning the key in the lock.

Facing Susannah, he stalked her.

"Leave me alone. Get out of this room." Her eyes were wide with fear as she backed herself into the far corner, near the writing table.

"You ungrateful wretch. Everything I have done for the last three years has been for you." He was consumed with rage. Damn her and her wily ways. He would have no more of it now that she was his wife. Nate pushed the chairs over and out of the way, and Susannah cried out in shock.

Ignoring her, he kept coming forward.

Susannah ran behind the chaise near the large-paned window. "Liar. You've done it all for you. *Your* political benefit. *Your* financial gain, no matter what you might say about my uncle. You don't care about me. You certainly don't *love* me."

She said the word like a taunt, and without thinking, Nate leaped over the chaise and pinned Susannah against the glass. He put both hands on either side of her and, on instinct, pressed his body against hers. Almost immediately, his anger dissipated, replaced by a feverish heat, a maddening desire to join, to meld, to fuse their bodies together. She was his *wife* now, after all. Through their bulky clothes, he felt every curve, every mound, every bend in her body, which seemed to melt into his like warm butter. He marveled at how well they fit, exulting in her warmth, her softness, her scent.

He would show her this wasn't a marriage of convenience. In a husky voice, he asked, "You think I married you for politics?"

She opened her mouth to answer, but Nate took his finger and slowly rubbed it across her lower lip, tracing the hot, plump edge of it back and forth, back and forth.

Her breath caught, her eyes riveted to his.

"There's nothing political about your beautiful, kissable lips, poppet."

The brown depths of her eyes swirled with passion, and Nate groaned inwardly at the temptation.

"You think I married you for money?" Nate slid his fingers down her chin and along the warm lines of her neck. Beneath her skin, he could feel her rapid pulse, and his responded in kind. "Your exquisite neck, your silky skin. God, Susannah," he said, his voice strained, "they are priceless."

Susannah closed her eyes and bit her lip. He could tell she was fighting him, trying not to succumb to temptation.

But Nate was determined to show her—not merely tell her—what she meant to him. He leaned down and tilted his head, brushing the tip of his nose against her neck, near her ear. God, she smelled divine. His body hardened in response. "How could I not care about you? You drive me wild. I would do anything for you."

She inhaled sharply, then stiffened. A second later, she pushed against him. "Liar." The word bit with accusation.

Nate stepped back, his passion quickly morphing into frustration. "Susannah…"

A wild look came into her eyes, more caged carnivore than skittish colt. "Liar," she said again, pushing away from the window.

He reached for her. "I meant what I said—"

"Stop," she cried out. Putting her hands to her ears, she screwed her eyes shut, then cried out, "Just…stop. Stop telling me you'd do anything for me. That it's all been for me. Because it hasn't."

"Poppet—"

"No." Adamant in her denial, Susannah dropped her hands, then came to Nate, tears streaming down her face. To his surprise, she put her hands on his chest and shoved him backwards a few steps. "Let me tell you what you did for me." Another shove. "You abandoned Isabela to that despicable landowner." Shove. "You abandoned me." Shove. "You broke my trust." Shove. "You broke my *heart*." Shove. "Worst of all, you abandoned Ben, your best friend, when he needed you most." Shove. "You let him die."

Her hands came up to shove him again, but Nate grabbed her by the wrists. "Good God, woman," he shouted, his voice rife with frustration. "Your brother is not dead."

CHAPTER 17

SUSANNAH FROZE, even as Nate held her hands against his chest, her clouded, angry mind trying to make sense of what he had just told her.

Ben is *alive?*

Her lips trembled, and her eyes overflowed with tears. He was lying again. He had to be. Her brother was dead. She'd buried him, for heaven's sake, or what had been left of him, which was only his officer's coat. Blood-soaked, burnt, and beyond saving.

Susannah blinked back some of the blurriness and scoured Nate's face, searching for truth, but seeing only resignation. In a quivering voice, Susannah said, "You're lying to me again. Why must you keep doing this to me?"

Suddenly overwhelmed by a frantic need to divorce herself from Nate's deceptions, Susannah struggled against him, squirming like a child who didn't want a bath. "Let me go," she pleaded. She tried to pull her hands from his, her movements primal and urgent, but the dratted man wouldn't release her. She began crying in earnest, her struggles never ceasing.

"Please release me. Please." She didn't care that she was begging. "I can't bear this from you anymore." Didn't he understand how the words and actions of him and his family tortured her? They thought they could make everything right by telling her what she'd wanted to hear—that they'd wanted her when no one else had. Even now, Nate stood before her confessing a fabrication so blatant and shameless, it was obviously intended to pull at her heartstrings and convince her to forgive him.

But that she could never do.

"Susannah, let me explain. Please."

She closed her eyes, shutting him out, and struggled harder, but she could not extricate herself from his firm grip. "Let go of me." She was sobbing now, her face wet with tears. The panic that had first surfaced at Nate's admission began rising within her like the tide, coming up higher and higher, covering her shoulders, then her neck, then her chin, about to drown her. Yet she refused to succumb. With renewed anger, she fought him with a burst of energy, like a dying man fighting for his last breath. "Release me!"

Nate squeezed her hands, then shook her. "Susannah! Good God, would you listen to me? I'm telling you the truth." He dropped her hands and stepped back, releasing a massive sigh that sounded of surrender. Shoulders slumping, he said in a resigned voice, "I'm finally telling you the truth."

Susannah stared at him incredulously. "Say it again," she demanded.

Nate looked at her, his eyes shadowed, dark, full of regret. "Your brother is alive." He turned away, one arm akimbo, the other rubbing his forehead. "Damn and blast."

Her instincts told her Nate wasn't acting. He wasn't

saying this to appease her. She raced around to face him, clutching his arms, digging her fingers into the fabric of his coat, shaking him in doubt and frustration, her heart bursting with hope. "Ben is really alive?"

He nodded.

"Oh, sweet merciful heavens." Susannah collapsed to the floor beside him in a crumbled heap, her hands covering her face, and she wept uncontrollably as three years of wretched sorrow were set free. *My brother is alive!* Her body shook with sobs as she struggled to suck in air, but the myriad of emotions swirling through her—relief, anguish, happiness, disgust—whipped her mind into a frenzy so uncontrollable, her ears buzzed. She was so full of questions, she could barely begin lining them up in her head. Where was Ben? What had he been doing? And why had Nate let her believe he was dead? The questions continued to whirl and spin in her head, almost faster than she could register them.

Through it all, her crying continued, huge wracking sobs, which tested the limits of her stays. Her hands grew wet from the painful tears she shed. And the entire time, Nate stood beside her.

Saying nothing. Doing nothing.

Slowly, after a time, Susannah's cries subsided, replaced with the occasional sniffle and gulp. Still on the floor, her body ached as if she'd been rung out with the washing.

Nate bent down next to her and gently put one arm across her back. "I think you needed that cry. Now…here. Take this, my sweet." With the other hand, he held out a handkerchief. "Dry your tears."

Susannah brushed aside the handkerchief. "Where is he?" she asked desperately.

"Susannah…" He thrust the fabric at her.

She scrambled to her feet, knocking his arm away

again, eyes burning. Susannah didn't want his gesture of kindness. "Tell me where he is. I want to see him. Where is Ben?"

Nate stood up and let go another resigned sigh. "I'm afraid you can't see him right now. His location has to remain secret."

After that confession…after all this time, she wasn't going to be able to see her brother? Susannah clenched her hands and shoved them against Nate's chest, once again making him the target of her frustrated and pent-up energy. "You owe it to me to tell me. I won't believe he's alive until I see him for myself." She pushed against him, knocking him slightly off balance.

"Good God, woman, curb your fists." Nate frowned, grabbing her hands and holding them in his strong grip, wrestling her arms down. "If you don't take a damper, I'm not going to tell you anything."

Her breathing labored, Susannah struggled to get her emotions under control. "If you think I'll be satisfied with half-truths right now, you're sorely mistaken. I want the full truth, Rain. Everything." She glared at him. "You've deceived me long enough."

"I may have, but it wasn't for any nefarious purpose, I assure you. It was to ensure your brother's safety. It is for that very reason that I cannot reveal his location."

"But is he in England?"

"Poppet." His voice held a note of warning. Nate squeezed her hands, willing her to accept his mandate.

Drat the man. Susannah wiped her wet face with the back of her hand.

Nate shoved the handkerchief at her again. "Good Lord, did that school teach you nothing?" He sighed. "Dry your eyes. And your nose." Nate gestured to the settee over by the fireplace, which he quickly righted. "Sit down, and I will answer whatever questions you have…that I can answer."

Begrudgingly, Susannah did as she was bid, mopping her face and nose with the now-wrinkled linen.

Nate walked to the wall and, to Susannah's surprise, pulled on a piece of wood trim, revealing a secret door.

"Where are you going?" Susannah rose, ready to follow him into the next county, if need be. "Where does that door lead?"

"Stand down, poppet." He rolled his eyes, then made a "be seated" sign with his hand. "This door leads to my suite. I merely want to get you a glass of brandy." Nate ran a hand through his already disheveled hair. "You need it. Damn, *I* need it. I'll return in just a moment, I swear." Then he started through the hidden door.

"Is he well?"

Nate pulled up short and spun around. "I'll answer all the questions I can in just a moment."

If Nate thought she was going to wait for answers, he was very, very wrong. Susannah dashed up behind him, grabbed his arm, and forcibly pulled him back into the room, her breathing hot and fast. "If I had just told you your sister was alive after supposedly being dead for three years, you wouldn't wait before dogging me with questions. So don't you dare put on that haughty attitude and think you can allay me for even a moment. I want answers, Rain. Now."

"I know. And I will give them to you. But not when you're acting like this," he said, making a sweeping gesture at her with his hand, his face showing annoyance. "So… uncontrolled. Undignified. What I have to reveal is serious, requiring discretion and circumspection. Your brother's life depends on it. But if you're going to be a screeching shrew, I won't tell you anything."

She stared at him, angered by his threat, but she swallowed her frustration…and her pride. "Very well. But I'm going to watch you here from the doorway."

Nate turned back to his suite. "So be it."

He disappeared into his room, which was dark, seemingly lit by only one candle. In the shadows, he walked over to a small table, which was outfitted with crystal glasses and decanters holding various liquids. Susannah heard the clinks of glass as he poured some into two brandy snifters and returned to her room, shutting the secret door with the back of his booted foot.

"Now tell me if Ben is alright."

"Drink first." Nate gestured to the settee. "Sit down. You'll be more comfortable."

Susannah did as he asked, and Nate handed her one of the glasses. Sitting beside her, he raised his glass in silent salute and pointedly stared at her drink. "Sip it, but slowly. It will help relax you a bit." In contrast, Nate downed the contents of his in one gulp.

"Is he married? Does he have children?"

"Drink, woman." Nate released a frustrated growl. "For heaven's sake, will you please take a drink?"

Goodness, he was such a bossy man. Susannah was far too agitated to think that any amount of liquor would calm her, but she did as he bid, taking a small sip of brandy, coughing as it burned its way to her belly.

He patted her on the back. "Go slow. Have another sip now."

She did, and the second one went down much more smoothly than the first.

"Finish it." Nate wasn't asking.

Frowning, Susannah sipped the rest down, and within seconds, a sense of relaxed warmth spread outward from her middle. She handed him the empty glass.

He set hers and his on a side table, then turned to her, one arm resting on the back of the settee, the other on his knee. His haggard expression gave her a bit of a shock, but she pushed the thought aside. Susannah didn't care a whit for how he felt right now.

Clenching her hands in her lap, she began peppering him with questions. "Well? Where is he? What is he doing?"

"As I told you, I can't reveal where Ben is. Only that he is alive and well. I heard from him only a few weeks ago. He's on an assignment for the Home Office, but it's low-risk."

"Is he married?"

Nate shook his head. "No. He's not married."

"Has he suffered any injuries? You're sure he's well?"

"As I said, he's quite well. No major injuries to speak of."

Susannah's heart leapt into her throat. "Major injuries? Then he's suffered minor ones?"

"Goodness, wife," he said in an exasperated tone.

The endearment took Susannah by surprise, and a thrilling flutter rippled through her belly. Lord, she was his wife. He was her *husband*. But she would think about that later. Her brother mattered most right now. Raising her eyebrows questioningly, she asked, "Well? Has he suffered minor injuries?"

"I can't say that he didn't cut himself shaving." He gave her a wry grin. "We generally don't discuss such trivial matters."

Nate's sarcasm annoyed Susannah. She frowned at his attempt at humor, but inwardly sighed with relief. Ben was safe, if she were to believe Nate. And surprisingly, in her heart of hearts, she did.

She closed her eyes and said a silent prayer of thanks,

grateful that her brother was alive. But as she did so, bigger questions started to form in her mind, dredging up all sorts of horrible memories of the last day she saw her brother years ago.

Glancing up at Nate, she fixed him with a pointed look. "I want to know what happened." She kept her voice steady, despite the tremors that coursed through her body. "Tell me what happened when you left the house with my brother that day."

Nate abruptly rose and walked to the fireplace, picked up the poker, and moved the coals around to create more heat. For a long time, he stared at the now-glowing coals, his back to her. He sighed and Susannah could hear the weariness in it, could see the surrender in his slumped shoulders.

But she still needed answers. "Well?"

"God, that was so long ago. I hated that night." Nate's quiet whisper could barely be heard. "That was the start of all of it, you see. For me." He continued staring into the fire, as if replying the entire night in his head, the poker clanging every now and then against the metal grate. "After we left your family's home, your brother came with me here to Rainsford House. He stayed a few days as we figured out what to do." He set the poker down, turned to face Susannah, and clasped his hands behind his back, his eyes dull, his face impassive. "My primary goal was to get your brother out of your uncle's house. Cressingham was itching for a reason to expel him. We were afraid he'd challenge your brother to a duel, or something equally stupid that would get Ben killed, and my only concern was your brother's safety. And as an extension of that, yours and Isabela's."

Nate began to pace back and forth in front of the fireplace. Susannah, her eyes burning, swollen, and tired from crying, tracked him, as if staring at him would compel him to reveal the truth faster.

"After a few days, it became clear we had to get your brother out of England entirely. The story I told you about your brother joining the army was just that...a story. I needed to tell you something at the time he left. And, of course, that's where your uncle thought he was headed."

Susannah's eyes dropped to the glowing coals, but she didn't really see them. She was reliving that day in her mind's eye. Her fingers nervously worked the fabric on her violet dress, twisting and pinching and turning the material, creating creases and wrinkles. That horrible day had been painted like a picture in her mind. Of Ben announcing his plans. Of his assurance that he'd return. Of Rain's promise that he'd protect Ben.

It seems he's kept that promise, you ninny.

A warm, comforting wave of relief washed over her, making her skin tingle in a pleasant way. It seemed her heart had decided that Nate wasn't the enemy anymore. But her mind wasn't quite ready to trust—or forgive—him.

Nate continued. "In order to get Ben out, we forged papers and shipped him off to the Continent. We were afraid your uncle would learn Ben was alive, so I had to make him disappear for good. Or give the illusion of it. Hence his death near Tordesillas." Nate walked to the settee and tipped her face up, his expression apologetic. "He was nowhere near a battlefield, poppet."

Susannah swatted his hand away, scowling. "Yet you never came to tell me what happened?"

"I couldn't tell you—"

Tears erupted once more and she stood, brushing past Nate. She crossed her arms, holding them tight against her middle, and paced the room back and forth and back again, replaying the awful day she'd received the news of

Ben's supposed death. Turning to face him, she shot out, "Did you have any idea how that news would affect me or Isabela?"

Nate ran his hand through his hair, then over his face, as if trying to wash away the memories. "There was so much going on at the time. I was working to keep Ben out of your uncle's sight. Cressingham had spies everywhere, watching every move I made. Besides that, it was imperative that I make myself an ally to your uncle, and if I showed any sort of preferential treatment to you or your sister, he'd see through my scheme."

The tears continued, long rivulets down Susannah's cheeks. In a barely controlled whisper, she said, "He was my brother, Rain. You left Isabela and me to fend for ourselves. With *him*."

"I know it seems that way." Nate came to Susannah, his expression earnest, and he put his hands gently on her arms, rubbing them. "But I assure you I knew exactly what was going on. In fact—"

Susannah's head shot up, her anger spiking. "If you knew what was happening, then how could you let Isabela marry that despicable man?" She swatted him away even as he tried to reach for her again. "Don't touch me." Stalking across the room, she stopped before the small writing desk, her fingers picking at the filigree on one of the drawer handles, her back to Nate. "You didn't know anything that was happening to myself or Isabela." Her voice was quiet, dejected. "And if you did, you certainly didn't do anything to reassure us."

"I take grave exception to that." Nate's indignation startled Susannah, and she turned towards him, her eyes going wide as he bore down on her, his expression dark and his finger pointed at her in accusation.

A twinge of fear shot up Susannah's spine, and she straightened to stifle it.

"I did everything—*everything*—I could to…to…*ingratiate* myself to your uncle," he said, his hands gesticulating wildly. "And it was, all of it, for you and Isabela."

Susannah opened her mouth to protest, but Nate cut her off. "No, you let me finish." He took a step closer, his large frame boxing her in against the desk as he stared her down. "I did everything your uncle ever asked of me, including 'getting rid of Ben,' all so he would trust me. So he would *listen* to me. And I used what little influence I had for you and Bela." He pressed his finger into her shoulder to make his point. "Unfortunately, your uncle had negoti-ated the marriage for her long before I tried to befriend him. That's what led to the fight between Ben and your uncle that day. He informed Ben of what he had planned for your sister, and Ben sternly disapproved, but because Ben wasn't quite twenty-five, and therefore not old enough to be your guardian, there was nothing Ben could do to stop your uncle from marrying Bela off. *Nothing*."

Nate turned away from Susannah, his face in profile, and for a brief second, a pang of guilt punctuated her heart, making it skip a beat.

Crossing his arms, Nate frowned. "But your uncle… he's a smart one. He knew that as soon as Ben achieved his majority, any control he had over you and your sister—and your dowries—would evaporate. And your uncle *wanted* that money, Susannah, so Ben had to leave. And after a time, we realized that Ben had to *die*, because your uncle wouldn't stop looking for him until he was sure Ben posed no threat to his plans."

She felt the anger of his words like a physical blow, heard their truth in his hard, labored breathing. The guilt was quickly replaced by remorse, the cold ache of it filling her body like Arctic water penetrating the hull of a sinking ship, weighing her down.

And yet Nate continued. "So I cozied up to your uncle. And when he asked me what should be done with you, because you weren't old enough at sixteen to receive your dowry, even if you were married, I suggested he enroll you as a boarding student at Miss Glover's School for Girls. Then I immediately went home and coerced Mama into enrolling the triplets."

At Susannah's raised eyebrows, Nate nodded. "The girls attended at the same time you did so they could keep you under watch, so to speak. I would ask them about you in the most innocuous way, but I knew that as long as you were talking to them, you were safe."

"Did your sisters know about this?"

Nate scoffed. "Of course not. I had other people at the school watching over you, as well, and reporting to me with regular frequency. Even after school I tried to protect you, encouraging your uncle to allow you to work as a companion for my reclusive great aunt in Northumberland until he determined what to do with you."

Susannah's remorse gave way to a certain peevishness. "So, you made sure *I* was looked after, but you left Isabela in the cold to fend for herself."

"No. Certainly not." Nate returned to the fireplace, kicking the iron grate that protected it with his booted foot over and over again, one hand clenching the mantel. Without looking at her, he said, "Remember the other day at your uncle's house? When we discussed the quid pro quo?"

To pretend she was in love with Nate? Susannah's face flamed at the thought, and she dropped her chin, trying to hide her reaction. She had loved him once, then for years she'd hated him, but here he was, exonerating himself right before her eyes.

"I remember," she said quietly.

"I revealed information to you about your sister. But I didn't receive any of that from your uncle."

She turned to him, her eyes wide. "Then who?"

"Since she married, my friend has been watching her. James Hedlington—Heddy—do you remember him? Another Beggars Club member."

Susannah nodded. "Yes, I remember."

"He's a captain in the Royal Navy. I arranged for him to be stationed in Jamaica, sailing in and out of Falmouth regularly, so he can watch your sister and report to me on her welfare." He took a breath, then let it out, still staring at the fire. "I couldn't stop your sister's marriage, but that didn't mean I couldn't look after her in her new life."

Susannah stood, mouth agape, trying to process this revelation. Nate had someone watching Isabela? "The entire time she's been away?"

Nate turned his head slightly, a weary smile forming. "The entire time. And much to Heddy's disappointment, I might add. He'd rather have been engaged in some sort of naval battle in the Americas than keep an eye on your sister."

The breath Susannah didn't know she was holding suddenly whooshed out of her. She collapsed into the chair near the writing desk. All this time. All these years. Nate had been watching over her and Isabela. The revelations were almost too much. She'd been so keen in her distrust of Nate, her downright hatred of him. And all the while, he'd been protecting their entire family.

He drew up another chair and sat next to her, their knees barely touching. She could feel the warmth between them, and her body responded as hot tingles traveled from her legs to her belly to her arms, filling every extremity. She cleared her throat to speak, but was interrupted by a knock at the door.

Nate frowned, his eyebrows coming together, and turned around in his chair. "What is it?" he asked in a gruff voice.

"My lord, I do beg your pardon," said a muffled Crimson from the other side of the door, "but I must speak with you. It is quite urgent."

They both rose, and Nate strode to the door. He pulled it open almost with a growl. "I asked that we not be disturbed."

"Begging your pardon, my lord," Crimson said nervously, "but Captain Cressingham is downstairs. He wishes my lady to return to his house at once. He is…quite agitated. I asked him to return in the morning, but he has refused and insists that his niece accompany him home at once."

Susannah's eyes widened, and a jolt of fear coursed through her. After everything Nate had told her this evening, she had no desire to return to her uncle's house. In a concerned voice, she asked, "Why is he doing this?"

Nate looked at her over his shoulder. "I did not tell your uncle we were marrying. It's complicated, but I will work it out. Trust me. You needn't worry about a thing." Nate turned back to Crimson. "Tell the captain I will join him presently. Please direct him to the study."

"Yes, my lord."

Nate shut the door and returned to Susannah's side, resting his hands gently on her arms.

Oddly enough, his action comforted her. She opened her mouth to ask a question, but before she could say a word, Nate put his finger on her mouth to silence her, then quickly pressed his lips to hers.

She stiffened in surprise. "Oh," she gasped.

Nate immediately drew back, then closed his eyes and pressed his forehead against hers, his breathing fast and shallow. "I'm sorry. I shouldn't have done that." He held her at arm's length, his eyes cloudy with passion. "But I've wanted to since the moment I saw you."

She felt it again…that magnetic pull that drew her to him. Only now it was stronger. How long had *she* wanted this? Wanted *him*? Far, far too long. For once, she would let her heart overrule her mind. Cautiously, she stepped closer and raised her arms to encircle his neck, then suddenly drew back, unsure whether she was being too forward.

"No," he said, shaking his head. "Don't step away." He guided her arms around his neck again.

This time, she threaded them about his neck to bring him close. "Alright."

Nate's eyes flared. Then with excruciating slowness, he dipped his head toward hers. He didn't close his lids, keeping his gaze on her. Did he think she'd change her mind?

Not this time.

Popping onto her toes, Susannah closed the distance between them, and their lips fused together. The heat sent a shock through her body, warming her skin, heating her blood, causing a pulsating throb between her legs, and setting her body on fire. Nate groaned, wrapping both arms around her and pulling her tight to him. She reveled in the feel of her body against his, noticing every bend, every bulge, every hard plane of him.

"God, Susannah," he said breathlessly as his lips nibbled hers. But no sooner had they begun than he was disentangling himself from her. He stepped back, her hands on his shoulders, his hands cupping her face, and he stared deeply into her eyes. "No, not now. I want to do this slowly."

Susannah's cheeks flamed and she nodded, keeping her eyes downcast.

"Look at me, poppet."

She did, easily able to see the desire and passion in his expression, and her heart did a little dance of joy.

"We will continue this later when we won't be interrupted." Taking her hands and holding them in front of him to create distance, Nate said, "I have something very important to tell you before I speak to your uncle." He lowered his voice. "What I've revealed to you about your brother is something no one knows except Secretary Lord Sidmouth. And I mean *no one*. Under no circumstances can you tell anyone Ben is alive. Not my sisters. Not yours. Not even Tradwick. At least not until your uncle is convicted. Your brother's safety depends on as few people knowing about him as possible."

Susannah nodded her head. "I understand."

Nate gave her a hard look. "Absolutely no one can know he's alive, Susannah."

Susannah covered Nate's hands with her own and gave him a look that she hoped conveyed reassurance. "I understand. Believe me, Rain, I have my brother back. I won't do anything to jeopardize that. I assure you."

He nodded, mollified. "I'm sure you have many more questions, but I need to speak with your uncle."

A niggle of fear gnawed at her insides. "You're confident everything will work out?"

"Quite." Nate gave her a quick kiss on the nose. "Now then, I have to convince your uncle that our marriage was the right thing to do." Nate's face grew serious. "Your uncle is a vicious traitor, and he won't hesitate to hurt you. Do you understand?"

His warning chilled Susannah, causing gooseflesh to rise on her arms. But she nodded. "I understand."

Nate cupped her cheeks, giving her a resounding kiss. "I will see you as soon as I can." He pressed his forehead to hers.

A warm, tingly feeling spread throughout Susannah's entire body, but she could only nod her head.

Nate left the room, closing the door silently behind him.

Susannah turned and faced the window, her hands rubbing her arms. She could say with certainty that when they had entered this room over an hour ago, she'd wanted nothing to do with Nate. But now? Susannah looked at the fireplace, entranced by the glowing coals. Now things were different. Of course she wasn't ready to wholly give her heart over to him. There were still too many issues for her to work out in her mind. Things to resolve. Feelings to put behind her. And several unanswered questions. But of one thing she was fairly certain…Nate was indeed worthy of her trust.

CHAPTER 18

NATE STOOD before the hall mirror near the top of the stairs and took a deep breath. This was an important moment. He not only had to convince Cressingham that marrying Susannah was the right thing to do, but that his reason had nothing to do with his attraction to her.

In other words, he had to lie like the devil.

He took another galvanizing breath, wishing he were as practiced at the art as Tradwick. Surely, though, he could pull off a few more lies in order to get this bastard arrested.

Nate looked himself over in the mirror, adjusting his neckcloth and straightening his coat. He pulled at the cuffs of his shirt until he was satisfied. His stomach lay in a tangle of twisted, tightening knots, his breath short and shallow, his mind anxious and active, but he would see this through.

He had to.

Squaring his shoulders, he descended the stairs and casually made his way to his study. Upon entering, Nate was surprised to find two formidable men flanking the door and Cressingham sitting behind Nate's large, polished desk. The captain's bony hands were alternately gripping and releasing the armrests of the leather chair, his back ramrod-straight, his expression so cold and calculating that Nate would have sworn he felt the temperature in the room drop. Fear skittered up Nate's spine like ice crawling across a glass windowpane at first frost, but he pushed it down.

Bowing slightly, Nate greeted him, offering Cress-ingham a *ton*-smile. "Good evening, Captain." He gestured to the two large men standing sentry. "Who have you brought with you?"

"They work for me. That is all you need know."

Nate shrugged, feigning nonchalance. "Very well then. To what do I owe the pleasure of this visit?" Nate walked to the desk, driving all of his nervous energy into projecting a calm and controlled demeanor.

The corners of Cressingham's mouth lifted—barely. "Sit, Rainsford." He gestured to the guest chair across the desk.

Nate crossed his arms. "I will…when you get out of my seat, Captain."

Cressingham grumbled, but did as he was bid. Nate lowered himself into the worn leather armchair behind his desk and crossed his legs, tenting his hands before him. He looked expectantly at Cressingham. "Well? I gather this isn't a social call."

"Of course it's not," Cressingham growled. "I had a very interesting afternoon following our little encounter this morning."

"Oh?" Nate played dumb, raising his eyebrows and cocking his head in mock-interest.

Cressingham narrowed his eyes. "Yes. I visited Doctor's Commons to secure a special license for my niece. My *ward*. Had the most enlightening conversation with the clerk there." His tone changed, becoming falsely incredulous, and the look on his face brightened in a mocking, jesting way. "Would you believe someone had already solicited a special license on behalf of my niece? And the individual lied about whether there were any impediments. The license shouldn't have been granted, for I, as her guardian, had not given permission for her to wed."

Nate shrugged his shoulders, playing along with Cressingham's game. "That is interesting. I wish you luck proving there was no permission, though, for if memory serves," he said, tilting his head and looking quizzically at the ceiling, then back at Cressingham, "you signed settlements a few nights ago. In fact, I have a copy of them."

Cressingham said nothing, his eyes narrowing, his mouth barely curving in one corner. "So you did it." It wasn't a question.

"Did you expect someone else would?"

"Where?"

Nate wasn't sure why it mattered where the wedding had taken place. "Marleybone. My mother and—" A discordant ripple of dread forked its way through his chest. *Tradwick's name is on the marriage license.* Hell and damn. They were supposed to be enemies. How had Nate let that happen?

Cressingham tented his fingers, drumming them against each other, and stared at Nate. "You were saying?"

Schooling his expression, Nate said, "My mother and sisters witnessed the marriage."

"Your mother and sisters. Of course." Cressingham's tone conveyed disinterest and the barest hint of disbelief.

That wasn't the reaction Nate expected, and the dread drifted lower, turning his guts to liquid. He'd predicted Cressingham would unleash a tirade of condemnation, but instead, the man acted about as interested as if Nate had told him where he'd gone for luncheon. Nate didn't like it. It was too easy. He felt the first bead of sweat pop out on his forehead as if it were a cannon blast and cursed inwardly for letting his nervousness show.

Nate rose from his chair and made his way towards the small sideboard, which held an arrangement of liquors, pretending to rub his brow in a contemplative fashion. He opened the cabinet and pulled out the bottle of Baron Otard. It was not the time for cheap cognac. Pouring a drink for himself, he looked over at Cressingham and held up the bottle suggestively. Cressingham shook his head, so Nate capped it and returned it to its resting place.

Swirling the tawny beverage in the snifter, he walked back to the desk, standing before it this time. Holding up his drink in salute, he said, "To Bonaparte." He took a sip, and although it should have gone down with a warm tingle, Nate was so anxious that it burned like acid. Yet he forced himself to smile in satisfaction. "I know you're eager for her dowry. It will be yours on Friday."

At this, Cressingham scoffed. The captain's demeanor had changed, turning dark. He frowned and sat forward at the desk. "You can quit dishing me this passel of lies, Rainsford. You don't do it well."

Nate's stomach lurched, but he tried to keep his face calm. "I'm not sure I know what you're talking about, Captain. We signed an agreement. I marry your niece and turn over her dowry. I intend to keep my end of the bargain."

"And...?" Cressingham made a "go ahead" gesture with his hands.

"And...what?" Nate shrugged his shoulders, but inside, he quaked, fearful that Cressingham knew the other reason he married Susannah. *Keep playing the game, mate. All the way to the end.*

"And you now have my niece right where you want her."

It was Nate's turn to scoff. "What the bloody hell do I need her for?"

"Oh, I don't know," Cressingham said, his tone suffused with syrupy sweet sarcasm. "Perhaps to get lost between her soft, fleshy thighs? Slide in and out of her honeypot?"

Nate's face flamed, and he tried hard to keep his countenance in check. Dipping his chin down and fixing a hard gaze on Cressingham, he said, "I can get that anywhere."

Cressingham rose and leaned forward, one hand resting on the desk, the other clutching his cane. Their faces were feet apart. The captain's eyes were bright with mischief, a disbelieving smile curving his lips. "But not from your best friend's sister...not without marrying her, at any rate."

Nate took a step closer, his tone hard. "Goading me isn't going to get you anything." He had to turn this around, had to take the focus off himself. Taking another sip of cognac, he set the snifter down on the desk with a thump and glared at Cressingham. "This isn't about me, in any case. For weeks now, you've been different. Sly. Secretive. I've waited patiently to see whether you'd let me in, and you haven't, except for finally agreeing to this marriage settlement. Yet I sense that you're even trying to cut me out of that." He took up the cognac again and swirled it. "The only reason I married her is to make sure you didn't cut me altogether. She's a bargaining chip."

Laughing, Cressingham sat back down. "Maybe you're more astute than I give you credit for. I've always questioned your allegiance, but you served a purpose, so I kept you on."

"What do you mean, 'questioned my allegiance'?" Nate narrowed his eyes, trying to look contemptuous. "I have done everything you've asked of me. Hosted parties for Whig sympathizers, including that parasite Harton and his featherbrained wife, ran messages for you, willingly agreed to hand over your niece's dowry…hell, I arranged for your nephew to be killed. All to support L'Empereur." He huffed and began stalking back and forth across the well-worn rug, shaking his head to make it seem like he didn't believe Cressingham's accusations. Stopping, Nate looked at the man. "You want proof of my allegiance? Fine. This morning, you asked for one hundred thousand pounds. I am telling you, right here, right now, I will honor that request, regardless of the settlements." He swept his hand wide. "I'm not sure what else I can do to prove my loyalty. You know that I'll do anything you ask of me."

Cressingham raised a skeptical eyebrow. "Anything?"

A flicker of fear made Nate's pulse quake, but he didn't hesitate. "Yes. Anything."

The captain pondered that for a moment, then gave a satisfied nod. He rose and began to limp towards the door, but he paused when he reached Nate. Holding out his right hand, he said, "I'm happy to hear you say that, Rainsford. Let us agree, as gentlemen, that you will do what I ask when I ask it."

The captain's eyes sparkled with mischief and something else Nate couldn't distinguish, but it made his chest constrict vise-tight. Still, he had to show Cressingham that he was on his side. Extending his hand, Nate grasped Cressingham's tightly, and the men shook.

When Nate tried to let go, Cressingham wouldn't let him. Pulling Nate towards him, he leaned in and whispered in Nate's ear, "When the time comes, Rainsford, I expect you to do 'anything I ask' or someone close to you —very close—will suffer." He gave Nate's hand one more punishing squeeze, then pushed him back and let go.

Nate's brows came together in confusion, followed quickly by a flash of fear. Who the hell was he referring to? Susannah? His sisters? Mama? "I'm sure I don't know who you mean."

"It doesn't matter," Cressingham said, his tone rife with exasperation. "Just remember that your full cooperation guarantees everyone you hold dear stays safe." He shrugged. "Well, almost everyone."

The flash of fear turned into a cascade, chilling Nate's blood. "Don't you dare touch a hair on my wife's head. Or my family."

"Then do as I ask." Cressingham smiled, but Nate could tell it was false. Neither man said a word, locked in a glaring battle of the wills.

A knock sounded at the door, but Nate didn't look away from Cressingham. "Enter."

The door opened, and Crimson took two steps into the room. "My lord, I beg your pardon, but you have a guest. Reverend Acland has just arrived from Sussex."

Andrew. Blast. He'd completely forgotten about his friend coming to London to officiate the ceremony. Unfortunately, he was too late for that. Nate nodded at Crimson. "Thank you. Please install him in a guest room upstairs and see that he has everything he needs to be comfortable. I will meet him in the Green Salon after he's changed."

Crimson bowed. "Very good, my lord." He began to back out of the room, but Nate stopped him. "Captain Cressingham and his friends are just leaving. Would you please see them out?"

"Of course, my lord." Crimson stood holding the door open, waiting for Cressingham to precede him.

Before he did so, Cressingham turned to Nate. "I'll see you tomorrow morning at nine-thirty at my solicitor's office. We can go from there to the bank."

"Tomorrow?" Nate frowned. "We agreed on Friday." How the hell was he going to get a hundred thousand pounds before tomorrow? Better yet, how was he going to get his spies planted at the bank in time? He'd told Rothschild to be prepared Friday.

"Consider me lenient. The settlements stipulated her dowry of ten thousand pounds. It shouldn't take two days to get together those funds. As for the rest of what you've offered…I can wait a few days. After all, you've promised to do whatever I ask."

Nate stiffened, standing erect, even though he'd rather beat Cressingham to a bloody pulp. "I have."

Cressingham turned to leave, motioning for his henchmen to follow.

Nate bowed, even though it was to the man's back. "I will send someone over early in the morning for the rest of Miss Cressingham's things."

Cressingham gave a small chuckle, then turned around at the threshold and waggled a finger at him. "Ah, ah, Rainsford. Not 'Miss Cressingham.' Lady Rainsford. And tomorrow is ideal. She won't need much this evening." He winked. "Have a…*pleasurable* night." With another devilish smile, he quickly left the room, Crimson trailing in his wake.

Once the door clicked shut, Nate collapsed into a chair facing the fireplace, the tension in his body coiling his muscles tighter than water-logged rope. Good God. Cressingham saw right through him. He knew Nate had a *tendre* for Susannah. And as if that weren't worrisome enough,

Nate had to come up with a hundred thousand pounds? He'd need Sidmouth's help with that, for he didn't have the money. How the hell was he going to explain all of this to Sidmouth. Nate's only chance at capturing Cressingham before the man demanded that huge sum was to have his men in place when the transfer of Susannah's dowry took place.

Tomorrow.

Nate took a deep breath and blew it out, rolling his head a bit to try to loosen the strain, but it was pointless. Dropping his head in his hands, he ran through the ever-growing list of items he had to take care of that evening in order to catch the bastard. A sense of futility crept into his chest and took hold, radiating out to every part of his body like a quickly-spreading disease. Would he ever be able to capture Cressingham? Uncertainty and resignation stirred his gut. Did it matter? For the first time in his life, Nate contemplated subverting the law and killing the man himself. It would make things so much easier.

He shook his head again. No, he couldn't do that. Wouldn't do that. It'd make him no better than that bastard, and he refused to stoop that low.

At least Susannah was safe.

Susannah.

Nate's heart clenched, the futility he felt being replaced by a longing to be with the woman upstairs. The woman who was now his wife. He wished he could snap his fingers and make the rest of the world go away. As crude as Cressingham was earlier, Nate *would* like nothing more than to get lost in the depths of her heat and warmth.

Focus, you fool. With another heavy sigh, Nate raised his head and slowly pushed himself to standing. He turned towards the study door and emitted a startled gasp.

"Hello, Rain." Andrew, his red-headed friend, stood at

the threshold, still wearing his dusty, travel-stained clothes. His blue eyes ran over Nate, and he whistled. In a jocular voice, he said, "I'd say you look better than when I pulled you off that cursed field at Albuera, but I'm not so sure." The look Nate gave him must have told him how serious things were, because Andrew's brow furrowed, his tone softening. "Are you all right?"

At Andrew's comment, Nate felt something in his body break, and the enormity of his precarious situation suddenly hit him like a physical blow. He shook his head, fearing if he spoke, his voice would crack.

Shutting the door behind him, Andrew made a beeline for the liquor cabinet. He poured two snifters of brandy and returned to Nate, handing him one. Raising his glass, Andrew offered a silent toast.

"Drink. And talk."

CHAPTER 19

Susannah stood at the top of the stairs, just out of sight, and listened as her uncle left the house. A shudder of relief swept through her, now that she knew she would not have to leave Rainsford House and return to her uncle's home. Should she go downstairs and speak to Nate about her uncle's visit? She sensed that there would be much Nate had to do in order to catch her uncle, but at the same time, this was her life and she deserved to know what her uncle said…in particular, how he'd reacted to the news of their hasty marriage.

Resolved to learn the truth, she began down the stairs, then paused when she heard heavy boots crossing the hall. She peered over the railing to see a red-haired man in travel-worn clothing make his way to the study door. He stood at the threshold and exchanged brief words with Nate that she could not hear, then went into the study and shut the door.

Susannah released an exasperated sigh. Who knew when she'd find out what her uncle and Nate had discussed. Turning to return to her suite, she came face to face with Juliana, Anna, and Minnie, whom she'd not heard approach, and drew a sharp breath, putting her hand to her now-racing heart.

"Goodness, you gave me a fright," Susannah said, coming up to the first floor landing.

"We're sorry, my lady." Anna held a small, white kitten in her hands.

Confused, Susannah's brows drew together, and she looked side to side in a quizzical fashion. "Who are you calling 'my lady'?"

Anna laughed. "Why, you, silly. You're the Right Honorable Countess of Rainsford. *Lady* Rainsford."

The very idea of being "Lady Rainsford" gave Susannah a tiny thrill of excitement, but an enormous wave of dread. "Please don't call me Lady Rainsford or my lady. Susannah is perfectly fine."

Minnie looked at Anna, giving her a slight nudge. "I told you she wouldn't put up with that sort of formality, but you wouldn't listen."

Waving her hand dismissively, Juliana turned to Susannah. "Never mind that. Mama thought you might like a cup of tea and perhaps some friendly company while Nate concludes his business." She leaned over and whispered. "She also thought you'd prefer our company rather than hers. Something about us being 'less threatening'?"

Anna nudged Juliana. "Do you really need to say that out loud?"

Susannah wasn't in the mood for company and was about to decline the offer when her stomach made the most obscene gurgling sound. All three girls' eyes widened, then they burst into laughter.

"Well, whether you want sustenance or not, I think your body needs it," Minnie said. "Anna, ring the bell and ask Mrs. Friars for tea. Do you mind if we join you, Susannah?"

She took a deep breath and exhaled. Perhaps having company right now wouldn't be a bad thing. It might actually take her mind off what Nate was discussing with the other gentleman downstairs, whomever he was. Smiling, she said, "Of course. But can we have it in there," Susannah said, gesturing to the room she'd been given, "where it's quiet and comfortable?"

"The countess suite? Of course." Anna smiled, holding the mewling kitten close to her chest and rubbing its head with her chin. "This is your suite now. We never get to use it. Or even go in it. Ever since Nate moved back to Rainsford House, he's kept this room unoccupied."

"Waiting for his future countess, I daresay," Juliana said. "I admit I never thought it'd be you, Susannah, but I'm so glad it is."

Her comment warmed Susannah. They all entered the room, and Anna rang the bell, then they made themselves comfortable in the chairs and settee by the fire.

Susannah was about to ask Anna, who seemed to always have some sort of animal scurrying about, where the kitten had come from, when Juliana spoke up. "Why was your uncle here this evening? We saw him when we came back from the church. I expected that he would have been there this afternoon, but he was not. Do you know why?"

"Jules, really," Minnie admonished, shaking her head.

Susannah's mouth popped open in surprise, but she quickly closed it. Well, Juliana certainly wasn't wasting any time with questions. Not that Susannah had the answers... or answers she could share, anyway. Or could she? The only thing Nate had asked her to keep secret was the news about Ben. Still...

"You needn't worry if it's something no one else should know. We won't say anything." Anna held the kitten in her lap with one hand and, with the other, reached over and patted her hand. "We're thrilled you're part of our family now. You can trust us."

Susannah mentally scoffed, but more out of the habit of not being able to rely on people than because she didn't believe Anna.

Minnie's brow puckered. "You don't trust us?"

Without even having a chance to reply, Juliana asked, "Why not? Is it because of what happened when your brother left?"

Good lord, Juliana was far too perceptive and quick with her words. Susannah would have to be very careful what she revealed to that particular sister. Still, she was unsure about whether she wanted to wade into the "trust" pond, so she deflected to their original question. "I'm not sure why my uncle was here, but I suspect it had something to do with our marriage. It seems that Nate didn't tell my uncle that we would be marrying today."

Naturally, Minnie had no reaction to this statement, but Juliana's and Anna's round eyes looked upon Susannah.

"Well, that would explain his gruff demeanor," Juliana said. "I thought…didn't your uncle and Nate sign settlements? The two of you intended to marry anyway." Her hands smoothed her dress as she spoke. "I can't imagine why your uncle would care when it happened. In fact, I would think he'd be thrilled that it happened sooner rather than later." She smiled. "At least now he doesn't have to be responsible for you."

"And she is such a difficult ward." Anna tempered her sarcastic tone with a generous smile.

"Oh, she is not." Minnie glared at her sister in protest.

Anna rolled her eyes and sighed. "Minnie, dear, you really must learn when one is teasing."

Susannah broke in to keep the peace. "I am quite happy not to be under my uncle's thumb anymore, I assure you." She then told the girls a slightly modified version of the truth Nate had shared. How her uncle wouldn't let her live with them after her parents died, despite Lady Rainsford's repeated requests. How Nate had convinced Cressingham to let Susannah attend the finishing school and the subsequent enrollment of the triplets. How Nate had arranged for Heddy to watch over Isabela. She did not, however, speak of her uncle's suspected treason, even though Minnie already knew about it. Susannah felt the fewer people who knew, the better.

"So that's why we attended Miss Glover's school," Juliana said. "I had always wondered."

Anna shivered, her face showing disgust. "What a horrible man. And how dreadful for you and Isabela." She crossed her arms, her hard-lined posture making clear her feelings about Cressingham.

The gesture sent a ripple of gratitude through Susannah's heart. She put her hand on her chest. "Thank you."

"I'm only sorry that Mama wasn't able to convince him," Minnie said, her eyes somewhat sad.

"It wasn't that she didn't try." Susannah played with the fabric of her dress, twisting it as she always did when she was pensive or nervous. Should she tell them the truth? No, absolutely not. Directing looks at both girls, she said, "There's more to this than I can tell you, but suffice to say I believe I'm a pawn in all of this."

"Oh, but you certainly are not," Anna exclaimed. "I see the way he looks at you, Susannah. I've known it from the start…this is a love match through and through."

Susannah put up her hands in protest. "No, it's—"

A knock sounded on the door, and Mrs. Friars and one of the housemaids entered carrying a tea tray and a small plate of assorted finger sandwiches and biscuits.

"Lady Anna, I do beg your pardon," said the housekeeper as she set down the tea tray on the table before the fire, "but if you have a moment, one of the kitchen girls scalded her arm. She would benefit greatly from one of your poultices."

Anna jumped up out of the chair she occupied, squeezing the kitten so hard it meowed. "Oh no, the poor creature. Of course." She gave the furry ball a kiss. "Sorry, precious." Turning to Susannah, she smiled apologetically. "I'm sorry, I really want to stay and chat, but I need to see about this."

Susannah rose. "Of course. The household is fortunate to have someone who cares so much and who is so knowledgeable."

"That she is," Mrs. Friars said, her head bobbing in agreement. "Always willing to help anyone in need. Lady Anna has such a generous heart."

Anna's face flushed with embarrassment, but she didn't dally. She left the room with the other maid trailing her, snuggling the kitten, and discussing the accident that led to the scald.

"Lady Juliana, your mama wishes to speak with you. She's in the morning room."

Juliana sighed, but she rose. "I'll wager she still wants to contrive some sort of wedding breakfast."

"Oh no, Jules. My wager is that you've done something —or said something—to displease her." Minnie wiggled her eyebrows in wry amusement.

"I doubt that." Juliana rose and gave Susannah a quick, awkward hug. "If you'll excuse me, Susannah." She marched out of the room, mumbling under her

breath. Mrs. Friars followed, then shut the door
behind her.

Minnie met Susannah's eyes. "Well, now that they're
gone, you and I can talk a little more…privately."

Susannah resumed her seat, a jolt of uncertainty
flowing under her skin. "I'm not sure what you wish to talk
about, Minnie." *Liar.*

Minnie gave her a disbelieving look. "Come, Susannah. After everything you learned today? Your head has to
be reeling."

So what if it was? It didn't mean she wanted to talk
about it. She was still sorting through everything Nate had
told her, things that Minnie didn't know. To say nothing of
her ever-changing feelings for Nate.

"I think I know what is bothering you the most. It isn't
that your uncle is a suspected traitor. That comes as no
surprise, to be quite honest. Anna was right. None of us
liked him, and we could never understand why Natey
socialized with him, but now that makes sense. What I
think is crawling under your skin are your conflicting feelings towards my brother."

"Minnie—"

"Let me finish," she said. "You don't completely trust
him. For goodness' sake, he's been lying to all of us about
his supposed falling out with Sir Philip. And apparently
doing all sorts of secretive things for the past few years."
Minnie stirred a lump of sugar into her tea and took a sip,
her eyes watching Susannah over the rim of her cup.

Susannah took her tea and sat back in her chair, her
eyes flitting to Minnie's, but she said nothing.

"You needn't deny it. I'm sure my brother's past actions
have done nothing to earn your trust. Particularly in
regards to your brother." She reached for a finger sandwich and took a small bite, examining the tiny pieces of

bread and the contents that lay in between them. "Mmm…smoked salmon. Cook does wonders with salmon." She popped the rest of the sandwich in her mouth and dabbed her lips with a napkin. "I think, though, you need to give my brother a chance."

Susannah had thought the same thing earlier, after Nate's confession, and while her heart was clearly willing to forgive him, her head wasn't quite ready. Susannah absently sipped her tea, her eyes unfocused once more on the fireplace.

Minnie must have sensed her conflict. "He changed a lot after Langley—er, John—died, you know."

The sudden switch in topics to Minnie and Nate's deceased older brother took Susannah by surprise. She frowned slightly. "I'm not sure what that has to do with trusting Rain."

Her new sister-in-law sighed wistfully. "Nate made a promise to protect John. It's why he went to war when John did. You know what happened to my brother, Susannah. That he died with Nate." She sat for a moment, not speaking, as if gathering her thoughts, or perhaps reminiscing. "Nate has talked of that day very little, but I do know he saw John get shot. Nate, who was supposed to protect John, had let down not only his brother, but our father, who had tasked Nate with keeping our brother safe. Father died shortly after he heard the news about John. Nate took the blame for his death, too. It was a tremendous burden on Nate and he became…lost…for a little while." Minnie's voice had turned melancholy. She picked up her teacup and swirled the contents, then sipped it. "We—Mama and my sisters—were afraid we'd never see the old Natey again. And to a certain extent, we haven't. He's different now, but in a better way, and that's because of Sir Philip and your brother. They gave him purpose, Susannah."

Susannah said nothing, her heart breaking all over again as she remembered eavesdropping on her brother and Sir Philip, listening to stories of Nate's fall from grace. Drunken nights. Drunken days, for that matter. His sense of worthlessness. His despair over letting down the family. And mostly how he felt he'd let down his brother. Each time she'd heard another story about Nate's struggles, her own heart had cracked and torn, leaving her emotions shredded. Finally, because she could take no more of the disheartening news about Nate, she'd suggested to her brother that Nate needed an occupation. Something to get his mind off wallowing in his own misery, and to give him purpose again.

It seems Sir Philip and Ben had taken her advice and offered him one...catching her uncle at his evil deeds.

Setting down her teacup, Minnie leaned forward and rested her hand on Susannah's knee. "I know my brother's actions of late have seemed suspicious. Deceptive, even. But now you know why." She paused. "I also know that you feel he was responsible for your brother's death. But Ben made his own choices, Susannah. Nate may have helped him get away from your uncle, but he didn't force Ben to go to Spain."

A pang of remorse reverberated through Susannah. If only Minnie knew what he'd done for her brother...that her brother was alive. She'd tell Susannah there was *no* reason not to trust Nate.

Minnie continued. "I know my brother's character. You have to trust that he loves you and will do whatever he can to protect you. And Isabela." She sat back, giving a slight giggle. "One need only see how he looks at you to know what's in his heart."

Susannah's face flamed. She'd seen how Nate had looked at her before he left the room earlier...like a starving man and she was the feast. The thought gave her pulse a jolt as a white-hot thrill coursed through her.

"Begging your pardon, but I'm going to be forthright. The combative approach you've used with my brother so far hasn't been very successful. He has things he has to do, and he will do them. If you want to know how he's going to catch your uncle, if you want his *confidence*, you need to demonstrate that you're on his side." Minnie's grin turned devilish. "Try a bit of honey instead of vinegar and see what it gets you. And maybe think about those tawdry books we read at school."

More flames scourged Susannah's cheeks.

Another knock sounded on the door, and both women turned towards it. Without waiting for permission, the door swung open, and Nate stood at the threshold, his eyes going directly to Susannah.

Minnie didn't even wait for him to speak. She rose from her chair. "Well, I've overstayed my visit." Looking at Susannah, she gave her a wink. "Honey, remember?"

Her face going red once more, Susannah could only nod. She rose as well and followed Minnie halfway to the door.

Nate gave his sister a discouraging look as she passed by. "What have you two been talking about?"

She patted her brother on the cheek. "Nothing of consequence. If you'll excuse me, I think three is a crowd." She slipped past him and into the hall.

"May I come in?" Nate asked.

Susannah nodded, unable to speak. Her throat had suddenly gone tight. He stood there, holding his coat over his arm, wearing only his waistcoat. Nate had undone his neckcloth, exposing a bare patch of skin at the base of his throat. Susannah couldn't draw her eyes away from it, her pulse positively racing.

He entered the room, closing the door behind him, and dropped his coat on a nearby chair, then turned the key in the lock with a resounding *click*. Leaning against the door, he regarded her from head to toe, that ravenous, starving-man look coming into his eyes again. He took a deep breath and exhaled, his white-hot gaze cooling slightly.

Susannah thought about Minnie's words. *Honey, not vinegar.* In her mind, she was still angry, but only a little bit, and only because Nate had deceived her for so long. Her heart, though—that pounding, pulsing organ—had already forgiven him in spades, and suddenly, she wanted to know what it would be like to be loved by Nate. Susannah thought back to the kiss Nate had given her just before leaving the room, and a warm glow spread throughout her body, settling deep in the depths of her belly, making her limbs feel heavy.

Remembering the promise to herself that she would let her heart guide her, she walked to Nate. Their eyes locked. Without words, she placed her fingers along one side of his cheek, then the other, framing his face between her hands, wondering at the scratchiness of his day-old scruff beneath the pads of her fingers. Remembering what Nate had done to her years ago, she gently ran her thumb over his lip and relished the feel of its plump warmth.

"Thank you, husband, for saving my brother."

Then, before she could second-guess herself, she stood on her tiptoes and placed a soft kiss on his lips.

CHAPTER 20

HUSBAND. His glorious, beautiful wife had just called him "husband." Her butterfly-like kiss, a tacit solicitation, was wholly unexpected, but no matter how chaste Susannah thought she was being, Nate interpreted it as a blatant invitation.

He wanted to make love to his *wife*.

It certainly was not what he'd expected when he'd come upstairs. Nate's conversation with Andrew had been edifying. With Cressingham's latest threat, Nate felt the pressure of his burden. He hadn't intended to reveal to Andrew the secrets about his work with the Home Office, but his friend's compassion and empathy had acted like a key, unlocking Nate's overwhelming worry. He'd revealed everything that had transpired since Ben's departure, including, despite a niggle of doubt, the fact that Ben still lived. Sharing with Andrew the precarious situation he was in, the threat to his family, Ben's tenuous position, and his challenges with Susannah had lifted a huge weight off his chest. Never mind that Nate would be sacked and likely drawn and quartered if Sidmouth ever found out he'd confessed everything to his friend. Some spy he'd turned out to be.

Despite the long list of things Nate needed to do to catch Cressingham, Andrew had encouraged him to go to Susannah first and confide in her his plan to catch her uncle. "The only way to earn trust, my friend, is to give it." Andrew's words ricocheted around his brain. Nate had always held his cards close to his chest, particularly in front of his family. Perhaps sharing his plans with Susannah *would* encourage her to trust him.

So he'd abandoned Andrew to find Susannah, intending to quickly share his burden, then leave to fulfill his tasks. Instead...*this*. To hell with conversation. The other demands could wait.

Standing before Susannah, his heart bursting and his groin throbbing, Nate cradled her beautiful face in his hands, still disbelieving that the woman standing before him was his. In a husky voice, he said, "If you're going to kiss me, poppet, do it right."

Nate lowered his head to hers, and like flint, their kiss sparked. He caught it like he was tinder, and a gentle flame formed between them both. He didn't waste time repeating her chaste offering, but plunged his tongue deep into her mouth, tasting and rubbing and sucking. To his delight, she didn't shy away, but used her tongue to parry with his. Nate's hands continued to frame her face as he turned them both around, backing her against the door, his hips pinning her there, while the dips and curves and mounds of her body pressing into his sent his libido into the atmosphere.

He quickly pulled all the pins from her hair, dropping them carelessly on the floor. With his fingers, he combed through her long tresses until they cascaded down like a chocolate waterfall. Snaking his arms around her, he slid his hands over her back and around her bottom while he kissed her senseless. Her scent, lavender and roses, invaded his nostrils, nearly driving him wild. Without stopping his assault on her mouth, he reached down and swept her up in his arms, cradling her against him, and made his way to the secret door. He pulled away from her long enough to whisper, "Open it."

She did, a shy smile lighting up her face. Without releasing her, he carried Susannah through the small corridor to his suite, heading straight for his bed, where he gently lay her down. Before she could say anything, he crawled on top of her, kissing her to the depths of her soul. She responded in kind, her tongue bravely meeting his, her fingers digging into his arms. Nate's hands were everywhere. They roamed down her front all the way to her legs, then back up again, pausing at the junction of her thighs, where he rubbed her through her gown. Susannah turned her head to the side and tried to push his hand away, but he wouldn't let her. Instead, he grabbed both her hands and held them above her head.

He looked down at her, flushed and breathless. The bedside candles flickered warm light over her flawless skin, and her intoxicating brown eyes were hazy with lust.

"You're so beautiful," he whispered. "And you're mine."

Her cheeks flushed pink, and she averted her eyes.

"Oh no, you don't," he said, chuckling. "I want you to look at me." While holding her arms in one hand, he lowered his head, kissing her gently, teasingly on the lips until she met his gaze. Then, with his other hand, he drew her gown and underclothes up to her hip. "And I want to touch you."

Susannah's eyelids fluttered closed, and she moaned as Nate slid his hand over her bare skin. He marveled at its silkiness, at her luscious and inviting curves. He could no sooner stop touching her than stop breathing. Sliding his hand to her knee, he pulled her leg up and wrapped it around him, then rubbed his hand over the bare patch of her backside that her lifted skirts revealed, her skin warm and soft and utterly tantalizing.

"My God, woman," he said as he licked and sucked the area below her ear. The little whimpers and sighs Susannah made in the back of her throat were more erotic than anything Nate had ever heard. He released her arms and slid her clothing up to her waist, pulling her other leg up and around him so that she cradled his bulging organ.

All at once, Susannah stiffened.

Nate, hard as stone, gritted his teeth and took a deep breath. Lord, he was ready to lose himself right now, but he could not. Brushing the strands of hair out of her face, he kissed her. "Let me worship you, poppet."

She nodded, and he felt her body soften and relax. Thank God.

Nate continued to pepper her with kisses on her lips, face, neck, and chest. Susannah responded by wrapping her arms around him, her hips wiggling, her hands pulling at his shoulders. He would not be able to take much more of this sweet torture.

"Rain," she whispered, kissing his ear. "Please, Rain."

"Poppet." Nate cupped her breast with one hand. Damned short stays. He wanted to *feel* her. Nate pulled back and rolled Susannah onto her stomach.

She sucked in a breath. "What are you doing?"

Nate leaned over and kissed behind her ear. "Patience, poppet." His hands worked quickly to undo the fastenings of her dress and petticoat. He slid them down her shoulders a bit to reveal her short stays. With deft fingers, he unlaced her, then backed off the bed. Standing next to it, his cock bulging in his breeches, he helped her into a sitting position facing him, her legs hanging off the bed and him right between her luscious thighs.

Susannah's cheeks were pink, but she kept her eyes on his face. Nate was torn between wanting to rip the clothes off her and wanting to take his time, to savor her slowly, like a good wine. He opted for slowly, for no other reason than this was her first time and he didn't want to scare her.

If he'd had his way, he would already be sheathed deep within her.

Slowly, he pulled the fabric of her gown and petticoat off her shoulders, letting them gather at her waist. She tried to cover herself as he expected she would, but he gently took her hands and held them out. "You're beautiful, poppet. Don't hide it from me."

She met his gaze, then nodded.

Nate trailed his hands gently over her almost-bare shoulders, and he smiled as goose pimples formed on her arms. Then he looped his fingers through the shoulders of her stays, pulling the confining garment down slowly as he had her gown. Her trusting gaze never left his, sending waves of erotic heat through his body. He ran his hand up her bare arm, reveling in the warmth of her skin.

Smiling devilishly, he asked, "Would you like to undress me?"

Her eyes widened, and her face flamed again—he would never grow tired of her blushes—but she nodded. "I...I would." She bit her lip. "Is that...appropriate?"

In a sultry voice, Nate said, "I am yours, Susannah. You can ask, say, or do whatever you want."

Nodding, Susannah stood slowly and put a tentative hand to his chest. She pushed him backwards a step, but grabbed his waistcoat so he couldn't go too far.

Nate's eyes opened wide, and he let out a laugh of

surprised joy.

"I want to see all of you, Rain," she whispered, leaning close. "I want to be your *wife*." She unbuttoned his waistcoat and slid her hands underneath to rub his ribs and back.

His joy quickly turned to smoldering lust. Where the hell had she learned that? He dropped his chin and gazed at her under his brows. "As my lady wishes." But first, he had to see her naked. With deft motions, he slid her gown and underclothes down so they puddled on the floor, gliding his hands over her sweet curves and bare flesh while he kissed her neck and shoulders and ear and chin.

"I...I want you to take this off," Susannah said, trying to shuck his waistcoat off his shoulders.

Nate complied, stripping himself of his waistcoat and shirt in a matter of seconds. They stood before each other, him in breeches and boots, her in stockings, and mutually admired the view. Susannah's hand came up, tentatively, and she fingered a scar on Nate's midsection. Her hand made small circles around the imperfection before she flattened her palm to his skin.

To Nate, it burned like an erotic brand. He put his hand over hers, moving it up until her hand covered his nipple. Then Nate did the same, cupping her breast, and Susannah's head lolled back, a moan of pleasure escaping her lips.

Swiftly, Nate scooped her up and laid her on the bed, pulling at the ribbons above her knees and quickly stripping off her stockings. He wrangled himself out of his boots, cursing at the boot jack, then his breeches, and he lay down next to her. Night had fallen, making the light in the room low, and the shadows from the candles created a seductive, private cocoon. Nate cradled himself between her thighs and slid down a bit, licking and suckling Susannah's breasts. She moaned, her hands rubbing Nate's back and shoulders, her fingers threading through his hair, and Nate turned his attention to her other breast, which he quickly plundered. He put his mouth on her breastbone and, using both hands, pushed her breasts towards his face, marveling at their mass as he gently squeezed her nipples with his fingers. He then alternated between each lovely mound, kissing and suckling.

Susannah writhed beneath him, her pants and sighs turning him on more and more. Her hands entangled in his hair, and she directed his mouth to her breasts. But Nate wanted to taste her very core. His mouth went lower, leaving a wet trail of kisses as he approached the center of her stomach.

"Rain, please," Susannah begged as he swirled his tongue around her navel.

"Please what?"

She sighed before answering. "Please don't stop."

God, Nate loved hearing that, and he wanted to make her his. But first he had to taste her. His head dipped lower, and after a startled spasm, Susannah grabbed his hair, trying to pull him up.

"What are you doing?" Her voice carried slight panic.

Nate slid his arms under her legs and rested his hands on her hips, his chin on her stomach just below her navel. He gazed at her, noticing the worry wrinkle on her brow. "I'm loving you, my sweet."

"But...surely not there. Not now. We haven't even—"

He gave a deep chuckle. "Oh, yes, now." He dropped his head and kissed his way to her magical center. The scent of her was intoxicating, nearly driving him to come on the linens. But he girded himself, brushing his chin against the stiff, dark hair at the apex of her thighs. He buried his mouth into each corner of her thigh, kissing and suckling and licking, and he reveled in the sighs and moans that his wife offered.

Then Nate dove towards her center. With one long stroke of his tongue, he licked her from bottom to top, causing Susannah to grab his hair once more and sigh. Unlike before, she held his head there now, silently encouraging him to keep going. Nate's passion spiked, his blood near boiling, his cock so hard it hurt. But he was going to give Susannah the pleasure she deserved before he took any for himself.

With agile tongue and long, lithe fingers, he alternated between plunging into her hot, wet core and licking the sensitive nub that lay just above it. Lick. Stroke. Lick. Stroke. Susannah's flesh was hot, a sheen of sweat forming over her. He could feel her muscles tense and loosen repeatedly. She'd already opened herself wide to him, her knees bent and pulled back, giving Nate a perfect view of her pink petals and provocative core. His tongue and fingers began to move faster now, as he could tell she was nearing climax. In and out, up and down, his fingers and tongue working her, while he tried like hell not to come himself.

Finally, with deft strokes, Nate drew the passion from Susannah, and she came, her whole body tightening, a deep, throaty scream escaping from her lips. Nate reveled in his triumph at her all-consuming climax, but it was quickly replaced with his own need. He crawled forward, kissing his way to her head, then taking her tongue in his mouth. His cock was parked at the doorway to heaven, and Nate pulled himself up on his elbows, looking down at Susannah.

She'd come back down from her high, her breathing still labored, and she ran her hands over his chest, his waist, his hips, his buttocks. "Make me yours, Rain."

Nate growled, dipping his tongue into her mouth and cradling her with his body. He slowly pushed his shaft into her. God, she was hot and tight and divine in every way. He pulled away from her mouth, alternating between kissing her neck and clenching his teeth, for he wanted to plunge right in, but didn't want to hurt her. For what seemed like an eon, he slowly slid in, then out, then in to her hot, wet depths, at last sheathing the full length of himself within her.

"Are you all right, poppet?" Nate asked in her ear.

"Move, Rain, please. I want you to move." She shifted her hips, trying to cradle him more, moving back and forth just enough that Nate lost all reason, his instinct taking over.

With strong movements, Nate drew out, then plunged in, again and again. Their bodies glistened with sweat, their tongues tangled, his skin slapping against hers, her legs wrapped around him, holding him tight. Again and again their bodies met, melded, drew apart, then met again, until finally, Nate braced himself on his hands, his eyes riveted to Susannah's shaking breasts, and with a series of fast, powerful thrusts, he emptied his seed in her, throwing his head back as a possessive groan escaped his lips.

He collapsed on Susannah, his energy spent.

It was like he'd died and gone to heaven. Nate lay there like a dead weight for several moments, unable to do anything except twirl his fingers in Susannah's glorious hair and try to get his ragged breathing under control. Eventually, he took a deep, satisfying breath, and a smile quirked his mouth.

If this is what heaven was like, he never wanted to live again.

CHAPTER 21

Susannah lay in Nate's large, four-poster bed and marveled at the feel of the very warm, very naked man who lay behind her, his hand running in slow, hypnotic strokes up and down her leg, over her hip, down and around her belly, and, most deliciously, under her breasts, just barely grazing their swell. She was still amazed at what had just happened between them. While she'd read those erotic books at school with Nate's sisters, she'd had no clue that it could be so powerful, such a sensual tidal wave of feelings, both physical and emotional. She'd never felt so close, so connected to another human being. As she cuddled next to Nate, she could practically feel her heart growing…in admiration, in desire, and—dare she say it?—in love.

His hands made another sweeping stroke down her body, and she sighed.

Nate chuckled, the deep rumble in his chest vibrating through her. "Well, someone is content. I gather you found it…satisfying?"

Susannah smiled into the pillow. "It was…" She

paused, unable to put into words what she was feeling. Or maybe she was unwilling. It had taken a remarkably short time for her romantic feelings towards Nate to rekindle, and it scared her. She wasn't quite ready to tell him how she felt, but she supposed it didn't hurt to tell him she had thoroughly enjoyed the physical act of becoming his wife.

Her non-answer must have made him curious, for he disentangled himself and rolled her onto her back, then leaned over, resting his elbows on either side of her head, pressing his weight into her as he settled himself between her thighs. His warm, caring, curious eyes caught hers, and Susannah's heart shifted in her body. Overwhelmed with feeling, she blinked rapidly to prevent the start of tears.

"Well?" he asked, gently brushing strands of her hair from the sides of her face. "It was…?"

She bit her lip, then smiled. "Wonderful? Beautiful? Breathtaking?" A flush crept into her cheeks. She tentatively put her hands on his muscled shoulders and wiggled underneath him, delighting in the feel of the light hairs on his chest and legs scratching against her skin.

"Is that all?" He winked at her, his tone carrying mock indignation. Then he grew serious, his eyes cloudy with passion. "It was more than that, poppet. It was earth-shattering." He leaned down and placed a gentle kiss on her lips, moving to her jaw, and sliding down to her neck, where he proceeded to nuzzle her.

She pulled her shoulder up and her head down, trying to push him away, and cried out with laughter. "Stop, that tickles."

"Good. Serves you right." He dropped a kiss on her nose.

They stared at each other, then Susannah, wanting to feel him on her and in her again, threaded her fingers through his hair and pulled him to her, opening her mouth to welcome him. Their kiss was passionate, their tongues lunging and parrying. She felt him harden between her legs, and a hot, pulsing throb began deep between her own.

Nate pulled away, groaning. "Poppet, we have to stop." He dropped his forehead on her chest, panting hard. "I have things I must take care of this evening."

Susannah stroked his back, letting her fingers gently run up and down over his damp skin, as their breathing returned to normal. She didn't like that he was taking on the burden of catching her uncle by himself. At least, that's what she thought, for he hadn't said anything about anyone else assisting him. Except Tradwick. She chewed on her bottom lip. While she didn't doubt Tradwick was helping in some small way, she wasn't sure he was providing the kind of support her husband—yes, her husband—needed. After all, they'd been playing enemies for years. What she did know now was that Nate had taken a lot upon himself. For her sake, for her sister's, and certainly for Ben's. To say nothing of the guilt he had felt after the death of his brother and father. An idea began to form in her head.

"Nate?" She brushed aside a lock of hair that curled over his ear.

"Hmmm?" He sounded sleepy, and Susannah grinned. "Nate—"

Before she could continue, he popped up on his elbows and looked down at her, a broad smile on his face. "What did you just call me?"

Susannah's face scrunched up, confused. "What do you mean?"

He gently brushed his hand over her forehead, as if he were trying to smooth it. "Answer the question. What did you just call me?"

"Um…Nate?"

His expression softened. "Nate." His tone carried a sense of finality. Of satisfaction. Then he gave her a quick kiss on the lips. "I wondered if you'd ever call me that again."

"It is your name." Susannah rubbed her finger in small circles near the scar on his shoulder.

"Yes, but you've addressed me as 'my lord' for most of the last few days. Maybe 'Rain' earlier. But I haven't heard 'Nate' since we were children."

Susannah shrugged as best as she could, given that she was pinned in Nate's protective hold. "It's who you are."

A slow grin spread across his face. "Yes, it is. And I love hearing you say it. Now," he said, peppering her face with tiny kisses, "what did you want to ask me?"

"Well," she said, continuing to turn her fingers in lazy circles on his arms, "I want to help you."

It was Nate's turn to look confused. "Help me what?"

Susannah bravely met his gaze. "I want to help you catch my uncle."

Nate stiffened, his eyes going glittering-hard. "No. Absolutely not." He quickly untangled himself from her and the bedlinens and got up, walking over to the wash-stand. He splashed water on his face several times, drying it with the linen towel that hung there.

Susannah was surprised by the quick change in his demeanor. She shifted in the bed and lay on her side, her head propped up by her hand, and watched as he went about the dimly lit room collecting his clothes and putting them on. His actions were crisp and business-like, almost militant, and she had to bite back a smile as he struggled to find the hole for the sleeve of his shirt.

"Nate—"

"No." His harsh reply took her off her guard.

"He's my uncle. He's hurt me in this, too. And Isabela."

Nate shook his head and huffed. "He is a vicious man who will stop at nothing—and I mean *nothing*, including hurting you—to get what he wants. Good grief, Susannah, he tried to sell you to the highest bidder." Brusquely, he stuffed his shirt into his breeches and fastened the fall. Looking around, he snatched his neckcloth up off the floor and returned to the mirrored washstand. "If I hadn't intervened and forced your hand, you might be married to someone else right now, and what happened here might not have been so pleasurable for you."

The thought sent a shiver through Susannah. She adjusted herself into a sitting position, wrapping the bedlinen around her, her mouth turned down pensively. "I understand that my uncle is dangerous, but I am worried about you, too. Who's to say he doesn't try to do something to hurt you?"

"I can take care of myself. I have so far."

She rose, dragging the sheet with her, securing it with her fist. Coming to Nate's side as he worked at tying his neckcloth, she met his eyes in the mirror's reflection. "That's entirely my point. You have done so much, beyond what I could have imagined. I am more grateful than you know for all that you've undertaken to help my family. But it's *my* family. Surely you can see that? I want my uncle to suffer for his misdeeds just as much as you do. Probably more so. And I want my brother back. But most of all," she said, squeezing his powerful arm with her free hand, "I want to help you."

She watched as he closed his eyes, clearly at war with himself. A hopeful rush coursed through Susannah. But then he opened his eyes, still hard as marble, and continued to tie his neckcloth. "No. I cannot. You mean far too much to me, poppet, and I don't trust him."

Somehow, she had to make him realize that she was firmly on his side, supporting him. That she had faith in his ability to handle her uncle. That *she* trusted *him*. She took a deep breath. *Did* she trust him? She thought back to the previous two hours, quickly reflecting not only on the things she now knew he'd done on behalf of her family, but also on what he'd done in the face of imminent danger to protect *her*. He'd blatantly thwarted her uncle's plan to marry her off. He'd been so gentle and caring with her in bed. And even now, he was adamant that she not be put in harm's way.

Of course she trusted him. How could she not?

She thought about Minnie's advice to use honey, not vinegar. And hadn't she read in those tawdry books stories about women who used their charms to entice men? Of course, it was probably wrong it was to do that, but Susannah was desperate to help Nate. She had to get him to agree. It was embarrassing to think that she would try to entice a man with her body, but perhaps it was the encouragement Nate needed.

She let the sheet drop.

Nate slowly stopped tying his neckcloth, his eyes riveted to her naked form reflected back at him in the mirror.

Susannah's cheeks flamed. In fact, it seemed her whole body flushed, but she leaned into his side, pressing her breasts into his solid upper arm. "Of course you do not trust my uncle, Nate. However, I trust you."

He stood statue-still for a moment, saying nothing, doing nothing, hands frozen on his half-tied neckcloth. The only movement was his eyes running over her body...up and down and up again.

A strange sense of power came over Susannah as she

observed her husband's mostly paralyzed state. Perhaps this *would* work. She rubbed one hand over his chest, the other across his back, almost hugging him, and met his gaze in the mirror. "Please, Nate. Let me help you."

Clenching his jaw and screwing his eyes shut, he shook his head. "I cannot."

"One time. Even if I just accompany you somewhere." With a surge of wanton courage, she ran her hand over his backside.

Nate groaned, stepping back from Susannah. "Enough, vixen." He exhaled through his nose like an irate bull. "I can't think when you do that." He stood silent for awhile, alternating between looking at her and every other surface of the room. Frowning, he said, "Perhaps you can be of help to me. I still want to disabuse the notion your uncle has that I'm attracted to you. If we're seen in company— acrimonious company, mind you—your uncle might back down a bit." Nate sighed heavily. "You can accompany me tomorrow to your uncle's solicitor. I'm to meet with him to arrange the transfer of your dowry. But that's the only thing I'm going to let you do."

Susannah's face lit up with a smile. "Really? You'll let me come?"

Nate shook his head resignedly, his hands dropping from his neckcloth. "Yes, I'll let you come. I can't believe I'm agreeing to this. But," he said, turning to her and pointing a finger at her nose before she could speak again, "you will do everything exactly as I tell you. This arrangement between him and me began as a show of political and financial solidarity. It has to look that way even now. I'm worried that he'll try to use you in some way against me. While we may be advertising our union as a love match in the eyes of the *ton*, we have to demonstrate when with just your uncle that there is no attraction between us."

She nodded, her heart skipping with joy at Nate's display of trust in her. "I understand." She grasped his face between her hands and kissed him quickly on the mouth. "Thank you. Thank you so much for trusting me."

He wrapped his arms around her and hauled her against his body, kissing her deeply. Sooner than Susannah would have liked, he ended the kiss, pushing her away from him. "Go away, minx. You're far too tempting."

Susannah grinned. "When do we leave tomorrow?"

"Nine-thirty. The offices are on the other side of town."

"I'll be ready." She walked to the far side of the room where his red banyan hung on a valet chair. Sliding her arms into the sleeves, she turned to see Nate watching her, his neckcloth still untied. She smirked. "Are you going to finish dressing?"

He mechanically raised his hands to his neckcloth, but kept his eyes riveted to her.

Susannah smiled, cocked a suggestive eyebrow, and flashed the banyan open, then quickly pulled it across her body, securing it with the tie.

"You *are* a minx," Nate said, turning his attention back to his neckcloth.

Susannah kicked her way back to Nate's side, trying to avoid tripping over the banyan. The entire garment was much too long—both in the sleeves and in length—but it smelled like Nate and, strangely, made her feel close to him. "What are you doing this evening?"

His neckcloth finally finished, he picked up his waist-coat off the floor and shook the wrinkles out of it, then slipped it on and began buttoning it up. "I have to meet with several people tonight to prepare for my encounter with your uncle tomorrow. I believe he has men following me, so I will be taking a very circuitous route to get where I need to go. I won't be back until late."

"What can I do?"

"You can stay here and entertain my friend, Reverend Acland, at dinner, which I will most certainly miss."

"Is that who you met with after my uncle?"

"Yes." Nate smiled ruefully. "Saved my life, too. He was on the same field where John died."

Susannah squeezed his arm in sympathy. "I vaguely remember him."

He sat in a chair and pulled on a boot. "Andrew knows your situation. Even most of what I need to do this evening." Wrangling the other boot onto his foot, he gave Susannah a sideways glance. "He's a fellow Beggars Club member."

Susannah couldn't help but giggle. They still referred to that silly group they formed when they were at Eton? "Really, Nate, you still call yourselves the Beggars Club?"

Nate stood and turned to Susannah, his expression serious. "Of course we do. I hope we always will. Those men are very special to me. Every one of them. I would do anything for them, and I know they would do the same for me."

"Then why aren't they helping you catch my uncle?"

"They are. Heddy, for instance, and Tradwick."

"Yes, but they're not actually doing anything."

Nate gave her a hard look. "They're doing more than you know. And that's all you need to know."

She opened her mouth to argue, but Nate held up his hand.

"No, I won't discuss this with you at the moment. Someday I'll tell you everything, as I have promised, but I don't have time now."

They were both quiet as he finished dressing. He stood

before her, the care and devotion in his eyes easy to see, and warmth spread through Susannah's body. His hands came to her arms, gently rubbing them, then they slid over her shoulders, down her back, and to her backside, where he pulled her tightly to him. "Do not leave the house tonight. At all."

"No, I won't." Suddenly overcome with worry, Susannah threw her arms around his neck and buried her face in his chest. "Please be careful."

Nate returned the embrace, dropping a kiss on the top of her head. "I will. I know you have your clothes, but someone will be bringing the rest of your possessions from your uncle's house early tomorrow morning."

She nodded against him.

"I would also ask that you not forget our guest, or my sisters and Mama. I don't doubt the latter group will be eager to spend time with you and make sure you're comfortable."

She returned the hug. "Your sisters already have."

Nate ran his warm hand along the curve of her cheek, and Susannah leaned into it. "Now, kiss me. I must leave."

Susannah drew him down to her. Their kiss was passionate and thorough, and it scorched Susannah to her bones.

He was the one to pull away first. Then he gave her a playful slap on her derrière. "Get dressed and play the hostess, my lady."

She moved to retaliate in kind, but he evaded her and slipped towards the door. Stopping there, he said, "I expect you to be in that bed tonight." He pointed to the one they'd just left. "I'll be back late, but I want you when I get home."

Desire coursed through Susannah's body. Oh, she

would be there all right. With a dainty curtsey and a saucy grin, she said, "Yes, my lord."

After one last, longing look, he exited the room, shutting the door behind him.

Susannah's thoughts immediately went to Nate as she wondered what things he would need to accomplish that evening in order to catch her uncle, and her stomach clenched in apprehension. She sent up a silent prayer that he would make it home that evening not only unscathed, but successful in completing whatever he had before him.

Pulling the banyan fabric to her nose, she inhaled deeply, and a warm, comfortable sense of peace came over her. Trusting Nate was the right thing to do. She was glad she'd listened to her heart instead of her mind, and she smiled to herself, surprised that the promise she'd made to herself in her youth—to marry Nate—had actually come to fruition.

But her smile quickly turned to a frown. That was all well and good, but if they couldn't prove her uncle guilty of his crimes, her newfound happiness might be very short-lived. Her blood chilled, and a cold sweat came over her.

She had endured far too much emotional pain to lose the man whom she'd just won.

CHAPTER 22

LONDON, THURSDAY, MARCH 9, 1815

NATE WAS A CANDIDATE FOR BEDLAM. That could be the
only explanation for allowing Susannah to accompany him
to the solicitor's office this morning. Although, from a
strictly male perspective, she could have asked him to steal
the royal scepter and he would have agreed.

Last night, after leaving Susannah's side, things had not
gone well. Sure that Cressingham had someone tailing
him, Nate had taken alternate routes around the city, slipping in the front door of taverns and ducking out the back,
jumping into hacks and taking them to innocuous places
like the British Museum, and then blending into the loud
and drunken crowds near Covent Garden. Anything he
could think of to get Cressingham's henchmen off his
scent. He'd eventually made his way to Sidmouth, fairly
confident that he hadn't been tracked.

After telling his lordship the events over the past day,
he'd almost wished he hadn't. Sidmouth had railed at
Nate, shaming him for overstepping his bounds, for making
promises he couldn't keep, and for generally cocking things
up, just as he'd predicted. His lordship had threatened

Nate once more with cutting him out and giving the assignment to someone else.

To Nate, it was a demoralizing meeting. For the second time in as many days, he'd been dressed down like a schoolboy, and this time, he couldn't help but flush under Sidmouth's harsh-but-not-inaccurate words.

To make matters worse, Nate had also been unable to notify in person the men he'd planned to use at the bank to tell them everything was moving up a day. Instead, he'd been forced to leave messages. Nate had no idea if the men would be in place today, or if Rothschild would even let them into his bank. The Austrian had been out to the theater and subsequent parties until very late the night before, requiring Nate to leave a note with the banker's butler.

The only thing that had made his night even remotely bearable was returning to Susannah's arms in the wee hours of the morning. They'd made love passionately once more, then both fallen into a deep sleep, only for Nate to be jolted awake when the footman entered to kindle the fire in his room, causing Susannah to duck, blushing, under the covers. He'd have to speak to Crimson about the footman's gaffe.

Now, sitting across from her in the carriage, he fingered his talisman, turning it over and over again in his fingers. His agitation and anxiety sent electric shocks through his blood, and he said a silent prayer for calm. Yet his fidgety fingers would not obey.

"What is that in your hand?" Susannah asked, trying to catch a glimpse.

Nate quickly folded his fingers around the button. No one knew about it. Not even any of the Beggars.

A hurt expression came over her face. "It's alright. You

don't have to tell me if you don't want to." She forced a smile and looked out the window.

But he did. Andrew had told him that to gain trust, he had to give it. Nate opened his hand and looked at the button, silver and shiny with a dragon over the motto *veteri frondescit honore* and the number *3* for the 3rd Foot. The Buffs.

"It was John's," he said, his voice pained. "I pulled it off his coat trying to drag him to safety."

Susannah leaned over and inspected it. "You keep it with you all the time, don't you?"

He nodded. "It reminds me of my purpose."

Covering his hand with hers, she squeezed. "I hope it gives you comfort." With a half smile, she said, "I wish I had something like that from my mama."

Nate cleared his throat, pulled his hand free, and dropped the button into his pocket. "Yes, well. Enough of that." He turned his attention to the window.

Susannah said nothing for a moment. Then she leaned forward, putting her gloved hand on his knee. "You're anxious about today, aren't you?"

Today? Yes. About her being with him on this stupid, dangerous adventure? Absolutely. There was no reason for her to be there. And damn if her beauty didn't distract him like the voices of Odyssean sirens on the hunt for sailors. He hoped he could play an uninterested husband, especially because the simple act of looking at her was likely doing his male parts irreparable harm. He was so hard, he was afraid he'd blow the buttons on his breeches. Pulling his hands from hers, he folded them on his lap, hiding his massive erection, and smiled what he hoped was a reassuring smile.

She returned it, her eyes crinkling with affection, and Nate's heart slammed against his chest. God, she glowed with life this morning, her face bright and fresh and light, as if illuminated from within. Her eyes were wide and curious, the tiny curls of her dark brown hair bobbing and bouncing against the sides of her cheeks as they made their way over the cobblestone streets, and her breasts, although covered by her pelisse, were round and firm and begging for his touch. He just knew it. And, of course, he could not fail to notice her eminently kissable mouth, which looked as inviting as anything he'd ever seen.

Forget Cressingham. The only thing Nate could think about was drawing the shades over the small glass windows in the carriage and plowing himself deep into her heat over and over and over again. He ground his teeth together, fisting his hands on his knees, and looked out the window, fighting for control.

She should not have come. At all.

He could still send her away. In fact, that's what he ought to do. Lock her in the carriage and order John Coachman not to stop until he'd returned her to Rainsford House. He was about to order the carriage to halt so he could give the appropriate instructions when it drew up outside the solicitor's office.

"Susannah," Nate said, taking her hand even as she slid towards the door. "I don't think—"

She shushed him, squeezing his fingers. "Don't worry, I will endeavor to look uninterested in you. Downright hostile, in fact."

"No, that's not—"

Thomas, the entirely-too-efficient footman, opened the door and let down the steps.

Nate groaned in frustration, pulling back on his wife's hand to halt her from exiting the carriage. "I don't want you going in there. It's too dangerous. I want you back home where you're safe."

She drew up, turning to face him, her expression hostile, just as she'd promised. "If you think I'm leaving you to my uncle's devices, you're quite wrong." Her hand squeezed his hard, but Nate doubted she knew she was doing it. "You made a promise, Nate, and I expect you to keep it. Don't ruin your perfect record with me now."

He blanched. Damn if she didn't hit him right in the emotional gut with that remark.

"Fine. But you're not going into the inner office. You can wait in the receiving room."

Susannah opened her mouth to protest, her expression indignant, but Nate put his finger over her lips.

"Listen to me, poppet. Your uncle does not know that you have been made privy to our plans, and were he to find out, he might nix the entire scheme. I can't risk that. It's bad enough you're accompanying me this morning—I don't know what I was thinking last night—but in front of your uncle, you absolutely cannot know what we are about to discuss."

She blew out a frustrated breath. "Oh, very well."

He pulled her hand to his mouth, pressing his lips to her gloved fingers. "Thank you. Now, time to act like the unaffectionate, uninterested, unloving couple we are." He winked at her.

Nodding and trying not to grin, she schooled her features. Nate was impressed at how well she made herself look dour. He had only to turn his thoughts to Cressingham for his demeanor to change, his muscles to tighten, his jaw to clench. Time to get this over with.

He came down from the carriage, placing his hat atop his head, and stepped onto the curb, letting the groom help Susannah, in case anyone was watching from the window.

Wrinkling her nose, she frowned. "The stench is awful."

"We're in a 'less desirous' part of town."

Holding her handkerchief to her nose, she said, "Of course my uncle would choose solicitors here. Get me out of the street, if you please."

Nate eyed her appreciatively. She was doing an excellent job so far of being difficult and demanding, exactly what she'd been in the first few days of their meeting, and entirely consistent with someone who was in an unwanted marriage. "As my lady wishes," Nate said, his voice heavy with sarcasm.

She looked up at him briefly, and he could see she was trying to hide a smile.

"Play the part," he whispered under his breath, and she responded by frowning and turning her attention to the building before them.

He led her up a short flight of stairs into a small, dusty office decorated with dark wood, a small chaise, and floor-to-ceiling bookcases filled with cracked, leather-bound volumes in a variety of muted colors. Stacks of papers littered the floor around the edges of the room, and the fireplace, which did not put off sufficient heat to ward off the morning chill, erupted with intermittent puffs of smoke.

At the far end of the room was a large door flanked on either side by two desks, and at each, a clerk. One kept his blond head bent over his desk, scribbling into a book. The other, a tall, gangly young man with mousy hair and thin, unmanly sideburns, rose to greet them both.

"Lord Rainsford." He nodded to Nate, offering to take his hat and gloves. "Welcome, my lord. I will tell Mr. Taylor you have arrived. Your lady friend can wait here." He gestured to the chaise near the fireplace.

Nate felt Susannah stiffen, and he wasn't sure if it was because she had to wait outside or because of how she'd been addressed. Either way, Nate thought it would show best if he ignored her.

The clerk took the hat and gloves Nate offered.

Addressing him, Nate said, "I assume Captain Cressingham has already arrived?"

"No, my lord. We have not seen the captain yet this morning."

The hairs on Nate's neck stood on end. Cressingham was never late.

The clerk set Nate's articles down on the edge of his desk. "If you will excuse me, I'll see if Mr. Taylor is ready for you." The mousy-haired man bowed respectfully, then turned and gave his colleague a punch in arm, whispering, "Tea." After a quick knock, he entered Taylor's office, closing the door behind him.

The other clerk rose from his seat, his face red. "Can I fetch the miss some tea?"

Susannah shook her head. "No, thank you."

Looking almost relieved, he dropped back into his seat and returned to his work.

A moment later, the first clerk emerged from the office. "Mr. Taylor will see you now. This way, if you please." He stood by the door, gesturing for Nate to enter.

Susannah took two steps towards the inner office, but Nate grabbed her by the arm, pulling her back.

Looking down at her, he said in mock-harsh tones, "This meeting doesn't concern you. Wait there." His eyes flicked to the chaise.

She frowned, her eyes flashing. "I will not. Surely there won't be anything to discuss that I can't hear. After all, this concerns my money, and I am entitled to know what you plan to do with it."

Nate pursed his lips, unsure if she was playing this card for show in front of Mr. Taylor, or because she really thought he'd let her into the room now that her uncle wasn't an issue. Nate didn't care...he still didn't want her in there. "You heard your uncle the other day. You're not entitled to know anything. That hasn't changed simply because we're married. Now go sit down and stop being so much trouble."

Apparently drawn by their squabble, a fat man with a ruddy complexion and beady, black eyes came to stand in the doorway. "Niall, what the devil is going on here?"

The mousy clerk stiffened. "Mr. Taylor." He wrung his hands apologetically. "Nothing, sir. There's nothing going on, not really." He must have decided that introductions would be easier than explaining their argument, because he turned to Nate and said, "My lord, you recall Mr. Taylor, Captain Cressingham's solicitor? Mr. Taylor, the Right Honorable Earl of Rainsford."

Susannah coughed delicately.

"And the Countess of Rainsford. Sir." Niall's cheeks pinked.

"What's the problem, Rainsford? Can't control your wife?" Taylor sniggered.

Nate's skin crawled with disgust. He'd met with Taylor intermittently over the years and had hated him from the outset, judging him to be a wheedling, scum-of-the-earth hell-bent on litigating his client's adversaries down to their last groat.

Before Nate could reply, Taylor made a "come in" gesture with his hand, then turned and entered his office. "She can join us," he called over his shoulder. "It will all be over her head anyway."

Double damn. With Taylor's tacit invitation, she would never stand for sitting in the main office. And despite what he'd said, Nate knew nothing would be 'over her head.'

Susannah gave Nate a smug grin and brushed past him

towards the office door. Reluctantly, Nate followed, the anxiousness that coursed through his veins beginning to harden like little pebbles, weighting down his limbs.

Taylor went behind his desk, creaking and squeaking from the stays attempting to hold in his large belly. He turned and made a vague gesture to a nearby chair. "She can sit over there."

Nate made a show of seating Susannah, then frowned at the solicitor. "Where is Cressingham?"

Taylor took a seat behind his massive desk, then steepled his fingers, resting them on his immense girth. "Not here. He wouldn't attend such a trivial appointment."

A sour taste of dread formed in Nate's mouth, followed by a flash of frustration. How dare he avoid Nate, especially after making such a point of moving Susannah's money today? This was not good. He clenched his hand in an effort to regain control of his raging mood. "Trivial?"

Mr. Taylor cast a smug look towards Nate. "That's what he told me," he said, holding up a note for a moment before letting it flutter back down to the desk.

Nate felt an overwhelming urge to punch that self-righteous look off Taylor's face. Instead, he huffed. "Then it seems Cressingham is not interested in the business we discussed. I have wasted your time this morning, Mr. Taylor." He turned to leave.

"Are you sure you don't want this?" Taylor waved a note sealed with blue wax.

Curiously skeptical, Nate took it, then turned his back on Taylor so he could read it privately.

Rainsford,

Enclosed you will find instructions for the transfer of funds in the amount of my niece's dowry, ten thousand pounds. I would be most obliged if you followed them to the letter. Failure to do so will result in disagreeable circumstances.

Your obedient,

Captain Alastair Cressingham

Well, it seemed Cressingham was going to keep his word. Nate looked through the attached sheet, and his heart nearly came to a crashing halt. Cressingham wanted her dowry, but he insisted Nate draw on his *own* bank for the entire sum, not Susannah's dowry account, then immediately present the draft himself to Coutt's Bank, rather than taking it to Rothschild's bank and putting it into the account Cressingham had there, as they'd originally agreed.

The dread pressed against his chest, seemingly suffocating him, and he concentrated on taking even breaths. There was no one at Coutt's who could monitor the movement of money. Hell, he didn't even have a relationship with that bank, and he doubted very seriously he could arrange for someone to be present in time, which meant that Cressingham's money would likely go to France undetected.

No, wait. My money.

Because Nate would be drawing the funds from his own bank, it essentially put his name on the whole scheme, and he didn't doubt Cressingham had his own people ready to turn this around on Nate, making *him* look like the traitor. The fact that he was on the outs with Sidmouth right now meant that, should things go wrong, the Home Office might decline to protect Nate.

And things were going very wrong.

"Is my uncle withholding my precious dowry?" Susannah's bitter, taunting voice made her sound pleased at Nate's discomfiture, but when he looked down at her, he could see the worry in her eyes as she clutched her reticule tight.

Nate pretended to dismiss her. "None of your business, wife." He let the last word bite for effect. All the while, his mind raced with regards to his next steps. What the hell could he do? Letting any money flow unencumbered to France would be a mortifying dishonor to his dead brother and the men who'd given their lives in Spain and elsewhere defending against that bastard Napoleon. It was quite simple: if there was no opportunity to track the flow of funds, Nate didn't want to do it.

He turned to face Taylor. "As I said, I've wasted your time this morning. Good day to you."

Taylor sat forward in his chair, his eyebrows nearly meeting his oily hairline. "So you do not agree to the terms of the letter?"

"No. Cressingham and I had another agreement, and I expect him to uphold it."

Smiling slyly, Taylor said, "Then I'm to give you this." He offered Nate another letter, this one sealed in red wax. At the same time, he took a similar looking one and held it over the lit candle on his desk, letting it catch fire, before dropping it into a pail beside his desk to burn.

Nate frowned, staring hard at Mr. Taylor before cautiously taking the letter from him. He opened it, and something small, round, and metallic fell to the floor with a *clink*, landing near the instep of his boot. Nate ignored that for the moment and began to read. After just a few lines, his jaw dropped and he broke into a cold sweat.

My lord,

As I expected, you are trying to control the situation. Indeed, it is out of your control. I strongly recommend that you follow the instructions I gave you. If you're reading this letter, it is because you refused to. Reneging on your promise so soon? Very well then. I must therefore threaten the safety of those whom you hold dear.

It's quite simple, sir. You either want this individual alive or you don't. Your actions will dictate in which way I should act. And just so you know to whom I refer—

Yours respectfully,
Captain Alastair Cressingham

Nate leaned down and picked up the circular piece of metal that had fallen to the floor. It was a ring splattered with tiny red dots. Turning it over in his hand, his breath stuck in his throat.

Tradwick's signet ring.

Bloody hell.

CHAPTER 23

CRESSINGHAM HAD TRADWICK. Nate swore again under his breath. This whole scheme was spinning out of control. He shoved the ring into his pocket, his muscles quivering with an unholy rage. Crumpling the paper, he threw it into the fire on the near side of the room, then turned on Taylor.

"You bastard—"

Susannah jumped out of her chair and planted herself in front of Nate. The concern on her face was easy to read. "What is it?"

He couldn't answer her question right now. He had to get to the bottom of this. Brushing Susannah aside, he came around the side of the desk and towered over Taylor, grabbing him by his grubby neckcloth and squeezing it so hard the man's face started to turn purple. "Where is he? Tell me!"

Susannah rushed up behind Nate and grabbed his arm. "Rain, let him go. You're choking him."

He shrugged her off and squeezed his hands harder. "Good. The bastard deserves it."

"Rain." She pulled hard on his arm, her voice pleading.

"My lord, I do not know," Taylor squeaked out as he struggled for breath, "to what you refer."

Nate shook him harder. "Don't lie to me."

Taylor made a horrible choking sound.

Susannah tugged at Nate's arm once more, hard. "Love," she said. "Love, please stop."

Nate glanced at her, his beautiful wife, her face fraught with concern, and he blinked.

She squeezed his arm again. "Love, let him go. Don't be like my uncle. Please."

Love. *Love.* She'd called him her love. He looked from her to Taylor's purpling, bulging face, and something seemed to reset within him. The last thing he wanted was to be like that bastard Cressingham. Nate released Taylor, pushing him backwards into his chair.

The man fell into it, wheezing, pulling his neckcloth away from his fat neck.

Before Nate could question Taylor, Susannah took his arm, turning him away from the solicitor, and whispered to him. "Please tell me what was in that letter."

Nate took a deep breath, running a hand through his hair. Tell her? Was she mad? He couldn't tell her anything anymore. Tradwick was another prime example of how poorly he was managing this entire debacle.

Susannah's voice wavered. "Is it about my sister?"

He gave a slight shake of his head, whispering in return. "No, it is not about Isabela."

"Ben?"

"No."

"Then what?" She searched his face. "What was in that letter?"

Nate could hear the worry in her tone. His stomach

churned as he recalled his brother, dead on the ground, shot through his brain. Then, after. The massive weight of disappointment that burdened him because he had not protected John. He'd failed. He'd let his family down. And now it seemed he was going to let down his Beggars Club brothers.

With great reluctance, Nate met Susannah's gaze. The compassion she showed nearly undid him. With a deep breath, he said quietly, "Tradwick is in trouble. Your uncle has him." Nate fished the signet ring out of his waistcoat pocket and showed Susannah. "This is his."

She nodded several times, her mouth forming a hard line. "I see." She looked up at Nate, her eyes gleaming, then tightly cupped her hands over his. "We must get him back, mustn't we?" Susannah turned to Mr. Taylor, making a "go ahead" gesture. "Get on with it, if you please," she said impatiently. "Tell us where Sir Philip is."

A wellspring of warmth and love flowed from the center of Nate's body to every extremity. This strong, amazing woman was his. *His.* And he would walk through the hottest fires of hell to give her everything she deserved, most especially a reunion with her brother and sister.

Nate re-channeled his anger and bore down on the solicitor, leaning over the massive desk, contorting his face into a snarl. "Yes, Mr. Taylor. Do tell."

Holding one hand out to keep Nate away and using the other to blot his perspiring forehead with a dirty handkerchief, Taylor said, "I don't know, I tell you. I am tasked only to give you letters. That is all."

"You seemed to know that the choices I made would lead to an undesirable result for me."

Taylor pushed himself back even further into his chair, distancing himself from Nate. "I knew Cressingham was changing the bank, but I had no idea he'd taken your acquaintance. Only that he seemed gleeful about the prospect of you not accepting the new terms." He patted his sweaty upper lip, fanning himself with the damp-looking handkerchief.

"Then why the devil am I here?" Nate spat out, before turning to Susannah. "We're leaving." He took Susannah's hand and drew it through his arm, then marched her to the door, his coiled rage barely able to prevent him from tearing the heavy door off its hinges.

Taylor's chair scraped across the wooden planks of the floor, and he issued a grunt. "But my lord, I have another letter."

Nate looked over his shoulder. "I don't have time for games. If Cressingham wants to change the rules, he can do it in person." Meanwhile, Nate had to notify Sidmouth of these developments and get all possible men focused on locating and freeing Tradwick from whatever filthy, rat-infested hold Cressingham had no doubt thrown him in.

But Susannah drew to a halt, forcing Nate to stop. "We should find out what is in the other letter."

"No. I don't give a damn. He can seek me out and tell me in person, the coward."

Susannah planted her feet. "We're not leaving until we know the contents of the next letter." Her mouth was set in a determined frown. "This is your friend, Rain. A fellow Beggar," she whispered. "We will find out as much as possible before we take next steps."

Nate certainly wasn't going to let Susannah take any "next steps" with him, but looking down at her, he was touched by the concern in her eyes. Of course, she was right. It would be short-sighted to not at least know Cress-ingham's proposal, whatever it was. This case, and Susan-nah's involvement, were clearly taking a toll on his good sense.

He turned back to the solicitor, whose color had returned to normal. "Very well," Nate said.

Mr. Taylor cleared his throat. "I beg your pardon, my lord, but I must know your answer to the previous letter. Do you agree to Captain Cressingham's terms?"

Sending his own money through Coutt's would likely mean he wouldn't be able to catch Cressingham red-handed, but Nate had to get past the singular objective of nailing the captain, particularly because Tradwick's life was at risk. "Yes, very well. I agree to the terms." He would figure out a way to plant spies at Coutt's bank if it killed him.

"Excellent, my lord." Taylor looked relieved. He opened his desk and drew forth another letter and handed it to Nate. While Nate tore it open, Taylor pulled another letter from his desk and set it on fire.

Nate stopped mid-tear and gestured to the now-burning letter. "What the devil are you doing there?"

Taylor dusted his hands off. "The captain said I should destroy at once the letter that represents the choice you did not make."

Nate didn't like that one bit. "What if I change my mind after reading this one?"

"You cannot change your mind, my lord."

Nate glared at the solicitor, then unfolded the letter and began to read, allowing Susannah to peer over his shoulder this time.

My lord,

I am so very pleased that you've agreed to our new arrangements. However, if memory serves, and I assure you it does, you promised me more than my niece's paltry dowry. Therefore, please have on your person this evening <u>ten</u> drafts, each for ten thousand pounds, the sum of which equals the amount you

committed to yesterday. All drawn on your bank. Surprised? Did
you think I would give you any hint as to where I will be taking
this money? Why, to France. Perhaps. And perhaps not. But I will
not have your spies at Rothschild's waiting for me.

One hundred thousand pounds in ten drafts, all from your
bank. Anything else will be considered unacceptable, and your very
good friend will pay the ultimate price.

Oh, do not bother contacting your friends at the Home Office
about this. My men will trail you—and your family and staff—all
day. I'll know if you mean to subvert me.

It's been a pleasure doing business with you.
I am your obedient,
Captain Alastair Cressingham

"One hundred thousand pounds?" whispered Susannah, her voice full of astonishment. "Good God, where are
you going to get money like that?"

Nate didn't answer. He had to figure out how to turn
this on its head. He thrust the letter at Taylor, an idea
forming. "This is all well and good, except I cannot draw
that much from my bank in such a short period of time.
My assets are tied up in the funds. It will take a day or
two." This was a bit of a lie, but he doubted Mr. Taylor
knew.

"The captain told me you might say that. He instructed
me to tell you that he knows you can get the money and he
will not accept anything less than the funds you promised.
Today."

Nate swore to himself. He would have to do some quick
thinking to figure out how to get around this. If he issued
the drafts, Cressingham could present them to any bank,
even private ones, and Nate would never be able to follow
them all—or even one—to say nothing of Nate's financial
ruin. It would reduce his family to indigence.

But if he issued the drafts and instructed his bank not to honor them, that meant putting Tradwick's life at risk, for the moment Cressingham discovered the drafts were worthless, Nate didn't doubt he would retaliate.

Nate wanted to kick himself for his stupidity and short-sightedness in underestimating Cressingham.

Susannah patted his hand. "You have to accept the terms, Nate," she whispered. "We can come up with an alternate plan later today."

He didn't like it, but he also didn't have much choice. Resolved, he glared at Mr. Taylor. "Tell Cressingham he'll have his money. Where am I to meet him?"

"The captain says he will seek you out later this evening."

"Very well. I'll await him…and *only* him. Tell that bastard that I will not hand over the drafts to some lackey." Then, before he could do something stupid like punch the man in his ruddy face, he drew Susannah's arm through his and stalked out of the office.

Once outside, he handed Susannah into the carriage, his mind spinning like an eddy as he thought about what to do. What he wouldn't give for Tradwick's counsel right now. The one thing Nate could do was secure the bank drafts. But he also had to notify Sidmouth. The challenge was in doing so without raising Cressingham's alarm.

Once seated in the carriage, Nate tossed his hat to the floor and threw his head back against the seat, sighing with frustration.

Susannah leaned over, putting her hand on his knee. "It will all work out. I know we'll come to a solution."

Nate looked at his beautiful wife, taking in her hopeful expression, her encouraging smile. Without thinking, he dragged her to his lap, his lips coming down hard on hers. He plunged and dove into her hot, sweet mouth, taking everything she offered. She responded in kind, winding her arms around his neck and pulling him to her.

Her faith in him—and her enthusiastic response—made Nate feel more vulnerable than ever. How the hell was he going to do this? Catch Cressingham? Shield his family? Find his friend? Protect his wife?

He had to figure out a way to find Tradwick and bury the bastard Cressingham, because there was no way on earth he would give up the treasure that lay in his lap—or his best friend—for losing either one would leave an enormous hole in his heart.

CHAPTER 24

LATER THAT MORNING, Nate sat slumped in the worn leather chair in his study, his coat hanging on the back, and turned his talisman over and over between his fingers. An untouched glass of brandy sat on the desk before him. He was still trying to come up with a plan that would both satisfy Cressingham's request for the bank notes, as well as protect his family. If he let Cressingham tender the notes, it would leave his mama and sisters destitute. But he couldn't let Cressingham get away with supporting Napoleon, either. Nate ran his hands through his hair and grunted in frustration. If Tradwick were here, he would no doubt be offering up plenty of ideas. But, of course, he wasn't.

A knock sounded at the door and Nate's pulse skipped. Was it Cressingham, changing the terms on him again? He straightened in his chair, slipped his brother's button into his coat pocket, and shuffled the papers where he'd scratched down some notes under another larger sheaf.

"Come." Nate's voice was hard and authoritative.

The door opened, and his mother poked her head in.

"Nathaniel? You've been in here all morning. Is everything well?"

Nate's pounding heart slowed to a more normal pace. He glanced at the clock on the mantel, surprised at the time. He would need to leave for the bank soon. "I'm sorry, Mama. I've had much on my mind and wasn't attending."

She opened the door and came inside, walking around his desk to stand next to him. With a gentle hand, she reached out and gave him a motherly caress on his cheek, her eyes crinkling with a sympathetic smile. "The last few days have been busy for you, what with the traumatic events at Sherry's and your hasty wedding."

"Yes, it has been." Nate patted her hand, then slid it away from his face, giving it a squeeze before releasing it. He stared at the tawny glass of liquor on his desk and sighed heavily. Almost without thinking, he slipped his hand into his pocket and pulled out his brother's button, mindlessly working it through his fingers. When the hell was Cressingham going to arrive?

"Susannah has settled in well. We received all of her personal possessions from her family home just a few hours ago and have arranged everything in her suite to her satisfaction."

"Good." Was Cressingham going to wait until late this evening? What sort of assurance would Nate be able to get from him regarding Tradwick's safety? He turned the button over and over and over. What could he do without Cressingham suspecting him of breaking their bargain?

"They delivered a baby elephant with her things, but we found room for it in the coal bin."

"Mmm-hmmm," Nate murmured.

Suddenly, his mother's hands covered his hand holding the button and pressed hard. "Nate."

He looked up at her, disoriented at first, like he'd just

awoken from a dream. Then he sighed. "I'm sorry, Mama. It's just… There's a bit of business that is proving…difficult."

"Well, if there's anyone who can take care of it, you can." She gave him a reassuring smile.

Nate only sighed again in return. Could he? Would he be able to get Susannah and his best friend out of this mess? He wasn't sure anymore.

His mother squeezed his hand again. "Nathaniel?"

Without looking at her, he returned the gesture. "Never mind me, Mama." He tried to wriggle his hand free, but his mama's grip was firm.

"It wasn't your fault, Nathaniel."

He glanced at her and was taken aback at the resolute gleam in her eyes. "What are you talking about?" he asked, frowning.

She squeezed his hands again, harder this time. "John. Your father. What happened to them wasn't your fault."

He furrowed his brows. What did they have to do with his current situation? Not that she had any clue what challenges lay before him.

"It wasn't your fault," she repeated, this time more slowly.

He stared at her, puzzled. She didn't know what she was saying. Of course, it was his fault. Everything was his fault…their deaths, Ben's exile, Cressingham's threats…it was all because he hadn't done enough to protect his family and friends. He still wasn't doing enough.

"It wasn't your fault." Her voice was soft, but it carried a tone of finality.

He opened his mouth to protest, but his mother held up a hand, cutting him off.

"No, you need to hear me. You are a wonderful man. An honorable one." Very gently, she pried the worn, silver

button from Nate's fingers, then held it up to the light of
the candles that flanked his desk. "This was John's,
wasn't it?"

Nate nodded.

She sighed heavily. "Your brother was a very stubborn
individual. I loved him as much as I love you, but your
father and I always knew he was going to do whatever he
put his mind to, whether or not we sanctioned it." She gave
a half-hearted chuckle. "Goodness, one only has to think
about the things he connived from your papa and me
throughout his life. That abominable horse, Demon. It
nearly killed him on several occasions. Or that hunting gun
your father gave him when he was ten? Your father insisted
it was too large for his little body, and sure enough, the kick
from it dislocated his shoulder. And I can't forget the
curricle that he drove like mad, racing his friends on the
road to Brighton. Your brother had his own mind, his own
idea of what he wanted, and he managed to convince us,
as well." His mama shook her head, her eyes glistening in
the candlelight. "I took grave exception to your father's
mandate that you protect him, though. Just how were you
supposed to do that? I admonished your papa about that
for weeks." She smiled gently, almost wistfully. "Short of
making yourself his personal bodyguard, there was naught
you could do except be there with him. And you were, to
the very end." Her eyes teared up.

Nate reached out and clenched her free hand.
"Mama—"

"No, let me finish." She took a cleansing breath. "As for
your papa, you did not bring about his death, Nathaniel,
however much you might think you had. He'd been seen
by a doctor several times in the months before you
returned home."

"What?"

She looked down at Nate, sadness in her eyes. "He was dying. His heart simply wasn't strong. We both knew it, although we ignored it, pretending it wasn't happening. But it was. We didn't want the girls to worry, or you or John, so we said nothing." She gave another heavy sigh. "Your father was devastated by John's death, and in his initial moment of grief, he laid the blame on you." His mama paused. "He always thought you were the stronger son. Much stronger than John in character and perseverance. You almost never ran headlong into mischief like your brother did. You're thoughtful and deliberate, and—"

"Mama." She had it all wrong. He was rash and shortsighted. Didn't his current conundrum prove that?

She held up her hand once more. "And no matter what you may think, Papa had the utmost faith in you." Mama shook her head ruefully. "He didn't blame you. Deep down, he knew John's death wasn't your fault. He wanted to tell you, too, but you vanished after that night you returned home with the news. And unfortunately, your father never got the chance."

Nate stared at the glowing tips of the candles on his desk. "Why didn't you tell me any of this before?"

She turned the button over and over in her hand, not saying anything at first. Then, "I think because I assumed you knew none of us blamed you, particularly after you stopped drinking and assumed your father's dignities. I thought you returning to us meant you'd absolved yourself of guilt. But seeing you the past few weeks—and in particular the last few days—like you're a man possessed, made me wonder whether you're still holding on to the past. To your notion that you failed him"—she held up the button —"and your father in some way." She set the talisman down on the desk next to the untouched brandy. "You haven't, Nathaniel. We, your father and I, were—are—so proud of you for doing your best, and we're so grateful to you that John didn't die alone."

Nate was unsure of what to say. Was she right? Could it be that he'd done his best and it was enough?

"Just remember," his mama said, patting him on the shoulder, "you have a beautiful new bride who adores you and a family who loves you." She gave his hand one final pat. "You have always put your family first. Even when you were lost for a time after your papa's death. You've always protected us. And I know you always will."

With those words, she kissed him on the forehead, then left the study, closing the door behind her.

Nate ran her words through his head again and again. He *had* done everything he could for his brother. And although he would have taken a bullet for him, Nate was grateful to be alive, because he had Susannah to share his life with. Damned if he would let Cressingham take her away. Or his best friend. He'd spent the last few weeks playing dancer to Cressingham's fiddle, but perhaps it was time for Nate to take the strings back.

He tossed back the brandy, then thumped the glass on his desk, right next to his brother's button. Nate's hand hovered over the familiar talisman, ready to snatch it up and pocket it, just as he always had. But he did not. Instead, he opened the top drawer of his desk and slid the button into it.

It was time to move on. Time to stop dwelling in the past. Time to live up to the faith his family had in him. Time to make a new future for him and his beloved wife.

He pulled a sheet of paper from the letter stand, dipped a quill, and began to write. He had an idea of how to catch Cressingham. He just hoped he could pull it off.

CHAPTER 25

THAT EVENING, Nate sat at the head of the table in the brightly lit dining room of Rainsford House. Two footmen stood like sentries on either side of the inlaid sideboard as if they were guarding the dishes that lay there. Their dark blue livery contrasted with the sky-blue silk that adorned the portrait-covered walls. A large fire blazed in the marble hearth, and Nate watched the animated faces of Juliana and Minnie from the reflection in the mirror that hung above the mantel as the girls' voices mingled with the clinking of silver against plate.

At the far end of the table, his wife sat barely touching the second course. Fiddling with his own fork, he tried to make a show of eating, pushing the food around on his plate, but he had no appetite, his mind far from the meal before him.

Ten bank notes, each written for ten thousand pounds, were burning a hole in his waistcoat pocket. But not because tendering them would leave Nate and his family destitute. Rather, if Cressingham presented them for payment, Nate's bank would not honor them. It was a calculated risk, but one Nate felt he had no choice but to take.

All afternoon, he'd had been on pins and pricks waiting for Cressingham to show up and demand the notes. And all afternoon, there'd been a multitude of callers and visitors, more than Nate had seen in days. Each bang of the knocker had sent his pulse into a gallop. Yet none of those visitors had been Cressingham. Nate had begun to wonder whether Cressingham was going to change plans on him again and come tomorrow or the day after. He certainly wouldn't put it past him. However, any delay on Cressingham's part meant more time to search for Tradwick. His gut wrenched with worry over his friend.

"Natey. Are you listening to me?"

Nate blinked, his mind returning to the present. He turned to Juliana, on his right. She was sporting a frown, her eyes drilling into his.

"You aren't listening. What on earth is wrong with you this evening? It's as if you're somewhere else."

He flicked his gaze to Susannah, who met it briefly, then looked down again at his plate. Turning to Juliana, he tried to smile. "I'm sorry, Jules. I was woolgathering. What was your question?"

Juliana snorted. "Woolgathering." She shook her head. "If you say so." Taking up her napkin, she patted her mouth, then laid it in her lap again. "I was asking you if we would be seeing Reverend Acland again?"

"You always ask about him," Anna said, knife and fork perched over her plate, a mischievous gleam in her eye. "It seems to me you're quite partial to the man."

Her face reddening, Juliana straightened her back. "Certainly not," she said indignantly. "He was here earlier today, and now he's gone." She shrugged and turned her attention to her silver-edged plate, cutting her food into minute pieces. "I am simply curious if he's left town or is visiting other friends this evening."

"He's returned to Langley Park." Nate took a sip of wine. In reality, Nate had conferred with Andrew about the new developments as soon as his friend had returned to the house that morning. He'd asked Andrew to seek out Sidmouth and inform him about Tradwick's disappearance so the Home Office could begin searching for him. Nate also requested Sidmouth plant as many men at as many banks as he could manage. He doubted Sidmouth would agree, but he had to try. Nate didn't dare contact Sidmouth himself, so the only errand Nate had gone on that afternoon was to his bank to arrange the drafts.

Andrew had readily agreed to undertake the task, going so far as to suggest that he pack his bags and head south on the toll road, as if he really were returning to Sussex, before circling back and making his way to White-hall. Nate just hoped Andrew had been successful and Sidmouth agreeable to the scheme.

"I declare, he wasn't even here for a full day." Mama rested her hands on the side of the table, her expression softening. "Such a sweet, gentle man. I do wish he could have officiated at your marriage, Nathaniel."

Nate twisted his mouth into a wry smile. "So do I, but I can't say I mind the result. After all, instead of sitting across from my fiancée this evening, I'm sitting across from my wife." He smiled at Susannah and raised his wine glass in silent toast.

She met his gaze and blushed.

A warm heat suffused Nate's limbs and his chest constricted.

On either side of him, both Anna and Juliana sighed.

"I told you it was a love match." Anna stabbed the food

on her plate with her fork, a decidedly superior expression on her face.

Minnie opened her mouth to retort, but Mama put up her hand. "So, Susannah," she said, her expression inquisitive, "have you thought at all about any changes you'd like to make to Rainsford House?"

Susannah dropped her fork with a clatter, her eyes widening. "Changes, my lady?"

"I hardly think she's had time to think about that, Mama," Nate said.

"Well, she's mistress of this home now." Mama smiled benevolently at her new daughter-in-law. "I fully expect you to decorate it to suit your tastes."

"My lady," Susannah said, pushing her plate away, "I have no desire to make any changes. In fact, I would be happy for Juliana to continue administering the household until…" She met Nate's eyes.

The fear and uncertainty he saw in them made his stomach cramp. "Until she's ready," he finished for her.

Susannah smiled gratefully, then addressed Juliana. "If you wouldn't mind, that is."

"Certainly. I would be happy to." Juliana nodded.

A loud knock sounded at the front door. Nate's heart tripped, and he and Susannah immediately locked eyes. He could see every wrinkle in her worried forehead, and his heart pounded in his chest, echoing in his ears.

Crimson, who had re-entered the dining room, bowed and left. Mama and the girls turned their heads to the doorway, expectant looks on their faces.

"Who might that be?" Anna turned to Nate. "Were you expecting anyone this evening?"

Nate didn't answer, his attention on the voices that echoed from the hall. The only sound in the dining room was the ticking of the ormolu clock on the mantel. He breathed deeply, trying to calm his racing heart. When that didn't work, he took another fortifying swig of wine, hoping the damn drink would kick in soon.

A short while later, Crimson entered the dining room, stood just inside the door, and bowed. "My lord, Captain Cressingham is here to see you and my lady."

His mother and sisters exchanged curious glances, looking between him and Susannah.

Nate ignored them, cocking his head to the side and frowning. "Susannah?" Why the devil would he want to see her?

"Yes, my lord. He is waiting in the study. I told him you were in the middle of supper, but he insisted you would see him."

Nate glanced at Susannah, who shrugged her shoulders, her eyes wide with the same confusion Nate felt. He'd best meet with the man by himself and get this over with. "Stay here and I will see to him." He set down his wine glass and rose.

But Susannah stood quickly, pushing her chair back before the footman could assist her. "He said he wished to see us both." She walked around the table and came to Nate. She pulled him aside, away from the table, so they could talk privately. Still, she spoke in a low whisper. "I don't want you to be alone with him. I don't trust him."

Nate rubbed her arms affectionately, trying to reassure her through his touch. "I don't either, but I think he's merely trying to incite trouble. Let me meet with him and soon this will all be over." He smiled down at her, hoping his false bravado would ease her fears, for he had no illusions about the depths of Cressingham's wickedness.

Susannah, her expression clouded with worry, opened her mouth to speak, but Nate put his finger on her lips. "Trust me."

She gazed into his eyes, searching, pleading, imploring, but soon she nodded. "Yes." She put her hands on his chest, staring at his cravat, then looked up at him and nodded once again, this time more convincingly. "Yes, I trust you."

A reassuring feeling washed over him, warming him like the sun after a storm. He *loved* this woman. And he was so happy that she was trusting him. He gave her a quick kiss on the nose. Glancing at Mama and the girls, he said, "This won't take long. Please continue your meal. I'll return shortly."

"Shall we invite him to dine with us?" Mama asked.

"No," said Nate and Susannah in unison.

"Good." Mama gave a huff of relief. "I don't want to sit at the same table as that odious man, but I also don't want to be censured for rudeness. We will wait here until you return." Turning to Crimson, who had taken up his rightful place along the wall in the dining room, she said, "I believe we're ready for the next course."

On those words, Nate strode out the door and to the study.

CHAPTER 26

NATE ENTERED, stopping just inside the door. As before, Cressingham sat behind Nate's large desk, his hands resting idly on the arms of the chair.

The captain looked up, then slowly shook his head. "You're not very good at following instructions, Rainsford."

Patting his waistcoat pocket, Nate said, "I have the drafts right here, just as you asked. Now where's Tradwick?"

Cressingham waved his hand absently. "We'll get to your friend soon enough. I'm referring to my niece, whom I asked to join us."

Nate walked further into the room and crossed his arms to make himself look intimidating. "She doesn't need to be here. She knows nothing of what's happening, so I don't see the point."

The captain let out a bark of laughter. "There's much you don't see." He rose to his feet and gripped his cane, which had been resting against Nate's desk. Using it like a conductor's baton, he pointed its marbled end towards Nate as he hobbled around the desk. "You certainly haven't seen the point of anything I've been doing. You're so distracted by Napoleon and your sense of duty and that hussy you think you've married that you haven't seen at all what I really want."

Nate's blood chilled. *Thinks I've married?* He narrowed his eyes. "I suppose you'll have to tell me then." His tone was cautiously curious.

Sighing dramatically, Cressingham hobbled over to Nate. "I don't understand what it is with men these days. So thick-witted. No sense at all. Would you agree, Jarvis?"

"Yes, sir," came a deep voice from behind Nate.

Nate turned halfway around, his arms uncrossing, and his heart came to a crashing halt.

A formidable man stood just inside the door, dueling pistol in hand, the barrel pointed right at Nate's chest. The man's scarred face and severely crooked nose made him look as if he'd gone a few rounds in the ring.

"Who the hell are you?" Nate whipped back around to the captain. "What sort of stunt are you trying to pull now, Cressingham?"

"No stunt. May I introduce Mr. Jarvis," Cressingham said, tapping his cane on the wooden floor authoritatively. "He's here to make sure you...cooperate."

Nate's temper flared. Ignoring Jarvis, he took two steps towards Cressingham, grabbed him by the lapels of his coat, and shook him. "I am done with your machinations, Cressingham," he ground out.

The captain, his eyes sparkling with mockery, did not fight back. He merely lifted his cane, and Nate heard the *click* of the hammer being pulled back.

Dammit. Every fiber in Nate's body vibrated with frenzied rage, but he released Cressingham and took a few steps away, not breaking his fixed stare. The damned man had the gall to smirk. Nate clenched his teeth so hard the tendon in his jaw popped, and he fisted his hands at his sides to stop himself from punching him.

In a deceptively even tone, Nate said, "You have changed the stakes at every turn, sir, and I have begrudgingly gone along." He raised a shaking finger and pointed it at Cressingham's smug face. "However, you're sorely testing my patience. I have the drafts and am prepared to hand them over. But in return, I expect you to release Tradwick."

Cressingham eyed Jarvis, and the hammer on the pistol clicked again to half-cocked. The captain began to limp in a circle around Nate, just as he'd done the other day outside Rothschild's. "About your friend." His cane tapped the floor at regular intervals. "I'm happy to see to his release. You have, as you've indicated, done all that I asked...so far. But there's one more tiny, insignificant request I have of you." Cressingham put his thumb and index finger together and held it near his eye, as if he were inspecting something small.

Nate lowered his chin and glared, saying nothing.

"One little request," Cressingham repeated. He came to stand before Nate, his forehead raised in a regal way. "What I want, Rainsford," he said, pressing the handle of his cane lightly into Nate's chest, "is your friend."

But...Cressingham had him. Had he been lying? He looked up at the captain. "You *have* Tradwick."

Cressingham laughed derisively. "Of course it isn't Tradwick." He spat out the man's name. "He was simply a pawn to garner your cooperation."

Nate frowned, then a deep, nagging uncertainty settled deep into the center of his body. *No, surely not.*

Cressingham leaned forward, his face inches from

Nate's. "The friend I'm thinking of is an old friend. A close friend." His eyes narrowed. "A dead friend."

A weight as heavy as a boulder settled in Nate's gut, but he said nothing.

"There's no sense denying his existence." The captain stepped back, shifting his stance onto his good leg and resting both hands on the end of his cane.

Nate clenched his jaw. "What do you want?" he asked brusquely.

"The only thing I want is to see my nephew again."

Nate swore to himself. How the devil had Cressingham learned about Ben? And what the bloody hell was Nate going to do about it? If he denied Ben's existence, Cressingham would certainly take his revenge out on Nate, and quickly, to say nothing of Susannah and Tradwick. Nate didn't doubt for a minute that the captain would also retaliate upon his mother and sisters. But if he gave Ben up? He might never see his friend again, and Susannah would never, ever forgive him. *Damn you, Cressingham.*

"Perhaps you need some incentive." Cressingham turned to Jarvis. "Tell Hungerford to join us."

Jarvis stuck his head out the door, spoke a few words, then returned, his pistol still trained on Nate.

Moments later, a thin, gangly man came into the room, his face scarred with deep lines, his eyes, which darted about the room, dark and hungry. The very personification of evil.

An uncontrollable shudder swept through Nate, and something primordial and primitive came over him. A deep-seeded need to protect everyone in his sphere from this living, breathing spawn from Hell.

Instinctively, Nate headed for the door, but Jarvis met him halfway, thrusting the metal end of the gun directly into his chest, stopping him in his tracks. "I'll thank ye to stay here in yer study. Wouldn't want to ruin yer nice, clean floors with bloodstains."

Cressingham laughed, a sick, sadistic sound. He gestured to the tall man. "Rainsford, I'd like you to meet Mr. Joseph Hungerford, an esteemed man of worth who owes me a favor or two."

Nate said nothing, but fixed his glare on Cressingham.

The captain ignored him and motioned to Jarvis. "Pull the bell. Instruct my niece to join us here."

"Don't you dare," Nate threatened, but the men ignored him.

Jarvis did as he was bid, keeping his pistol trained on Nate the entire time.

When Crimson entered the room, Jarvis was standing behind Nate, the pistol hidden. Bowing, the butler asked, "Yes, my lord?"

Nate didn't say anything, but he glared at Crimson, his eyes flicking to Cressingham, hoping his trusty butler would get the message. Any message.

Cressingham left no time for that. "Tell my niece to join us at once," he said, then made a "go on" motion with his hands.

Crimson looked at Nate for confirmation.

Nate paused, then Jarvis shoved the barrel of the gun in his back even harder. *Blast.* Reluctantly, Nate nodded. "As the captain says, please, Crimson."

"Very good, sir." He bowed and turned to leave. As he walked out the door, he gave a backwards glance.

"Now we wait," Cressingham said, sighing. "I hope she doesn't take too long."

In fact, it was no time at all before Susannah entered the room, her expression fraught with worry. "Nate?" She began walking his way, but Hungerford reached out and grabbed her by the arm, pulling her to him.

"No," shouted Nate.

She stumbled as Hungerford held her arm. "Unhand me, sir," she commanded, pulling at his fingers.

Hungerford ignored her.

Cressingham gestured to his niece. "Pretty, isn't she?"

"She'll do," Hungerford said in a deep, demonic voice. He forcefully turned Susannah to face him and with his bony hand, stroked her cheek.

"Let her go." Nate's voice was threateningly dark.

"Oh, shut up," Cressingham said with a scowl.

Susannah glanced at Nate, her eyes scared. "Nate? Why do you stand there?"

"Poppet..."

Jarvis stepped to Nate's side and pressed the barrel into Nate's temple.

She gasped and her eyes widened. "No, you can't." She pulled against Hungerford, twisting to try and free herself.

Swiftly, Hungerford slid his hand down Susannah's neck. When he reached her throat, he tightened his fingers, and Susannah cried out. He pushed her entire body backwards a few steps until she collided with the doorframe and pinned her there.

Susannah wrapped her hands around Hungerford's wrist and pulled hard, her body writhing, a half-choke, half-sob escaping her lips.

Nate clenched his fists, breathing hard. "Get your bloody hands off my wife!" He stepped forward.

Jarvis grabbed Nate by the collar of his coat, moving the end of the gun to just under Nate's chin. "Not another step, milord."

The captain wagged a finger at Nate. "Ah, ah, ah... she's not your wife." He then turned to Hungerford. "Release her. You'll have her soon enough. You have an obligation to fulfill for me first."

Hungerford grumbled, but released his hold on Susannah.

She sucked in a ragged breath, then fell forward to the floor on her hands and knees, her body consumed with dry, wracking coughs and gasps of air.

Oh, thank heavens. Nate sighed with relief. God, how he wanted to go to her, to hold her, to reassure her. He hated standing there, helpless to protect her.

Susannah's coughing slowly subsided. She sat on her knees, her hands resting on her thighs. Turning to her uncle, she choked out, "What do you mean I'm not his wife?"

"Not yet, niece." He held up a dismissive hand. "First, Rainsford is going to tell me where to find my nephew."

Susannah's worried eyes met Nate's, then she turned her focus on her uncle again. "Ben is dead. I buried him. You know that."

"You buried nothing except a bloody coat."

Susannah started to protest, but Cressingham thumped his cane on the floor. "Don't bother. Rainsford won't lie now. There's far too much at stake, and he knows it." He cast a speaking glance at Susannah. "The only thing he has to do now is reveal my nephew's whereabouts."

"No," Susannah said in a scratchy voice. "Don't say a word." She looked up at Nate, and her expression nearly did him in. Tears streamed down her face. Her throat was red from being squeezed. And her eyes…her beautiful, brown eyes were desperate and pleading, begging him not to reveal anything.

"I have to." He hated doing it, but he had no choice. Before she could argue, he turned to Cressingham. "He's not been in London long, so I don't know where he resides. He picks up messages that I have delivered."

"Nate," Susannah croaked, "don't do this. Please."

But he ignored her. Ben was smart. Resourceful. And he had connections. Their situation was bad enough. Nate had no leverage, and Cressingham knew it.

"Where do you drop the messages?" Cressingham asked.

"At the Red Lion brewery, near the docks."

"Very well, then. I hope he doesn't expect it in your handwriting." To Jarvis and Hungerford, he arched an eyebrow. "Now, shall we share what we've learned about their marriage with the rest of their family before we depart?"

"Susannah isn't going anywhere," Nate said.

"You're hardly in a position to dictate terms." He inclined a head to Jarvis. "Get him moving." Cressingham walked around everyone and hobbled into the hall, his cane tapping the floor as he went.

Susannah and Hungerford followed Cressingham out the door, Hungerford's hand around the back of Susannah's neck, guiding her.

"Slowly, milord," Jarvis said to Nate, giving him room to move. "Nothing fast. I have an itchy finger." Jarvis waved his pistol towards the hall. "Just follow the captain at a nice, slow pace, and everyone will be fine."

His muscles as tense as wire, Nate slowly walked down the hall with Jarvis behind him.

Fine, indeed.

CHAPTER 27

"GOOD EVENING, LADIES." Cressingham entered the dining room in his characteristic faltering strides and walked around the corner of the table to stand before the fire.

Nate's mama and sisters dropped their cutlery with a clatter. They began to rise, but Nate made a "sit down" gesture. Thomas and Jacob, flanking the sideboard, stared wide-eyed, and Crimson frowned.

Hungerford, who had taken his hand off Susannah's neck, kept it at the small of her back, maneuvering her to the opposite side of the table from Cressingham, near the windows. Her frightened expression made Nate's gut clench.

Nate stood just over the threshold, near the foot of the table, stopped from going further into the dining room by Jarvis, who had pulled on Nate's collar. He felt the press of the pistol in his back as a warning.

Cressingham clasped his hands together. "I have an announcement. An unfortunate one, I'm afraid."

The girls had resumed their seats, looking around anxiously, but Mama stood. "Captain," she said with stiff formality, setting her napkin down. She managed to pull back the corners of her mouth to form a not-quite-polite smile. "I didn't think you were joining us." She eyed Hungerford up and down. "Or your friend." She motioned to Crimson. "More settings, if you please."

"Sit down, Lady Rainsford," Cressingham said tersely. "We are not joining you. I am here to share a delicate piece of news which, if it were to get out, could mean ruin for my niece, your son, and, by extension, your daughters."

"I beg your pardon," Mama said, the ire evident in her voice. "There is nothing you could say that would hurt my family, including my new daughter-in-law."

Cressingham's eyes glittered, and his mouth formed a twisted grin, making him look like the Devil at the gates to Hell. "Except that she is not your daughter-in-law, because she is not legally Rainsford's wife."

The startled gasps of Mama and his sisters filled the room. Susannah, primed for the news, said nothing, but her cheeks quickly suffused with heat, her eyes flashing with anger.

Nate stifled a growl and glared at Cressingham. "You're lying." He clenched his hands at his sides. "Lying through your ruddy teeth."

Cressingham feigned disappointment. "I'm afraid not. There is no record of the marriage in the parish register."

"But we all signed it." Susannah's voice, although scratchy and hoarse, had a hardness to it.

Turning to his niece, he said, "You signed *something*, but it clearly wasn't the register."

"You…you…*bastard*." Nate's muscles tensed, ready to attack. The small thump in his back, a stark reminder of Jarvis and his pistol, was the only thing that kept him in check. He barely noticed the protests from his sisters and Mama. "What did you do? Burn it?"

Cressingham put his hands out, palms up, his expression apologetic. "For shame. I did nothing of the sort. I merely visited the church to verify that this blessed ceremony took place, as any good ward would do for his niece, only to find...nothing. No page in the register with your name or my niece's."

Nate seethed with anger, his pulse primed like a cannon about to go off.

"But...what does this mean?" Mama asked. "You are not legally married?" She stood by the table, clutching the back of her chair, her face drawn tight with concern. "Why did Reverend Acland have to leave today. I'm sure he could straighten out this misunderstanding in a trice."

"I'm sure he could," Cressingham said in a capitulating tone. "In any case, this is very easy to resolve." He turned to Nate. "You and your"—Cressingham paused dramatically—"fiancée need only come with me to the church again. The special license is not in question, nor the vows. Merely the signature on the register. My friends here"—he gestured to Jarvis and Hungerford—"and I can witness the nuptials. We'll be back in time for tea."

The hairs on Nate's neck immediately stood at attention. So. *This* was Cressingham's plan. Get him and Susannah out of the house with no fuss or fight. Nate began to wonder whether or not Cressingham was lying about their marriage being invalid.

He glanced at his wife, who stood like a statue near the windows. Her face had turned ashen, proof that she, too, wasn't fooled by Cressingham's ploy.

There had to be a way to circumvent Cressingham's plan. He did *not* want Susannah leaving the house. Nate ground his teeth in frustration, mindful that he still had to save Tradwick, too. Turning to the captain, Nate said, "I will send an express to Reverend Acland and ask him to return to London to officiate. A few days won't matter." He gestured to the door, hoping he could pressure the captain to leave. "Shall we continue the rest of our conversation in private? Or do you wish to share the details of that with the ladies, too?"

Cressingham shook his head, clearly disappointed. "I was hoping you two would come quietly so we could get this rectified."

"We will get it rectified." Nate's tone was unyielding. He threw his shoulders back and dropped his chin, sending Cressingham a daring glare. "And it will be done by a rector whom I know will ensure everything is done properly."

"Shame, shame, Rainsford. You're assuming I'm comfortable with a niece who is living in sin here at your house." Cressingham gestured to Mama. "I am not."

"She is not living in sin," Mama countered. "I can assure you, Captain, your niece will be adequately chaperoned in our home until their marriage is legitimized."

"This isn't an argument I'm willing to engage in, my lady."

Mama's cheeks reddened. She clenched her hands at her sides, her eyes narrowing. Taking a step towards the captain, she pointed an accusatory finger at him. "For years, you have run roughshod over me and my family, as well as Susannah's. You have ignored my requests. Ignored what's best for your wards. Frightened off your nephew. Drove him to his grave. And yet here you are again, trying to exert your authority where you *have none*." She spat out the last few words. "I will not be intimidated by you anymore. I will not be ignored, either. Susannah is a part of *this family*"—she pounded her fist into her palm—"and no one will take her, or my son, anywhere."

Cressingham glared at Mama. "I don't take orders from others, particularly a cow-faced windbag like you."

The girls gasped.

"How *dare* you." Nate charged towards Cressingham, fists raised. "I am going to shove those words back into your mouth."

"Oh no you're not," Jarvis said loudly. He cocked the hammer of the pistol and pointed it at Susannah. "Not if you want your lady love to live."

Susannah gasped, and Minnie and Jules, sitting closest to Susannah, shrieked and jumped out of their chairs, scurrying to the head of the table.

Nate stumbled to a halt and dropped his fists.

Cressingham threw back his head and laughed. "I admire you, Rainsford, standing up for your mama like that," he said mockingly, then waved Nate away with his hand.

Jarvis trained his pistol on Nate and jerked his head towards the door.

Nate, his heart pounding in his chest, begrudgingly backed away from Cressingham and moved towards the entrance to the dining room. Jarvis half-cocked his pistol and thrust it in Nate's side.

The captain turned to Mama, took a step towards her, and forced her back. "As for you, *my lady*." His expression darkened. "I put up with your repeated requests to take on my nieces. I ignored you, hoping you'd get the message. Yet you kept nagging me, over and over and over again, until finally I sent the girls away." He took another step forward, Mama another step back. "The one thing you haven't been able to get through your thick, female brain is that I have never given a damn about my nieces, and I certainly don't give a damn about *you*." He turned his back on her, fuming.

The girls sucked in another shocked breath, and Anna's hands flew to her mouth.

Mama stood motionless, glaring at Cressingham with pure hatred, her lips drawn in a tight line.

Nate clenched his teeth. His face burned with pent-up rage, but that wouldn't suit. His mama had to back off, or the captain would hurt her or the triplets. He took a deep, calming breath. "Mama, you've trusted me, haven't you? Trusted me to protect this family?"

She looked up, somewhat startled, but she nodded.

"Trust me to take care of us." Nate held her gaze. "*All* of us."

His mama nodded again, then went to stand by Minnie and Jules, dragging Anna with her.

Nate turned his attention to Cressingham. "We married in good faith, Captain. This does not need to be rectified now. We can continue our meeting in the study while the rest of the household resumes dinner."

"No, we cannot," Cressingham said matter-of-factly. Turning to Jarvis, he said, "It's time to go."

Jarvis nodded, then called out over his shoulder into the hall.

A moment later, Nate heard the heavy tread of boots, and he stiffened. What the hell did Cressingham intend to do now?

Two large men entered the dining room. They were the captain's thugs from before, only now they were wearing soldier uniforms. No doubt to make this whole ordeal look "official."

"Natey, what are they doing here?" Anna's voice was small and shaking.

At the same time, Susannah said, "Uncle, what is this? What are you doing?"

Her pleading tone nearly undid Nate, and his anxiety

changed into full-on panic. He took an instinctive step forward, his protectionist tendencies telling him to put himself between the men and the ladies at the table, but Jarvis grabbed him by the collar of his coat.

"No, milord," he said, pushing the pistol into his back. "Yer fine right here."

Nate halted, but still yelled to the men, "Get out of my house," and pointed to the door. Jarvis poked hard with the pistol, but Nate ignored him. "Crimson, Jacob, Thomas. See them out. All of them."

But as Nate's trusty staff jumped into motion, Jarvis grabbed Nate by the neck of his coat again and propelled him forward. He raised the pistol so it could be seen by everyone in the room and pressed the muzzle into Nate's temple. "It seems I have to threaten your master, too." Glaring at Nate's staff, he said, "If you'll be kind enough to leave these gents alone, I'll not find it necessary to make a mess of your master in this lovely dining room."

A chorus of cries echoed around Nate, and Juliana and Anna began weeping.

"Sir," Crimson said in shock, then to Jarvis, "here now, release his lordship."

While the other two footmen backed against the wall, Mama, in tears herself, ordered Cressingham to stop, and Susannah pleaded with her uncle to release Nate.

"Take care of the ladies, Crimson," Nate ordered breathlessly. "Mama, it will all be fine."

The two "soldiers" came up behind Nate and grasped his arms, pulling them behind his back so forcefully, Nate cried out in pain. Sweat broke out on Nate's brow, and he cursed under his breath. The men quickly coiled rope around his wrists to keep them behind his back, then one of them stood to the side and extended his foot, while the other man pushed Nate from behind.

He fell forward onto the floor, landing with a thud that knocked out his breath. As he struggled for air, his sisters cried out in protest, their high shrieks and vigorous sobs tearing a hole in Nate's heart.

Jarvis pressed his knee painfully into Nate's back, and one of Cressingham's thugs began tying his hands together in earnest. Nate winced at the taut rope digging into his skin, but refused to give Cressingham the satisfaction—or his family more worry—by protesting. When they were done, the men grabbed Nate by the arms and pulled him to standing.

Cressingham looked at Hungerford, gesturing to Susannah. "Now then, if you'll bring her with us, we'll get this all straightened out."

"No," Minnie shouted, dashing from her spot at the table to grab Susannah by the hand and pull her back.

Cressingham's lips curled in a snarl. "Get your bloody hands off my niece."

"No." Minnie's determined gleam made Nate momentarily proud, but Cressingham's threats were very real. It would be enough for Nate to worry about Susannah.

"Let her go, Min," Nate said, still out of breath. "I'll take care of her."

His sister looked at him, pain in her eyes, but to Nate's relief, she dropped Susannah's hand.

Cressingham's scornful laughter filled the room. "Indeed. I'm sure you will take good care of her."

Minnie glared at Cressingham, but she quickly moved to stand near her distressed sisters.

Cressingham looked pointedly at his mama and sisters. "Your precious Rainsford must be held to account for what he's done to my niece, stealing her fortune and virtue." With a nod to the uniformed men, he said, "Out. Now."

"Don't you dare remove my son or daughter-in-law from this house." Mama's voice was as hard as iron.

Cressingham laughed. "Shut up, or the next time you see your son, he will be dangling from a noose."

Mama fisted her hands at her sides, but Nate saw her begin to crumble.

"Take care of the girls, Mama," Nate said, as he was forcibly pushed from the room. "You trust me. I know you do."

His mama was clearly trying to be strong, but Nate heard her sob, and Anna rushed to her side, consoling her. Nate turned his head a bit more to meet Minnie's gaze and gave her a speaking look. He needed her to be the strong one, the smart one, the one who would hold the family together until this was resolved. She must have gotten his silent message, because she nodded, then set about reassuring Mama and her sisters.

Cressingham led the procession outside and down the steps. Turning to one of the "soldiers," he said, "Stay here. No one in or out." The man nodded and took up his position by the door.

The captain proceeded to the awaiting carriage. He gestured to Jarvis, who shoved his gun into his breeches, then awkwardly thrust Nate into the vehicle.

Nate managed to right himself on the seat without using his hands. Hungerford pushed Susannah in next, then climbed in himself, his manacled grip still holding her by the arm. Nate tensed, his breathing ragged as he took in Susannah's fearful expression and occasional winces of pain.

Cressingham stood outside with Jarvis, giving orders. As he did so, Hungerford's hungry and lecherous gaze roamed over Susannah.

Nate's body tensed, coiled like a spring.

Susannah squeezed her eyes shut and leaned away, but Hungerford grabbed her by the chin, forcing her to look at him. "Don't shy from me."

She opened her eyes, her expression hardening. "Don't touch me," she said furiously.

"Get your filthy hands off my wife, you bastard," Nate growled. His fingers twitched with the need to beat the hell out of Hungerford.

He gave Nate a glance, his mouth forming an evil grin. "Did Cressingham tell you why she's here?" He reached up and stroked Susannah on the cheek, but kept his eyes on Nate, taunting him. "She's to be my traveling companion. Among other things."

Susannah gasped.

Hungerford looked down at her and forced his mouth down on hers.

Like hell! Nate exploded in a burst of fury. With a ferocious roar, he lunged at the man, head-butting him and landing on his lap. Nate swung his head into the man's face repeatedly, using his skull and shoulders to inflict whatever damage he could. He would kill the bastard if he had to bite him in the neck and watch him bleed out.

Hungerford shouted, letting go of Susannah to block Nate.

Susannah began beating Hungerford too, using her puny fists to bash him wherever she could.

"Jarvis!" Hungerford called out. "Jarvis!" He pushed Nate off him and against the opposite seat, then grabbed Susannah by the hair and twisted sharply.

She cried out, pulling at Hungerford's hands. "Let go of me."

"Release her," Nate yelled. He drew up his booted foot, but the carriage door flew open and Jarvis wrapped his arms around Nate's leg before he could make contact with

Hungerford's groin. Jarvis pulled so hard he dragged Nate onto the floor of the vehicle, half his body hanging out of it.

Nate grunted at the impact, thrashing his legs to keep Jarvis at bay. But Cressingham's other "soldiers" managed to encircle his legs. They jerked him out of the carriage and threw him to the ground.

Nate landed on his back, his head bouncing on the pavement, and he groaned at the hard fall. Jarvis straddled him, his weight grinding Nate's bound hands into the cobblestones. Nate grimaced, clenching his teeth, and swore, bucking as hard as he could to unseat Jarvis but, with his hands behind him, could not. A mixed crowd of young, well-dressed men, older workers in tattered clothing, and scrawny boys with dirty faces all surrounded Nate, mocking and jeering at him.

"Get 'im."

"What'd he do?"

"Tear 'im up. Bleedin' nob!"

Nate glared at Jarvis in the dim lamp light. "Get off me, you pig," he said through his teeth.

Jarvis merely laughed. "Goodnight, my lord." He raised his fist, then slammed it into Nate's face.

His world went dark.

CHAPTER 28

"Nate? Nate, can you hear me?" Susannah was trying very hard to be someone Nate could depend on, if he ever woke up. More tears dripped down her face. She raised her shoulder to wipe them as best she could, but with her hands bound behind her, there was little she could do.

"Nate, please answer me."

The only sounds were Nate's even breathing mixed with the noise of children's whines, crying babies, sharp-tongued women, and drunken men in the rooms around them. The stench of human excrement and decay that wafted up from the narrow streets nearly made her retch.

Susannah looked around for the hundredth time. Last night, her uncle and Hungerford had taken them deep into the rookeries of London, ultimately giving up the carriage when the streets became too tight. They'd dragged Susannah past dirty hovels while Jarvis followed, Nate hefted over his shoulder. Despite passing numerous people, no one met Susannah's eye, and when she'd asked for help, she'd received a powerful slap from Hungerford, forcing her into silence.

She'd been led into a narrow building and up a rickety set of stairs to the small, attic room where she now sat on the floor, hands and feet tied, leaning against the back of her slumped-over husband. His hands and feet had also been tied, and another rope had been cinched over their arms and around their waists, to ensure they couldn't move.

After her uncle left last night, Susannah had begged Nate to wake, but the knock on his head must have been severe, for he never stirred. She'd then cried out pleas to the people she could hear through the paper-thin walls in the rooms around her, yet no one came. Her fingers had lost feeling hours ago, and her back ached from the awkward position she'd been sitting in all night. She'd shivered in the dark, dank, chilly room, despite Nate's body warmth, but now she didn't even have the energy to do that. Judging by the light around the edges of the covered windows, it was early, just after daybreak, and she could start making out the contents of the room around her.

"Nate." God, if only he would wake and answer her. She needed to know he was all right. She'd felt his slow, even breathing all night, but hearing his voice would reassure her tremendously.

Susannah had never seen anything so frightening as Nate's limp form tossed back into the carriage last evening, his head bleeding profusely either from being thrown to the cobblestones or from that man punching him. She'd reached out to help him, but her uncle, sitting beside her in Hungerford's place, had pulled her back, ordering her to leave him alone. Then he'd laughed. Susannah had never heard such a crazed, maniacal sound, and it had sent chills through every fiber of her body. With the blinds drawn in the carriage, she hadn't been able to see where they'd gone, but she'd listened to the sounds of their trip. They hadn't crossed bridges of any length, nor had she heard the sounds of water, so they must be north of the Thames. Still, that gave her no comfort, for the rookeries were dangerous and vast.

The light in the room continued to brighten, and Susannah could now see two chairs scattered about. One was lying on its side and broken, the other standing near a small, rickety table that had been pushed up against the wall to her left between the windows. An open stair along the wall facing her led down to the lower floors, and two smaller windows were situated to her right, on what she assumed was the back side of the row house.

The street noises grew louder, and Susannah took a steadying breath, trying to bolster her heavy heart. They would get through this. They had to. She finally had in her life the man she had always loved. What's more, he loved her. She was sure of it, even if he hadn't said the words. She wanted nothing more than for the two of them to walk away from this and live their lives together, but... Her heart clenched, a near-sob escaping her lips. If sacrifices had to be made, she knew he would make them. And she would do the same.

Susannah shuddered at the thought. She called to him again, leaning her head back, trying to make gentle contact with his, but his was slumped forward. "Nate? Nate, wake up."

He groaned, the vibration rumbling through Susannah's body, and a flood of relief washed over her, her heart bursting with hope. Fresh tears popped from her eyes as she called his name again, unashamed of the desperate note in her voice. "Nate. Nate? Wake up."

More groaning.

Susannah decided to try a different tact. She took a deep, steadying breath, concentrating on removing all anxiety from her voice. In what she hoped was a come-hither tone, she said, "Wake up, my love. I want to hear you. Come on now…open your eyes."

Nate grunted and sighed, then took a deep breath, which caused the ropes around Susannah's waist to pull taut.

"Good God," he mumbled. "Ugh, my head."

Susannah whispered a prayer of thanks through trembling lips. "Hello, my love." She turned her head to try and see him out of the corner of her eye.

He was still slumped over, shaking his head like he was trying to clear it. Then he brought his head up, moaning loudly. "Susannah." He sucked air through his teeth. "God, my head. I can't see very well. Everything is…distorted."

Oh, good heavens. "That dreadful man hit you last night. I'm right here behind you." She inclined her head so it touched the back of his. "See? Right here."

Nate grunted. "My hands and legs are bound."

"Mine, too. What hurts you?"

"Everything. Mostly my head. And my vision is blurry." He moved around, pulling taut the ropes that encircled them, then turned his head towards hers. "Are you well, poppet?"

Of course she wasn't, with numb hands and a stiff back, not to mention their precarious position, but she was the last person to tell him that. "Yes, love, I'm fine. None worse for the wear."

"Do you know where we are by chance?"

"In one of the rookeries north of the Thames, I think. I didn't hear any of the usual sounds of the river last night."

Her comment was met with silence. She felt him

breathing behind her, his breaths coming fast and deep. Yet her pulse ticked up. Why didn't he answer?

"Nate." She wiggled against him. "Nate, don't fall asleep again." Her voice quivered with worry.

"I'm awake." He began to struggle between them, where their hands were tied. "We have to get out of here. Ben. And Tradwick…" The desperation in his voice made Susannah wince.

"Wait. You've been unconscious all night. Give yourself a little time to adjust."

The tenor of his voice changed, becoming frantic and worrisome. "There is no time. Cressingham may have your brother as we speak. And God knows what he's done with Tradwick."

Susannah turned her head. "A few minutes won't matter. Take some deep breaths. It might clear your head."

He did as she instructed, then groaned again as his head fell forward.

Susannah's breath hitched. "Nate? Nate?" she asked, her pitch rising.

There was no response. Merely the movement of Nate's chest as he breathed in and out.

"Nate?" Had he passed out again? She craned her head to see, but her hair, coming loose from its pins, obstructed her vision.

"I'm sorry." Nate sniffed. "So very sorry for putting you in this situation."

She tried to speak, but her throat constricted. Was he *crying*? Good God, surely he did not feel guilty for what her uncle had done to them? As if Nate had had an alternative.

She found her voice, and it was firm. "Nathaniel Edward Kinlan, don't you dare blame yourself for what has happened. It is entirely my uncle's fault. Do you hear me?"

Nate didn't say anything for a moment. Then he gruffly cleared his throat. "John would say the same thing, you know."

His brother. Susannah's chest clenched, but she kept her tone strong. "I'm sure he would." She knew in her heart that Nate had to confront that day in Spain. Goodness, he'd succumbed to its horrors when the riots started at Sherry's house. More than that, though, it was time for Nate to discard the mantle of guilt that he wore like a stifling cloak each and every day.

She spoke in a near-whisper. "What happened in Albuera?"

Again, he was quiet. Then he gave a scornful laugh. "Albuera. God, that day. I'll never forget it. Ever." He sighed heavily.

Susannah gave him the space and time to speak, simply waiting patiently until he was ready.

"We came under fire from the French. I was leading a company of men around the right flank, and John was in the middle, coming right up Boney's center. Boney had lines of snipers taking out our men, our horses. But we kept pressing. Then...chaos." He stopped, his breathing ragged. "It began raining. Positively pouring buckets of rain—and then the hail started. We couldn't see anything. Not the columns of men in front of us. Not our hands in front of our faces. Men without helmets were knocked out by the apple-sized hailstones." He breathed deeply, his voice steady and even. "Naturally, our rifles wouldn't fire. Our cannon went quiet. Yet somehow Boney's men were able to keep at it. The entire battlefield turned into a wet, muddy slog of..."

Silence.

Susannah waited for several moments, but all she could hear was his labored breathing. In a soft voice, she said, "And John didn't make it."

Nate sniffed. "I got shot in the side. It wasn't mortal. And quite honestly, my well-being was the last thing on my mind. The only thing I gave a damn about was finding my brother. I'd promised my father I would protect him, you see. So I had to find him. And, unbelievably, on that mess of a battlefield, I did."

Tears pricked Susannah's eyes.

"That feeling of seeing him standing there, waving at me? God, it was euphoric. I was jubilant, so happy to see he was safe." He laughed, but his laughter quickly died away. "Then…"

She knew what happened next. A tiny flame of ire sparked inside her. Nate had to accept that he wasn't to blame for John's death. He could not divine the hand of God, ordaining who lived or died, just as he could not control her uncle's actions now. "Your brother's death was not your fault." Susannah's voice carried conviction. "You cannot blame yourself. And it was entirely unfair for your father to put that kind of responsibility on you. Were you to have died in John's place, we never would have married. We never would have shared that beautiful night together. You never would have saved my brother." Her voice trembled with passionate conviction. "And I would likely belong to someone other man right now, instead of the man that I love so *very* much."

Her appeal was met with silence.

The muscles under her skin jittered with apprehension. Had she said too much? Not enough? She wasn't sure if his silence was damning or affirming.

"My love?" she asked in barely a whisper. She turned

her head, but her dratted hair blocked her view. Please let him not be mad at himself. At her.

Nate chuckled, the vibrations shaking her body. "I love you, Susannah." He sighed. "You and my mother must have been talking. She said the very same thing to me yesterday morning." He cleared his throat. "John would be proud of me for what I've done for your family, and so would my father."

Susannah nearly cried with relief. "Of course they would. You are the best man I know, Nate." The pride in her voice was unmistakable.

"And I had better continue to make him proud. And you." His voice lowered. "You are the best woman I know, and I promise you—"

"No, Nate. No more promises." She wouldn't let any more vows hinder their future together.

"I promise to love you, Susannah. That is a promise I can keep."

It was Susannah's turn to sniff, her heart overflowing with affection. "I promise to love you, too. Because I do."

"Good. That's settled. Now," Nate said, becoming businesslike, "we need to get out of here."

"But your head. How is your vision?"

"I still have no peripheral sight, but at least I can make out what's in front of me."

Susannah felt an odd pressure on her fingers, and she tensed. "Something is touching my hand."

Nate chuckled. "It's me. I'm stroking your fingers. They're quite cold."

"I'm not surprised. They're probably blue. I haven't felt them for hours."

Nate began to shift around between them, his movements intermixed with the occasional curse. As he wriggled, he said, "That was quite devious of you, my love, distracting me like that so I'd sit still."

"You're welcome. What are you doing?"

He issued an oath, followed by more fidgeting. "I'm trying to free my hands."

"My bonds are too tight." She had tried to free herself when they'd first been brought here, but hadn't been able to. She hated being so helpless...so useless.

"I think I've got it...just a few...more..."

The heavy tread of footsteps sounded on the stairs, and Susannah gasped. Nate's movements stilled, and a moment later, three men seemingly rose through the floor as they came into the attic room.

"Well, well. It seems we're all awake now."

CHAPTER 29

CRESSINGHAM, the bastard. Nate stopped squirming against Susannah. He'd managed to free his hands just as their damned footfalls sounded on the stairs, but he'd not had time to untie his feet, and he and Susannah were still bound around the waist by another rope.

"If you can, create a distraction," Nate whispered to her.

"What?" She turned her head towards him.

"Create a distraction," he hissed.

"Oh, how charming," Cressingham said with syrupy-sweetness. "The lovers are exchanging words."

Nate, still facing away from the stairs, craned his neck to see who else had come up with Cressingham, but the sharp movement caused a twinge, and he had to lower his head. He cursed under his breath. Jarvis's fists had affected him more than he thought.

Heavy footsteps sounded on the wooden floor boards, and Nate blinked, trying to get the room, which had started spinning again, to stop. He looked up slowly to see Cressingham standing before him, thumbs tucked into his waistcoat pockets. Just behind him were Jarvis and Hungerford.

The captain looked from Nate to Susannah. "Good morning, esteemed guests. I hope you spent a comfortable night."

Nate's blood simmered under his skin. Contemptible prig. "It was lovely, the hospitality second to none. I'll be sure to recommend your accommodations to all my friends." His tone bit with sarcasm. Behind him, Susannah shifted on the floor, and Nate's frustration grew. If only he could *see* her. He had no peripheral vision, and what he could see wasn't very sharp.

Cressingham laughed at this remark, then limped over to the table and snagged a chair. Dusting it off with his fingers, he leaned on it, testing its sturdiness. He must have been satisfied, for he sat down, relaxed against the back, and crossed his bad leg over his good one, his cane held loosely in his hands.

"My, my, you are full of wit this morning, aren't you, Rainsford?" He shifted in the chair, and it creaked. "You'll be happy to know that your friend—your *other* friend—has agreed to meet us at the Spread Eagle."

Susannah stiffened behind him, but Nate squeezed her fingers in a silent plea to stay quiet. He just hoped she could feel it.

"Now then," Cressingham said, his tone upbeat, "the only thing left to do here is to kill you and give my blasted niece to Hungerford." He motioned to Jarvis. "Untie her and hand her over."

"Don't you dare touch her." Nate's voice cut through the room.

Jarvis and Hungerford laughed at them.

"Have I told you what's in store for her?" Cressingham stood, cane in hand. "I don't think I have." He tapped his cane on the floor authoritatively. "She's going to be Hungerford's companion as he sets out for New South Wales, taking her far, far away from me"—he deepened his voice—"and everyone she holds dear."

Susannah sucked in a sharp breath. "No, I won't go."

Nate's nostrils flared. "You will do no such thing," he ground out. Behind him, Susannah's body shook with little tremors. Nate grasped Susannah's hands tightly, willing her to be comforted by him. He would get her out of this. He had to.

Jarvis strutted over to them and began to unwind the rope from around Nate and Susannah. Nate clenched his hands together, schooling his racing breath. He wanted to strangle the life out of Jarvis, but he couldn't. Not now. The timing wasn't right. Carefully, Nate fisted the loose rope that had encircled his wrists in his fingers, his pulse pounding. He hoped Jarvis didn't notice his hands were free.

When Jarvis finished with the rope around them, he untied Susannah's feet, then pulled her upright and thrust her at Hungerford, her hands still bound behind her.

Nate shifted on the floor. He turned his body and tucked his legs under him, resting on his heels. His rackety pulse careened through his veins. Nate now faced the men, his hands hidden behind him.

"As promised, Hungerford," Cressingham said, then put up a warning finger. "But you can't have her until you've killed her brother."

"Don't you dare," Susannah said in a venomous voice.

But Nate threw his head back and laughed loud and long, hoping it sounded sincere. It better, because the action nearly made him fall over with dizziness.

Everyone's eyes turned to him, even Susannah, their expressions perplexed.

Nate lowered his head, his laugher subsiding. He locked his blurry gaze on Cressingham and shook his head scornfully. "You're a coward, Captain, ordering other men to do your dirty work. Afraid to get blood on your hands?" He was desperate to say something—anything—that would set Cressingham off-balance.

Cressingham's eyes narrowed, but he scoffed and waved his hand dismissively. "Of course not. I merely detest the mess. Not to mention it's entirely too damned convenient when there are men like him willing to do it for me." He gestured to Hungerford.

Nate tsk'd. "Some protege of Boney you turned out to be," he said in a blistering tone.

Cressingham shrugged his shoulders. "He was an excuse to get rich—and a distraction for you I'll bestow a token gift on L'Empereur, which will ensure I can live in France in peace and be protected from righteous English bastards like you. Which reminds me." He hobbled over to Nate, leaned down, and dug in Nate's breast pocket until he found the drafts. "Thank you." His eyes gleamed.

Turning to Hungerford, Cressingham said, "Bring her with you to wait for my nephew, but no violence—yet. I want to see the reaction on my nephew's face—and hers— when he realizes his fate." His smug look made Nate want to hit him.

Susannah issued a chorus of protests, and Hungerford shook her, saying, "Shut up, you shrew."

Nate cast Cressingham a dark look. "Don't you dare remove her from this room or you'll regret it." He was not making an idle threat.

Ignoring Nate, the captain motioned to Susannah, adding, "You best untie her. Where you're going, she can't look like a prisoner." He pulled a small knife out of his boot. "Use this to keep her in line."

Hungerford took the knife and slid it into his own boot. Then he began to untie Susannah.

Her eyes met Nate's and sparkled with fire. A surge of hope swept through him. They might be able to pull this off. Mindful not to draw attention to himself, he mouthed the word "distraction" then held his breath. Would she get his message?

A flicker of recognition crossed her face, and Nate wanted to shout in triumph. Instead, he breathed deeply, his body coiled and ready to strike. With as much stealth as possible, he slid the ropes from his hands and hid them beneath his boots.

Susannah, embracing her role, complained loudly to Hungerford about his treatment of her, which he ignored. He untied the last knot and as soon as her hands were free, she ran for the stairs.

Bravo, my love!

"Wench!" Hungerford reached for her, but missed.

Jarvis, who stood closer to the stairs, took a step and lunged for her. He managed to snag her dress, fisting it in his hand. "I've got her," he said breathlessly.

"No," Susannah exclaimed.

Both men tried to grasp her wrists, but Susannah fought like a banshee, arms swinging, legs kicking, teeth biting, and screaming like a woman possessed. Cress-ingham limped over to assist, and the three men swore out loud, trying to restrain her.

It was the distraction Nate needed. He quickly untied his legs. Once free, he stood. The blood rushed to his head and he swayed slightly. Reaching out, he steadied himself on the wall.

He took two steps towards the fray, his arm raised and ready to drive into someone's face.

Hungerford caught Susannah in the cheek with his fist,

delivering a knock-out blow. She dropped to the floor, unconscious.

"Bastard," Nate cried out, but he didn't slow down. Changing his tactic, he lowered his arm and plowed his shoulder into Jarvis, the nearest target, shoving him into the wall as hard as he could. Jarvis's head made contact, severely denting the plaster, and his body rattled against the wall as Nate collided into him. Nate grabbed Jarvis's pistol, hanging from his breeches, but the man clenched Nate's wrist and wrenched it. Nate swore and dropped the pistol. "Damn you," he ground out, and slammed Jarvis into the wall once more. Jarvis moaned as he fell to the floor, and Nate collapsed on top of him.

Behind him, Cressingham shouted at Hungerford. "Take her and go."

No! Nate couldn't let her leave. He pushed himself off Jarvis and scrambled to his feet as Hungerford hoisted Susannah over his shoulder and raced down the steps. The captain slowly hobbled towards the stairs after them.

Jarvis groaned, still on the floor.

Nate turned his head to see Jarvis reaching for his pistol. *Hell and damn.* Nate quickly doubled back and leaned down to grab the weapon, but Jarvis's grip was already around the stock. Nate slammed his boot on Jarvis's hand, grinding it into the floor, and Jarvis swore, releasing the pistol. Nate kicked it out of the way and dropped to his knees. "Your turn, you bastard." He thrust his fist solidly into Jarvis's jaw and the man fell over, unconscious. A twinge of satisfaction came over Nate. That was for threatening his sister.

Nate turned back to the captain, who stood at the top of the stairs. It was high time he paid for what he'd done. Nate scrabbled on his hands and knees and reached for Cressingham, but the captain side-stepped him and swung out with his cane. Nate recoiled and put his arm up to block it, but the cane still made contact, hitting him hard in the ribs.

Oomph. Nate moaned and fell onto his backside, his hand covering his side. He tried to take a breath, but a searing pain shot through his chest. Had Cressingham cracked his rib? "Damn you," he said through clenched teeth.

Cressingham laughed. "Then I suppose I'll see you in Hell." He started down the stairs, one hand on the wall for balance, his quick step-hop, step-hop indicating he had to take them one at a time.

Nate blinked several times, trying to catch his breath. He *had* to stop Cressingham. Ignoring the pain in his side, he scrambled to his knees, a sense of desperation giving him a burst of energy. He could do this. He reached out for the collar of Cressingham's coat. *Just a few more inches.* But before he could grasp it, Jarvis tackled him, throwing all of his weight onto Nate. *Oooof.* Nate groaned, the wind knocked out of him.

Jarvis rolled Nate to his back and straddled him, his narrowed eyes full of spite. "Going to do it right this time, you prig." He threw punch after punishing punch to Nate's upper body.

Nate gasped, wincing at each hit. He put up his arms to block Jarvis's attack, but the man's fists came hard, one smashing into Nate's cheek, the other delivering a stunning uppercut to Nate's jaw, a third connecting with his good side. Nate cringed with each powerful punch, the awful agony permeating every bruised and battered fiber within his body. His vision began to darken around the edges, and a flurry of panic made his pulse thump. *I'm going to pass out.* Nate glanced to the side, desperate for any leverage against Jarvis, and saw the dull glint of metal nearby.

I can do this. I must *do this.* With renewed vigor, Nate clenched his teeth and planted his feet on the floor, determined to get out from under the bastard this time. When Jarvis drew back to punch again, Nate pounded his fist into the fall of Jarvis's breeches.

Jarvis threw back his head and issued a high-pitched cry, his hands lowering to cup himself.

Nate thrust his pelvis upwards as hard as he could and swung his arm into Jarvis's chest, unseating him. Jarvis fell to his side, hands still covering his groin, moaning. Nate flipped onto his hands and knees, crawled towards the pistol, and grabbed the stock. He stood and turned around, pointing the weapon at Jarvis's dark, hate-spewing eyes.

"Shoot." Jarvis's whispered dare was laced with malice.

I will, but not you. Nate moved swiftly towards Jarvis, flipping the pistol in his hand as he did so, and slammed the stock into the side of his head. *Crack.*

Jarvis didn't issue a sound. Blood pooled around his head and his rapid breathing soon slowed, then stopped altogether.

Nate dropped the pistol and lay on the floor, panting from exhaustion. He turned away from Jarvis, the man's injury too fresh a reminder of his own brother's death. *Susannah. Ben.* He couldn't rest yet. Groaning, he rolled onto his side and got onto his hands and knees. Nate grabbed the pistol and tucked it into his coat pocket. He struggled to stand, forcing himself to breathe slow and deep so he wouldn't pass out. Like an old man, he hobbled to the stairs, hands out for balance. His vision was still slightly blurry and even more distorted as his eye began to swell shut. He licked his lip, tasted blood, and spat on the floor. His head was pounding, his side ached with each breath, and every muscle in his body protested the slightest movement. God knows what he looked like, but there was no time to clean himself up. He descended the steps to the ground floor and out the door.

A few women in tattered clothing, their hair stringy and greasy, sat on steps leading into the building across the way.

Nate stumbled over to them. "Where am I?" Nate asked hurriedly, wincing at the sound of his croaky voice. "What part of town?"

They looked up, and their expressions registered shock. "Law, mercy, look at 'im, Peg," one of the women cackled, first elbowing her friend, then pointing to Nate. "'E's right dun up, 'e is."

Nate frowned, then grimaced from the pain. "Yes, thank you, I've had a bit of a rough night." He put out a hand to lean against the wall. "But where is this place?"

"Saffron 'ill, milord," answered Peg, a gap-toothed woman with streaks of dirt on her wrinkly face.

He nodded. "And which way is the Thames?"

All three women pointed down the alley.

"Did you perchance see a tall man carry a brown-haired lady in that direction a few minutes ago, followed by a man with a cane?" Lord, he hoped they had.

"Aye, milord," said the first woman. "The long shanks cull been draggin' a smock faced gentry mort yond 'ere." She pointed down the alley as before.

Nate closed his eyes, sighing with relief. He quickly stepped towards them from the narrow, muddy lane, his arm holding his side, and dipped his head. It was all he could do. "Thank you, ladies." His words came out in a *whoosh*. He reached into a hidden waistcoat pocket, drew out a guinea, and held it up.

The women brightened, their eyes sharp.

"Do me a small favor?"

"Aye, milord. Anyfing." Peg held out her hand.

Nate nodded. "I need one of you to call down to Bow Street to collect the man in that building over there." He gestured across the alley from whence he'd came. "His name is Jarvis. Also tell Bow Street that Rainsford is at the Spread Eagle." Nate enunciated all the names.

The women nodded.

Nate held the coin higher. "And two of you to make sure no one but Bow Street goes in or out."

"'E's a clinker, is 'e?" asked the first woman, rubbing her hands together appreciatively.

"Yes. A dead one," Nate replied.

"Oh, 'es dead, is 'e? 'E won't go nowheres," Peg said. "On me honor." She thrust her hand out again.

Nate drew two more coins from his pocket and held them aloft. The women squealed with delight. He cocked his head inquiringly. "Repeat it to me, get it right, and I'll give you each one."

Peg stood. "On me way to Bow Street. Jarvis, 'es dead." She pointed at Nate. "Yer Rainsford. At the Spread Eagle." Then she pointed to the building behind Nate. "No one in er out."

Nodding, Nate placed the coins in their hands. The ladies shrieked and tucked their coins away. Peg darted down the lane, and the other two ladies situated themselves on the doorstep across the way, crossing their arms and scowling. Well, at least they weren't running off with his coin...yet.

Nate turned and gingerly made his way down the alley. *I'm coming for you, my love.*

CHAPTER 30

After Nate left the rookery, it had been devilishly hard to hail a hack. The tradesmen, workers, and domestics that crowded the pavement had stared pointedly at his bloodied, bulging face and stained and tattered clothing, and it wasn't until Nate had held a guinea in the air that a jarvey finally pulled up, willing to take him on.

Nate was grateful for Cressingham's blunder when he'd revealed the location of where to meet Ben. But when he'd gotten into the hack and inspected Jarvis's pistol, his gratitude changed to anger. There was no powder in the pan. Jarvis had threatened Nate's life with the pistol, and it was nothing more than a club. The revelation made Nate's hands shake with fury as he held the near-useless weapon, his mind racing to come up with a strategy against Hungerford and Cressingham that didn't involve shooting one of them.

The hack stopped a few doors down from the Spread Eagle and Nate peered out the small window. Gracechurch Street was busy at this time of the morning. Taking a fortifying breath, he opened the door and lumbered down to the pavement, ignoring the aches that penetrated every part of his body, then tossed up a coin to the driver. "Wait here. There's more where that came from."

"Yes, milord." The crusty driver doffed his cap, eyeing Nate nervously.

Ignoring the stares from the people on the pavement, Nate lowered his head, trying to look as inconspicuous as possible without wincing, and strode to the Spread Eagle.

He entered into noisy chaos. Two stages were preparing to leave for Kent, and the main room was busy with passengers caching a last drink, porters carrying bandboxes and portmanteaus, and the owner shouting and barking orders to seemingly everyone.

Keeping his head down, Nate ascended the stairs to the dimly lit hallway that led to the hired parlors. They afforded privacy, something Cressingham would want.

There were six parlors in total, and every door was closed, indicating all were likely occupied. Cressingham had to be in one of them. Taking a deep breath, Nate went to the first door on his right, his hands shaking with fear of what he might find, and gingerly lifted the latch. It opened without challenge, so he let it quietly drop back into place. Cressingham would have surely locked the door. Silently, Nate moved to the next door, opposite the first, and tried the latch. Unlocked. He went to the next one, and the next.

At the fourth parlor, he reached out for the latch, when the door suddenly opened and a burly man stood on the threshold.

Nate gasped in surprise, his heart thudding in his chest like a drum. He took a quick step back, then turned away from the occupants so they couldn't see his marred face.

"What's this?" asked the man, his voice hard and full of accusation. "This parlor is taken."

A woman's voice sounded in the background. "What is it, Percy? Who's there?"

"Begging pardon," Nate mumbled over his shoulder, "wrong one."

"I should say so." The man huffed, then turned back to his female companion. "Come, my love. We must depart."

Nate pretended to inspect the numbers on the two remaining parlor doors as the man and his squawking lady made their way down the hall and then, finally, down the stairs.

He looked over his shoulder. They were gone, and the door they'd left open shed a little more light into the hall, not that Nate needed it.

Ben and Susannah had to be behind one of the two remaining doors. He tried the latch to his right. Unlocked. That left the room on his left. He stood before the door, his breath coming in fast pants. He reached out, his hand shaking, and tried the latch.

Locked.

Nate drew in a deep, shuddering breath. His entire body quivered with tension, his pulse skipping under his skin. He prayed that Cressingham had Ben and Susannah behind this door. Reaching into his pocket, he drew out the pistol and gripped it by the barrel as he had earlier. One more deep breath. *Steady, mate.*

He banged on the door a few times. "Service, milord," he said loudly in his best Cockney accent.

From the other side of the door, Nate heard deep voices and the sound of boots on the floor. He adjusted his grip on the pistol, tensed and ready. This *had* to work.

The lock clicked, the latch lifted, and the door opened a few inches, revealing a sliver of Hungerford's face.

Yes.

Before Hungerford could react, Nate shoved his

shoulder into the door, opening it wider, raised his arm, and brought the stock of the gun down on the top of Hungerford's head, hard.

Instinctively, the man's hands covered his head. Nate swiftly kicked, his boot connecting with Hungerford's groin, and the man dropped to his knees, moaning.

Pushing the door open even more, Nate slammed the pistol onto Hungerford's head again and again until the wretched man collapsed to the floor, out cold. He took a shuddering breath.

"Nate! Watch out," Susannah shouted from further inside the room. "Uncle has a knife!"

Nate glanced up in time to see Cressingham charging him, dagger in hand, and no limp.

What the deuce? Nate's shock at seeing the captain striding swiftly across the room slowed his own reaction time. Cressingham slashed with the knife. Nate tried to side-step him but tripped over Hungerford's prone form and landed on the floor with a grunt, the pistol skittering out of reach.

Cressingham pounced on Nate, half straddling him, his blotchy face and frenzied eyes giving him a crazed look. "You're dead, Rainsford." He raised his arm and plunged the knife at Nate. "A dead man!"

Nate gripped Cressingham's wrist with both of his hands to push the blade away. The damned man was strong, and Nate felt the first press of panic building inside him. *He can overpower me.*

"Nate, I'm coming," Susannah said from across the room.

The captain used his weight as leverage to push the knife closer and closer to Nate's chest, and Nate didn't dare try to look at his wife. "Stay...where you...are." He could barely get the words out.

A drop of Cressingham's sweat landed on Nate's face and he winced. Nate pushed against Cressingham's arm with all his might, but the knife came closer and closer, the glint of the blade shining brightly. The muscles in Nate's arm were shaking...weakening.

Susannah cried out, and Nate flicked his eyes to her. She was seated in a chair near the fireplace, her eyes filled with worry.

She's safe there. Nate wanted to tell her, but he didn't think he had the breath. His arms shook from the exertion even more, and Cressingham must have felt it, because his expression changed. The bastard was *gloating* like he was going to win.

I can't let him.

With a deep breath and a mighty grunt, Nate heaved against Cressingham, shoving the man off him and to the floor. Nate rolled over and dropped onto the captain's beefy body before he could get away, grasping his wrists tightly. Digging in with his nails, Nate twisted the captain's skin like he was wringing a wet cloth. The knife clattered to the floor, and Nate gave him a wicked half-smile. "Bastard. It's my turn."

Cressingham ground his teeth, trying to wrest his hands free, and the two men grappled. They rolled over and over on the floor, knocking against furniture as each attempted to get the upper hand, snarling and growling like a pair of wild dogs. The captain, using his solidly built frame as leverage, wrestled Nate onto his back. He broke Nate's hold and immediately went for Nate's throat, clamping it tightly with both of his bony hands.

Nate tried to suck in air, but there was none. He pulled at Cressingham's hands, writhing like a trapped snake, but his growing panic made his movements jerky and ineffectual.

Cressingham's dark, devilish eyes stared down into Nate's. "You pompous prig," he said through clenched teeth. He gave a huff of laughter and spittle shot out of his mouth and onto Nate's face. "You thought you'd best me, did you?" He squeezed harder as sweat dripped off his puffy, red face like condensation on glass.

Susannah.

Stars began to flicker in Nate's vision and the edges grew dark. He felt an immense pressure in his face and head, pounding like rapid cannon fire, and a shock of realization came over him.

He was going to die.

He did not have the strength to best Cressingham. He would be letting down his friends and his beautiful, precious wife. A tear trickled out of his eye and he closed them, hoping the captain hadn't noticed.

But he had. He chuckled and said in sing-song, "Oh, the poor little spy is crying. Boo-hoo." Eyes gleaming, he added, "You're going to lose your precious wench and her bastard brother, as well."

"No he's not," Susannah said, her voice gritty.

Nate's eyes flicked up, looking over Cressingham's shoulder.

She stood behind him, her wrists dripping blood, holding his cane like a cricket bat. Before Cressingham could turn around, she swung it hard. It whistled through the air and the marbled end hit the middle of Cressingham's back with a solid *thwack*.

The captain cried out, wincing, and he loosened his hold on Nate's throat.

Nate sucked in a breath of air, then coughed. *Bloody well done, poppet.*

Cressingham glanced over his shoulder, frowning. "You

damnable wench. I should have killed you years ago," he snapped.

Susannah had already drawn back for another swing. Nate clenched the lapels of Cressingham's coat so he couldn't move and in a scratchy voice, whispered, "Again."

She let the cane fly and it made contact with his back once more. The captain flinched, but didn't cry out. "Let him go, uncle," she panted, winding up a third time.

Cressingham turned to face Nate again, his eyes burning with hatred. He raised his fist to strike, but Nate, still holding the man's lapels, thrust him to the side, then climbed on top of him.

"Susannah, the cane," he whispered, extending one hand while the other pressed against the captain's neck. He could feel Cressingham's resistance building. Nate didn't have much time before the man would be able to topple him.

She quickly reached over and handed the cane to Nate.

He grabbed the ends and pressed it against Cressingham's neck.

The captain took hold, pushing against Nate, and the two men wrestled for control.

Then Nate leaned forward, putting his weight behind his efforts, and stared down at the mottled, sweaty face of this human parasite, this cockroach, this conniving, thieving, lying brute of a man, and his anger grew to epic proportions. Flashes from the past—Ben's removal, Susannah's hatred, Hungerford, Jarvis, the threats to his sister—stirred inside Nate like a toxic stew. Heat suffused his face and burned in his chest, and like dry wood on an already raging fire, Nate's power grew.

He glared down at Cressingham, his lip curled in disgust. *No more.* Nate would have no more of this man in his life, or anyone's. With renewed strength, he leaned forward harder and pressed the length of the cane across the captain's neck.

Cressingham tried to push Nate off, but Nate adjusted his stance, exerting even more force, and made a series of downward thrusts against the man's neck, using his body weight as leverage.

The captain's eyeballs bulged in their sockets and he tried to suck in air.

"Doesn't feel good, does it?" Nate asked with a sneer. He thrust downward again and the captain made a choking sound.

"Your days tormenting my family are done." Another thrust. "It's time for you to rot in Hell." Another thrust, and Nate heard a bone in his neck crack.

"Nate," Susannah said in a worried voice. "Don't be like my uncle. Please."

But Nate kept his gaze riveted on the man beneath him. Sweat beaded on his brow and dripped onto Cressingham's forehead. Nate pressed once more and the captain pounded his boot into the floor repeatedly as if begging for mercy.

Except Cressingham didn't deserve it.

"Nate?" she said with a sob.

"No, poppet," he snapped breathlessly. "I promised to protect you." He kept his gaze on Cressingham and watched impassively as the captain's eyes registered anger, then panic, then fear. Nate leaned down closer, pressing the cane down on the man's neck even more, and whispered harshly in his ear. "Finally, you bastard. You're finally getting your comeuppance. You'll never hurt my family again, and the world will forget you ever existed."

The captain's struggles grew weaker. Nate gritted his teeth and pressed with all his remaining strength, anxious to be done with this bastard. After what seemed like an age, Cressingham exhaled his final breath, but Nate didn't release the pressure.

He had to make sure the man was dead.

After several seconds of stillness, Nate finally sat back on the man's prostrate form, panting heavily from his exertions. Sweat streamed down his face, and he wiped at it with his bloody coat sleeve. He threw the cane onto the floor next to him, then slid off Cressingham's body.

He looked up at Susannah. She stood over him, tears running down her face. *His beautiful wife, safe at last.*

Groaning with the effort, Nate rose, grimacing at the pain that shot through his body. But he didn't care about that right now. He wanted to touch his wife. Nate reached for Susannah, took her in his arms, and kissed her hard and deep, running his hands around and over her back.

She responded in kind, wrapping her arms around his neck and melding her warm, soft body to his. Her mouth took and gave as much as Nate's as she threaded her fingers through his hair.

Nate drew back, his hands coming up to frame her face. "My beautiful poppet." Then tears pricked his eyes and he dropped his head, resting his forehead against hers.

"No," Susannah cooed. "Don't. Please don't, or I will, too." She took his face in her hands, forcing him to look at her. With eyes hard as steel, she said, "I should not have asked that of you. To not be like my uncle. Because you aren't, Nate. You're nothing like him, no matter what you do." She wrapped her arms around him and squeezed gently. "I love you, Nate. Always and forever. I promise."

Pulling back, Nate took her hands and pressed them, palm down, to his chest. Staring deep into her eyes, he said, "You have my heart, Susannah. Always and forever. I promise."

TWO WEEKS LATER, Nate stood at the altar of the small, stone parish church of his Sussex estate, Langley Park. Flowers decorated every inch of the small space, filling it with a glorious springtime scent. Branches of candles cast a warm glow everywhere. His mama and sisters sat in the first pew, smiling broadly at him. Nate returned it, then did a double-take as something crawled over Anna's shoulder. *What on earth?* She turned her head, then reached up and plucked the little lump off, cupping it in her hand. Grinning at Nate, she uncovered her hand, and Nate recognized Samson. He rolled his eyes and gave a chuckle. God forbid his other sisters discover the little rodent, or they'd all go screaming from the church.

"What are you laughing at?" Tradwick asked, leaning over. He stood with Nate as best man, his arm in a sling and his lip still a little swollen from the beating he'd received at the hands of Cressingham's thugs. Sidmouth and his men had managed to find Tradwick, but not before the captain's men had wrung him dry attempting to extract information from him.

Nate shook his head. "It's nothing." He glanced over at Andrew, fidgeting nervously at the altar. "Are you well, Drew?"

Andrew looked up, startled, and pasted on a smile. "Yes. Of course. Why wouldn't I be?"

"Just checking." Nate pulled out his pocket watch for the twelfth time. "What the devil could they be doing?"

The doors to the church swung open, and as at Marleybone, two figures stood in silhouette at the entrance. Nate's heart beat a primal rhythm in his chest. Without taking his eyes off his bride, he shoved his pocket watch back into his waistcoat pocket.

Susannah walked slowly down the aisle on the arm of her brother, Ben, who hadn't a scratch on him, the bastard. By the time Ben had made it to the Spread Eagle to meet Cressingham, Sidmouth and the Home Office, as well as Bow Street, were there, arresting Hungerford and taking away Cressingham's body. While everyone had been thrilled to learn Ben was still alive, he'd received no end of ribbing from Andrew, Nate, and Tradwick for "missing out on all the excitement."

Nate's eyes flicked to Ben, who wore a proud smile, then returned to Susannah. She was beautiful, even though her eye was still a yellowish-purple and a brownish bruise marred her delicate neck. She wore elegant lace gloves that Mama had made, which loosely covered the rope burns Susannah had gotten when she'd wrenched herself free from her bonds. She smiled at Nate, her eyes glowing with happiness, and Nate's heart lurched. God, he loved her.

Susannah and Ben approached the altar, and Ben quickly handed his sister off to Nate, but not before giving her a kiss on her cheek. "Be happy, sister," he said affectionately, then sat down in the nearest pew.

Nate and Susannah faced each other, their fingers entwined. He basked in her warmth, which crept up his arm and across his chest, sliding deeply into every corner of his body. She was going to be his wife. Legitimately and for all eternity. He gave her a suggestive smile and a wink, then turned to his friend.

"Marry us, Drew."

EPILOGUE

LONDON DOCKS, TUESDAY, APRIL 12, 1815

NATE STOOD at the foot of the gangplank, holding Susannah's hand tightly. He was about to keep a promise to his wife. They were set to board the *Lady Sarah*, which would take them to Falmouth, Jamaica, where Isabela resided. He looked around, amazed at the turnout for their departure. Ben, Tradwick, Nate's sisters and Mama, Sherry, Andrew, and even Captain Lord Whitsell, who had assisted Nate during the riots, had come out to wish them well.

"I'll miss you, brother," Susannah said, pulling her hand free from Nate's and giving Ben a hug.

Ben wrapped his arms around her. "You take good care of Isabela. She'll need you. I know she will." He released her and stepped back, then put his hand out for Nate. "Rain, if anything—"

Nate laughed, pushed his friend's hand aside, and gave him a hug, pounding him on the back a few times. "Nothing will happen." He lowered his voice so only Ben could hear. "We'll visit Isabela and I'll try to convince her husband to let her come back here with us. Don't worry." He released his friend.

Ben put his hands up in protest. "It's not that I worry. It's just that…"

He didn't need to finish. Nate knew what concerned him. For years, Ben hadn't been able to see his sister, and now that he was back in Susannah's life, Nate was taking her away. Albeit temporarily. "I'll keep her safe. And Isabela. You'll see them again."

"Thank you, Rain."

Nate's mama stepped forward, a handkerchief to her eyes. "Oh, Nathaniel. Must you take Susannah on this voyage?"

He smiled down at her, then met Susannah's eye and winked. "Yes, Mama. I promised. And I always keep my promises."

She embraced him, sniffing as she did so. "Be safe. And come right home as soon as you may."

"Yes, Mama." He hugged her tight, then kissed her cheek. He loved her dearly and would miss her terribly. He had worried that she wouldn't be able to handle the girls without him, but the way she had stood up to Cressingham, then bossed and commanded and given orders about Nate and Susannah's care and recuperation after they'd returned home, left him with no doubt of her ability to keep the girls in line.

His mama stepped back, taking Susannah's hand in hers, and pulled her aside for a private word.

Nate's brow furrowed, wondering what she could be saying to his wife, when his sisters fell upon him, wrapping their collective arms around him and squeezing him tight. He returned their embrace, kissing each of them on their bonneted heads.

"We'll miss you, Natey. Are you sure I can't come?" Anna asked, looking up at him with a hopeful expression.

"Don't be silly," Minnie said. "Of course you can't go."

"I wouldn't want to." Juliana sniffed. "I hear the weather is dreadfully hot there. I can barely stand the heat here."

"Pooh." Anna frowned at Juliana. "You have no sense of adventure."

"All right, girls," Nate said. "Treat your sister-in-law to the same love you just showed me, then we must be off." The girls disengaged themselves and crowded around Mama and Susannah.

"We have a gift for you, Susannah." Minnie's smile widened and she reached out for the small wrapped box that Whitsell had been holding. She handed it to her. "We, including Mama," she said, gesturing to her sisters, "all thought you'd like to have this while you're on your trip." She placed a hand on Susannah's, who held the box. "And of course we will make a permanent place for them at Rainsford House."

Susannah's mouth turned up in an inquisitive smile. "I'm curious what you could have given me."

"So am I," Nate said, moving to stand behind her.

"Help me open it, my love."

He stood before Susannah and held the box while she untied the ribbon and lifted the lid.

"Ohhh," she breathed. "Oh, sisters." There was a catch in her voice and Nate peered over her shoulder to see what could cause that reaction. There, nestled in soft fabric, were the miniatures of her family that had been on the hall table at Rainsford House.

Nate met his sister's eyes one-by-one. "Thank you. This is...it's wonderful."

"Oh, it is," Susannah said. She hugged Mama and each of his sisters in turn, whispering in their ears. Then she took the box from Nate and showed Ben the little portraits of their family.

"Thank you for keeping them," Ben said, his eyes a little misty.

"Of course." Anna patted Ben's arm. "You're part of our family now, you know."

"Wait a minute," Tradwick said. "Why is no one showing me such 'love'?"

Anna, flanked on one side by Sherry, waved a dismissive hand at him. "Oh, pooh, Sir Philip. You're not going anywhere."

He cocked a single eyebrow. "Oh, but I am." Tradwick pretended to brush dust off his coat sleeve. "I just received word this morning that I have been recruited for a special assignment by the Duke of Wellington."

The group was speechless, staring at Tradwick with wide eyes of astonishment.

"Well?" He put his hands out expectantly. "I believe congratulations are in order? Wishes for luck? Goodwill? Godspeed?"

Nate was the first to step forward, offering him his hand. "Congratulations, Tradwick. It's quite an honor, and justly deserved. I'm very proud of you, and very thankful for all that you have done for me and my family." He squeezed Tradwick's hand, which was once again bearing his signet ring. "I mean that. I wish you every success."

Tradwick met Nate's eyes. "Thank you, friend. I'm here for you anytime."

"I know. But do watch yourself. That bastard Boney is out for blood. Be safe."

His friend nodded.

Then the others jumped in, offering their congratulations and wishes for good luck.

A bell rang on the ship's deck and their crowd quieted. Nate turned to Susannah and held out his hand to her. "Come, my love. It's time to sail."

Susannah smiled at him, putting her hand in his, and clasped it tightly. Nate escorted Susannah up the gangplank. Once on deck, they turned and watched as their friends waved them off, laughing at Ben's hysterical—and loud—warnings about bad food, rough seas, and naughty sailor talk.

Nate stood behind Susannah, his mouth near her ear. God, she smelled divine. "This voyage is going to take six weeks, you know." He pressed himself into her back, willing her to feel his hardness through their clothes. "I wonder what we can do to pass the time?"

She wiggled her bottom enough to let Nate know she received his message. Turning her head, she looked up at him. Love—and the first sparks of passion—illuminated her beautiful brown eyes. "I was wondering the very same thing."

"I love you, poppet." He meant it with every fiber of his body, and he meant to show her in every way possible, starting with a detour to their cabin.

"I love you, too, Nate." She leaned up and gave him a quick kiss on the lips, and their friends on the dock cried out in mock horror. Susannah laughed and pulled away from him, hiding her reddening face in Nate's shoulder.

They watched as the sailors cast off the lines and pulled in the gangway. The sails unfurled, and soon, the ship was headed away from the docks, down the Thames. Nate and Susannah waved to their friends and family until they couldn't see them anymore. Then Nate took Susannah's hand and pulled her close. "I have something for you," Nate said. "I'd meant it as a wedding gift, but with everything that has happened, it never seemed like the right time to give it to you." He wasn't sure how well Susannah would take what he was about to offer, but he owed it to her.

She smiled broadly. "What is it?"

Nate reached into his pocket and pulled out a sheaf of letters, tied with a navy ribbon. He took the small box holding the miniatures from her and handed over the letters.

"What are these," she asked, a wrinkle across her brow.

"They're letters from Heddy. About your sister. I saved all of them."

She looked up at him, tears forming in her eyes. "Really?" Her eyes dropped to the letters, and he heard her sniff.

"Yes." Nate covered her hands with his. "It's not all happy news, you know. Her husband is…well, I've told you. But you will at least know how she's fared these past few years. Heddy was very thorough in his communication."

Susannah nodded. "I understand." After a few seconds, she turned her head up and met his eyes. "Thank you for trusting me with these."

Nate leaned down and kissed her gently on the lips. "Of course." He stepped back and coughed. "Well, I suppose you want to read them." He gestured over to the captain, who was speaking with the bosun. "I'm going to put this in our cabin," he said, lifting the box with the miniatures, "then speak with Captain Kirkby—"

"Before you go, I have a present for you, too." Susannah handed Nate the packet of letters. "Can you please hold those for a moment?"

Nate nodded, tucking the letters into his coat pocket as insurance against the gusty wind. He wondered what Susannah could possibly have gotten for him? Or why?

She turned away from him slightly, slipping her reticule off her wrist. Nate watched as she dug into it and extracted something, which she quickly hid in her hand. When she turned to face him again, her cheeks were flushed and a coy smile flashed across her face. "This is for you," she said. "Hold out your hand."

Nate extended it, and into his gloved palm, Susannah dropped a coil of red silk cord.

His eyes widened and he gazed at her, his mouth curling into a mischievous smile.

She clasped her hands before her demurely, rocking slightly back and forth, and looked up at him, her expression deceptively innocent. "I read in a book once that being tied up could be pleasurable. And I think learning how to extricate myself from bondage without shredding my wrists would be a good skill to learn...in case we're ever abducted again."

Nate was speechless. His wife was asking to be tied up. By him. With silk cord. But... "What about your sister's letters?"

"I trust you that Heddy is watching her. So I'll read them. Later." Susannah headed towards the stairs that led belowdecks. Just before descending, she turned, looking at Nate over her shoulder. "Are you coming, husband?"

That was all the invitation he needed. Grasping the cord tightly in his fist, he raced to catch up with her.

Inside their cabin, he dropped the box on the small table, threw off his gloves and hat, and shucked his coat. She removed her gloves and bonnet, then unfastened the buttons of her pelisse, shrugging out of it. The came together, arms entwined around each other, and Nate stared down into her eyes, which glistened like pools of liquid chocolate. "Do you know how wonderful you are?"

"Just merely wonderful? Or especially wonderful?" She laughed, throwing her head back, the deep-throated sound making Nate instantly hard.

"Magnificently wonderful," he replied. "Spectacularly.

Justifiably. Incredibly." He dropped kisses on her nose, her cheek, her neck.

"So are you," she whispered, returning his affections. "I love you, Nate."

"And I love you, poppet."

"Promise?"

"Promise."

The End.

WANT to read more of Nate and Susannah? Sign up for my newsletter on www.justinecovington.com to receive the FREE prequel to the story you just read.

You'll also get updates on new releases, early access to prequels for the next novels in the Beggars Club series, links to free stories, funny anecdotes, contest info, historical tidbits, book recs, and more.

Thank you for reading! If you're so inclined, I would appreciate a review on Goodreads or Amazon. They are the lifeblood of any author. Thank you!

COMING SOON...TRADWICK'S STORY

HIS LADY TO HONOR

Bound by duty, caught between honor and desire...

The last thing Sir Philip Tradwick wants to do is hunt down the Duke of Wellington's missing goddaughter. But if he fails at this mission, he can bid his hard-earned promotion a fond farewell. Fortunately, bringing her home to her father shouldn't be challenging. Keeping the scandalous—and maddeningly beautiful—young lady from stealing his heart, however, might just prove impossible.

Lady Catherine Jenico has no interest in romance. Being ruined by a rake and banished in the wake of a pregnancy scandal effectively rid her of any childish romantic notions she'd ever had. Her only desire now is to find the baby that was stolen from her. He's all that matters. Except...she never anticipated how beguiling the agent ordered to bring her home would be...

It's not long before Tradwick realizes there's much more to Catherine than meets the eye—and Catherine realizes there are still men of honor left in the world. But when all is said and done, will their love be strong enough to overcome all that stands between them?

Coming in 2020.

ACKNOWLEDGMENTS

This book, my first, would not have made it to its current state without the keen eyes of my two critique partners and best friends, Jenn Windrow and Lisa Heartman. Thank you, ladies, for your input, our Regular Red Robin lunch dates, late-night Group Me chats, and everything in between. I'd be lost without you.

I'm grateful for my editor, the amazing Alida Winternheimer, whose expertise helped find story holes, inconsistencies, and missed opportunities. Thank you for helping me seriously raise the bar on this book.

To Jennifer Crusie and the Eight Ladies...you were there when I got on and started riding this writing train, and I'm incredibly lucky to have had you with me for the journey.

Mom, Dad, and Danielle, I will forever be grateful for your encouragement to write the books I love to read. Thank you with all my heart.

My sweet boys WH and STP have endured countless PBJ and MYO dinners as I worked long hours and weekends (they've also gotten a fair amount of game time, so there's that!). Thank you for all the encouraging words you gave me when I said, "I finished a chapter today!" It means so much to me that you support me achieving my dream.

Lastly, to my husband. Thank you for believing in me, encouraging me, listening to me discuss story minutae, taking on the kids and the house, and otherwise being the best man a woman could ask for. I love you.

ABOUT JUSTINE

A lifelong history lover, Justine used to play "Laura Ingalls Wilder" in her backyard as a girl, making corn cakes and other "pioneer" food in her sandbox. She fell in love with the Regency when her grandmother introduced her to Johanna Lindsey at age fourteen.

Twenty-five years later, Justine decided it was time to write the Regency historicals she loves, rather than simply read them.

When not writing, Justine enjoys reading and spending time with her family. She has an unhealthy addiction to office supply stores and calls Phoenix home, where she lives with her husband, children, and mini-Schnauzer Chewie.

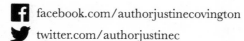

facebook.com/authorjustinecovington

twitter.com/authorjustinec

goodreads.com/justine_covington